SHERLOCK HOLMES

THE AUSTRALIAN CASEBOOK

SHERLOCK HOLMES

THE AUSTRALIAN CASEBOOK

EDITED BY
CHRISTOPHER SEQUEIRA

echo

echo

A division of Bonnier Publishing Australia
534 Church Street, Richmond
Victoria Australia 3121
www.echopublishing.com.au

First published 2017
Printed in China.

Cover design by Design by Committee
Page design and typesetting by Shaun Jury
Typeset in Garamond Premier

National Library of Australia Cataloguing-in-Publication entry:
    Creator: Sequeira, Christopher, author/editor.
    Title: Sherlock Holmes: The Australian Casebook / all new Holmes stories.
    ISBN: 9781760404673 (hardback)
    ISBN: 9781760404680 (ebook)
    ISBN: 9781760404697 (mobi)
    Subjects: Holmes, Sherlock—Fiction. Detective and Mystery Stories. Short stories, Australian.

🐦 @bonnierau
📷 @bonnierpublishingau
f facebook.com/bonnierpublishingau

To Jacqueline Amy Sequeira. To me she is always THE woman.

To my children: Valentina, Daniel and Anita; and my grandson, Hunter.

And to my late mother and father, Josephine Sequeira and Jack Sequeira, who were always proud of anything their children attempted, no matter how trivial, no matter how outré; here at last is a work they would have both willingly read even if I hadn't been involved with it!

A Note to Readers

This book depicts situations and characters that are reflective of the year 1890, and principally, the institutions, laws and social customs of some groups of people living in Australia at that time. The writers, editors and publisher are all well aware that certain language, attitudes and even laws would be completely unacceptable if they prevailed today, yet if those events are not included in the narratives herein the content would fail to convince of its period setting. Readers are asked to please take this into consideration; as, in some cases, the very things that will offend our sensibilities now are specifically the issues this book wishes to emphasise were scenarios that were, sadly, typical, and commonplace at a time over a century past.

TABLE OF CONTENTS

INTRODUCTION

Bill Barnes

E IGHT OF THE sixty original Sherlock Holmes stories contain an Australian connection. Most of these are a direct mention of a location as part of the story; a couple are a general reference to Australia; and one is an oblique association via a remark about a British company that had its operations in Australia. Perhaps the most interesting of these references occurs in *The Sign of Four*, set in 1887 or 1888, when Sherlock Holmes and Dr Watson visit a house where the grounds have been dug up in search of a treasure and Dr Watson remarks that he has seen something similar at the gold prospectors' diggings near Ballarat.

One of Dr Watson's most famous statements also occurs in that particular story when describing a young woman who has come to Holmes for help (and who eventually becomes Watson's wife), he says, 'In an experience of women which extends over many nations and three separate continents, I have never looked upon a face which gave a clearer promise of a refined and sensitive nature.' The previous reference to Ballarat has provided fuel to Sherlockian commentators for close to ninety years as proof that Australia was one of the 'three separate continents' where Dr Watson gained such valuable experience. Renowned Australian Sherlockian, the late Professor Lionel Fredman, surmised in his 1961 piece 'A Note on Watson's Youth' that he had holidayed in Australia in about 1883 (which would have been when Watson was in his late twenties). Other writers have made the case that Watson spent part of his schooling there.

Ken Methold's 1991 novel *Sherlock Holmes in Australia* recounted how Holmes and Watson travelled there after receiving a note in London delivered by a member of a visiting Aboriginal cricket team. Methold subtitled their subsequent investigation through Queensland, New South Wales and the South Pacific *The Adventure of the Kidnapped Kanakas*. In this book Holmes not only displays his legendary problem-solving acumen but also his social conscience as he takes up the fight to improve the lot of the sugar-plantation labourers.

One of the notable villains in the Sherlockian Canon (as the original sixty stories are fondly known) is Henry 'Holy' Peters, whose speciality is impersonating a clergyman and beguiling lonely ladies to donate funds to his fictitious overseas missionary endeavours. In the case recorded by Dr Watson as 'The Disappearance of Lady Frances Carfax' (set in the late 1890s/early 1900s) Holmes recognises Peters' modus operandi, confirms his suspicions, sight unseen, from a description of the 'clergyman's' damaged left ear and informs Watson of his true identity as an Australian conman. In doing so Holmes displays more than a passing familiarity with the antipodean criminal class. Another of the early, great Australian Sherlockians, the late Alan Olding, argued persuasively in his 1994 article 'Holmes in Terra Australis Incognita – Incognito' that Holmes gained this knowledge by travelling to Australia on a secret commission for the British government during the 'missing' three years ('The Great Hiatus') following his 1891 confrontation with Professor Moriarty at Reichenbach Falls in Switzerland.

Well, as the accounts in this book now remarkably reveal, Holmes and Watson also visited this part of the world in the year before the Swiss incident. In your hands, or on your ebook reader, you have an excellent collection of stories from a talented bunch of writers, very nicely illustrated by gifted artistic hands, covering the great detective's exploits from that time in Australia. In these tales Sherlock Holmes is at the height of his powers and it seems that wherever he and his companion and chronicler, Dr John Watson, go there is crime aplenty to be found. Holmes's reputation naturally precedes him and people with problems seek him out. Murder, robbery, kidnapping, bribery and extortion are on the cards in a land far from England, but all are caused by an array of criminal motivations that the British Holmes and Watson are nonetheless very familiar with – almost all of the seven deadly sins are covered in these stories.

As well as visiting major cities like Adelaide, Hobart, Melbourne and Sydney we also find our intrepid duo in places like Bunbury, Dirranbandi, Queanbeyan, Tennant Creek and Ballarat, and on a ship from Australia to New Zealand; each of the eight states and territories currently part of Australia is the location for at least one case in this volume. Settle down, read on, and as you turn the pages learn about Holmes's battle with a Chinese demon; a dark and very deadly secret amongst a brotherhood of monks; supernatural effects in a beachside cave; a boy risen from the dead; an apparent accidental death in the outback; a 'locked cellar' mystery; and a venomous sea creature, among others.

You will enjoy the time you spend reading this collection of tales of the world's greatest detective investigating mysteries on the world's greatest island.

Bill Barnes
Captain (President), The Sydney Passengers –
incorporating The Sherlock Holmes Society of Australia
BSI (Invested Member, The Baker Street Irregulars)

FOREWORD

I SUPPOSE IT WAS something of an inevitability that the cache of documents I have come to call 'The Antipodean Case Files' came into my possession a few years ago.

I have a small (uncharitable folk might say 'deservedly small') reputation for being a subject matter expert on the celebrated histories of Mr Sherlock Holmes and Dr John H. Watson, who were involved in numerous high-profile criminal investigations largely between 1881 and the start of World War I.

My personal obsession with Holmes and Watson's work grew out of three childhood events: discovering Watson's literary agent Dr Conan Doyle's collection of four of Holmes's most complex cases in one volume at my school library; watching the local Sydney TV station re-runs of Basil Rathbone and Nigel Bruce's 1940s adaptations of some of Watson's writings; and reading the visually powerful, two-part 1975 Marvel Comics graphic-novel adaptation of Holmes's greatest case, the Baskerville affair, by the late Archie Goodwin and the wonderful and kind (I have his autograph on my copies!) Val Mayerik. The final nail in my proverbial *idée afixed* coffin was when my researches into the Holmes-contemporaneous crimes of the 1888 'Whitechapel Murderer' revealed to me that a forensic witness was one Dr George W. Sequeira (one of my middle names is George), and this led to some startling discoveries about Dr GWS (another subject, for another day). If I was not irrevocably preoccupied with Victorian-era criminology and mystery before that final event impacted me, I was now addicted more unremittingly than Holmes was during his early years to his seven per cent solution of cocaine! So it was no surprise that I later, in adulthood (please, no smirks) joined the largest Sherlock Holmes society in the country, and would periodically write of the detective and doctor's work for that society's journal. I later also adapted some of the investigative duo's previously unpublished cases to dramatic formats such as short prose stories and graphic novels, so my profile as a Holmes and Watson aficionado residing on this continent became reasonably well established.

So it was then, that when a large assortment of notes was uncovered in an auction of a deceased estate in Sydney a few years ago and the contents appeared to be related to Holmes and Watson, the buyer was directed through two or three parties, eventually to me. I examined the collection and was astounded (still am!) to see it was an assortment of notations, diary entries, newspaper clippings, the odd photograph and other pieces of ephemera relating to Mr Sherlock Holmes and Dr Watson's visit to the shores of Australia for a period of several months in 1890. I was intrigued, for, as many a scholar of Holmes knows, 1890 was a year where previously little data on the duo's affairs appeared to be extant; I now knew why. It seemed that, to use the parlance at which all Australians actually cringe a little, in 1890 Holmes and Watson were 'Down Under'!

Apparently Holmes had been summoned to undertake an important and sinister case involving another well-documented figure of his day, the notorious master criminal Dr Antonio Nikola (subject of five book-length historical accounts by former assistant to the mayor of Adelaide in South Australia, Guy Boothby). Nikola was sometimes known as 'Doctor Diablerie' because of his menacing aspect and (obviously fraudulent) claims to have a mastery of 'occult' energies, and it appears he and Holmes had a set of adversarial encounters in Australia before matters came to a dramatic conclusion. Holmes prevented a catastrophe from occurring, and so I suspect it was concern for the public's peace of mind that caused the government of the day to ever-so-gently place pressure on the local newspaper proprietors to avoid mention of the great detective's presence on *Terra Australis* and his grappling with Nikola's perfidy. The press, in fact, overreacted by avoiding almost ALL specific mention of Holmes and Watson during their Australian visit and their investigation of many another matter while here, which thus explains why public records and references relating to them for the time period are scant.

It was also interesting to see from the cache I was given that Holmes and Watson journeyed all over the country, even circling back through major cities like Sydney and Melbourne more than once. While they enjoyed less attention than they would have in London, their names and their successes were known of here, meaning that no matter how they attempted at some berths to keep to themselves, word quickly spread and privacy was never theirs for long. This may have accounted for them visiting so many different places and staying at a variety of hotels even in the same cities. In addition, Holmes was clearly committed to adding to his incredible (previously firmly well-documented) mental storehouse of knowledge about sensational and unusual crime, and this, combined with the grapevine of the various state police forces telling one another a 'detective genius' was in the country, meant that the British consulting detective and his doctor friend were specifically approached and appealed to for help with many unusual cases that presented a challenge to local law enforcement; the details of which have been lost to history.

That is, until the deceased-estate find that prompted me to talk to a publisher about releasing an assemblage of some sort.

Unfortunately, Watson's notes were not only unpolished (written 'on the road' as it were), but also significantly water-damaged in places; parts were virtually indecipherable. To edit, research the data to cover missing portions, intelligently speculate about missing portions and then cast all into a dramatic format was beyond my resources in the short term. Then a colleague of mine suggested I enlist the help of other, skilled writers with sharp minds; a brilliant idea! The call went out, and with the help of the incredibly supportive Angela Meyer from my publisher, who backed the entire project, a team of great authors was assembled, each of whom was happy to reveal a Holmes and Watson case!

So, that brings you to the book you now read. I have taken some (but far from all; there are plenty more insightful and inspiring documents in the cache) of the Australian cases Watson docketed and given them to over a dozen acclaimed and gifted writers, who have rendered them into engaging, dramatic prose form. Pleasantly, I can say that for this volume an example was able to be deciphered of a case in geography corresponding to every one of the current states and territories of Australia, and one involving a short voyage the two men took to New Zealand.

If you are new to the exploits of these seekers for justice and have only picked up this volume because of your interest in Australiana, well, I envy you; you are in for a treat indeed. If, on the other hand, you are already a 'Sherlockian' (or 'Holmesian') I trust you shall be equally entertained as you discover how two quintessential Englishmen adapted their unique collaborative investigative skills to the landscape of the nation that was the most removed, unruly child of Great Britain; the former Aboriginal homeland forcibly saddled with a convict settlement known as Australia. The intrigue will not escape you, nor will the ironies of the extended sojourn to Australia of this historic pair of detectives – a case of a land artificially super-populated with untrustworthy criminals being visited by the greatest criminal-hunter of his age, accompanied by his very trustworthy associate.

Christopher Sequeira
Burwood, New South Wales, February 2017

The Play's the Thing

Meg Keneally

'OH, PLEASE DON'T concern yourselves. The theatre is a place for inflamed passions, even in one such as Louisa Fraser.'

I watched as Hamish Drake produced a lacy, feminine handkerchief from his breast pocket and bent to wipe the spittle from his shoe. It had been ejected a minute earlier from the mouth of a dourly dressed matron who had stalked up to Drake, glared at him and then wordlessly made her opinion of him known.

'We are not concerned in the slightest,' said my friend Sherlock Holmes, watching the woman's stiff back as she made her way through the theatre's ornate doors.

'Somewhat odd, though,' I said. 'I can't remember the last time I saw a lady spit.'

'One gets used to oddness here, Doctor,' said Drake. 'Everything reversed, nothing as it should be. One of the many reasons I'm so delighted they built this place, it brings some much-needed culture. Tell me, what did you think of our little Eden here?'

Holmes and I had met Hamish Drake at the New South Wales Club. Dr Thomas Farrier, with whom I had served in the Afghan war, had made the introduction.

'I wish you the best of luck,' Farrier had whispered to me.

Drake, who described himself as a theatre impresario, had dragged a chair to our table – without invitation, as he seemed to think none was needed – and had spoken with such delight of Her Majesty's Theatre that it almost sounded as though he had built it himself.

'The place is my home,' he had said, 'and the management love me. I may come and go as I please. You must let me give you a tour.'

The tour, as it turned out, had been as much of Drake's career as it was of the building itself.

'You know Janet Achurch was in *A Doll's House* here in Sydney last year. The dear thing insisted I come to her dressing-room after – we had a long acquaintance in the West End, you see. Sarah Bernhardt's intending to come next year; she sees hope in the place now I'm associated with it. Begged me to set something up for her, but I'm sadly too busy,' Drake said as we trailed him through the theatre.

I had made polite noises of admiration. Holmes had not so much as pretended to listen, minutely examining the elaborate plasterwork that framed the boxes, and rapping his cane on the boards of the stage to assess the acoustics.

'Quite extraordinary, the equal of any theatre in London,' I said. 'Have you had many productions here yourself?'

'Well, not quite yet,' said Drake. 'Important to take the time to get these things right, don't you think? Takes quite a bit of money, you know. One needs the right partners.'

Now, with his shoe cleaned, Drake smiled and shook first my hand, then Holmes's.

'Poor woman, I see her in the foyer from time to time. She does not come to see plays, though. Simply sits there, watching people. Her husband died under… well… troubling circumstances. I suspect she may be somewhat unhinged.'

He bowed and took a florid leave of us, striding down Bligh Street with the air of a man who had far too many calls on his time. I made to walk in the other direction, towards our lodgings, stopping when I realised Holmes was not following.

Holmes, instead, was staring at the doors of the theatre, frowning.

'They are doors, Holmes. Surely not even you can divine some sort of deeper meaning from them,' I said.

'Not from the doors, no. From the woman who passed through them.'

'Ah. The expectorating enigma.'

'Alliteration is used by those who wish to divert attention away from the fact that they have nothing to say,' said Holmes. 'And she is no enigma. Did you not note that our friend Mr Drake applied a name to her?'

'Yes. Mrs...'

'Fraser, Watson. Fraser. Does that not kindle something in one of the corners of your mind?'

'No. Should it?' I asked.

'Tell me, Watson. Those newspapers you hold in front of your face each morning at breakfast. Do you actually read them, or do you simply use them to avoid having to converse with me?'

'Both. Not that it matters, you invariably steal them anyway.'

'It's as well that I do,' said Holmes. 'Otherwise I could not have read of Mrs Fraser last week.'

'Read of... you don't mean to say she was in the newspaper?'

'Yes, and it seems our new friend is not the only one to have displeased her. She was the subject of an accusation, you see, by a former servant. Man says the woman beat him with a broom.'

'Good Lord. I'll take care not to anger her, then. Mind you, not much chance of encountering her at the New South Wales Club. Shall we take lunch there?'

'Truly, I'd rather not,' said Holmes. 'Our last visit brought us here. God knows where we'll end up if we chance it again.'

THE NEXT MORNING I was only a few sentences into the *Sydney Morning Herald* report on the lawn tennis when the paper was snatched out of my hands.

'You're approaching your theft of my newspaper with more than the usual enthusiasm, Holmes,' I said. Truly, this habit of his was getting tiresome. He did it from time to time at Baker Street, but here in Australia it had become almost a compulsion, as though he needed to scan the international news to reassure himself London still existed.

Now, though, Holmes was not settling down at the table to read. He was ushering in my colleague, Dr Thomas Farrier, who looked to have come in some haste judging by the sheen on his skin. Farrier, unable to get a foothold on Harley Street, had moved to Australia a few years earlier to gain some colonial experience, and probably to collect stories with which he could regale dinner parties on his return. I had seen him under fire, betraying far less agitation than he was now showing.

'I thought you'd like to know… I'm on my way to… Well, I thought you might like to come,' Farrier said, taking a seat next to me and leaning forward as he spoke.

'Certainly, if you'll tell us where,' I said.

'To the theatre.'

'But we were only there yesterday.'

'Not to a play, man! I've been asked by the police for my professional opinion on a matter concerning Mr Drake. As you spent yesterday morning in his company, and as you are familiar with police from what I understand, I would appreciate your company.'

Holmes was already gathering his things as well as mine.

'What has Mr Drake become embroiled in?' Holmes asked.

'I've had a short but rather graphic report, and… well, probably best you see for yourself.'

There had been no-one on duty to admit Holmes and myself to the theatre when we had visited the day before. Today, though, there was. A young constable opened the door, with far less flourish than a doorman might have.

'They're still on the stage, Dr Farrier,' he said. 'Best hurry before they cut him down.'

Farrier led us along the central aisle towards the stage, past seats littered with *Hamlet* playbills, where a man in a cheaply made suit, notebook in his hand, was standing next to a stepladder and staring up at an object dangling at the end of a long rope from the stage's catwalk, just feet above the stage itself.

The thing had eyes which stared at nothing, and a purple cast to its skin.

Given the location, it would have been easy to mistake it for a prop, had it not shared the features of Hamish Drake.

'Dr Farrier,' the man on the stage said. 'I haven't seen you since the last hanging.'

'Yes… Inspector Mobbs, I do wish we could meet under more pleasant circumstances.'

'I too, but not all of us are cut out for the New South Wales Club,' said Mobbs, looking sideways at Holmes and me. 'Your friends, though, seem the type. They are…?'

Holmes stepped forward, holding out his hand which Mobbs reflexively grasped.

'Sherlock Holmes, consulting detective, Baker Street, London. My colleague is Dr John Watson, formerly of the Fifth Northumberland Fusiliers.'

'Holmes… I may have heard… never mind. You can stay for now, but nothing you see here can be discussed outside, is that understood?'

'Quite.'

'I had him under investigation for fraud, you know,' said Mobbs. 'I believe this investigation will be more straightforward.'

He went over to the stepladder and climbed it until he was face to face with the corpse.

'As you gentlemen are here, I don't suppose you'd mind assisting me in getting our friend down? If you're not too squeamish, that is.'

'Not at all,' said Holmes. 'Watson, go to it.'

I glared at Holmes, then moved over to the corpse, put my arms around Drake's waist and braced myself as Mobbs took out a pocket knife and sawed away at the rope.

Drake had enjoyed his food, and the sudden weight when the rope broke sent both him and myself sprawling onto the stage.

'Do be careful, Watson,' said Holmes. 'Evidence, you know, can be a delicate thing.'

Farrier extracted some opera lorgnettes from his breast pocket, knelt and began examining Drake's neck.

'Would have taken some strength, I imagine,' I said. 'He is not a light man, I can attest to that myself. Someone would have needed some muscle, or some help, to get him up to the catwalk and drop him off at the end of that rope.'

Holmes looked down and touched Drake's leg with his shoe.

'Oh, he wasn't killed here. Nor did he die of that rope around his neck. As Dr Farrier is about to tell us.'

Farrier looked up.

'You're quite correct,' he said. 'There is nothing like the bruising I would expect from such a fall, had he been alive at the start of it. I would say he's been smothered, going by the bluish tinge to his lips. And he reeks, by the way, of liquor.'

'And nothing like the flexibility you would expect, had he been killed here,' said Holmes.

He nudged Drake's leg again with the toe of his shoe. There was no movement at all.

'You would expect at least some movement still, had he met his death on this stage.'

'Holmes, rigor can set in quite quickly, you know.'

'Not quite this quickly, Watson. You would expect, wouldn't you, that I would be able to shift his leg even by an inch or two, less than eight hours after his death.'

'How can you possibly know it's been less than eight hours?' Mobbs asked.

'Inspector,' said Holmes, 'do you suppose he was placed here in full view of the audience? Or, perhaps, while the stagehands were still at their work after the play?'

'Of course not. But it's a little after 8 a.m. now, surely there would have been no one here by around midnight.'

'Not necessarily, inspector. *Hamlet*, was it, last night? One of Shakespeare's longest.'

'Indeed. Four thousand lines, and then a few,' said a voice that had clearly been trained to carry to the very back of the theatre. 'And I can deliver every one of them, could do so now.'

The inspector looked up towards the man who had spoken. He was wearing a scarlet smoking jacket, and had pomaded his hair to the extent that it gave me the impression he was trying to disguise its paucity.

'That won't be necessary, Mr Harbin,' said the inspector. 'If you could enlighten us as to when you delivered the last one yesterday evening, though, I'd be grateful.'

'Of course, but first you must introduce me to your new friends.'

'My new… oh. Well, I'm sure they are capable of making their own introductions.'

'A consulting detective, how exciting,' said Harbin after Holmes introduced himself. 'I suppose that means you get to pick and choose which cases you work on. Nothing boring. Must be marvellous.'

'At times,' said Holmes. 'May I know to whom I'm speaking?'

A scowl crossed Harbin's face for a moment, submerged almost instantly by his professional joviality.

'Charles Harbin, sir. To be at your service in my capacity as humble manager of this establishment – I hold the lease, you see, as well as working for myself in my capacity as an actor.'

'And how came you to know the number of lines in *Hamlet*?' said Holmes.

'Well, by speaking them several nights a week, of course. I considered taking on Polonius, you know. Thought I might be getting a bit old for dear Hamlet, but everyone insisted, they said nobody was equal to the task except me, so here I am, still playing a prince half my age, and nobody seems to mind.'

'I imagine the play ended quite late last night then,' I said.

'Oh yes, past eleven. And I like to stay until the stagehands are finished, so I didn't leave until a little after one.'

'And you didn't see Mr Drake?'

'Last night? No, haven't seen him since that business with *The Silent Lover*.'

'*The Silent Lover*… that is a play?'

'Yes, Drake was trying to get it made, you see. Took it round to some of the wealthier types here, seeking investment.'

'And he was unsuccessful, I presume,' I said.

'To a point. He was able to line up some investors. But not quite enough, he said. And when they asked for their money back, it had mysteriously vanished. Most hadn't put in enough to be seriously affected but one, a fellow who was very keen to increase his social standing, lost almost everything. He… Well, he was the last hanging. From the rafters of his kitchen. His wife found him.'

'How appalling! Must be impossible to recover from that sort of thing.'

'For most, I'm sure it is,' said Harbin. 'But this woman, a bit of a harridan, is not one to show weakness. She had to move, of course. And she mostly withdrew from society – she was never as keen as he was anyway. But whatever her feelings, she is still a formidable presence when she does venture out. And she mostly ventures here or to one of the other theatres, to haunt the lobby and try to confront Drake. Not one to be crossed, our Mrs Fraser.'

'Mrs Fraser…' I said. 'You don't mean Louisa Fraser?'

'Ah, you know her!'

'Yes,' I said. 'In fact, we should probably tell the inspector…'

'That we intend to call on her later today, to bring her this news,' said Holmes. 'I don't suppose Mr Drake asked you for money?'

'Not money, no. He wanted to trade on my reputation. He told everyone I had agreed to have the play performed here.'

'And had you?' I asked.

'Absolutely not! Hard enough to turn a penny here without getting a reputation for staging dross. I asked him to stop, several times, but he ignored me, the scoundrel.'

Holmes had moved toward the body and was now kneeling beside it. 'Inspector, what was in Mr Drake's mouth?'

'Who's to say there was anything in it?' said Mobbs.

'Mr Drake himself, as it happens,' said Holmes. 'His mouth is gaping, more even than you'd expect under the circumstances, and his cheeks are distended.'

'As a matter of fact,' said Mobbs, 'it's none of your business what was in there. I've not met you before but here you are, taking over the investigation as though you were the superintendent.'

'I only wish to assist,' said Holmes. 'Still, if you would prefer, we will of course leave you in peace.'

'Have a care, Inspector Mobbs,' said Farrier. 'Holmes and Dr Watson are both reasonably famous in London policing circles. Your superiors might take a dim view if you were unable to reach a conclusion in this case, and they found that you had rejected help from such a well-regarded source.'

Mobbs flicked his eyes between Farrier and Holmes, who was taking more pains than usual to look contrite.

'As I'm short staffed… Very well. I need everyone's word, though, that none of this will be discussed outside this building. That includes you, Mr Harbin.'

'I wouldn't dream of it, dear boy,' said Harbin. 'Not much of a gossip, you know. One gets told more secrets that way.'

'All right,' said Mobbs, walking over to a satchel at the side of the stage. He extracted a wad of crumpled paper the size of a fist, and tossed it to Holmes.

'Don't know how much sense you'll get out of it, seems like raving to me, the little I've seen,' he said. 'And I've not much time for reading. But if men of such splendid education as you think you can shed any light on it, please feel free to try.'

The papers were thin, and some of them still moist from the inside of Drake's mouth. In many places, the ink had been smudged beyond legibility. But, judging by the way the writing on the pages was structured when Holmes unfurled one of them, it looked to be a scene from a play.

'Mr Harbin,' said Holmes, 'Do you recognise this?'

Harbin glanced at the page.

'Looks like Alistair Sinclair's writing, actually. Makes sense, I suppose. He was the one who wrote the play that Drake was trying to raise funds for. Sinclair was working on a more polished version. I said we'd wait for that before making any decision.'

'I see. And you know where this Sinclair is to be found?'

'I confess, no. He did have a room in one of the better boarding houses – he had some success on Drury Lane, you see, and used it to fund his move here. But I suppose the funds ran out. I haven't seen him for some time.'

'Very well. And we also need to find Louisa Fraser.'

'I can assist you with that,' said Farrier. 'I was her husband's physician. I have made many visits to their home, particularly after they moved to a smaller one, following the business with the play, when George Fraser was always after what he called "nerve tonics". If you wish, I can take you there now.'

'I do hope we find her in,' I said.

'Highly likely,' said Holmes.

'Quite an assumption, Holmes, from one who rails against the making of them,' I said. 'Just because she has turned her back on society, it doesn't necessarily follow that she never leaves the house. She lurks around theatre foyers, that much we know.'

'Yes,' said Holmes. 'But did you not note her pallor? In this climate, even ladies who habitually carry parasols have signs of the sun on their skin, and she had no parasol.'

'Perhaps she left it at home?'

'Perhaps not. I see you opening and closing your fingers when you don't have your cane. People who are used to carrying an item unconsciously look for it. Her hands, though, were not searching for anything.'

'You're quite right, as it turns out,' said Farrier. 'She does not frequently go abroad, and is not a woman of many friends. Not easy to get along with, as you will see.'

MRS FRASER LIVED in a cottage in one of the less fashionable parts of town. She retained the means to employ a maid, though not a very good one. The girl answered the door wearing an apron that bore one or two smudges, and her cap was askew.

She nodded wordlessly when Farrier gave all our names, and wandered off, presumably to see if her mistress was amenable to a visit.

Mrs Fraser received us in a tiny parlour, neat but with very little in the way of decoration save a small table over near the window bearing a decanter, and a tea set and cup on another table in front of her.

Her hair was scraped back tightly into a bun. She wore a well-made but drab dress, and even the buttons were covered in grey fabric, preventing them from relieving the monotony of her gown.

She received the news of Drake's death calmly.

'It does not surprise me in the slightest,' she said. 'The worst of charlatans, that man. I could never believe that George couldn't see it. Or didn't want to. The governor's wife had told him that she so admired patrons of the arts, and he didn't have the funds to endow a museum or gallery or the like.'

'What did you think of the project your husband did endow?' Holmes said.

'Unutterable tripe. I don't think he even read the play, even though Drake left us with a copy. It was enough for him that there were others also putting up money. He adored fantasising about the opening night, about the praise for his generosity, but he had no actual interest in the play itself.'

'You did read it, though,' said Holmes.

'Of course. Honestly, it was the most poorly constructed, trite and boring piece of work I believe I have ever read. The man did not even have the decency to present it well; he had deplorable handwriting. Mr Drake said the playwright was working on another draft, a better one. I doubt it though. Drake was an expert in telling people what they most wanted to hear.'

'Did you meet the playwright yourself, Madam?' I asked.

'No, and nor had I any desire to. Reading his words was enough of an introduction for me.'

'And on the subject of those words,' said Holmes, 'do you still happen to have the copy of the play Drake left with you?'

'Yes, and I'd be grateful if you took it. I certainly have no further use for it. Especially now that the man who used it to destroy us has himself been destroyed.'

Holmes was leafing through the pages as the door of the Fraser home was closed behind us, with unexpected energy, by the maid.

'Well, she hardly seemed devastated by Drake's death,' I said. 'Perhaps we should be looking more closely at her in connection with causing it. Best not read that as you walk, by the way. You may be accompanied by two doctors, but our powers are not unlimited.'

'Louisa Fraser is not our murderer, Watson,' said Holmes, tucking her copy of the play under his arm as we walked back towards the theatre. 'That much I can guarantee you.'

'You can guarantee nothing of the sort!'

'I believe I can,' said Holmes. 'To begin with, Mrs Fraser does not possess the requisite strength to attach Drake to that rope, let alone to overpower and smother him, with or without the aid of alcohol.'

'Perhaps she had help?'

'Where would a recluse like her, someone who is universally disliked, find someone to assist her?'

'Perhaps we should look into the other investors. The answer may be there.'

'Indeed it might, but it is not sitting back in that cottage. Because, as well as needing a willing accomplice, someone who conceived such a plan would need a clear head, something that Mrs Fraser does not possess.'

'She seemed clearheaded enough to me, Holmes.'

'Did she indeed? You failed to notice, then, the teacup in front of her. It was dry, the leaves plastered to the bottom. Put there hastily, to give us the impression of a sober woman.'

'I must say, Holmes,' said Farrier, 'I've never had the slightest concern about Mrs Fraser's sobriety. Never smelled so much as a whiff of alcohol on her breath.'

'Nor would you, Dr Farrier, if the alcohol in question was gin. Which it was.'

'How could you possibly know?'

'About the alcohol? Did you note how she kept her hands folded in her lap? But when she went to the sideboard to get the play, they shook, so that she had to steady the hand extracting the paper with her other hand. As to the gin, there was a decanter on a side table, you may recall. A fair way from where she was sitting, over by the window. But the legs of the table had left indentations in the carpet right next to her chair. That table, I assure you, was hastily moved when she was informed visitors were arriving.'

'I wonder,' said Farrier, 'whether we should be discounting Harbin?'

'Oh, yes, I think so,' said Holmes. He took a leaf from a nearby tree, crumbled it in his fingers and smelled it before throwing it into the gutter.

'Drake was threatening the reputation of his theatre, though. It's even possible he might gain financially from the death; there are plenty with a macabre streak who would want to visit a theatre where such an event had occurred,' said Farrier. 'Like Mrs Fraser, Mr Harbin did not seem at all distressed at Drake's death, and he was the last to leave the theatre, by his own admission.'

'Well, you have hit on something there, Dr Farrier. Very well observed – the fact that Harbin did not show any concern about the death. That in itself, to my mind, is almost exculpatory.'

'How could it be an indicator of the man's innocence?' I asked.

'Because Harbin, Watson, is an actor. And I would imagine that if he had been the murderer, we would have seen a performance of grief from him to rival Hamlet's reaction to Ophelia's death. I'm willing to keep a slightly open mind on the matter of Harbin, but I do feel our efforts are best bent towards one particular individual.'

'The playwright? Possibly,' I said. 'But we haven't the faintest idea where to find him.'

'Ah,' said Farrier. 'I believe I know someone who may be able to assist us.'

JAMES MCGREGOR SHUT the door of his office against the noise and pipe smoke that were the two overwhelming characteristics of the *Sydney Chronicle* newsroom. He looked like a man who had long ago abandoned the respectable practice of wearing a jacket at all times, and had no concerns about being seen in his shirtsleeves. Some rickety chairs had to be hastily pulled out from under the posteriors of newsroom journalists so that our party could confer with him around his desk.

'You know, I hadn't heard from Sinclair for months,' he said. 'He took out some ads for his play – *The Silent Lover,* was it? – and paid for them out of his own pocket. They ran, of course, a sort of teaser to get other investors interested. But then Drake seemed to lose interest, and the money that was supposed to be there suddenly wasn't. Sinclair begged me to refund him for the advertisements, but of course I couldn't. The space had been sold and used. Went on for weeks, too – he'd be here every morning when I arrived. He must've given up, though, because I hadn't seen him for months. Until today.'

'He contacted you in connection with Hamish Drake's murder?' I asked.

'After a fashion, Doctor. He presented me with a piece for publication. An absolute excoriation of Drake, claiming that he was a charlatan, that he had never intended to produce a play, that he was a blight on the cultural life of this colony and of Sydney in particular. All sorts of other unsubstantiated rot as well. I didn't publish it, of course. Entirely inappropriate, just after the man's death. I never took Drake seriously, but I would not see anyone treated thus, even if they're not around to be hurt by it.'

'That makes you a rather unusual newspaperman, in my experience,' said Holmes.

'This is not London, Mr Holmes. If you offend someone on Monday, you are likely to need them on Tuesday. Some of those who invested in Drake's little venture are still powerful people, and would prefer not to be reminded of their lapse in judgement.'

'You weren't concerned about offending Sinclair?'

'Him? No, he's a spent force.'

'And you wouldn't happen to know where he is lodging?'

'Haven't the slightest idea, but I do know where he can be found. He enjoys expounding on his views on life and philosophy from on top of a crate in the Botanic Gardens. And today just happens to be fine but not too hot – his favourite weather. I'll wager if you take a turn through the gardens, you may find him.'

THE HARBOUR THAT day was well behaved, an almost violent blue but still and calm, although Holmes and I knew from the crossing that the Tasman Sea beyond the Sydney Heads could produce waves to match any that the North Sea could throw at a vessel.

Well-bred ladies strolled through the gardens, ignoring statues of naked nymphs as they made their way to the Art Gallery of New South Wales to look at similarly underdressed statues of figures from Greek and Roman mythology. Had they been so inclined, they could have availed themselves of a free lesson in philosophy from the man standing near the park's entrance.

'The mercantile classes are destroying our art,' he yelled. 'Culture has become a commodity, my friends, traded alongside bales of wool in the marketplace.'

Holmes, Farrier and I walked slowly up to him. His audience was small and transitory, people stopping for a moment before moving on after they noticed the febrile gleam to his eyes and were assaulted by the pitch of his voice. They may very possibly also have noticed his unkempt hair, the small red veins on his face and the buttons missing from his shirt.

The three of us waited until the speaker paused for breath, then Holmes stepped forward.

'Alistair Sinclair?'

'Yes!' the man said, jumping down from his box. 'You are English, I perceive. Perhaps you have seen one of my plays performed in London?'

'Sadly not, although I'm sure I would find the experience quite illuminating. No, we have come on the matter of Hamish Drake's death.'

'I hope you will not be inviting me to the funeral, as I shall not attend. The man is a confidence trickster and a barbarian. He took my best work and used it as a prop to defraud people of their money. He is nothing more than a vandal.'

'Your best work. This would be *The Silent Lover*?'

'You have heard of it!'

'Yes, but sadly I have been unable to peruse it as yet. May I ask, what is it about?'

'It concerns a man who falls in love with a woman who is mute. She returns his feelings, but cannot communicate them. He takes her silence as disdain. It is only after she is carried off by consumption that he finds letters she has written to him, confessing to her true feelings.'

'Ah. A tragedy, then.'

'No, a farce. It is the subverting of these assumptions about which play fits into which category that makes this work so fresh – makes it so, if I may say, revolutionary.'

Holmes examined Sinclair's face, perhaps searching for any sign of sarcasm. He appeared to find none.

'I am sure it is a most interesting work,' I said.

'It is now, yes. I have redrafted it, you see. Wanted to emphasise the pathos, contrast it more plainly with the comic elements. I feel confident, you know, that had Hamish Drake waited for me to complete this work before showing the play around, it would be on a stage today.'

'He was unwilling to wait?'

'Yes. He said if I wanted any opportunity to work with him, I would let him show around a draft. He promised me he would emphasise the fact that the play would improve. But honestly, I believe he cost me an opportunity, one which I am unlikely to have again. I shall have to seek employment as a clerk now, you see. I did my part to promote the play to investors, and it cost me most of my livelihood.'

'You must detest Drake, then,' said Farrier.

'He is merely a symptom of a wider disease,' said Sinclair. 'His excision from the cultural corpus of Sydney will go some way towards curing it, but I fear the patient is still doomed.'

'Well, Sinclair is aware of Drake's death, then, at least,' I said as we walked away. 'I'm sure the theatre grapevine is very efficient, but did not Mobbs tell us to refrain from talking about it? There has not even been time for our friend at the *Chronicle* to publish a story about it.'

'Yes, that was rather interesting,' said Holmes. 'Although there may as yet be an explanation. But now, Watson, I am afraid that you and I have a most distasteful duty to perform this evening.'

'Pity,' said Farrier. 'I was going to ask you to dine with me.'

'Very grateful to you, Doctor, but I'm afraid we will have to decline for now,' said Holmes. 'Dr Watson and I have a play to read.'

IT WAS WELL past eleven before we finished, squinting in the low light at the cramped, spiky handwriting of the draft we had been given by Louisa Fraser, the pages spread out before us on the dining table of the boarding house.

'She was right,' said Holmes. 'Unmitigated tripe.'

'Give the fellow the benefit of the doubt, though, Holmes,' I said. 'He did say it was an early draft.'

'Watson, I find it hard to see how redrafting can rescue this.'

'So do I, to be honest.' I rose. 'Well, this has hardly been revelatory. The only thing I've learned is that my eyesight is failing. I'm for bed, Holmes. Even Harbin will be offstage by now.'

'Oh, we are not finished. Not quite.'

I sighed and sat down again. 'What else could we possibly hope to achieve?'

Holmes had extracted the pages that had been stuffed into Drake's mouth from his case, and was smoothing them out on the table.

'We should, at least, read these.'

I picked up a page.

'It's the same play, Holmes. Just with a little more saliva.'

'Nevertheless, reading it may be a little more… What was the word you used? Revelatory.'

'And you will give me no peace until it's done, will you?'

'Certainly not. Best just get it over with.'

Holmes divided the pages between us, and I slumped over on the table, supporting myself by my forearms, feeling my eyes begin to close at the prospect of re-reading a bad play.

After a page or two, though, they snapped fully open.

'Holmes… You recall the scene where the man finally realises his love has been returned all along,' I said.

'Yes. A more pathetic attempt at melodrama I have yet to read.'

'Well, I happen to have a rather more overblown piece of melodrama here. The man simply walked away at the end, didn't he? Put flowers on her grave, and wandered off.'

'Yes. Hardly the most compelling of endings.'

'Well, he's not walking away now. He is wailing at her headstone, lying down on top of her grave, begging fate to take him, resolving to stay there until cold, hunger or thirst finishes the job.'

Holmes snatched the page with far more vigour than he'd ever applied to relieving me of my newspaper.

He scanned it, scanned it again, and stood.

'Come along, Watson. The police never sleep. We'd best try to find Mobbs.'

'To tell him what? That Sinclair has managed to revise a bad play into a worse one?'

'Sinclair said Drake would not wait for him to complete his revisions. We have no indication that Drake had even seen the changed version. Which means neither had anyone else. The only person who could have had access to these pages, Watson, who could have placed them in Drake's mouth, is the playwright himself. We are going to tell Mobbs that we have found his murderer for him.'

'HE CONFESSED, IN the end,' said Farrier. He stopped in front of the space where Sinclair's makeshift podium had been. The past few days had brought vehement rain, which had now eased enough to make a stroll through the Botanic Gardens feasible.

'I'm sure he did,' said Holmes. 'No point in doing otherwise, not since we discovered the discrepancy between the two versions of the play.'

'He did smother Drake, then?' I asked.

'Yes. Invited him round to his lodgings – in a part of Sydney which Drake would usually never be found in, I might add – by saying he had located a potential investor who wanted to meet. The mythical investor was running late, so Sinclair kept topping up Drake's glass until he started to doze. Then Sinclair simply held a cushion over his face. He had a friend who was a carter, who helped him get the body to the theatre and string him up. And of course Sinclair couldn't resist the final flourish, stuffing the pages in Drake's mouth.'

'We haven't heard from Mobbs,' I said.

'And you may not,' said Farrier. 'With the confession, your testimony may not be needed.'

'What were you expecting, Watson? A thank-you note?' said Holmes. 'He will not be thanking us. They never do.'

'Well, I, for one, would like to show my appreciation,' said Farrier. 'What about this evening? Some sort of diversion? What do you fancy?'

'Oh, anything, anything at all,' said Holmes. 'Except perhaps the theatre. Plays these days. They are not what they used to be.'

A Wild Colonial

Kerry Greenwood & Lindy Cameron

N O DOUBT HOLMES would be wondering what was keeping me from the hotel, as it was I who'd been desperate for a cool drink, but a necessary walk across the dusty yard to the outhouse had thrown more strangeness in my path in five minutes than we'd encountered in the previous two weeks.

It began when I exchanged words with a gentleman of previous acquaintance and ended with me sitting in the dirt in the adjacent paddock, being snorted at by a ship of the desert.

The curious and the eventful were norms in the life I shared with my friend Sherlock Holmes, but the previous fortnight had been unusually empty of interest. I should clarify that it had been devoid of diversion for Holmes; I had found charming company in the other passengers on the ship, enjoyed games of cards and backgammon, and marvelled at the savage beauty of the rugged southern coastline.

Holmes, meanwhile, had endured two days of violent sickness a week into the sailing from Melbourne, caused not by rough seas but by the rough rum he'd imbibed with the crew below decks. Not willing to endure that again, and with no other stimulants on board, England's foremost consulting detective had taken to inventing elaborate crimes, committed by our unsuspecting fellow passengers, just to pass the time.

And now here I was, miles from anywhere, on a continent thousands of miles from everywhere, waylaid by a coincidence of rather epic proportions, locked out of the hotel by a firmly bolted back door, and accosted by a man insistent on selling me a pocket watch. While the last was not itself strange, I was almost certain he was the same man who had spoken to Holmes at the port of Adelaide two days before.

After politely refusing the man's goods I headed for the side of the hotel and a way back to the rather confidently named High Street. The hotel, a general store and post office, and a blacksmith comprised the town's entire commercial centre. In fact, as the store and forge also had adjacent cottages these formed the entire town of Oakwood – named for the hotel.

As I clambered through a rough-hewn fence I was assaulted by a familiar stench and the recall of a memory so strong I altogether forgot where I was until a voice, urgently asking if I was hurt, drew my attention to my position on the ground. It seems I'd tumbled into the corral where horses and other beasts of burden were tethered to feed and rest while their owners did the same indoors.

I understood well the connection between memory and smell but it had previously only been the whiff of gunpowder that had taken me back to Kandahar.

I sat up, accepted the assistance offered and, once righted, stared into the faces of two men: one a bearded cameleer, and the other the Englishman I'd already greeted in front of the outhouse. As I'd last seen Captain Harcourt on a battlefield on the far side of the world it perhaps explained, by association, my melodramatic reaction to the funk that wafted from the dozen camels not six feet from where I now stood. Harcourt, it seemed, was the owner of the herd, the turbaned Nazeem was his lead cameleer, and his business was now a trade route north and into the centre of the country.

Moments later I pushed open the front door of the Oakwood Hotel to discover it was unlikely Holmes had noticed I'd left the bar, let alone been gone nearly quarter of an hour. My friend, in shirtsleeves, his coat held gingerly by a young lad, was engaged in a contest of arm wrestling with a mountain of a man dressed in baggy trousers and an undershirt. Money had been wagered and six raucous men cheered on the outcome they thought was a forgone conclusion. Unbeknownst to them, Holmes was deceptively strong and possessed a stubbornness that matched his opponent's drunken bravado.

I retreated to the table we had chosen on arrival and enjoyed the rest of my ale. When my travelling companion rejoined me, victorious of course, I realised just how bored and restless he must be so very far from the congenial surroundings of Baker Street. When Holmes resorted to taking part in pointless manly challenges or, worse, engaging sociably with strangers, then his brilliant mind was clearly verging on the deranged. Watching him cope with a month on a pastoral station far removed from civilisation, or what passed for it in the colony of South Australia, was a situation I decided I could do without.

'I think we should rethink our plans, Holmes.'

'They were your plans, Watson. We journey to the wilds of Penwortham for a reunion with another of your brothers-in-arms. They've certainly spread themselves around the world in the years since your war.'

My war. I took another drink. I hated my war.

In that very moment, ex-Captain Harcourt entered the bar, glanced around, including in our direction, and without acknowledgement stepped up to the bar.

In a flash, Holmes's wrestling partner crossed the room, swivelled the empty chair opposite me and straddled it. 'So, Mr Holmes, what do your skills tell you about the blighter who just walked in?' The man then turned to me. 'He picked me good, you know. Knew I was a shearer, and where I was from an' all. Bob Sykes is the name.'

I shook his offered hand. 'John Watson. And my friend is most adept in such matters.'

Holmes smiled and studied Harcourt. 'He is a gentleman of determination and rigorous discipline. Once a soldier, either here in the colony or, no, a European battlefield; most likely the Crimean War.'

Usually adept. Perhaps the colonial air was confusing his senses.

Sykes, however, was nodding, so I wondered what lies Harcourt had been telling in his new life to make amends for his old one.

'Given his gait and dress he is now employed in trade along the new route from Adelaide and the great Port of Augusta –'

'Port Augusta, Mr Holmes; there's no of.'

'Right, Mr Sykes. The man's gait and bowed legs suggest he has spent a lifetime in the saddle and even now spends days on horseback plying his supplies to towns further north.'

I frowned at my friend. Perhaps it was the colonial ale. Sykes too cocked his head as if he now doubted the detective's talents.

'May I cut in?'

'Go right ahead, John,' Bob Sykes insisted.

'I think you'll find the man's posture, while it confirms a life in the saddle, is more indicative of a man accustomed to camels rather than horses.'

Holmes raised an eyebrow at me in surprise before returning his attention to the 'stranger' at the bar. 'Ah,' he said. 'The somewhat backwards lean of his stance; an acquired habit rather than a natural occurrence. I believe you're right, Watson.'

'Well colour me impressed.' Sykes got to his feet. 'And good luck, Mr Holmes, in your hunt for our strange creatures.'

'His accent was from Derbyshire and he smelled of lanoline?' I asked my friend after the shearer left.

'Very good, Watson. No skill in the obvious though. Oh, I mean no skill on my part.'

'As you say, Holmes: the obvious is obvious.'

'So, a camel rider?'

'I met his camels outside.'

Holmes laughed. 'Anything else?'

'Ex-Captain William Harcourt. Fought in the Second Anglo-Afghan war. Never set foot in the Crimea. Shipped out here direct from India.'

'Another one of your cohorts then, Watson.'

'I'm afraid so.'

'You don't want to take time to discuss old war wounds?'

I scowled at Holmes. 'Once the shock of recognition wore off, it took but a moment to recall we had not liked each other. At all. He was an unremarkable soldier, by which I mean he did the least he could in order to ensure his survival. The rumour, never proven, that he was profiteering from goods removed from the company stores, resulted in his redeployment to a different unit.'

'Such malefactors would once have been transported to this country as convicts,' Holmes observed. 'Oh Watson, I am quite encouraged in my Australian quest, as Sykes informed me that in the waterways around Penwortham we might just come across the curious ornith–'

All conversation in the establishment was silenced as the door banged open dramatically and a dog entered. It was closely followed by two members of the constabulary: one rotund and unhealthy; the other rangy, fit and alert, though marked with a small scar below his left eye. Both were dressed in the navy-blue uniform of the trooper, rather casually worn by the tall sergeant, and in this instance covered by the red dust that was no doubt the curse of the local mounted police.

The quiet was short-lived as most patrons were unperturbed by their presence. I say most, because I noticed Holmes had also noticed all these details, and probably more, but his attention swivelled between the sergeant and my erstwhile comrade in arms.

'Your man is likely still involved in questionable business practices,' said he.

'Harcourt does look like a cornered animal,' said I. 'The trooper, however, seems more intent on slaking his thirst than on any level of policing.'

'As did we on our arrival, Watson. That did not mean we weren't alert to the possibility of any wrongdoing.'

I glanced at my friend and wondered, not for the first time, if he was ever not alert to the potential for misconduct in any room or situation.

'But he does have business here too, my dear Watson, as you will soon see.'

Given I had no doubt Holmes was correct, I simply waited for what he could already see coming. Sure enough, as soon as the sergeant had quenched his thirst, in one swallow, it should be noted, he thumped the bar and turned to his fellow patrons.

'I have here two new Wanted posters,' he began, yanking the once-rolled papers from the button-less gap in his jacket. 'One for a blackguard who's been doing wrong by several women in the region, and one for the outlaw gang known as the Red Boys. The latter have returned to our fair colony to terrorise and rob decent citizens on our roads. Respite from their attacks was a seasonal thing, it seems, for they struck outside Port Wakefield two weeks ago, and yesterday they were seen hightailing it from a brutal assault on Bill Cooghan, the baker from Leasingham. Many of you know Bill, and that poor man is still unconscious and may not live to see his young wife bring their first child into the world.'

'An effective way of cajoling information from a crowd not usually inclined to help,' I noted.

'I heard those bastards scarpered into the Skilly Hills.' It was Bob Sykes who offered the information.

'You heard right, mate,' the sergeant said. 'It was Mick and I who chased them there. We lost their trail in Skillogalee Creek.'

Holmes raised a finger to let the trooper know he wished to view the posters, which as it transpired, could have been portraits of anyone hereabouts, even my good friend in one of his disguises. The thin-faced man wanted for unnamed crimes against respectable women sported bushy sideburns, and the attending information on the bushrangers simply said that the Red Boys were four tall bearded Irishmen, at least one of whom had red hair.

'I'll wager the facial hair has gone with these being posted about,' Holmes said, offering the back of his hand to the trooper's dog – a handsome black and grey-blue creature that stood by his side.

'You'd think that,' the sergeant said. 'But around here that would make them stand out; not unlike your good shaven selves.'

I stroked my moustache to ensure it was where I last left it; Holmes tried not to snicker. A glance around the room, however, showed that apart from the youths, all the men sported facial hair of various lengths. Even the sergeant's close-cropped beard could hide a multitude of sins.

'I've never heard of seasonal criminals,' Holmes said. 'Unless perchance they use snow skis as a means of escape.'

The sergeant laughed. 'It's the best explanation I have for these bushrangers plaguing us at the same time every year for the last three.'

'What else is seasonal in these parts?' I asked.

'Wheat harvesting, sheep shearing, vine planting and grape picking. Hmm, you think these blokes maybe have a legitimate sideline?' The trooper looked impressed.

'In the grand scheme of things,' Holmes said, 'one would hope the bush-ranging – not being in the slightest an intellectually criminal pursuit – would be the sideline. Or perhaps they simply use the influx of workers as a cover for their low deeds.'

The driver of the bullock cart that was to provide our transport for the last ten miles of our journey tapped on the half-open window behind Holmes. 'We need to be heading out now, Dr Watson.'

'You're travelling with Teddy Draper,' the sergeant said. 'Are you hitching a ride north, or actually making for Moonadarra Station?'

'Moonadarra,' I said. 'I'm Dr John Watson and this is my friend, Mr Sherlock Holmes. We're calling on Stephen Brookes, with whom I served in India.'

The trooper nodded enthusiastically. 'Stephen's highly thought of around here – a big deal for a bloke who ain't been here a decade. Tell him we'll be calling through in a couple of days. I'm Robert McKellar. And no doubt I'll see you again. If you've come all this way to see an old friend, I don't imagine it will be a short visit.'

FIFTEEN MINUTES LATER Holmes and I were perched atop a well-packed but hideously uncomfortable dray being pulled by six snorting bullocks loosely handled by the charming Teddy Draper, a talkative grey-haired working man in the employ of my friend Captain Stephen Brookes, British Army retired. We had barely travelled a hundred yards when a horseman approached along a crossroad and hailed us.

'You heading back to Moonadarra, Nick?' Draper asked the dapper gentleman.

On close inspection – which Holmes was giving the rider – he was overdressed rather than fashionable: neat as a pin, in a dark green frockcoat and waistcoat, long black boots and white riding breeches.

'That I am, Teddy. Just been visiting my cousin in Watervale. And you'll be Mr Brookes' guests all the way from England. The name's Nicholas Arandale.'

Holmes completed the introductions and then, after running his hand through his hair, asked the most peculiar question. 'I wonder if your barber is local enough for my friend and I to attend him. It seems most men in the colony favour the beard and dishevelled look. After days on the road I fear we will soon be indistinguishable from the locals and may not recognise each other.'

Arandale preened like a dandy. 'There are only two gentlemen I trust with my grooming, Mr Holmes. One is Surtees Ward of Hindley Street, Adelaide; the other happens to be Dougal McTavish, one-time Edinburgh barber, now station manager at Moonadarra.'

'Excellent,' Holmes said, and then strangely – by which I mean in a manner un-Holmes-like but quite deliberate – he affected a casual stroking of his cheek and jaw.

Interestingly, Arandale copied the gesture across his own clean-shaven face and then quickly dropped his hand. He withdrew his fob watch, checked the time, and returned it to his waist pocket. 'Well gentlemen, I must be off. I'll need some sleep before hitting the boards with the last flock tomorrow.' He urged his horse forward into a trot then a canter, and within moments had disappeared on the road ahead.

'Nasty piece of work.'

'What's that, Mr Draper?' Holmes asked.

'Disagreeable little toad, that Flash Nick, and I make no apologies for speaking ill of him.'

'He seemed quite–'

'The charlatan, Watson,' Holmes interrupted.

'My dear chap, this country is the place for reinvention. Mr Arandale clearly dresses above his station, but here in the colonies the lines between those stations are somewhat blurred.'

My friend looked at me as if I'd taken leave of my senses and Teddy Draper laughed like a rum-soaked sailor. Clearly, I had missed something.

'He fancies himself quite the toff, that's true,' Draper managed to say. 'And he might be one of the district's gun shearers but he's mean enough to kick a dog, sly enough to cheat at cards, and rake enough to treat women like they owe him their time.'

'You deduced all that?' I asked my friend.

'Of course not, Watson. I noticed only his costume and his grooming. And, of course, that he was a shearer, for the same reason as I knew Bob Sykes was a shearer.'

Holmes stood, balancing expertly despite the roll and drop of the dray, and rearranged a couple of smaller sacks to make something of a wide armchair for us both.

It proved passably comfortable for the next two hours, at which point Mr Draper suggested we all climb down and walk for a while. The road, inasmuch as it could be so designated, seemed like a never-ending meander edged by wild grasses and towering eucalypts. It was daunting to recall how unbelievably huge this country was, and that so much of it was untamed and so very foreign to the sensibilities of two Englishmen who, though well travelled, were more accustomed to William Blake's green and pleasant land.

Stretching the legs and back for a mile proved to be a sensible idea, though it brought us closer to the bush – as Draper informed us the vegetation was called; all of the vegetation everywhere, apparently – and the reptilian dangers that lay therein.

'Watson, do you hear that?' Holmes stopped in his tracks. 'It sounds like a large man running after us.'

'Several men,' I agreed, and totally without shame leapt back onto the cart. As Draper had been regaling us with tales of giant lizards that ran on hind legs, I had no desire to be knocked down by a gang of them.

Holmes, on the other hand, stood stock still in the middle of the potholed road as if pretending to be a tree would save him from a giant marauding–

Teddy Draper was laughing raucously at both of us.

Oh – a giant marauding bird. It thundered out of the bush, veered around the bullocks and came to a swaying stop one inch from, and at eye level with, Mr Sherlock Holmes. The ridiculous ostrich-like creature bobbed its head with large beak and beady eyes back and forth, stomped its oversized talons as if daring Holmes to run, and then, with equal melodrama, ran off into the trees. It was followed a moment later by another eight of its kind.

'Emus,' Draper managed to say between guffaws, as he climbed back onto his seat. 'T'was a good idea to remain still, Mr Holmes.'

England's great consulting detective, a man rarely given to fear or astonishment, turned to face us, a pallid tinge retreating from his aquiline visage and a look in his wide grey eyes I could only describe as startled. He returned silently to his place on the wagon beside me. 'Well, that was exhilarating,' said he.

I rolled my eyes. Only Holmes would register terror and describe it as thrilling. 'I suppose this only enhances your desire to find one of those *Ornitharapuss?*'

'Honestly Watson, you know full well it's *Ornithorhynchus anatinus.*'

'Actually, Holmes, I know it as a duck-billed platypus – which hints at its comical appearance far more accurately than the Latin.'

'Riders coming up behind,' Draper stated. 'Oh, dear.'

Oh dear indeed, I realised at the same moment, and reached into my pocket for my revolver. My companion touched my arm and whispered, 'Do not engage with them, my dear Watson.'

Do not engage with the three armed and dangerous bushrangers?

The men – long-bearded and masked by kerchiefs – rode to a rowdy stop, one in front of the bullocks, and the others either side of the cart. Draper had no choice but to pull his beasts to a halt. It seemed the Red Boys had chosen us as fair game.

'Hand over yer money and anything of value and we'll be letting you go on yer way – unharmed,' said the man in front. The two beside him brandished pistols but were otherwise silent.

Draper, his hands out in plain sight, waved to indicate he would reach for something. Holmes, likewise, pulled out his pocket watch, then reached carefully into his coat for his wallet and handed both to the robber beside him. With no choice but to follow suit, I handed over my purse of pound coins and my own watch.

'Any flour or sugar in your supplies?' the lead bushranger asked.

Draper nodded and turned to us. 'You'll have to give up your couch there, gentlemen. And the one near the back, on top, is a bag of sugar.'

Holmes handed over the two sacks of flour we'd been reclining on and crawled back for the other. All the while, he was studying the bushrangers for every possible clue that might later help Sergeant McKellar and his constable. As was I, of course.

True to their word, the Red Boys took only what we offered up and rode off in the same direction we were going.

'Curious,' said Holmes, as the wagon lurched forward on its way again.

Draper, only a little perturbed himself, smiled at my friend. 'You're a strange one, Mr Holmes. You find a giant running bird exhilarating and robbery-under-arms a mere curiosity.'

'It's not our first robbery,' I explained. 'And it was likely the bushrangers themselves that Holmes found curious. But you don't seem too troubled by the incident, Mr Draper.'

'Not my first robbery either, Dr Watson. While it's true some bushrangers are ruthless, many are just poor and hungry, travelling the roads having lost all on the goldfields. Mostly, if you do as they ask, no one gets hurt.'

'One can only wonder, therefore, what the baker from Leasingham did, or did not do, to that same gang to be beaten so badly,' Holmes noted.

'Curious there were only three of them.'

'Perhaps the fourth Red Boy was indisposed, Watson; or their robbery of us was one of happenstance,' Holmes noted. 'I assume the small sacks we handed over were easily reached tokens designed to acquiesce to any possible robbery, Mr Draper.'

'You don't miss a trick, do you Mr Holmes?' Draper grinned. 'They got the second bag of flour only because you rearranged the cart. It was Mr Brookes who suggested the idea.'

Ten minutes later we spied a man limping along the road towards us. Despite his dishevelled state, it took but a moment to recognise the fellow as the dandy who had cantered away from us in the township of Oakwood.

'Bloody Flash Nick,' Draper said.

I jumped down from the cart to give Mr Arandale a hand, just as he was about to slump to the ground. 'Good grief my man, what happened to you?'

Arandale's once-white breeches were red with dirt, his waistcoat torn at the buttons, and there was blood and a blossoming bruise beside his mouth. Put together with the limp and the lack of horse...

'I see you too met the Red Boys,' said Holmes.

'Damned bushrangers,' Arandale said.

'You argued with them didn't you, you fool,' Draper said. 'There ain't nothing you own that's worth your life, Nick.'

Arandale shrugged and then allowed me to help him up onto the cart beside Draper. 'I know that now. But I liked that watch.'

'The watch?' Holmes was surprised. 'It wasn't your horse they stole?'

'No. And I'm hoping that Bessie returned to Moonadarra after they knocked me off her.'

Holmes studied Arandale from behind, amusement tugging at the corners of his mouth, then glanced at me with a promise of a later explanation. There was something amiss in the young man's account, though I could not see what it might be.

'Do you suppose those bushrangers were originally convicts from the east?' Arandale asked, reinforcing the misconception that a free-settled colony would mean no criminals. My partner in crime-solving and I had already discussed this delusion.

'They were Irish sailors, possibly pirates, turned to a life of crime on the land,' Sherlock Holmes stated, as if it was obvious. 'Correction: their leader was Irish. As the other two did not speak, I cannot vouch for their heritage. And, as the wanted posters describe them all as Irish, when perhaps they are not –'

'Then that would be a reason for them not to give themselves away by speaking,' I said.

'P… pirates?'

'Yes, Mr Arandale,' said my clever friend. 'Shipless brigands, if you like. All three had swallows on their forearms, which alone signifies men of the sea. The bushranger I handed the sacks to was at least a boatswain, as evidenced by the anchor between his thumb and forefinger; and I believe I saw, between the open collar and the scarf of the Irishman who did all the talking, an image of the uppermost rigging of a sailing ship – the boast of a man who has rounded Cape Horn.'

'But what –'

'The already mentioned scarf is the link to their life as privateers, Watson. The Irishman's was well worn but clearly silk of a deep blue.'

When I shrugged at the significance of the scarf, my friend explained that even in our modern era pirate dress was a deliberate insult to the notion of a society organised by rank and privilege. 'From the great seafaring days of the mid-1500s, swashbucklers took delight in flouting the so-called Elizabethan Sumptuary Laws regarding clothing. As you know, Watson, only royalty was permitted to wear purple or gold, but further to that only the upper classes could wear silk or velvet, and colours such as dark blue, crimson and violet were banned from the lower classes. Pirates wore such things to further flaunt their lawlessness.'

A mile down the road, a painted sign nailed to a tree announced that Penwortham was four miles ahead and Moonadarra Station two miles west. Three hours later the bullock cart clunked across a livestock grid and the pastoral station that was our destination finally opened out before us. Three days of hot sticky weather, biting insects and dust faded from memory amongst the greenery that surrounded the homestead. Young ash and beech trees formed a tranquil stand of England in this dry and dusty colony, and the planted shade trees also included palms and fruit trees. I wondered how much of this great continent would be thus transformed.

Arandale muttered a goodbye, slid from the cart and limped towards the large sheds on the far side of the yard next to the house. Other buildings of various sizes stood apart from the main residence, while the geometric garden beds before it were replete with roses, petunias and lavender. I could tell Holmes had also caught the glorious smell of water in the air, and the sound of ducks and geese suggested a source of reasonable size, perhaps a lake or even a brook.

As we clambered from the wagon, a hubbub of voices and barking accompanied the crowd that approached us. Three dogs led the way, followed by my dear friend Stephen Brookes, two other men and a collection of children. One of the children abandoned not only his cricket bat to greet us, but also the ball just bowled by a heavily bearded man who, it must be said, fitted perfectly the description of the Wanted poster's redhead.

I nudged Holmes, who said, 'The resemblance to the absent Red Boy bushranger is noted, Watson. Likewise, the same could be said of the man about to greet us, were he not devoid of chin hair.'

Stephen Brookes – older by a decade since we last met, and sporting a substantial ginger moustache to go with his thick red hair – shook my hand with great enthusiasm. 'Watson, my friend, you have come at last. And this must be Mr Holmes.'

There were handshakes all around, while Brookes ushered us forward. 'Welcome to our home, you must be bone weary. My wife Euphemia has made tea and fresh lemonade.'

'Such interesting architecture,' Holmes noted as we stepped up onto the broad, vine-covered verandah.

'I see you've adopted the Indian style of building to combat the climate, Brookes,' I added.

'And merlot?' Holmes questioned.

Brookes glanced between us, not knowing which one to answer first. 'The experiment with merlot grapes is going well. Some varieties really do not like the heat. The vineyard has two years' growth. And yes, Watson, as you well know the pitched roof and deep verandah all around keep the interior considerably cooler. This will, I think, become the Australian architecture.'

We entered the house through wide double doors to find a tall and queenly woman awaiting our arrival. Brookes introduced his charming wife who, as was the colonial custom, took our hands.

'I am guessing there are only two things you want right now; it's up to you in which order you require them,' she said. 'Refreshments await you in the parlour and a cool bath has been drawn for you.'

'A bath to scour ourselves of several layers of travel dirt would be excellent,' Holmes said. 'Watson?'

'Indeed. I too am desperate for water in any form after a day on that hellish cart.'

The lady of the house smiled. 'Peter will carry your bags to your room and then escort you to the bathhouse. There you will find robes and slippers.'

AN HOUR LATER, clean as whistles and considerably lighter, Holmes and I joined our hosts in the parlour for a spread of sandwiches, scones, rose jam and clotted cream, an aromatic fruitcake and a generous selection of beverages.

We had just taken our seats when the younger Brookeses entered the room. Five children – a boy child in an overall, the cricket-playing youth in baggy trousers, two girls and a young lady – did their polite best and then escaped; all but the young lady, the elder Miss Brookes, who loitered long enough to be invited to play mother. She took great delight in pouring tea for her parents and me, and black coffee for Holmes.

'Delightful,' Holmes said. 'Perfect coffee served by a delightful hand.'

'I trust, gentlemen, that you won't think badly of Australia because of your unfortunate experience on the road here,' Brookes said.

Holmes raised an eyebrow. 'Mr Draper told you of our meeting with the bushrangers.'

'As well he should,' Brookes said. 'I don't know why you didn't mention it.'

'In truth, my friend, being held at gunpoint is nothing new for us,' I admitted.

'You've met bushrangers before?' It was an excited question from the Brookes' elder son Harry, who'd returned surreptitiously to the room and was perched on the piano stool beside us.

'We encountered a highwayman on a cold foggy night outside London,' Holmes explained. 'It was an irritating experience rectified by our unmasking of the criminal at a house party just two days later.'

Young Harry's eyes were wide. 'Perhaps you'll catch the Red Boys while you're here, Mr Holmes.'

'Perhaps. But there was a greater mystery involved in the unveiling of the Goodnight Highwayman than there would be in merely apprehending the armed thugs who accosted us.'

'There has been such an influx of menacing robbers of late,' Brookes said. 'And our constabulary is a fledgling thing; the founders of our colony having mistakenly believed we would not need a police force at all.'

Holmes nodded. 'Watson and I debated this before we were bushwhacked, that an absence of convicted and transported felons would not mean an absence of crime or criminals. The absence of our watches now being proof of that.'

'Nor would our being a free-settled colony stop convicts and other ne'r-do-wells from ranging into South Australia from the eastern colonies,' our host stated. 'Especially once our governor encouraged the search for gold to stop our population from heading east to the rushes in Victoria. Our own diggings now lure the best and worst of men, or as the editor of *The Register* said, "attract lawyer and larrikin alike". The rush at Teetulpa continues. Sergeant McKellar says close to five thousand miners were trying their luck up there, before last year's discoveries of gold at Mt Ogilvie and Mongolata.'

Holmes steepled his fingers and looked at me. 'Interesting that McKellar didn't cite gold as a factor for his theory of seasonal crimes,' said he.

I nodded. 'Though Mr Draper equated unlucky prospectors with an increase in bushranging.'

My travelling companion was unable to keep silent on the matter. He pointed out that, goldrushes aside, criminals are present in every level of society everywhere in the world; one just has to know where to look. 'The fact that they have not yet been caught does not mean they do not work in your field, your bank or your parliament.'

'Like that horrible Mr Anderson at Parakoo Station,' Harry volunteered. 'Teddy and Hans say he hits his wife and his horses. And that's a crime, don't you think so, Mr Holmes?'

'Harry!' cried Euphemia Brookes. 'Our guests do not need to know the business of our neighbours.'

'But Harry is quite right, Mrs Brookes,' Holmes said, and I caught him winking at the lad. 'A man who hits a woman has no character, and one who harms a horse has no hope of redemption.'

'No redemption, Holmes?' I asked.

'A man who beats an animal in his care will likely treat the people in his dominion the same.'

'There's lots with no character or hope around here then.'

'Harry!' his mother said again. The youth drew a finger across his mouth to imply silence. Holmes seemed oddly amused.

In fact two hours later, after I roused myself from a nap, I found Holmes on the verandah playing chess with young Harry. 'Did you know they have a venomous spur on their back feet?'

'I did know that, Harry. It's why I find them so fascinating.'

'Do you want to collect some for your poison collection?'

'What diabolical thing are you planning now, Holmes?' I inquired.

'Scientific research, nothing more, Watson. Harry may be able to find me a platypus.'

The venom. His obsession with the strange creature now made perfect sense. I don't know why it hadn't occurred to me before.

NEXT MORNING AFTER a splendid breakfast of bacon, sausages, eggs and fresh-baked bread, Holmes and I were treated to a tour of the homestead by young Harry. My friend seemed to find great entertainment in the company of the lad, who it must be said showed a keen intelligence.

The house was flanked by what Harry called the ladies' and blokes' quarters. 'Of course, I can't take you in where the women live and do sewing and the like, Mr Watson,' Harry said with a chuckle.

'And we three would have no reason to go in there,' I declared.

Holmes seemed amused and when I asked what was so entertaining, he said, 'I heard the delightful sound of a woman laughing, Watson, I suspect at someone else's expense. It must be contagious.'

Harry next pointed out the kitchen, bakery and laundry, each in small buildings behind the house – kept apart to avoid losing everything should they catch fire.

Mrs Brookes, Mrs McKenzie – the cook – and a young woman emerged from the kitchen and crossed the grass to the house, quite preoccupied by something that seemed significant.

'Such music,' Holmes declared, distracting us from the fact that what bothered the women was not our business.

Harry grinned. 'They're our magpies singing their water song. They come for the washing.'

Strung between the laundry room and a stand of gum trees were rows of ropes on which hung the household wash and there, hopping on the ground beneath, were several black-and-white birds warbling an exquisite melody.

'They sing for the water that drips from the clothes,' Harry said. 'And for the bits of mutton Hans gives 'em when he slaughters a sheep.'

'You have your own butcher?'

'We do, Mr Watson. He made the breakfast sausages you liked so much. He does cuts for Mrs McKenzie's cooking and mince for her delicious pies, and makes food for the dogs at Pembroke Station over the way.' Harry pointed in an easterly direction.

'What about your dogs?'

'The butcher at Pembroke makes the meat for ours, from their cattle. Can't have working dogs getting a taste for the animals they're meant to care for. Hans took the last mutton for this season over yesterday and came back with beef for our mutts.'

'Interesting,' said Holmes.

'Sensible,' said Harry, and he led the way across the wide yard towards the shearing shed.

'Fresh meat, fruit and vegetables, other supplies only a few days away,' I noted. 'You have everything even a gourmet could desire despite being so far from civilisation.'

'Dad says this is a great country, better than England, for growing stuff, especially with Bonnie's Creek yonder; it never runs dry. Bluey McTavish reckons Dad is trying to grow everything known to man – except coffee and cigars. Them we haul in.'

'Thank goodness,' said Holmes. 'Is that the same McTavish who cuts a fine head of hair?'

Harry self-consciously pushed an errant strand of his collar-length hair behind his ear. The action reminded me there was something I needed to ask Holmes. 'How would you know that, Mr Holmes?'

'Mr Arandale told us he was a fine barber.'

Harry scuffed his feet in the dirt and scowled. 'Ordinarily I would tell you not to believe a word Flash Nick says, but in this he happens to be right.'

'I suspected there was something not quite right about that man,' Holmes said.

Harry leaned closer to us both and said, 'That Flash Nick is one of them you'd say had no character and no reception.'

'Redemption, Harry,' Holmes corrected.

'My sister Amelia is taken by him. I fear she has no brains at all.'

Holmes laughed. 'Unlike you, young Harry.'

'You already know I am quite smart, Mr Holmes.'

'And humble,' I noted.

Our destination was the shearing shed but Harry took us by the pig paddock occupied by seven large black Berkshires rolling joyfully in a quagmire; the dairy and its milking yard, empty until dusk; and the butcher's shed and adjacent blacksmith forge from which a *whit-whit-whit* could be heard accompanied by a baritone singing 'Ach du lieber Augustin'.

Harry introduced us to the singing blacksmith, a powerful broad-shouldered German wearing a leather apron over his undershirt and trousers. It seemed Hans Schwartz, who was sharpening a collection of shears, a daily task during this shearing season, was both butcher and blacksmith. He asked Harry to take the bag over to the shed and see if there were more shears for him.

Shearing was well underway for the day; it was, after all, past ten o'clock. The spectacle that greeted us was one of sweat and toil, an organised chaos of sheep after sheep being dragged from pens across the boards to one of twenty men armed with large blade shears. The time each man took to relieve a sheep of its fleece was obviously a matter of pride and fierce competition.

Flash Nick, as he was universally known, was front and centre, what they called the ringer, and his speed and skill were indeed impressive. He handled two of the sturdy Merino – a Spanish breed that thrived in the colony – for every one and a half shorn by his fellows.

In amongst the raucous men and the animals that passed through their hands were the tar boys who darted in to apply tar to any cuts inflicted on the sheep in the process. The fleeces were then gathered up by the roustabout who cast them onto a wool table for classing.

'That's Bluey over there.' Harry pointed at the giant red-haired Scotsman who'd been shouting encouragement, the same man with whom Harry had been playing cricket the previous day. 'He's our wool classer too, does the skirting to get rid of any burrs and inferior wool from the edges, and grades it all. The main line or best of the fleece goes into those bags, the skirtings get bagged over there, and any damaged wool, from dags or pests, ends up in the dead wool bin.'

'How many sheep do they shear in a day?' I asked.

'Flash Nick's best is two hundred and sixty a day; the others maybe two hundred. But, there's a story of a bloke in Queensland with a record of three hundred and twenty-one in just under eight hours.'

'That is an extraordinary number for such backbreaking work,' I said.

'And the ringer does not seem at all impaired by his run-in with the notorious Red Boys yesterday.'

'True, Holmes, but this is his element and, as you well know, a man can do anything when his livelihood or reputation are on the line. I've no doubt he will limp out of here at the end of the day.'

Holmes asked why the shearers here were not yet using the modern shearing machinery. 'After all, the revolutionary method was patented by an Australian pastoralist.'

Harry marvelled at all the things Mr Holmes knew, but when he said Bluey could answer that question, I left my friend to his fact gathering and went in search of Brookes.

WHILE CHANGING FOR dinner that evening I finally asked Holmes about his sudden interest in local barbering, whereon he regaled me with his theories about the clearly questionable character of Mr Nicholas Arandale.

'You may recall, Watson, when we first met the pretender outside Oakwood, he claimed he'd been to Watervale to visit a cousin. This was patently untrue, as his horse had obviously already been ridden for longer that day than the mere two miles to Oakwood. Given his desire to present, by way of dress, as a gentleman shearer, he paid scant attention to the residue on his neck that marred his otherwise impeccable grooming.'

'Residue of what?'

'Spirit gum I believe, Watson. The kind used for attaching facial hair as a disguise.'

I pondered what this could mean for a good two minutes, and finally asked Holmes to explain.

'Sergeant McKellar was looking for bushrangers and… ?'

'A blackguard doing wrong by local women.'

'Indeed. Whether McKellar meant that in terms of financial, emotional or physical harm, we do not know. But coupled with Harry's opinion of Flash Nick as a man of no character or *reception*,' Holmes smiled, 'and Mr Draper's statement that Arandale is a reprobate when it comes to women, I am inclined to wonder what else he hides behind that dandy façade.'

Holmes was about to elaborate on his theory when the gong sounded for dinner, which was a raucous and amusing two hours of fine food and conversation, followed by a blessedly short piano performance by Miss Amelia.

Later that evening Brookes and his lovely wife and I were enjoying a brandy and conversation on the verandah alongside Holmes and Harry, who were again playing chess and talking about poisons.

'Such a fine mind, Brookes. Have you considered sending Harry to study the science of medicinal drugs? I noticed a Yorkshireman, one Francis Faulding, has established a pharmacy in Adelaide.'

Brookes laughed. 'I agree she is intelligent, Watson, but I doubt the world is ready for a female pharmacist – even in this new frontier.'

She?

Oh my.

I did not look at Holmes, who would no doubt be annoyingly gleeful at my expense, and at my questionable powers of observation. I wondered where on earth my mind had been that I was fooled so easily. Perhaps it was because the girl's clothes were not worn as a disguise. Harry clearly dressed as a boy because she enjoyed it.

'You're right, my friend. Medicine would be a better option. There are more than a few women studying in London, Edinburgh and Boston, and I believe even the University of Sydney Medical School has admitted women. Harry need not even leave the colonies.'

'Bravo Watson,' Holmes said. 'Well saved.'

I pointedly ignored my friend but smiled at Harry, who leapt to *her* feet, announced she'd rather be an astronomer, and excused herself from the game and our company. 'I will be back, Mr Holmes, but I must catch Amelia before she retires.'

Harry's elder sister had just strolled off the far end of the verandah, heading towards the kitchen, although the darkness soon swallowed her completely.

'And I,' announced Euphemia Brookes, 'shall rouse Mrs McKenzie from her crochet to make us all some coffee.'

Left alone with a thoughtful Brookes and a highly amused, at my expense, Sherlock Holmes, I hid my desire for retribution behind a copy of the *Adelaide Advertiser*. It was two weeks old but nonetheless an article I had read earlier provided an instant conversation point.

'Holmes, my dear chap, I do believe this news article makes reference to you.'

'How so?' His question was cautious, as if he guessed my intent was to insult.

I read part of the article aloud. *There is here and there a misanthrope who shrinks from the society of his fellows, hates correspondence, votes telegrams a nuisance, and whose idea of a happy life is to be far away from the active bustle of the world –'*

'A misanthrope? Really Watson?'

I shrugged and continued. *'Such characters may have found small satisfaction in last week's absence of intelligence from other countries, but even they probably have had about enough of it.*

'The breaking of the cables has been felt by everybody to be an unmitigated

vexation. It is bad enough to be suddenly switched off in the midst of a telephonic conversation and to obtain no response to successive rings and calls, but the deprivation we have lately experienced is ten thousand times worse.

'*It is only at such a time that we discover how closely the copious and prompt information we are accustomed to receive from distant lands is interwoven into our daily life, and how much of our interest in life is bound up with it.*

'*This ordinary situation has been reached by a gradual and sometimes an almost imperceptible process, but its abrupt alteration produces a kind of mental shock. There are many who scarcely knew how much they were concerned in watching the progress of events until the reports, for which they had become accustomed to look every morning, suddenly ceased.*

'*A much larger number are eagerly anxious for their daily news, and its absence has been a keen disappointment. The greater part of the community has got to regard it as a principal part of the daily pabulum, supplying food for thought and topics for conversation, besides keeping up a pleasant sense of knowledge as to how the world is going on.*

'*Our reliance has been on a slender strand of copper wire, which parted without warning, and the result of it was, for a time, complete isolation. We have felt as completely cut off from the rest of the civilised world as though we had been mysteriously transported to another planet.*

'*The more frequent and regular mass communication of late is little compensation and no substitute. It is the news of the day, or of yesterday at latest, that we want, and to do without is an unpleasant deprivation.*

'*It is strange and almost amusing how many things people wanted to know about, and at once, when the flow of news was interrupted,*' I finished.

'And oh, my dear chap,' I said to Holmes, 'you would have been desolate about the following:

'*For instance, how were the Cricketers getting on. They had had a somewhat-chequered career and suffered some serious defeats, but scored a splendid victory at Leicester, and were in the middle of a match with Gloucester when the cable broke. They had begun excellently, and of course people were anxious to know how they sustained the colonial reputation.*'

'Amusing, Watson.'

'It was quite dislocating indeed,' Brookes stated. 'The Overland Telegraph commenced operation only a decade before we settled here. Ordinarily it would not have troubled us too much, as news still takes time to get to Moonadarra, but McTavish and I were in Port Augusta getting supplies and awaiting news of our last shipment of wool to England when the line broke. We had a taste of what life was like when news from England took six months to get here. If the ship was wrecked taking our cargo with it, we might not have known for a year.'

Holmes steepled his fingers and proceeded to dig into the infinite library that was his mind. 'It was an incredible feat of engineering, Watson, to build a two-thousand-mile telegraph line across the forbidding centre of this country from north to south, and to meet the undersea cable being laid from Java to Darwin. And much of the heavy lifting was done by men like the Afghan cameleer you met in Oakwood.'

I waited for even more information but my friend stood abruptly and announced a walk was in order. With no invitation to join him, I assumed Holmes needed time to himself and indeed, though he crossed the wide yard towards the shearing shed, he avoided the men gathered around a large fire and singing vibrantly of a shearer's life.

Mrs Brookes rejoined us, followed by the cook carrying a tray with the coffee and a selection of small cakes. Our conversation turned to the Afghan cameleers when it was commandeered by the sight of Holmes striding across the yard in the company of the misses Harry and Amelia. Bluey McTavish meanwhile, after a quick word from Holmes on the way by, headed for the shearing shed.

'Holmes, my dear fellow, what on earth –'

'Do not be alarmed, gentlemen, Mrs Brookes, we are not injured.'

'Harriet!' Mrs Brookes exclaimed, rushing off the verandah to tend her daughter.

I followed close behind to check everyone for wounds because, despite my friend's protestation, Harry's face was smeared and her shirt soaked in blood, and Holmes's hands were red with it. Miss Amelia, though unsullied, looked to be in shock.

When everyone was safe on the verandah, Brookes asked again what had happened.

'It was that bloody Flash Nick!'

'Harriet! Honestly.'

'Allow her this moment, Mrs Brookes,' Holmes requested. 'Harry just saved Miss Amelia from the rough and inappropriate attention of Mr Arandale.'

Harry's eyes, I noticed, were shining brightly and she wore the same expression of exhilaration and triumph I had often seen in Holmes after an encounter with danger. I had an inkling of the woman she would become, for even at fourteen Harriet Brookes was formidable.

Her father, meanwhile, was on his feet and demanding to know all, Mrs Brookes was fussing over Amelia, and Mrs McKenzie had reappeared to find out what all the ruckus was about. Holmes, standing beside Brookes, whispered a few words in his ear that calmed him considerably.

The elder Miss Brookes, it seems, had taken a stroll – straight into the clutches of Mr Arandale. That the meeting had been prearranged by the two did not make the man's behaviour any more excusable. And Miss Amelia was now mortified that her innocence had been tested in the worst possible way. If Harry had not followed, the evening would have turned out much worse. Holmes and Harry recounted the events, as the poor young lady was weeping silently into her mother's shoulder.

Accustomed – as Teddy Draper had hinted – to getting his own way with women, Nicholas Arandale had tried to molest Miss Amelia, first by stealing a kiss and then by grabbing hold of her when she objected that he was much too forward. When Miss Amelia tried to extricate herself – just as Harry entered the shearing shed from the other end – Arandale pushed Amelia backwards and pinned her against the wall.

'Couldn't you cry out, Miss Amelia?' It was Mrs McKenzie doing the asking. She had a comforting hand on Mrs Brookes' arm, but her fierce expression hinted at something more than tonight's incident. Indeed, when Miss Amelia moved from her mother's embrace and touched her throat, we could all see the bruise forming there. Mrs Brookes muttered to her cook, 'You were right, Jeannie.'

'Even if he hadn't had his dirty hands around Amelia's neck,' said Harry, 'the men were singing so loud around the fire outside they wouldn't have heard her – so I ran at him.'

'And I…' Miss Amelia quickly lifted her knee in demonstration.

'Good thinking,' I said, and Brookes agreed. 'But where did all this blood come from?'

'From Flash Nick, Dr Watson,' Harry declared. 'He was just getting up off the ground from where Amelia put him with her knee, when I jumped on him. He just flung me away like I was nothing, but somehow – and I really don't recall how they came to be in my hand – next I knew I was up and sticking him good and proper with a pair of shears.'

'Oh my lord!' said Mrs Brookes, while her husband looked both shocked and proud.

'Not that he deserves it, but does the man need medical attention?' I asked, realising now why Holmes had dispatched McTavish to the shed.

'He ran off, Dr Watson,' Harry said. 'He just ran out into the dark night like the coward he is. I hope he dies out there before we even go looking for him.'

I glanced at Holmes, who nodded. 'There was no sign of the blackguard when I arrived to find young Harry still holding the gory shears. There was enough blood on the floor to suggest he'd not make it beyond the creek, that being the direction he went, but as Harry says it's too dark to go searching.'

Now this seemed a strange thing for my friend Sherlock Holmes to say, because for him the thrill of the chase comes second only to the unravelling of a mystery. I therefore decided that for Holmes not to be out there tracking down the assailant, there must now be a greater mystery attached to this attack.

A long low whistle that curled around the exuberant singing of the shearers was noticed only by Holmes and myself, the others on the verandah being too occupied with matters at hand. Bluey McTavish – quite visible in the light of the fire he'd returned to – tucked his pocket watch into his waistcoat and gave a casual thumbs-up.

'Mrs Brookes, Mrs McKenzie, this morning you were engaged in a conversation that seemed fraught and of great concern to you. I guessed at the time it had something to do with the young lady also in your company; your daughter Ivy, I believe.'

Mrs McKenzie nodded. 'Aye. You're an observant one, Mr Holmes. My daughter Ivy was out the back last night, collecting an extra loaf, when she was grabbed around the throat by a man who… who then grabbed her in other places he shouldn't. It was in the pitch dark beside the bakery so she couldn't see his face.'

'Euphemia, why didn't you tell me?' Brookes asked.

Mrs Brookes shrugged. 'What would you have done, Stephen? If it was one of the shearers you would not have sent him packing, so close to the end of the season. Especially as it now seems likely it was your ringer.'

Brookes could not deny the way things would have gone but he did seem troubled, perhaps by the realisation that the likelihood of him overlooking the harm done to the cook's daughter would have allowed the same to happen to his own.

AN HOUR LATER the household had retired, though I doubt the Brookes family got to sleep any sooner than Holmes and I. My friend paced our room like a man in search of a way out, until I finally begged him to at least lie down and cogitate.

He sat on the side of his bed. 'I am troubled, my dear Watson.'

'I would never have guessed.'

'There is something – a clue, a piece of the whole – that is just beyond my reach.'

'A clue to what, Holmes? We know the truth of Nicholas Arandale. Perhaps not his whereabouts or the state of his health but his bad character has been revealed.'

'Oh, I know exactly where Mr Arandale is, Watson. And the man is quite dead.'

I sat up and stared at Holmes. There was nothing else to do.

'There was too much blood on the floor for the man to have gone anywhere, let alone run from the shearing shed and out into the night.'

'But he was not there. You didn't see him.'

Holmes gazed at me. 'No Watson, I did not see him. But there was no blood trail leaving the shed. There was a pool of the stuff where Harry stabbed him, a few splashes as he no doubt stumbled away gripping his wound, and a smear on the floor.'

'The word "smear" has never sounded so mysterious,' I said.

'I am almost certain Harry rolled Arandale's body into the dead wool bin.'

'Good grief, Holmes. What if the man isn't dead?'

I swear Sherlock Holmes shrugged at my question as if it mattered not. 'Harry stabbed him in the heart, Watson. She re-enacted it for me, and her sister, shaken as she was, verified it.'

'But that's no reason–' I began and then found myself quite without words.

HOLMES TOOK AN early-morning walk the next day but returned in time for breakfast, a rather subdued affair. The younger Brookes children still had much to say, but the adults were quietly entertaining their own thoughts. Miss Amelia was still in bed, and Holmes was chatting to Harry about gunpowder. The young girl seemed untroubled by the previous night's misadventure; quite extraordinary, given it may have involved her killing someone.

We had just polished off Mrs McKenzie's aromatic bread when a hullabaloo with the farm dogs heralded a visitor. Brookes excused himself from the table, but as we all needed a distraction from the tense atmosphere, we followed.

Although she stood quite tall – in her boy's breeches and suspenders – and bold, I noticed that Harry had taken hold of the hand of Mr Sherlock Holmes, perhaps displaying trepidation that of the five visiting horsemen only one was not a policeman. Sergeant McKellar, true to his word to visit Moonadarra, was accompanied by three mounted troopers, and a man – not unknown to Holmes and me – who was cuffed by his hands and tied to his horse.

McKellar dismounted, whereon his blue dog came bounding back from a run around with the farm hounds – all circling Hans Schwartz as he rode towards the gate – licked her master's hand and then took off again, nose to the ground.

Mrs Brookes offered the troopers refreshments and, like everyone else gathered around, including Bluey McTavish, eyed the captured man.

'I see you have caught the Red Boys' lone Irishman, Sergeant.'

'We have, Mr Holmes. But how did you know only one of 'em, as it turns out, was Irish?'

'A simple deduction. He was the only one who spoke when they held us at gunpoint on the road here.'

'You was robbed by these blighters?' It was McKellar's overweight constable who spoke, and then took delight in smacking the bushranger in the back of the head.

'What of the others?' Brookes asked.

'Dead,' McKellar said, matter-of-factly. 'Two of 'em anyway. No sign of the fourth member of the gang.'

'We encountered no fourth man,' Holmes said.

It would be an understatement to say that everyone in the know gave me a look of utter incredulity when, clearly without thinking, I added, 'And Mr Arandale said it was only three who robbed him too.'

Harry stepped behind Holmes, Brookes coughed in shock, McTavish pulled out his pocket watch and I was rather hoping an emu would run through to take the attention from me. Sergeant McKellar noticed none of this as his own next statement could have produced the very same reaction.

'You don't say? He's doubly unlucky then. We've actually come to arrest your ringer, I'm afraid. Arandale's been identified as the man who behaved quite inappropriately with Miss Imogine Clark over at Pembroke Station late yesterday. We reckon he's the man on our Wanted poster.'

Well, there was a revelation that surprised none of us, although the astute attention of Sherlock Holmes was switching between Bluey McTavish and the handcuffed bushranger.

'Our ringer scarpered last night,' McTavish said. 'He tried the same with one of our girls and was caught. He took off a couple of hours before midnight with just the clothes on his back.'

'Did anyone see which direction he went?' Sergeant McKellar asked.

'South-west, we think,' Brookes replied.

McKellar scowled. 'Likely heading for Port Augusta and a boat out of the colony then. We'll take rest and refreshments, thank you, Stephen, and then be on our way. We might even catch the blighter.'

'Gotta check the dogs,' Harry muttered, but Holmes held her tight by the hand and declared they were fine. While I wondered when my friend had become an expert on canine behaviour, the creatures began acting quite strangely; they were following the lead of the sergeant's dog, who stood atop the deck outside the shearing shed, barking as if she'd found…

Oh dear.

'Go see what's got Ruby's tail in a twist, Mick,' McKellar ordered. He led the rest of his company into the shade on the far side of the garden, where he dragged the bushranger from his mount and retied him to a tree trunk. His constable, meanwhile, demonstrated why he carried more weight than his fellows, by trotting his horse over to the shed to investigate.

The moment the constabulary were out of earshot we retreated further away to the verandah. In the next few moments I learned that my friend Stephen Brookes honestly thought Arandale had fled into the night after being stabbed by his daughter. When Harry, Holmes and McTavish gave me looks that each said 'do not say a word' I took their advice. And while Holmes and McTavish likely knew something Harry did not, I now suspected there was more they knew than I did.

Even so, Holmes surprised me when the question he asked the big red-headed Scotsman was how long he had owned his pocket watch.

McTavish grinned like a loon. 'Nothing gets by you at all, does it, Mr Holmes?'

'What does Bluey's watch have to do with–'

'Everything, Mrs Brookes. Although I was worried all this fresh antipodean air had quite dulled my senses,' Holmes replied gleefully. 'But I'm now convinced there was one among us even more villainous than I suspected.'

Bluey McTavish raised his hands as if in surrender when we all stared at him. 'Not me. He ain't talking about me.'

Holmes laughed. 'Of course not. I do believe, however, that particular timepiece belongs to Mr Arandale.'

'It does,' McTavish nodded. 'Found it on the… along with two others in his swag. I'm guessing they really belong to you and Dr Watson.'

I announced my confusion and found I shared company with Brookes and his wife. Harriet, on the other hand, was jumping up and down on her chair.

Holmes smiled. 'Yes Harry?'

'Flash Nick was… is… the other bushranger, isn't he, Mr Holmes.'

Holmes was gloriously pleased, as much with his own realisation as with the fact that Harriet had come to the same conclusion. He glanced, only somewhat apologetically, at me. 'Do not fret, my dear Watson. Harry and I had more to work on than you; we had discussed some incongruities that now turn out to be clues.'

'Dirt on the front of his breeches and not on the back, even though he said those bushrangers knocked him off his horse,' Harry said, as if she was the one who had sat behind Arandale on the bullock dray.

'With no injuries to his hands,' Holmes continued, 'I first assumed his horse had run off, and he had been robbed while on foot and without putting up a fight, merely dirtying himself a little to cover the embarrassment.'

'That could still be true,' I said. When Holmes raised an eyebrow, I added, 'Ah, except for his watch.'

'And you recall the evidence of the spirit gum?'

'You thought Arandale was adopting a disguise to take advantage of women.'

'And you recall what the good sergeant said when I noted the bushrangers might shave their beards to reduce their likeness to the Wanted posters?'

'That it would make them stand out more.' I frowned. 'Oh! You mean Arandale wore a false beard as one of the Red Boys.'

'But why?' Brookes asked. 'The man has a sound reputation as a top shearer. And how can you truly know this?'

'For some, a criminal life is more exciting than the humdrum of hard work,'

I said, nodding at Holmes to hurry up and explain his theory, for I too thought he was taking a leap of deduction.

'It's now clear to me that after assaulting the baker in Leasingham, the Red Boys separated. The next morning, Watson, Draper and I met Arandale first on the outskirts of Oakwood, and again barely three miles from here. In the original encounter, I noticed the remnants of a possible disguise on his neck, in the second he claimed to have been robbed by the same bushrangers who had beset us. While I am still inclined to think he met his bushrangers while standing on the road, I now suspect he had been waiting for them. Barely fifty yards further on from where we picked him up, I saw evidence – a disturbance in the dirt made by hoofprints. And don't raise your brow like that, Watson, you know well what we have deduced from such things.'

'I'm with Dr Watson on this,' said McTavish. 'Even our remote bush track is much travelled.'

Sherlock Holmes, as is his custom, ignored the doubters. 'Three sets of hoofprints, from the direction we all travelled, made a stop where it was obvious one man had been pacing for some time. There was evidence of a second set of boot prints, on the ground just long enough, I believe, for the owner to punch Arandale in the face and hand over our watches, and perhaps other booty. That man remounted, collected a horse that had been tethered for some time to a large gum tree, held it close to his own mount and released it where the track bifurcates between Moonadarra and Penwortham.'

'And Bessie did what she would do naturally, and came home,' Harry said.

We all watched as Trooper Mick rode back through the yard after his investigation at the shearing shed, and Mrs McKenzie was met halfway across the garden by Sergeant McKellar. On her return to the house, the smiling cook informed us that when Mick had followed Ruby the dog into the shed – straight to the dead wool bin – the lads over there had informed the constable that a sheep had been accidentally killed by an overly enthusiastic young shearer, who'd stupidly tossed the carcass into the wrong bin.

'Is that true, Bluey?' Brookes asked.

'I believe,' said Holmes quickly, to save McTavish from putting his foot in anything unnecessary, 'that the blood in the bin belongs to a certain missing shearer. When I found Harry and Amelia, there was quite a mess on the floor. I myself reached into that dead wool bin to pull out some fleece to clean the worst of it. Mr McTavish, I believe, cleaned the rest. It's not surprising that Sergeant McKellar's skilled dog would pick up the scent of blood.'

'Perhaps Ruby could track the man into the bush,' said Mrs Brookes. 'What if he comes back?'

'He's unlikely to return, Mrs Brookes,' Holmes said. 'If he's not dead out there somewhere – much like his bushranging cohorts – then he's halfway to Port Augusta already. In my opinion he is not worth the effort of a search.'

It was settled then, to avoid any complications over the veracity of the various stories regarding the missing Nicholas Arandale, that no one would further enlighten Sergeant McKellar. When McTavish returned to his shearers and Harriet and her parents retreated inside, Holmes and I took a stroll through the garden. Only then could I ask my friend if Arandale was indeed deceased, and if so what on earth had become of his body.

A look of barely supressed amusement graced Holmes's angular face although, as he closed his grey eyes to compose himself, I caught a moment of self-reproach. When he drew my attention to something that had occurred earlier – in plain sight of all, including the police – I realised why the great Sherlock Holmes considered his mirth inappropriate. We agreed however, before he left me to my thoughts regarding the departure of Herr Schwartz – the blacksmith and butcher of Moonadarra Station – that justice had been served in the cases against the blackguard Nicholas Arandale. It bothered me a little that the dogs of Pembroke Station might be dining on the remains of a bushranging violator of women, but then Teddy Draper had said Flash Nick was also inclined to kick dogs.

Ten minutes later I spotted Holmes and Harriet Brookes heading towards the vineyard. 'Where are you off to now?'

'Harry says she has something special to show me, Watson.'

'I do hope it's an *Ornithorhynchus anatinus*, so you can be done with that obsession, Holmes.'

'No Dr Watson. It's a *Xylocopa*,' Harry said.

I waited for an explanation – knowing one would be forthcoming whether

I asked or not. But Holmes was engaged by the chatter of the young woman who walked beside him.

I finally called after him. 'Well?'

'A green carpenter,' Harry said, with a smiling backward glance.

My sigh was quite audible.

Holmes didn't bother turning, though he stabbed his cane rather joyously in the air. 'A bee, Watson. A wild colonial bee.'

Phil Cornell
2016

Shadows of the Dead

Kaaron Warren

THERE ARE TIMES, such as these, when a pleasant convalescence in the quiet of my own home seems too far away.

I mentioned this to Holmes in passing, and his comment, 'Well, then, onto the next boat with you. Or would you like me to warm your slippers?' reminded me not to expect sympathy from this friend. Ten years now since I was invalided home, and it is only on the rare occasion I remember my injuries.

'Are you bewildered by all we have encountered, Watson?'

'I miss my home and my wife, Holmes.' I did not add *something you will know very little about.*

'I, too, miss London, Watson,' he said. 'We shall return in due course.'

He had surrounded himself with the accoutrements of home, travelling with as much luggage as the flighty young ladies we observed on our ocean journey to this far side of the world. He had his violin, of course, and his pipes, which sat lined up on the mantelpiece of our rented yet somewhat lavish accommodation at the top of Collins Street in the city Holmes chose to call New London (or Surrogate London), being Melbourne, a thriving metropolis I would have been delighted to share with my wife. Much as was my desire to go home, there was much to explore in the city.

It was odd for us to walk the streets and be relatively unknown, and just as odd to sit in our lodgings without any expectation of our regular Scotland Yard supplicants arriving at our door. While enjoying the elements of the city itself, Holmes found himself undistracted from the boredom of being 'not at work', so he took to travelling on the trams of Melbourne to exercise his deductive talents. He would return to me in great excitement, although of course his deductions could not be proven.

'Today I saw a paperboy. He stood with one hand thrust deep into a pocket, one toe lifted off the ground. He only had one newspaper remaining. He wore a scarf around his neck. Clearly, Watson, he is a boy at the end of his day's work. His hand clutches his fare in his pocket, hoping not to pay but ready should he need to. The scarf is dusty around the edges and the back of his hair mussed, leading me to understand he has taken some rest during the day. He is carrying this last newspaper home to his father. I could see that the pages were bent; he could not sell this copy and would not have to pay for it.'

Holmes nodded, pleased with himself.

'There were a number of men carrying lacrosse sticks. Not young men, Watson. These were not college students out for a game. They were men taking time out from work and from their responsibilities. They sat cross-legged. The toes of their boots looked scuffed. Under the seat rested a large box. They barely spoke and all were rather grubby, so it is simple to surmise that the game was completed rather than upcoming. I felt a moment's envy for that quiet camaraderie.'

'I played lacrosse at Barts, you know,' I said, and was unsurprised when Holmes did not respond.

Instead, he recommended we take tea at the rooms lower down Collins Street, and I could think of no reason to refuse.

I did enjoy seeing Holmes at play in this way. It seemed to me he was lighter in spirit, for the time being at least.

The Sunday following we had been told we were to have goose for dinner. Holmes took off just after eleven in the morning, and had not returned within the timeframe our wonderful lady of the house hoped for.

He arrived at four, quite agog. Our hostess was perhaps a little sharp with him, because the goose was well ready and, as she reminded me more than once, it would be 'on her' if the bird was dry. I did not assume that Holmes was hoping to avoid the bird altogether, although since the case of the Blue Carbuncle, we have both been wary when eating goose.

'What is it, Holmes? You seem agitated.' There are times when I refrain from delving into his state of mind, but he did not seem in any way unnaturally affected.

'Watson, I have been travelling by tram.'

'Yes, you have, Holmes, most days for a week.'

'And time and time again I have assessed my fellow travellers with ease. This one an accountant, that one a guilty conscience, this one nearly wed.'

'Yes, yes, Holmes, you are indeed clever.'

I was eager to eat and, to be honest, a little tired of my friend's cleverness.

'Yet today I find a paradox. A woman of the near to middle forties, showing all evidence of being a doctor. Not a nurse, Watson. A doctor.'

'A woman?' I said. 'Quite sure?'

'Quite, quite sure. I tell you, Watson, this flummoxed me for some time. The information seemed contradictory. Will you think ill of me if I tell you I followed her, only to discover that my assessments were correct? Only my prejudices were wrong. She is, in fact, a doctor. You might find that interesting.'

I recommended to Holmes that rather than follow the poor woman, he should have been at table, where I had been waiting, and with that we set upon our goose with gusto.

I relented the next day and assisted Holmes in his inquiries. We discovered that his lady doctor was Dr Constance Stone, late of Toronto University and the Society of Apothecaries in London, and the first lady doctor registered in Australia.

'Remarkable!' Holmes said. I wondered if I was seeing the first romantic inkling I had witnessed for some time from my friend, but he professed a mere professional interest.

She worked one day a week in Dr Singleton's Mission in Collingwood, and it was to here we repaired the next morning. I had some professional interest also, in that we shared a degree.

What a remarkable woman. She was delighted to make our acquaintance and had, indeed, heard of Sherlock Holmes, which was most gratifying to him. We shared tea and some rather tedious ginger biscuits and then she said, 'Would I be forward in presenting a case to you? If you hadn't expressed a certain boredom I would not even mention it, but it strikes me as the kind of thing that might appeal to you.'

Such a powerful woman! She had none of the diffidence many women feel or display when they are exposed to the Holmes intellect.

'A young man presented to us from Sydney. He was sent to stay with his mother in Collingwood, she being considered the best carer for a man in his condition.'

'Condition?'

Dr Stone continued, 'There are no previous signs of insanity. While I would call this man intrepid in the extreme, I would not say he was foolhardy or deluded. A war hero, invalided out, and you know what that can do to a man.'

I did indeed; in the years since my injury precipitated an early departure from battle, I had not yet regained my physical confidence.

'He claims that in a cave in Manly, New South Wales, he saw the shadows of the dead dancing on the walls, and that he is partially blind because those shadows now dance in his eyes.'

'No previous incidents, you say?'

'Not on record. We referred him to an ophthalmologist because there was little we could do, but he came back with the prognosis "little reason for the supposed occlusions". Sometimes, these experts…!'

Sherlock Holmes concurred.

'Sadly, he will be incarcerated if we can't find a solution soon. Once the authorities decide you are unfit to care for yourself there is little to be done.'

'I am intrigued, and would like to hear more of the man's story,' Holmes said.

'Excellent. I'll call for him. Tomorrow at the same time?'

Holmes was quite excited by this development and as we travelled home he expressed all he knew about the beachside suburb of Manly in Sydney and the caves therein.

ON OUR ARRIVAL at the clinic the following day, the subject was clearly identifiable amongst the dozen or so people waiting. I did not need Holmes to point him out, and yet point him out he did, whispering through the side of his mouth, 'There is our man, or I'm sadly mistaken.'

The patient was a scrawny man in clothes that hung loosely upon his frame. 'He has lost weight recently,' I whispered to Holmes, and he nodded curtly, as if I had stated something very obvious. The man's hair sat flat on his head and had not been trimmed for some time, and neither had his beard, which was marked with grey. He squeezed his eyes shut, rubbed them, squeezed them again. He startled a number of times, glancing sideways as if catching something from the corner of his eye.

Once in the treatment room, Holmes spoke. 'Dr Stone has told us a little of your condition, but perhaps you could explain it to us. Dr Watson has much medical experience and I have been known to solve puzzles such as your own.'

'I am not mad. There are ghosts in that cave, I swear it.'

'Can you tell us about this cave?'

We had researched much about this place, including a brief history of Manly itself, which was incorporated only in 1877. A brand new city, no less. An army general was beaten to death in 1872 and his remains thrown into the cave. This much is on record. Others say the same thing happened to pirate Blackjack Vaughan, who they say was dismembered and dumped there.

The patient said, 'The place is haunted. You ask anyone. They blame my failing eyesight, that I could not see properly and therefore I saw shadows. But I could see perfectly well before. There was nothing wrong with my eyes before I went into the cave. You ask anyone.'

He seemed to struggle with beginning his story.

'Tell us how you came to be in Melbourne. You are a postman, are you not?'

The man looked surprised.

'With both a slump to one side and a particularly calloused finger, your occupation is apparent,' Holmes said quietly.

'They sent me down to my mum. But all she can do is say *Never mind. Never mind.* All very well, isn't it? But how do you never mind when you've got an eyefull of the shadows of the dead?'

His very words sent a shiver running through me. I glanced at Holmes; he was transfixed.

'Tell us how you came to be in the cave.'

'I can't believe you're listening to me. Others refuse. I work at the General Post Office in Sydney as an investigator for their so-called Dead Letter office. In the quiet times I will help to track down the addressees of lost letters, but mostly I investigate crimes committed by mail.

'We received a series of parcels marked for the *Quetta*, a ship that sadly sank, taking near a hundred and fifty lives and all the mail onboard. As that vessel no longer existed, those parcels came to us. Amongst the many items – love letters, newsletters, photographs, you know the sort of thing – we discovered a large package containing the dismembered limbs of a man. Investigation showed that they once belonged to a postman who had disappeared from the Manly area.

'It was the local paper that put two and two together and came up with the cave where both a pirate and an army general are said to have been dismembered. It seemed as good a place as any to investigate.

'I was warned; don't go there. "It is haunted," children told me. "You should never go in there or you'll never sleep again."

'It was with little trepidation that I travelled to the cave. I am not a fearful man, and the stories I'd been told seemed mostly foolish. I tell you this so you will understand I am not a fanciful man. In fact I have been accused of having very little imagination. I did not enter expecting to be terrified, and yet…'

It was very sudden. He collapsed at our feet, as if the very thought of the cave made him seek unconsciousness! I stepped forward to help, as did Holmes, who placed a cushion under his head, and I saw, as few did, the kind man who resided within the cool, calculating, brilliant one.

The patient revived.

'I can't sleep at night for fear of the dancing men.'

'Can you tell us about them? The more I know, the more I might be able to understand.'

'When first you enter, there is a warmth to the place that feels unnatural. Once inside, I saw a glow, but it was low enough I was glad I'd brought my lantern to light the way.'

'What did you expect to find? What were you looking for?'

'Evidence that our postman had been there and had perhaps left something behind to help us find his killer. There was a silvery glow…'

Holmes interjected. 'Mercury, perhaps?'

'I don't know. But as I stepped further inside, a terrible thrumming began. Rhythmic, like the heartbeat of a giant. My heart matched its beat and as it sped up, so did my pulse.

'And then…'

He held his head. I had him sit up straight, hoping to avoid another faint.

'Upon the wall, shadows appeared. I swear to you there were no men dancing, and yet those shadows danced. I watched, transfixed, confused, until the shadows severed and the arms, the legs, the heads – all were severed and danced alone.

'At that point I ran in sheer horror. Perhaps it doesn't sound so bad in this bright room, but I can tell you the sense of violence, of death, was pervasive.

'They live in my eyes now, the shadows.'

He held his eyes open wide with his fingers and I do believe I saw smudges there.

HOLMES AND DR Stone went into consultation. I did not mind being at one remove; this was far from my remit and I wanted to make no diagnosis.

'Watson, we are off to New South Wales. We must bid Collins Street and Melbourne farewell and go north.'

'Will you be looking at the cases of the pirate and the army general too, Holmes? Do you think there is a connection?'

'That we would do if we indeed believed in ghosts. But we do not. We are not seeking salvation for lost souls; we are seeking a modern-day murderer with evil proclivities.'

'Why did you ask about mercury, Holmes? Are the caves in that region known for it?'

'That we will discover. What is known, and perhaps you will dredge it from your early learning, is that mercury poisoning can lead to smudges in the eyes. That is a known fact and perhaps where we will begin.'

'That accounts for some of it. But what of the dancing men?'

'We shall have to see them for ourselves.'

WE TRAVELLED TO Sydney by the train. I do not believe Holmes slept at all. His brain was far too engaged on what we had heard and what lay ahead.

I missed my wife more than ever on the journey. We would have spent the time deep in conversation, and she loved an overnight sleeper train.

Instead, Holmes kept up a steady patter as he was wont to do on occasion. I was not sure he was aware of my presence at all; he may well have been talking to himself, although he mentioned me by name every now and again.

'So, the *Quetta*. How many lives were lost, Watson?'

'One hundred and thirty-four, with one hundred and fifty-eight surviving. All mail was lost in the Torres Strait.'

'A tragedy not only for those lost at sea and their families, but also for those many affected by the loss of mail. It is something we perhaps underestimate, the importance of our daily delivery,' he said, although we both knew very well how he anticipated the postman's arrival each day.

'To say nothing of the murdered postman,' I said, and Holmes nodded.

We were silent for a while as the miles passed us. I was reminded of my great fortune, for all my complaints, as we observed families by the tracks, their belongings at their feet.

'Hard times ahead,' Holmes said.

WE SETTLED OURSELVES in an adequate domicile. Holmes promptly vanished for two days and returned in that state of mind I hated to see him in. It was almost unbearable and, in fact, I left him alone in our lodgings rather than hear his babbling, to say nothing of the aroma that arose from him.

Still, as ever he recovered himself by the next day and we made the journey to Manly. There we made enquiries, hearing rumours that the beach itself was a haven for opium users, which was cause for great concern.

There were thirty-four steps down to the beach where the cave sat. 'Do you remember that there are seventeen steps in Baker Street, Watson? How very odd that here should be exactly double.'

This was not the last oddity.

As we approached the cave, we saw evidence of failed men, slumped in the sand, flesh exposed to the sun's rays.

'Ah, the poor souls,' I said. 'Those lost to opium are lost to life, with very little chance at redemption.'

'More so than any other?'

'Indubitably. Sinking into the life of opium is sinking into a miasma. Sadly enough, these victims barely notice and cannot draw themselves out. A loved one may be able to achieve it, but my word it will take some determination.'

Holmes was quiet. We did not discuss his… interests. I wondered if he was imagining who might pluck him from the abyss, should he sink there.

'Poor souls, as you say. And yet, each one a person with the ability to choose their own future, and the responsibility for that is theirs alone.'

'This is true.' At that moment, I caught a glimpse of the great self-control Holmes exercised. I thought for a moment of how tempting that oblivion might be, how gloriously empty.

One man called out to us in his damaged voice, 'Don't go in there, not if you want to live. Not if you want your soul to save.'

His words brought a shiver to my spine, regardless of his circumstances.

We now stood at the mouth of the cave. On advice, we carried lanterns, the brightest we could find. Holmes removed his deerstalker cap. 'If there are bats, I would prefer the damage be done to my head, not my hat, in this place of mediocre millinery.'

We entered the cave. At first, the pleasant warmth seemed almost comforting, but within moments I found the air cloying and hard to breathe. Our lanterns seemed barely to penetrate the darkness and yet there was a brightness too, not so much flashes as flickers of light.

There were shadows on the wall.

Perhaps I am being fanciful here, but the shadows seemed human-like and no mistake. Dancing, shaking, shivering. Hypnotic, you might say. I reached for Holmes, dizzy at the sight, because I could not draw my eyes away from them. It was as if all else had vanished, and all I could see were these dancing men. They were long dead, I was sure of it, and as I watched their limbs seemed to sever…

I felt choked. Blinded.

The drumming came deep and strange. I could not imagine the sort of hands that could manage it. It was so odd I felt ill, as if some rhythm inside me was disturbed.

Not since the Baskerville case have I been so terrified. There was a palpable air of evil.

'Holmes!' I said, wanting his assurance, or wanting to leave these awful confines. 'Please, can we leave?'

We stepped outside, where I drew deep breaths. My eyes pained me and I thought that clouds had fallen over the city.

I was to discover I was wrong in this.

'Horrifying. Simply horrifying.'

'I don't know,' he said. 'I've seen worse puppetry.'

'Puppets!'

He smiled as I spluttered that these were not puppets but the shadows of fully grown men.

Holmes said, 'Do you not recognise these shadows?'

'Had I known those poor murdered men, Holmes, then perhaps I would.'

'Ah,' he said. 'Have you not heard of the shadow puppets of Java? I believe if we can find someone who has travelled to those parts and learned to make the puppets, we will be well on our way.'

It is difficult for me to report what followed because my eyes seemed to fail me altogether and I remember nothing more until I awoke in a hospital bed (tended by the inimitable Dr Stone, who had travelled up from Melbourne to see us both). I experienced a moment of panic, but fortunately the nurses had since removed the bandages from my eyes. I can only imagine my terror if I'd thought myself blind.

I lay there for a moment assessing myself before I spoke. I wanted that at least.

Tremors. Emotional lability (irritability, shyness, loss of confidence, nervousness), memory loss. Weakness. Headaches. 'Stocking glove sensory loss'.

Flu-like symptoms. Vomiting, diarrhoea.

Clearly this was mercury poisoning.

I said as much to Dr Stone, and she assured me that our poor Dead Office investigator, who had drawn us into the cave, had been treated and seen great improvement.

'Then it was all imagination?' I stuttered, sure that I was not capable of such dreaming.

Holmes laughed then, a sight most will never see. I would have felt offended if I didn't enjoy his merriment so much.

'Watson, no. You saw all you thought you saw. You heard all you thought you heard. But there is a mechanical explanation for it all, as a very small investigation revealed. I was correct about the Javan shadow puppets. They were manipulated, will you believe, by a large mouse on a wheel, with strings tied to both legs.

'The drums were set up in a natural crack in the cave, where a sea breeze drifted in sporadically. This helped the shadows to flutter, too.

'All of this was to conceal our killer's second crime. The cave was full of mailbags and other people's letters. Some had clearly had money and gifts removed; this must be a lucrative endeavour. And there was, as we all now know, mercury running down the walls.'

'But who, Holmes? We must stop them before they kill again.'

'Events have played themselves out, Watson. I needed to move quickly. I established an understanding of those who might have been in Java, and who now lived in the local area. There was just one: a lower-level diplomat who had been released from the Foreign Service for conduct unbecoming. From all reports, he very much enjoyed the benefits of being a diplomat in a country where a small amount of money can make one seem very wealthy. He returned to Australia poorly positioned, unhappy to be "poor" again. Some mail washed up as he walked along that very beach you and I walked along, Watson. Was he there seeking the false release offered by opium? That I cannot say. He opened this mailbag and found remnants of money in it. From here, he hatched his plan. It went well for many months, until the postman discovered him. In a panic, or so he says, he killed the man. I have a feeling there was a sense of power enjoyed, however, and can imagine him reoffending. He mailed the pieces to the *Quetta*, before she sank, thinking his package would travel around the world and never be opened. Pure chance that the vessel was shipwrecked. There is a certain justice, don't you think? That the same style of shipwreck that set him on his path also led to his discovery. I confess I am almost more offended by this randomness than I am by the murder.'

'And so?'

'And so, we discovered that the culprit is en route to Java again. Never mind; we have sent word of his arrival, and he will be caught before long. Would that we could fly through the air, Watson, and meet our killer as he lands.'

Dr Stone peered into my eyes then and declared me cured. 'The ghosts are gone,' she said, and I do believe she and Holmes shared a small laugh at my expense.

'I will be glad to return to the depravities of home,' I said.

The Sung Man

Raymond Gates

W E HAD BEEN in Australia for some months when we found ourselves in the bleakest, most godforsaken part of the country. I had experienced the desolate, unforgiving climates of Afghanistan and Asia, yet the physical challenge in withstanding the scorched, red earth that made up the interior of Australia was even greater.

What possible interest Holmes could have had in coming here was beyond my comprehension. We had joined a group of Afghan cameleers in Adelaide who were travelling north through the interior. For days we followed a route marked by the Overland Telegraph Line, which ran from Adelaide in the south to Palmerston in the far north, and had seen, I often thought, nought but an abundance of nothing. But, in fairness, the countryside of that strange northern realm does on occasion include copses of vegetation, strangely beautiful mountain ranges, and unique fauna. However, after enduring mile after mile of discomfort on the back of the particularly smelly, sour, temperamental beast that was our transport, my interest in these sights paled in comparison to my desire for a comfortable bed enclosed by four walls, with nary an insect to be seen or heard. Clearly, I was no longer the hardened young solider I had once been!

Holmes, infuriatingly, took it all in his stride. He had exchanged his deerstalker and Inverness cape for the head-wrap the Afghan cameleers favoured, atop which he set a wide-brimmed hat from which corks had been strung at regular intervals. Many station hands and miners had adopted the headwear as a means of keeping away the black flies that infested this land. Though it looked ridiculous, I must attest to its effectiveness. Holmes did not seem at all bothered by the insects, whereas I always seemed to find at least one (I suspect the same one) had made its way beneath the netting of my pith helmet, forcing me to remove it at regular intervals to swat the creature away, much to Holmes's amusement.

Eventually we arrived at Stuart, a place that barely earned its township status, being comprised of a population of under a hundred, and touting little more than an inn, a boarding house and a general store. That it existed at all was only due to the recent influx of gold prospectors, fuelled by stories of rich finds amongst the ranges. The only thing close to the area was the relay station for the telegraph. I had hoped to use it to send word back to Mrs Hudson – if only to let her know we were still alive and dissuade her from cleaning house in our absence – prior to setting out again. Holmes was determined to strike out west in search of some monolithic rock in the desert he had heard tales about. Spectacle though it may have been, I for one would have been just as happy to enjoy what little comforts the inn and boarding house might offer, for I had seen enough rocks to last a lifetime.

Given the town's remoteness, I had expected that the appearance of two Englishmen would be the most unusual occurrence of the day. I was soon corrected.

We arrived in the midst of a commotion between two groups of people. On the one side were three men mounted on horseback – miners, I surmised from their dirty and somewhat unkempt clothing – while on the other side a uniformed constable stood in front of two cowering natives, a man and a woman, naked but for their ginger hair and iron shackles that bound them hand, foot and neck to each other. The lead miner was yelling at the constable, his anger punctuated by the finger he jabbed towards the natives. Each man beside him held a rifle, pointed skyward. The constable stood firm, holding his hands up in a placating gesture and trying to get a word in edgewise.

Our approach distracted the men, but for only a second; however, that was long enough for Holmes to slide off his camel and stride towards the confrontation.

'Constable. Gentlemen.' Holmes's voice was at once genteel, yet imbued with an air of superiority. 'May I offer some assistance?'

For a moment, the men seemed too stunned to speak. Finally, the constable spoke. 'And you are?'

'Holmes,' he said, bringing himself between the two parties. 'Sherlock Holmes. The man approaching us is my associate, Dr John Watson. And you are?'

'I'm Constable Andrew Davis, and normally I'd be pleased to make your acquaintances, Mr Holmes. However, as you can see, I'm a little preoccupied, so I have to ask you gentlemen to move along.'

Holmes gave the man a thin-lipped smile. 'Yes, I understand perfectly, Constable.' He turned to the mounted men. 'May I ask your names, gentlemen?'

The man closest to Holmes had lowered his rifle and stepped his horse closer. He glanced back at their leader.

'Best take the copper's advice,' the lead man said. 'This ain't got nothing to do with you.'

Holmes took a step forward. Both armed men trained their rifles towards Holmes, a gesture that made me wish I had my service revolver at hand. All I had on my person was a leather sap in my pocket, and while I could produce it fast enough, I certainly would not beat the speed of a bullet.

'Yes, you are quite correct, sir,' Holmes said. 'Though as a consultant to Scotland Yard, more than one royal family of Europe and a number of the local Australian authorities during our travels here, upon seeing your heated dispute over what appear to be two incarcerated natives, I thought either yourselves, or the good constable here, might benefit from our assistance.'

The man spat and turned towards Davis. 'Just give us the coons and let us be done with it. You know they got to pay.'

'You know I can't do that. It's up to Willshire to decide what to do,' Davis said.

'Willshire. He's not here, is he?' The lead mounted man's horse shied at his outburst, and he pulled back hard on the reins to keep it steady.

'We're taking 'em,' he said. 'One way or another.'

The constable glanced at the natives, then turned back to the mounted men. His shoulders slumped, and I expected him to give in to their demands.

'I'm not sure that's such a good idea,' Holmes said, stepping forward to approach the constable and his captives. He addressed the constable. 'This Willshire you mention. Would he happen to be William Willshire, by any chance?'

The constable squinted. 'You know him?'

'I haven't had the pleasure of his acquaintance, no,' Holmes said. 'However, I do know that he is the Warden of the Goldfields here, and as such has jurisdiction over all matters of law in the area. Including the handling of prisoners. These two aborigines are your prisoners, Constable Davis, are they not?'

Davis nodded.

'Then, by extension, they are prisoners of the Warden of the Goldfields, and being that they are natives, they are by further extension within the custody of the Protector of Aborigines of this state. Is that not correct, Constable Davis?'

The lead miner snorted his derision. 'What the hell is this? Who do you think you are? These two killed one of my men! And they're going to pay for it. It's that simple.'

'That may be true,' Holmes said, turning towards the man. 'But if there has indeed been a murder, and the warden has not been able to investigate it to his satisfaction before *retribution…*' Holmes smiled, '…excuse me, *justice*, is meted out… well, that's the sort of thing that could lead to a deeper investigation.' Holmes arched an eyebrow. 'One that could lead to the suspension of mining activities until a full investigation can be undertaken.'

The miner rubbed his stubbled face, his eyes ablaze. 'You got no idea what you're talking about. No one gives a curse about these coons. You need to be minding your own damn business.'

'The Englishman's right.' Davis spoke up, and I noticed he had unholstered his pistol. 'Willshire will be back tomorrow. He'll decide then. Until then,' he said, waving the barrel of the gun towards the trio, 'it'd be best for you fellas to go back to your claim. Willshire will be out to see you once he's back.'

The armed men looked to their companion. The miner stared first at Davis, then at Holmes, then at the frightened natives. 'You'll get yours,' he said, and spat at the ground again. He then wheeled his horse around and galloped westward, followed promptly by the two. I let out a breath I felt I had been holding since we arrived.

'So then, Constable Davis,' Holmes said. 'Who is it that was murdered?'

THE CONSTABLE'S STATION was little more than a small, single-roomed cottage, furnished with only a simple desk, two chairs, and an iron pot-belly stove. Davis explained that the attending constables only used this as a work area, and that they resided at a camp at a place called Heavitree Gap. There were no holding cells, so the natives had their chains shackled to an iron ring embedded in the wall outside. The constable assured us that as natives of the land they were used to being exposed to the elements. Despite the plausibility of his statement, I could not help but pity the poor creatures.

Holmes and Davis sat at the desk, and I leaned in one corner of the station. It seemed cooler there, but only slightly, and I still felt the wetness of my shirt clinging to my back. Davis had offered us tea served in metal cups. It was terribly bitter; however, it was certainly the best we could expect.

'You fellas are a long way from home.' Davis relaxed back in his chair, sipping at his tea.

'Yes, we are,' Holmes replied, his own cup steaming on the table. 'Watson and I are trying to see as much of this land as we can during our time here. Make the most of it, so to speak.'

Davis nodded. 'Well, things are different to merry ol' England out here, Mr Holmes. Ain't much in the way of law or civility. Don't get me wrong, it's coming. Why, there was nothing more than dust here only ten years ago.' He leaned in close. 'But this is harsh country, Mr Holmes. People disappear out here all the time.' He paused. 'I don't want to see that happen to you and your friend here.'

'Trust me, we don't want that either,' I said. 'In fact, the sooner we get to Palmerston, the better, in my opinion.' I glared at the back of Holmes's head; however, he did not respond. Instead, he withdrew a small jewelled box from his top pocket and opened it. The aroma of tobacco wafted through the confined space.

'What happened here, Constable Davis?' Holmes took a pinch from the box, held it to his nose, and inhaled sharply and deeply. He offered the box to both Davis and myself before returning it to his pocket.

'There's a claim, about sixty miles east of town,' Davis said. 'Those three fellas that were here? That's where they're from. There was a fourth man with them. Gordon Hendricks. He's the one that was killed.'

We waited for him to go on.

'It happened over at Wallis's store. I saw it myself. Hendricks had come into town for supplies for the claim. He brought those two,' he said, indicating towards the natives outside, 'with him to help carry the goods back.'

'Is that typical?' Holmes asked.

'Some of the claims use the aborigines for labour.'

'As slaves?' I asked.

Davis gave me a sharp look. 'You've got to chain them up or you'll bloody well lose everything,' Davis said. 'They steal anything they can get their hands on, and they'll run off in the middle of the night.'

'Yes, I'm sure it's a concern,' Holmes said, with a sarcasm lost on Davis. 'You were explaining how this man Hendricks was murdered?' he continued.

'He was talking with Wallis, boasting how they'd just found a fresh seam. I only noticed something was amiss when Wallis asked him what was wrong. I turned to look and he just dropped to the floor. I rushed over to him and turned him over. He was limp, like a sack of flour. He wasn't breathing. I tried shaking him, shouting at him, even pounded on his chest a couple of times. He was gone. Just like that.'

'What was the cause of injury?' I asked, stepping forward.

'Them,' he said, gesturing outside.

'Who?'

'Those blacks. They killed him.'

'I'm sorry, I don't understand,' Holmes said. 'How did they kill him?'

Davis stared into his empty cup for several moments before answering.

'They sung him.'

'What did you say?'

'They sung him. Those two, out there. They sung Hendricks, and he died.'

'What the devil are you talking about, man?' I asked.

'They sung him! It's something the blacks do. Part of their rituals or black magic or whatever you want to call it. If you cross them, they sing you and you die.'

'Did you hear them?' Holmes asked.

'Hear them what?'

'Sing to Mr Hendricks.'

'Bloody hell. They don't sing *to* you.' Davis stood and began to pace. 'They just sing. Like a chant. Mitchell – the man who was doing all the talking today? He says he heard them the night before. Singing in that gibberish tongue of theirs. He heard them, and the next day Hendricks dropped dead.'

Holmes turned to me. 'As the only doctor present, what do you think, Watson?'

'Preposterous,' I said, unable to hide the disdain in my voice. 'A man doesn't die because someone sang some kind of morbid lullaby.'

'Well, I saw it with my own bloody eyes,' Davis said, rounding on me.

'Be that as it may,' Holmes said, standing and stepping between us. 'It does seem unlikely that a song alone could kill someone. Was there any evidence he may have been poisoned somehow?'

'Poison?' Davis stared at Holmes as if he thought him mad. 'He wasn't poisoned. He wasn't sick or anything. He was as strong as an ox, and twice as mean-spirited when the mood took him. You'd need a lot of bloody poison, mate.'

'Were there any marks on him? Something that could account for an injury?'

'No. Nothing.'

Holmes cupped his chin between his thumb and forefinger. I could practically see his thoughts jumbling around behind his eyes.

'Look,' Davis said. 'This really has nothing to do with you. I think you fellas would be best on your –'

'What was their motive, Constable Davis?' Holmes asked.

'What?'

'Why did they do it? Why would they want Hendricks dead?'

'You mean apart from slavery?' I muttered.

Davis leaned against his desk, took a deep breath and let it out slowly.

'There was a rumour Hendricks was availing himself of the woman.'

'Availing himself?' I said, unable to believe what I was hearing.

'He means he was having sexual relations with the woman,' Holmes said. 'Most likely against her will, I imagine. I understand it's almost a common practice here. Is that right, Constable Davis?'

Davis stared at the floor, unable to meet our gazes.

'In case you hadn't noticed, it's pretty remote out here,' he said. 'Not many women around, apart from the gins. They don't seem to mind.'

'Don't seem to mind?' I was appalled. 'Good god, man, you're talking about rap–'

Holmes cut me off with a raised palm. 'So, Constable Davis,' he said. 'You're saying they had both means and motive. May I ask, what happened to Hendricks' body?'

'He's been stored until Willshire gets back.'

'Stored?'

Davis moved to a window and gestured across the street. 'Wallis's store has a stone cellar, built over a well. He uses it as a kind of meat safe. To keep things as long as possible. We put him in there.'

'Brilliant,' Holmes said and strode towards the door. 'Come along, Watson. I've a task for you.'

'What task?' I asked as I followed him.

'You're going to show me how a man dies from song.'

THE STORE OWNER, Wallis, seemed a reasonable fellow, and to my surprise only baulked slightly at Holmes's request to inspect Hendricks's body. No doubt that was only due to Constable Davis accompanying us and explaining that I was a doctor who had come to identify the cause of death of the former miner.

Holmes requested several items from Wallis: a chisel and hammer, a hand drill, and a knife that any butcher would have been proud to wield. I dreaded to think what Holmes had in store for me. With the purchase made, Wallis showed us outside to the cellar doors. He threw them open and the stench of death rose to assail us. I decided there and then I wouldn't be partaking of anything other than dry goods from the store.

Holmes, Davis and I made the short climb down into the cellar. The temperature difference was immediately made apparent by the gooseflesh that rose on our exposed skin. The opened doors let enough light in to see by. A number of animal carcasses – rabbits, sheep and several kangaroos – hung from the ceiling, odorous but not rancid. In the centre of the room was the well: a simple hole in the ground with a brace, winch and bucket line above it. Against the far wall was a table, on which the late Mr Hendricks lay, shrouded with a bolt of linen.

'Don't be down there long,' Wallis called from above. 'You'll cause it all to spoil!'

Holmes moved towards the body and flung the covering from it. Hendricks's skin had begun to mottle, but he was otherwise reasonably preserved. I knew there was no point delaying the inevitable, so I moved to examine the body.

'Right then,' I said, and began undoing the man's shirt buttons.

'That won't be necessary, Watson,' Holmes said, and handed me the knife he'd purchased. 'We already know there were no external injuries. What we're looking for is in here.' He tapped the end of the chisel against Hendricks' forehead.

'Hey!' Davis shouted, the sound reverberating around the stone walls. 'What do you think you're doing? I can't just let you desecrate this man.'

'Fear not, Constable Davis, Dr Watson here is a highly skilled surgeon and I'm sure will not do any more damage to poor Mr Hendricks than is required for us to determine the cause of his death.'

I leaned in close to Holmes. 'Are you mad?' I whispered. 'You want me to perform some kind of crude post-mortem on this man? In these conditions? With these tools?'

'I just need you to open Mr Hendricks's skull, Watson. I'm sure the answer will reveal itself.' He smiled that supercilious smile which I knew meant he thought he already had the answer. The trouble was, in my experience, I'd yet to see him be wrong.

Though reluctant, I turned to the task at hand. At least the knife was sharp, and sliced through the skin and tissue of the forehead with ease. Had I had access to a bone saw I would have made a larger incision and simply removed the top of the skull. As it was, I did not relish trying to pry open the man's head with a miner's chisel, so I made a small cut, a half a finger's length, about two inches above the left eye. With the bone exposed, I opted to use the hand drill to bore a hole through to the brain. The bone was slick and it took some effort to have the drill bite in; however, once it had it proceeded with moderate effort. There was a slight pop as the bit cut through and into the soft tissue below.

I removed the drill and a great gout of blood, dark and viscous, erupted from the hole. I was taken aback, and I thought I must have cut into a major artery of the brain. However, when I recovered from my initial shock, I realised what must have happened. I took Mr Hendricks's head in my hands and turned it so that the exposed hole pointed towards the floor. More blood, thick and clotted, escaped from the hole onto the floor.

'Well, Watson?' Holmes said. 'What's your diagnosis?'

I stepped back, picked up the linen that had been cast aside and wiped my hands. 'I would have to say death by apoplexy.'

'Apoplexy?' Davis said, his voice choked in what I imagined to be an attempt not to disgorge his stomach contents.

'A massive bleed in the brain,' Holmes said. 'Most likely an artery had been ballooning in his head for some time and finally burst. Not all that common, but common enough for the Royal College of Physicians in London to determine it as an insidious anomaly of anatomy.'

'A what?'

'An accident, of sorts,' I said. 'Something that just happens when an artery is blocked off or otherwise damaged. It doesn't always kill. Sometimes it leaves the victim devoid of speech, or movement, or rational thought.'

'But sometimes it kills you instantly,' Holmes said. 'Just as it appears to have killed Mr Hendricks.'

'You're saying he was just walking around with this going on in his head? Until it just decided to burst and kill him?'

'Sadly, that's how it often happens,' I said. 'Any one of us could have this going on in our brains and we wouldn't know it.' I locked eyes with Davis. 'You could have one about to burst right now.'

Maybe it was just the dwindling light, but Davis appeared to turn a shade paler than he had been. 'And this is what you would have me tell Willshire and those other men? That an artery burst in his brain for no reason and killed him stone dead?'

Holmes turned towards Davis. 'Would you rather believe that a man could be murdered by a song?'

I ASKED WALLIS for some twine and a baling needle and managed a crude but effective job of sewing the newly formed wound in Hendricks's head closed. We then rewrapped his body, and bade Constable Davis a good evening as we sought to retire at the local boarding house. Holmes had promised to explain everything to Willshire upon his return the next day, after which we would depart westwards to explore this great rock he was determined to visit. Constable Davis appeared shaken but ultimately satisfied with this, and after ensuring his prisoners were secured, he took a horse and left for the police camp at Heavitree Gap.

Sleep found me with ease, and I don't even remember my head hitting my pillow before I was out. At some early hour of the morning I awoke to a creak on the stairs. When I investigated, I found Holmes sneaking into his room. In his hand was the hammer and chisel he had procured earlier. I thought to ask what he was up to, but being no stranger to his nocturnal meanderings, I dismissed it and yielded to the call of my bed.

When morning came, we secured some horses and supplies and prepared for our journey. I reminded Holmes that we had planned to await Willshire's return. He brushed it off, stating that Davis could inform him of what happened, and that we could always follow up upon our return when we headed back this way again much later.

We mounted up and turned our horses westward. As we passed the constable's station I noted that the two natives were absent. Further, I noticed several broken chain links near where they had been held.

'They've escaped,' I said to Holmes as we rode by.

'It would appear that way, wouldn't it, my dear Watson?' He doffed that ridiculous hat and kicked his horse into a canter.

'Come along, old fellow! Adventure awaits!'

The Prima Donna's Finger

Will Schaefer

HOLMES AND I had been nearly a week at the port of Fremantle, and had a further week to wait until our ship was ready to put to sea again. The heat was intense, and the close air of our small hotel room was not amenable to reading. I had therefore taken to long walks along the beach and the wide, handsome river, finding them most pleasant in the afternoons especially, when the ocean breeze blew its cool refreshment inland, and the city breathed again.

I returned from one such afternoon reconnaissance to find Holmes in an armchair, looking considerably agitated.

'What is it, Holmes?' I asked.

'This was delivered by post an hour ago,' he said, gesturing towards a bundle of plain wrapping paper on the table. A human finger lay at the centre of the papers. I recoiled at once. Certainly, this was not the first time that Holmes and I had been the recipients of gruesome packages, but the smell of decay was overwhelming. From its odour I knew then that the finger had been removed from its owner some time ago, perhaps a month. It was only after pressing my handkerchief to my nose that I was able to examine it more.

The finger was slender, doubtless that of a woman. The pattern of wrinkles suggested it had belonged to a younger rather than an older woman.

'What do you make of it, Holmes?'

'Pray, sit down, and I shall read you the letter which accompanied the package.' I did as he bade, while he sat in his armchair.

Dear Mr Sherlock Holmes,

You will forgive my dramatic gesture in sending you a person's finger in the post, but the matter is important, and I am obliged to ensure your full attention, for I have exhausted all alternatives.

My name is De Vries. I am one of only two detectives in my city, which lies approximately one hundred miles to the south of Fremantle, which I believe you have already arrived at, or are due to arrive at shortly. Our city, Bunbury, which has insisted on a slow rate of expansion over the last sixty years, has grown quickly of late as the vast timber resources of the area have been exploited more determinedly. You may rightly intuit that it is a rough town far remote from the civilising gravity of polite society, where brute force instead of law is more often the governing power.

The police, who have few resources in the western two-thirds of this continent, are not yet able to sufficiently man the station in Bunbury. Furthermore, there is little training available for detectives in this part of the world, and as much as I am pained to admit my own inadequacies, I confess that I am ignorant of the best course of action on this matter. Nevertheless, while you are known even here as probably the finest solver of police problems anywhere in the world, it would not have occurred to me to write to you unless the owner of the finger, Mrs Godfrey Norton, who was entrusted to my protection, had not talked of you so incessantly prior to her disappearance last week.

I now knew the reason for my friend's uncharacteristic agitation. In the mansion of his mind, Mrs Norton, formerly Miss Irene Adler, occupied a special throne, however much he declined to admit it, and he would suffer much until he had assured himself of her safety. She had been a famed prima donna in the Imperial Opera of Warsaw, in Poland, but her intellectual brilliance was such that she was one of only a few people who had ever bested Holmes.

No doubt, prior to my arrival, Holmes's thoughts were halfway to that awfully described city of Bunbury, where they had excited a maelstrom of conjecture that even he had been unable to master.

Holmes continued reading the letter.

The facts of the case are straightforward enough. Mrs Norton was in town with her husband, Godfrey, who was engaged in speculation upon minerals from the area, and the establishment of profitable trading businesses. But he had underestimated the speed with which his sophisticated English manner made him enemies among the rough merchants and pioneers, and he further underestimated the violence of the growing criminal underground of the town, which has already staked considerable claims in the arenas of gambling, horseracing and the retail of hard drink. Having run foul of these parties, he resolved to wind up his business in Bunbury as soon as possible and return to England. However, the process of disentangling himself from the locals proved more complicated than he assumed, and it was with some weeks to go before his business was concluded that his safety was endangered. He approached me personally and entreated me to protect his wife.

Knowing the criminal element of the town as I do, I agreed to provide her with lodging at the station while he travelled to some of the new satellite towns to pay some debts. He stated that he would return within a fortnight. But four weeks elapsed, and I had heard nothing of him. For the most part, Mrs Norton took the protracted absence of her husband with commendable calm. In the evenings she would sometimes sit with me and my wife, charming us with stories of her life in England. As I have mentioned, she appears to have held you in high esteem, for your name frequently entered into her tales.

My wife and I agreed readily that she was a fine lady, a gentlewoman of rare quality with whom we were privileged to associate, and we quickly grew to very much value our evenings with her. I would, in fact, venture so far as to say that the three of us became friends, with my wife particularly impressed, as she is from a family of more significant standing than mine and was even gladder for the civilised company than I. You can imagine her distress when she called on Mrs Norton one afternoon to invite her in for tea and discovered that not only was she was missing, but also that some horrible violence had been dealt her. There was evidence of a struggle, with her room in disarray, and the finger lay upon her writing table. Beside it lay a typewritten note addressed to her husband:

You have until next Wednesday to pay. You shall not see her again unless you do. You know where to find me. Signed, B.

As you will appreciate, violent noises are commonplace about an overcrowded gaol such as Bunbury's, and the conflict in Mrs Norton's room could easily have occurred unnoticed. It thus did not surprise me when my enquiries among the men on duty that day revealed that none had seen anything out of the ordinary.

Even my investigation of the local underworld, which I had presumed to know at least to some degree, has met with no success, for I have been unable to identify or locate 'B', the infernal author of the note. To make matters worse, I have heard nothing of Mr Norton. I fear that he may have either met his fate in the bushland that surrounds Bunbury, and in which his body would probably never be found; or he has approached 'B' of his own accord in town, and suffered some other grisly fortune such that his corpse is stuffed into a beer barrel and is buried at the bottom of a slagheap.

To some it matters not. The station is severely undermanned, and the township overflowing with more arrivals each day. I thus have much pressing work. My superiors have ordered that I attend to my other duties without delay, and stop immediately my investigation into the disappearance of Mrs Norton.

My poor wife, of course, has been beside herself since this black day. She is finding it difficult to sleep. Only her charity work, which busies her mind, brings her any relief. It is for her health's sake, as much as for the sake of my professional obligations and my friendship with Mrs Norton, that I now beseech your aid. Are you in a position to come here posthaste? I would welcome your assistance at once. Be assured that we would meet your expenses and arrange for other compensation as required.

Yours faithfully,
Edward de Vries
Bunbury Police Station
Bunbury, Western Australia.

'Intriguing, Watson, is it not?' said Holmes.

'More so than the usual,' I said, 'if only because the stakes of this case mean so much to you, personally.'

'The stakes are of little importance. The issue is one of principle. Now tell me, what do you make of the finger?'

I picked up the awful-smelling object again and examined it carefully. 'I believe it to be that of a woman aged no older than forty.'

'Precisely. From the general size and shape it is apparent that this finger is that of a woman of approximately Mrs Norton's age. Naturally, that fact does not in itself confirm her rightful ownership of this digit. But do note the absence of work-callused skin tissue on the palmar flesh of the finger, and the integrity of the varnished fingernail, from which it may be deduced that this appendage is that of an uncommon woman, specifically, not merely one who has never performed manual work, but one who can additionally afford the expensive ointments necessary for preserving the youthful appearance of her skin.'

'Yes, I follow. Important when one notes that Mr de Vries stated that society women are rare in Bunbury.'

'Correct. One may then deduce that such a finger would not be easy to obtain, unless one were to separate it from someone such as Mrs Norton.'

'Not necessarily, Holmes. Suppose for the sake of argument that the finger belonged to another woman, who sold it in desperation.'

'A sound question, my dear Watson, but I have anticipated it. Firstly, we have established that the finger must have belonged to an uncommon woman. An uncommon woman is almost by definition not likely to succumb to an offer of money in exchange for something so precious as a finger.

'That, for our intents and purposes, eliminates the possibility of the finger having come from some other wealthy woman, especially as a town such as this Bunbury, which is noted for its rough constituents, is not likely to yield pampered women in great abundance.'

His tone was determined. I took this to mean he was no longer interested in sailing out of Fremantle. 'You wish to leave for Bunbury, don't you?' I said.

'My bags are packed. Should you prove agreeable, I would be much obliged to you if you would accompany me.'

OUR TRAVEL ARRANGEMENTS were made as quickly as possible that very afternoon. Cables were sent to De Vries. We booked the first available ship and left the hotel an hour after dawn.

It was more than a hundred miles by sea to Bunbury. As the vessel cleaved the sparkling seas, I had ample occasion to admire the astounding, clean whiteness of the beaches, so unlike the shores of our homeland, and the dryness of the land behind. Curious about the geography of the region, I made company with the ship's captain, a gentleman by the name of Collins, and asked of him the opportunity to look at maps of western Australia. He gave me the run of his cabin and all of his charts and maps, which were, fortunately for us, numerous.

Ignoring the sea charts and concentrating on the land maps, I learned much in a short time. There were few markers of civilisation, no railways outside of the Swan River area and only a smattering of towns. There was even less evidence of permanent water. Collins told me that Bunbury would not have held more than two and a half thousand inhabitants, with the villages and settlements in its forested hinterland perhaps offering the same number again. I saw place names that were quaintly familiar: Guildford, Midland and York. Others, however, were entirely alien: Meckering, Merredin, Boyup, like the strange eucalyptus trees that corkscrewed their way out of the parched dirt inside the coastline, their leathery leaves drying like old meat in the sun that belted them without mercy for eight months of each year.

I confess that the sheer scale of the country became somewhat unnerving to me. For hour after hour we passed by nothing but wilderness, baked dry and devoid of all but the sparsest signs of habitation. But as we neared our destination the thrust of people towards this Bunbury was obvious. There was foot traffic on the wide beaches, carts and wagons ferrying cargoes of ragged-looking souls across a river of hot white sand. The horses were larger and leaner than their English counterparts. I felt as if they owed some of their monstrousness to their battle with the elements of this inhospitable country, where even the soil has succumbed to the blistering sun, and is now the colour of bones.

Holmes remained lost in thought for much of the journey, and did not seem especially to care for observing the delights or registering the dangers of the Australian bush. He was in this state of mind when we reached the docks at Bunbury.

It was only when the ship docked that Holmes seemed to come alive. He stood at his full height, his eyes darting from object to object, no doubt noticing the same things I could see, only in greater detail. The jetty held a mass of dusty people, mostly sun-weathered men in wide hats, their leather faces breaking out of matted beards, and firm-faced women. The absence of gentry was immediately noticeable, not only in dress but also in the conversations that we overheard, where the language was dependably coarse and direct. Our refined clothing attracted stares. I did not fear for us, for Holmes is one of the most formidable boxers I have yet encountered, and I have had much experience myself.

'Our lodgings,' he said after we collected the trunk, 'are at the police station, which may be found this way, according to the map I studied on our voyage. Let us take a carriage.'

The change in his mood was remarkable, and I said as much to him.

'My dear Watson, it is all perfectly clear to me now,' he replied, 'and it will become clear to you very shortly.'

De Vries was a stout fellow, barrel-chested and reliable-looking, with a pronounced moustache. After some minutes of formality, in which he was effusive in his gratitude for our coming, he said, 'There has been no word of anyone, I'm afraid. Nothing of Mr or Mrs Norton, nothing of the kidnapper. It is as though they had never existed.' He had no sooner arranged for our things to be taken into the rooms when Holmes asked if he could see the room where Mrs Norton was abducted. My friend seemed particularly interested in the doors to the rooms.

'These are, I take it, the only means of entry and egress to the dormitory?'

'They are, sir, yes,' said De Vries.

The answer seemed to please Holmes, who smirked. 'May I see the kidnapper's note, please?'

'It's back in my office.'

In De Vries' office Holmes studied the note carefully, then looked around the room until his eyes fell on the detective's typewriter. 'Watson, my dear fellow, pray let me dictate something for you to take down on the typewriter there.'

'I should expect it to be easier if I simply take notes by hand,' I said, reaching into my jacket for a pencil.

'Please, use the typewriter,' he said, with a detectable firmness.

Perplexed, I sat down and fed a sheet of paper into the machine as De Vries looked on. 'Very well,' I said. 'What's this message to be?'

'You have until next Wednesday to pay,' said Holmes, reading from the ransom note. *'You shall not see her again unless you do. You know where to find me. Signed, B.'*

'There,' I said, giving the finished note to Holmes.

My friend sat down with both of the ransom notes and was lost in thought for a few moments. 'It is as I feared, detective. Each note is identical. The note left by Mrs Norton's kidnapper was written on this very typewriter.'

De Vries gasped. 'That cannot be! Let me see, at once!'

Holmes gave the papers to him, not deigning to move from his chair. 'It is simple, detective. Due to idiosyncratic patterns of use, a particular typewriter will develop its own distinctive signature over time. Even machines manufactured with identical parts in the same factory on the same day will perform differently within a short while. In this example, note the slight angle of the small letter *a,* the manner in which the capital *W* is lifted from the base level of the other letters, the abnormally large space between the capital *Y* and the lower case *o*. These are but three of the many examples of signature in the first note. I suggest you examine it yourself. All that was required was a specimen of the same words from the same machine to confirm my suspicion.'

The detective bristled as he took the papers from my still-seated friend. 'Mr Holmes! Surely you do not mean to suggest that I was a player in this dreadful event?'

'On the contrary, my good fellow. I have considered you wholly innocent from the moment I received your note. It is your wife I wish to question further.'

'My wife?' thundered De Vries. 'Are you mad?'

'There are sound reasons for my request, sir. She will not mind in the slightest if my instincts are untrue.'

'Edward,' said a lady behind us, suddenly. She looked dejected, her head low.

'Elizabeth!' cried De Vries. 'What's the meaning of all this sneaking about?'

'I have been listening at the door. Mr Holmes is quite correct. The note that was found in Mrs Norton's room was typed on your machine.'

'Come, my darling! How could you possibly know that?'

'Because I typed it.'

De Vries had to steady himself on the edge of the desk. He had turned the colour of a starched cloth. 'I'm afraid I don't understand,' he said weakly.

'Why don't you sit down, Mrs de Vries,' I said, offering her my chair. 'I'll fetch you some water.' Mrs de Vries was a handsome woman, and she spoke with the unmistakable air of a well-bred young lady.

'It'll do you much good to tell us everything, right from the beginning,' said Holmes.

The poor woman let out a long sigh, and began. 'You know, my darling husband, that I never meant to injure you in any way.'

'I am sure, Elizabeth. But do tell me your story.'

'Well, you know how much I have missed the company of even middle society out here. I was beginning to grow very unhappy about it, wondering if my lot were to be reduced to dead-ended conversations with provincials about laundry and cooking for the rest of my life. Then Mrs Norton appeared. Almost instantly I felt I was back in England and the trees and lawns were green and I had a friend again, a real friend with whom I could share my thoughts on books and music and plays. We became very close.

'But then I noticed some affection in her voice at the mention of your name, Edward. And I confess I caught a glimmer in your eye when you were in her company. Let me be frank. I was furious at you both for it. In my mind I was set to lose the only friend that I had made since I arrived here. To lose her to you, my dear husband, would have made it almost unbearable. Mrs Norton was aware of my turmoil, I am certain. I began to suspect that she was avoiding me out of shame, which, in my heightened anxiety, only confirmed that she was guilty of betraying me.'

Mrs de Vries paused, wrestling with emotion.

'You confronted her, didn't you, Elizabeth?' said her husband.

The woman nodded. 'I went to her rooms…'

'But your visit did not transpire as you'd planned, did it?' said Holmes.

'No. I told her I wanted her to leave before she ruined my marriage. She laughed and said she didn't know what I could possibly mean, but I took this to be one of her manipulations, and became livid. Suddenly there came a moment when I could not stop myself from attacking her.'

De Vries buried his face in his hands.

'Yes. I'm very sorry, Edward.'

Momentarily I assumed the incident resolved, but Holmes spoke firmly. 'There is considerably more to the story than that, Mr de Vries. Have no fear. Your wife will tell us when she is ready.'

Mrs de Vries took half a minute to compose herself, then began again. 'As it transpired, I had hit her harder than I thought myself capable. By the time I arrested my movements, Mrs Norton was on the floor, completely still. I panicked. I was mortified with myself, and terrified at the thought of what would happen if her murder were traced to me.

'I put her into one of the big laundry tubs and covered her with wet linen. That afternoon I asked a pair of young labourers to load the tub onto the back of the wagon I use for my charity work, which I took out to the dumps.'

'And that is where we will find her?' asked De Vries.

'That is where I left her. I rolled her into an abandoned squatter's shack in the forest.'

'The note was wholly your idea,' said De Vries, without passion.

'It was, Edward.'

'And the finger?'

'My idea also. I knew you would not believe me if I said she had suddenly gone of her own accord. It occurred to me that I could lie about her receiving news of her husband's fortune, but I realised that you would make enquiries, and these would make you suspicious. I thought the finger would lend weight to the idea of a struggle with violent criminal figures.'

'Where did you obtain the finger?'

'From the hospital. It was easy enough once I had found the right room. A woman of roughly Mrs Norton's age had died during childbirth a few hours before.'

De Vries paled, no doubt imagining his wife removing the digit from the hand of an unfortunate mother. 'Then you are confessing a murder, Elizabeth,' he said sadly.

Mrs de Vries began sobbing. 'Oh, my darling! Whatever have I done?'

Shortly thereafter, Mrs de Vries led the three of us to the shack into which she had rolled the body of Mrs Norton. I thought Holmes had taken the news of her death well, considering the depth of his attachment to her, for he retained a relatively bright manner.

'In here, I presume?' he said.

'Yes,' replied Mrs de Vries.

'I shall investigate myself. Watson, with me, if you please.'

The two of us entered the shack, a half-collapsed structure made mostly of branches, sticks and scraps of tin sheeting. 'Fear nothing, Watson,' whispered Holmes. 'There is no Mrs Norton here. Observe.'

I was surprised at my friend's confidence in the face of what we had just heard from Mrs de Vries, but I ought to have trusted him more, for there was no sign of Mrs Norton's body.

'How could you possibly have known?' I asked.

'All will be clear in an instant, my dear Watson.' At that moment he struck a match and waved it gently around the shack, as though he were looking for something on one of its walls. Something small and metallic shone in the flickering light. 'Here! It is just as I expected!' he cried, pocketing the glinting prize before I had a chance to see it myself. I followed him out into the daylight, where the detective and his wife were waiting.

'You appear satisfied, Mr Holmes,' said De Vries.

'Only to the extent to which I have confirmed the validity of my instincts about this matter,' replied Holmes. 'There has been no murder. Nor has Mrs Norton ever been assaulted by your wife. She has lied to all of us.'

De Vries looked puzzled to the point of pain. 'Elizabeth... I don't understand. Is this true?'

'I cannot say yet,' said Mrs de Vries, avoiding the eyes of all parties.

Holmes said, 'If you please, detective, I can provide you with a full explanation of the events as I see them.'

'That would be appreciated.'

'You and your wife formed a legitimate friendship with Mrs Norton. There is no question of the sincerity of her affection for you both. But her mind is devious, and not beyond the use of you as tools with which she may accomplish the designs she has formed. Let me, for example, ask of you why it was me and not another expert you summoned for help?'

'Your reputation is famous, even here,' replied De Vries without hesitation.

'But why was my reputation sufficiently impressed on your imagination?'

'Well, there are the stories about you that I have heard from visiting detectives who have worked in the bigger cities. But then, Mrs Norton brought your reputation into conversation many times,' said De Vries.

'Precisely! Now, pray tell me, without revealing any details that you may regard as too intimate, what is the precise quality of your wife's family's financial situation?'

'Mr Holmes! Are you suggesting that –'

'It is simple, Mr de Vries. Her manners are refined, and her clothes are of high quality, but they are out of fashion, even for the town of Bunbury. Although well made, they are in need of repair that is quite beyond her own ability with a needle, and thus their true age is betrayed. Why would a family of high standing neglect to provide for one of its daughters for so long? I deduce it has lacked the means for some time, possibly since the time of your marriage, which would explain their willingness to permit your matrimony – no doubt a financial relief to them.'

The detective was aghast.

'You are shortly thereafter acquainted with Mrs Norton, an Englishwoman of substantial means, who is missing her beloved husband in a colonial wilderness where few are able to help her. She cultivates a friendship with the two people in the district most able to assist her, and during this process discovers that one of them is from a once-respectable English family that has recently come upon financial ruin. She foments a plan to enlist more specialised aid: me, if you will pardon my immodesty. To this end, my name is mentioned to you several times in connection with the successful resolution of exceedingly difficult mysteries. Then she offers the more desperate of her new friends a sum of money that is sufficient to restore a measure of the honour that has been surrendered by her family in its descent, and it is irresistible. You, my dear Mr de Vries, are then convinced of the sudden kidnap of Mrs Norton, but due to lack of evidence are unable to resolve the novel mystery. Your wife is distressed by the fate of her new friend, and you yourself grow concerned more with each day. Your wife begins suggesting the use of her family's funds to secure the services of Mr Sherlock Holmes and you assent, not knowing that it was Mrs Norton's money that you would in fact be using.'

'I am not convinced, Mr Holmes,' said De Vries. 'Would it not be simpler for her to contact you herself, especially since you know her personally?'

'Mrs Norton knows full well that I have no need of her money, and that I am inclined to mistrust any direct approaches from her. It would only be a question of her life or death as raised by a legitimate authority that would arouse my interest in travelling this far. And in this, I must admit, she was surely successful.'

De Vries's mouth was now open. He looked, amazed, at his wife. 'Elizabeth… is any of this true?'

Mrs de Vries flung her arms around him. 'Do please forgive me, my darling husband. It is all true.'

'Oh, thank the Lord!' he exclaimed as he returned the embrace. 'But how much trouble you could have been in! The thought of arresting you for murder! And why did you not tell me of your family's misfortune?'

'Oh, Edward! I would have told you everything as soon as I could! But the whole thing was so important for her – the only way she could find her husband again.'

'Tell me then, whose finger was sent to Mr Holmes?'

'Mrs Norton gave it to me. She never said whose it was. She forbade me from asking questions. She wouldn't even tell me why the note had to be written with your typewriter. And she insisted that I confess nothing of the truth until Mr Holmes had emerged from the shack!'

'The answers will follow soon, De Vries. Mrs Norton was kind enough to visit the mineshaft only long enough to leave this for me,' said Holmes, fishing something out of his jacket and showing it to De Vries. It was a heart-shaped silver locket on a chain. 'It will further confirm the correctness of my reasoning, and your wife's innocence. Observe,' he said, opening it.

'There are two photographs in here,' said De Vries. 'One of Mrs Norton, looking much as I remember her. And the other is of… you, Mr Holmes!'

'Well done!' I said to my friend.

'It was simple, my dear fellows. The facts never lie.'

De Vries said, 'But what a dreadfully elaborate ruse! A summons from the frontier. It can only mean she wants you here very much indeed, Mr Holmes.'

'A logical deduction. As I have said, it is my estimation that she requires my aid in locating her husband, whom she genuinely cannot find.'

'She must love him immensely to go to such lengths,' said Mrs de Vries.

'Indeed,' said Holmes, averting his eyes to the ground. 'Probably more than anything in her own life.'

I marvelled at my remarkable friend, who had probably solved much of the mystery by the time we arrived at the harbour.

'Well, Mr Holmes, I am supposing you've some idea of what the locket may mean,' said De Vries.

'Correct, Mr de Vries. I am the one who gave it to her some years ago.'

De Vries looked perplexed. 'I confess I am lost. How does it help us determine where she may be at the moment?'

Holmes smirked. It was imperceptible to all but me. 'My good sir,' he said, 'it is all perfectly simple, and I shall explain it in the morning when all is well again. Now if you will indulge me, I require transport back into the town, where I will take my leave.'

TO MY SURPRISE, Holmes requested that the buggy stop at the busy intersection in the middle of Bunbury. After reassuring our puzzled companions that he was in no need of assistance, he bade them farewell, dodging the carts and carriages on his way to a bustling footpath. He did not acknowledge my entreaties for an explanation. Instead he surveyed the long, wide streets around us, before exclaiming in triumph, 'Ahhh!'

'What do you see, Holmes?'

'Behold, Watson. The Wellington Hotel.'

A handsome brick hotel of two storeys, faintly reminiscent of buildings at home, stood on the far side of the intersection. Although of elegant design, to me there was nothing instantly remarkable about it; the town had numerous other specimens.

'What does it mean, the Wellington Hotel?'

'Mrs Norton awaits me inside there, Watson.'

'There is a reason you are certain of this, I assume.'

Holmes fished the locket from his waistcoat. 'I must disclose an embarrassing failure of mine, Watson. You no doubt recall the evening in London when we were followed to Baker Street by Miss Adler whilst she was disguised as a young man? I regret to reveal that I later became aware she had effected a stealthy burglary of our premises, by conniving Mrs Hudson when we were out! And the only item she took was something that belonged to me.'

'My Lord! What did she steal, Holmes?'

'She took this,' he said, the locket dangling from his hand, 'from an envelope on my dressing table. The envelope was clearly labelled with the arms of the Wellington Hotel in Waterloo. After a few moments I understood the locket to be a signal to meet her at a local venue of the same name. I asked our hosts to drop me in the centre of the town, reasoning that it would be the logical place to begin inquiries into the location of such a hotel, and found, as you have, that the hotel exists immediately here.'

'You could have asked De Vries to tell you where it was.'

'Consider, Watson, the trouble she has undertaken to limit police involvement thus far. It is patently clear that her husband is in some measure of difficulty with the law as much as he is with parties outside it. I deduce that Mrs Norton needs me to come alone.'

'I see. In that case I shall take refreshment in these tearooms here until you're done. Or shall I meet you at the police station?'

'I am of the opinion that I shall need you before long, Watson. But please do refresh yourself here and watch the doors and windows of the Wellington Hotel.'

The waiter had scarcely brought my tea before I saw Holmes leave the venue with a shabbily dressed woman. Pressing a generous sum into the surprised waiter's hands, I saw them waving for a coach to pick them up, and had no choice but to push my way through a mass of coffee-parlour patrons onto the street.

The woman looked furtively in several directions, as though afraid of an ambush. Was this Mrs Norton? She had succeeded mightily in her disguise if so; in her dusty clothing and defeated stoop she was indistinguishable as a woman of good birth. The pair entered the cab and made off to the north. With considerable difficulty I flagged a cab and kept my mark. At my behest the driver followed at a distance which was modest enough for me to avoid declaring my presence but close enough to respond to any change in my quarry's bearing.

It was fortunate that I had done so, for there were several startling changes in direction, first to the right, then left, then right again, until the buggy stopped amid a shambles of lean-to buildings and rickety tin-sheet fences by the timber-loading docks. My first thought was that I had better close the gap between myself and the duo I followed, for tracking them through this maze of rusting tin would likely prove impossible.

Paying the driver, I stood down some fifty yards from them, undetected as far as I knew, before I saw my quarry drift into the darkness of an alleyway between two buildings. I broke into a trot, suddenly aware of how foreign Holmes and I were in our gentlemen's outfits in this shantytown, and how my running was attracting the stares of the fierce-looking men who stood idle near one of the doorways.

In the alleyway I became concerned. Holmes and Mrs Norton were nowhere to be seen. Like bones on a fish spine, the innumerable other lanes and alleyways radiated from the alley – their sheer number making it impossible to all but guess in which direction the pair had gone. Sensing shadows behind me, I turned to see that the rough-looking locals had followed me and were now blocking the way I had come. My service revolver was with me; I would use it if I had to, I told myself as I took firm steps deeper into the alley. The ruffians behind me quickened their pace.

It was not long before the alley stopped and I was trapped. The coarse tin walls around me were devoid of windows and were too high for climbing. On the verge of drawing my pistol, I observed the flimsiness of sheeting in parts, and discovered that one sheet was easily bent in such a way as to permit my escape.

I squeezed through the gap and pulled out my pistol. Seconds later the torso of one of my pursuers, a man with savage sunburn, appeared through the hole. I pressed my revolver into his temple.

'I cannot but conclude you are following me, sir,' I told him. 'You will turn around at once.' He did not move. Behind him there were scuffling noises, exclamations and the sounds of punches and bodies falling inert on the ground. The sunburnt man's eyes widened noticeably.

'Who is that?' I asked him. He turned, slowly, to see what was behind him.

'It's a man. And a woman,' he said.

'Holmes! Is that you?' I asked.

'Ah, Watson,' came a familiar voice. 'Come now. We near the end of our stay here.'

'What about this man here?' I said.

'He shall not be the source of further trouble, I assure you,' said Holmes. The sunburnt man was jerked from the hole out of my sight. By the time I had made my way back through the gap, Holmes was standing over the man's prostrate body, dusting his jacket off.

'Excuse my having lost you. Rather a labyrinth in here,' I said.

'An advantage to many,' said Holmes. I noticed then in the shadows nearby the woman who had accompanied Holmes from the hotel. Her stoop was gone;

before me was a woman of fine confidence, her previous physical attitude being as much a part of the charade as her clothing. The difference was remarkable. I believed her to be utterly comfortable with the recent violence around her. She stepped from the shadows, suddenly a strikingly handsome woman.

'Dr Watson,' she said.

'Mrs Norton.' We shook hands.

'Do please follow me now, gentlemen,' said Mrs Norton, looking pleased with herself.

We made our way through the maze of sheds and leaning walls, which she seemed to know well, until we reached a cramped brick house. From where we stood, the little house looked deserted, a window or two broken, its tiny yard strewn with rubbish.

'Mr Norton is being kept in that room there,' she said, nodding towards one of the rooms at the side of the building. 'For some reason his captors refer to him as Mr Cundall.'

'It is probable that Mr Cundall is the moniker that he gave them for business purposes. Their continued ignorance of his true name suggests two things,' said Holmes. 'One, that their intelligence is limited, which puts us at an advantage immediately. Two, your husband has not succumbed to the tortures imposed on him. Most commendable.'

'Six other men are inside,' continued Mrs Norton. 'There are two guns, one shotgun and one large revolver.' The curtain of the room seemed to open a fraction, a sliver of dark behind the dirty window.

'I see,' said Holmes. 'Come, let us not discuss our tactics in so public a venue.' He led us up the road somewhat, effusive with ideas.

Within three minutes I was knocking on the door of the house. After the fourth knock, a voice called.

'Whaddayou want?'

'My name is Watson. I believe there is an injured man, a Mr Cundall, in the house.'

'You got the wrong house,' came the reply. 'Get lost.'

It occurred to me that Mrs Norton had been brave indeed in her earlier attempts at negotiating with these men.

'But this is the house of Mr Cundall, is it not?' A pause.

'What's it to you?'

'I am a physician. Dr Watson.'

'Dr Watson from where?'

'From London, sir.' A long pause.

'What, London, England?'

'That is correct.'

'Look, there's no injured man 'ere. Shove off back to London, England.'

'Sir, I insist that you allow me to examine the injured man who is in the kitchen this very moment. He has a fractured left cheek, extensive bruising about the ribs and possibly spinal damage as well. Mr Cundall himself will appreciate it.'

'There's no Mr Cundall here,' said the voice, faltering enough for me to know I now had an advantage.

'Mr Cundall is prepared to pay for the privilege of 15 minutes of medical attention,' I said.

There was a long period of quiet, then footsteps and whispering voices tense with feeling. ''Ow much is 'e think it's worth then?' said a different voice.

'Half of what is being asked to spare his life.'

'An' you got that much on you?'

'I do, sir. In this bag.' I patted Mrs Norton's handbag, which was filled with nothing but newspapers that Holmes had collected from the street just moments ago, and my pistol.

'Two steps back and stop. No tricks, or you get shot, England.'

I stepped backwards, noting the gun barrel trained on me from the front room. It lingered, as though contemplating whether or not to shoot me on the verandah of the house, before disappearing. The door opened suddenly. Two bearded men stood there, one pointing a box-pattern hunting shotgun at me, the other a Webley revolver.

'Put the bag on the dirt,' said the man with the revolver, 'and keep them hands up.'

'As you say,' I said.

The revolver stepped forward slowly onto the verandah, the shotgun covering him from the doorway. The man with the shotgun did not see Holmes until it was too late. Holmes simply held a little pistol (Mrs Norton's derringer, I assumed) under his chin and took the shotgun from him. My friend's mouth moved to utter a command, the bearded man raised his arms in surrender and addressed his comrade.

'Fitch.'

Fitch turned, then gaped at the sight of Holmes having disarmed his companion, offering me ample time to retrieve my own pistol and point it at him.

'Hands high, please,' I said. He did as I bade him at once.

Out of the door came Mrs Irene Norton. She was supporting a bloody-faced, half-conscious man who had severe trouble walking on account of injuries to his legs. From the way he cradled his side I assumed there was damage to his ribs as well. Mrs Norton looked extremely concerned for him, hardly registering the four of us until she was near the front gate.

'Good day to you, gentlemen,' she said. 'One day I shall repay you for your kindness.'

'No doubt, Mrs Norton,' said Holmes, ushering Fitch and his villainous friend into the house.

'Might I take a look at Mr Norton, Mrs Norton? His condition appears to warrant a hospital bed.'

'Very kind of you, Dr Watson, but we must be going now. We have an engagement with some people who are going to sail us a long way, very quickly.'

'A moment then, Mrs Norton,' said Holmes with firmness. He shut the door of the house and with long strides made his way to the married couple. 'It is possible you may need this.' He took the locket from his coat and handed it to the former prima donna.

'Thank you, Mr Holmes. If we are desperate for funds it may fetch a few shillings at the flea market in Zanzibar.'

'It will fetch considerably more than that,' said Holmes, smiling, as he checked the action of the shotgun. 'As you well know.'

'Yes, which is why I jest,' she said. 'But I shall not be parting with it, for any sum. I have only met my intellectual match twice; once it was a woman, and once a man, Mr Holmes, and that man was you, who has aided me in my hour of need. I value the keepsake,' she said, over her shoulder. And with that, Mrs Norton led her husband away.

Holmes watched them for a while. 'We shall give them a start of several moments, Watson, and ensure that none leave this building in the meantime. Let us observe from the shade over here; this heat is infernal.'

'I take it all went according to your design in there?'

'Precisely! Your distraction at the front door was masterful, the firearms rapidly converging there, as expected. During this time, Mrs Norton once more proved most adept at opening windows without making superfluous noise, and our entry to the building was undetected. From their unforgivable devotion to the incorrect name "Mr Cundall" I had already deduced that these were no John Clays, no men of brains, but common thugs; there would be no orchestrated policy of patrol, or any danger of meeting a coordinated defence of the dwelling. As anticipated, I was able to deal with each of them separately, and hardly required more than a few moments. Shortly thereafter I came upon the criminal holding the shotgun, and the rest you are aware of.'

'A straightforward case, then,' I said.

Sherlock Holmes shook his head. 'On the contrary,' he said. 'Considering it involved The Woman's artfully contrived means to absolutely ensure that I, personally, would engage with this matter, I would have to judge it as anything but elementary.'

The Adventure of the Demonic Abduction

J. Scherpenhuizen

IT WAS ON a voyage from Melbourne to Adelaide that I met a woman who was, perhaps, the most beautiful and enchanting I had ever known, up until that point. I did not know it at the time but she was soon to be the centre of one of the most disconcerting cases Sherlock Holmes and I were ever to encounter, and her charms were, no doubt, the central motivation for the crime it concerned. We were strolling along the undulating deck of the *Christopher*, as it plied the waters off the coast of South Australia, when Mah Ling and her venerable father came into view. Holmes had been holding forth most animatedly on the subject of the many varieties of rope and how a specific knot in a particular variety of hemp twine had led him to a lascar who was the villain in one of his early encounters. I was never quite able to muster the same amount of enthusiasm for the subject of string as Holmes, and he soon saw that my attention had wandered. He followed my gaze which had fixed upon the lady in question who stood with her father pointing out to sea, speaking with some animation.

Curious as to what could cause such excitement, we made our way to the rail to view the scene for ourselves. A little convoy of dolphins had decided to accompany us on our journey. The lady's delight was easy to comprehend. For loveliness and novelty, it was a sight to compete with any in the world as these extraordinary beings coursed through the waters beside our vessel like the very embodiment of freedom itself.

Holmes immediately launched into a dissertation on the creatures and the subject of cetaceans in general. If the lady already knew they were not fish but mammals, she made a good show of pretending that all of this was new and fascinating to her. Having overcome our excitement at this natural spectacle, we recovered our composure sufficiently to make the suitable formal introductions.

Mah Ling's English was perfect and it transpired that her youth had been mainly spent in Australia where her father, An Ling, had thrived as a merchant catering to the many Chinese who had flocked to that country's goldfields since the 1850s. He had also conducted a considerable trade with the broader public, for the Australians' desire for all things Chinese was no less voracious than that of the Europeans of the past hundred years. Mr Ling was a delightful gentleman himself, who had done and seen much in his travels, and we spent a good deal of the rest of the journey chatting about a diverse variety of subjects. Although his English was broken and heavily accented, we communicated with ease. He was an animated raconteur who spiced all of his tales with a pleasing concoction of fact, fancy and humour.

While Holmes and I had only planned a short stay in Adelaide on our way further to the west coast, Mr Ling was planning a stay of a couple of weeks, to be spent in the pursuit of certain matters of commerce upon which he did not elaborate. It was with some reluctance that we parted ways with the Lings on the docks at Port Adelaide, for they had already planned to stay with a business associate in North Terrace while we had arranged to stay at the Hotel Richmond in Rundle Street. We had agreed to meet for a final dinner the following day and had therefore exchanged addresses so we could contact one another, should the necessity arise, to change our plans due to some unforeseen eventuality.

Holmes abandoned me for the evening, being taken with a sudden desire to dress himself in the most insalubrious manner imaginable in order to haunt the unsavoury neighbourhood around Light Square in the West End. For my part, I dined with a Dr Cavendish, an old friend of mine from my medical school days who had set up shop in Adelaide. Thus, mutually satisfied, Holmes and I met over breakfast the next day. Having finished a very fine repast, we were about to quit the dining room when we were accosted at its door by our foreign friend from the voyage who had been directed to us by the hotel staff.

To say that the man we had met on our voyage was transformed is an understatement, though the change was in no way for the better. While the Mr Ling we had known was a fellow full of confidence and vitality, the man now before us seemed defeated and aged beyond his years.

'Goodness,' I exclaimed. 'My dear Mr Ling, what on earth has befallen you?'

'Mr Holmes, Dr Watson, I am so glad I find you here,' the venerable Chinese managed, his voice a cracked whisper. 'The most terrible thing has happened.'

Immediately we conveyed the worthy gentleman to our suite where he might tell us of his woes in the comfort of our drawing room. I poured him a stiff brandy as he was clearly in need of fortification. Mah Ling's absence troubled me and I feared that the bad news involved her, for what else could have affected her father so? I encouraged our guest to finish his liquor before commencing his tale. He winced at the fiery draught, set his glass down and launched into a startling narrative.

It transpired that the Lings had enjoyed an extremely pleasant evening at the North Terrace home of their host, a Master Xian, with whom Mr Ling was negotiating the final phases of a lucrative business alliance. They had retired for the night to their adjoining rooms and Mr Ling had fallen into a heavy sleep. Around two in the morning he was awakened to the sound of screams coming from his daughter's chamber. Frantically he dashed out of his own room and to his daughter's door, which resisted his every effort to gain entry, though Ling was physically modestly endowed and well past his prime, so it would not have taken much to barricade him out. He was about to go for help when, but moments later, his host appeared accompanied by a hefty bodyguard. Master Xian was about to try the door himself when, seeing his burly servant approaching, he wisely stood back and allowed him to make the breech, which with his massive frame was achieved in short order.

The screams had ceased a good half minute earlier, which far from relieving Mr Ling made him all the more desperate to see his daughter safe and well. The most he could hope for was that she had fainted, yet what greeted him upon entering his daughter's room was a scene of the utmost terror. Mah Ling's dressing-gown lay upon the floor and it and the entire room were bespattered with blood. Yet the chamber was empty. Running to the window, Master Xian threw the curtains aside – yet the window was closed and the clasp down. Furthermore, the room was on the second storey. Xian gasped with surprise, causing Mr Ling to join him just in time to see a 'demon' halfway across the courtyard.

At this point I felt compelled to interrupt the narrative.

'Excuse me, Mr Ling,' I stammered. 'May I ask what you mean when you say, "a demon"?'

'I mean, one from what you would call hell.' Mr Ling winced at his own words. 'I have seen many pictures of them. A terrible being with wild hair, a distorted face with tusks and horns. Taloned hands…'

'Yet, that is impossible,' I insisted. 'Surely you don't believe such beings exist in reality?'

Mr Ling sighed. He knew he had an argument to win and it was plain to see that he barely had the energy for it. While I was certain of my perspective, he was equally sure of his own and was in the unenviable position of a man with perfect sight having to convince the colourblind man of all the colours of the rainbow. However, despite the onerous nature of the task, he girded himself manfully and plunged into the attempt.

'East and West are two different worlds,' he said carefully. 'We Chinese see things differently. While many of you in the West say you believe in the world of spirit, many of us see it, we feel it. Ghosts are all around us, everywhere. We feel our ancestors by us every day. And I am particularly sensitive to such things, even for one of my race.'

Ling was right. He was, indeed, talking about two different worlds. I understood his words but could not take them seriously. For me, what he spoke of was mass delusion, but I could see how for him what I advocated was joining the mass spiritual blindness of a culture different to his own. I could not help but think of my very good friend, Dr Doyle. Although that worthy gentleman is the most rational of men in nearly all matters, he is also an inveterate séance-goer and unshakeable believer in a super-sensible realm. As I pondered this ideological impasse, Holmes, ever practical, took the opportunity to interject.

'Let us allow Mr Ling to tell his story in his own way without further interruption,' he suggested. 'There will be time enough to entertain other interpretations of events when he has finished.'

Holmes was talking undoubted sense, yet I must confess to feeling more than a little reluctant to let that particular bone go.

'So you saw this demon…' Holmes prompted, and Ling took up the tale afresh.

Over the demon's shoulder, the blood-spattered body of the young girl was draped. Mr Ling was in no doubt it was his daughter whose nightdress and slippers he recognised and whose exceptionally long hair was unmistakable. The demon leered back at the witnesses for one moment before disappearing from the courtyard in a plume of smoke! Mr Ling was about to quit the window when fresh screams erupted from the far end of the courtyard, some thirty yards from the window, and a man and a woman, in a somewhat dishevelled state, ran from the stable there. Master Xian leapt into action at once. Snatching up a sword that was clasped in the hands of a costumed manikin in the corridor, he led the charge downstairs and, accompanied by his formidable bodyguard, raced down the courtyard and entered the stable, ordering Mr Ling to wait outside, fearing something too dangerous for him to face awaited them in the outbuilding.

Yet, upon hearing the exclamations of the others, our friend could not contain himself long and followed them inside. On the floor of the stable glowed a luminescent circle that had been marked there with some sort of paint or chemical, which Mr Ling took to be magical: the device by which the demon had first been summoned and hence had used to make his escape. Of Mr Ling's daughter and her abductor there was no trace, though an infernal stench still hung heavy in the air, which Mr Ling attributed to a demonic transportation of some nature.

'My daughter is gone,' Mr Ling announced despairingly, 'taken to the underworld.'

I looked at Holmes, confounded, and when he did not object to this preposterous story I felt compelled to do so. 'With all due respect, Mr Ling,' I cried. 'You have been tricked, sir. Someone has concocted some elaborate scheme to deprive you of your daughter. You have been duped!'

'You think me a fool?' Mr Ling said, more tired than insulted. 'Yet my host Master Xian confessed he is in a struggle with one of our countrymen who uses sorcery. I am unfortunate enough to be caught in the middle of their conflict. You see, my host has a daughter of his own who was away at the time. Mah Ling was given her room. The demon must have taken Mah Ling by mistake.'

'Who is this person with whom you were staying?' I protested. 'How well can you trust him? If he had designs on your daughter then no one else is better placed than he to concoct such a plan and carry it out.'

Mr Ling looked dubious. I was about to launch into further remonstrations when Holmes held up his hand, somewhat imperiously, and I held my peace. Turning to Mr Ling, he spoke evenly.

'Sir, let us not concern ourselves with metaphysics which cannot be proved nor disproved. Let us say, for the sake of argument, that demons exist and are capable of doing what you believe. If that is the case, your daughter is lost and we have no hope and no recourse to action or remedying the situation. However, it is possible that even if such arcane forces do exist, they are not involved in this case, and you have witnessed a counterfeit demonic attack rather than a genuine one. Let us say that some trickery is involved and let us investigate the case in such a manner. Then at least we have some hope.'

'I see the sense of what you say,' Mr Ling mused. 'I do believe in gods as well as demons but, as you say, the hands of neither may be in this crime; however, the hands of the gods may well be in its solution. For it is a wonderful coincidence indeed that at this time in my life, when I have been the victim of a most remarkable crime, the world's most remarkable detective is my friend.'

'I am indeed.' Holmes smiled warmly.

'That is why I am here,' Mr Ling said. 'In such an hour, one seeks out a friend.'

'And I gather you have not involved the police?'

Mr Ling hesitated briefly. 'East is East and West is West, even here in Australia, although the geography of that saying becomes muddled. If I believed that a crime had been committed, I would still hesitate to call the police. In our society we keep our own law, we have our own enforcers.'

'And I imagine Master Xian is just such a one?' Holmes said.

'True,' Mr Ling agreed, clearly impressed with the detective's insight. 'He is a prominent person in the community here and the leader of a local Yee Hing – a society devoted to helping our countrymen. It is to him I would go in such a situation while in Adelaide. He assures me that his rival is the source of this trouble.'

'Yet, if he is the source of the trouble…'

'Then perhaps we need the police.' Mr Ling nodded. 'But Xian presented himself as my friend, and if I suggest world's greatest detective be allowed to investigate, he could not refuse without showing his guilt. I do not believe police could do so much as an independent man of your trade and skills, Mr Sherlock Holmes. If you fail, sir, there is no need to involve them.'

'I agree,' Holmes said. 'We shall not involve the police unless we require more manpower and such an expediency as a forced search of the premises. But an investigation of the scene of the disappearance should reveal more data. Let us not jump to any conclusions, Watson. If there is, indeed, skulduggery involved, it might be that Mr Ling's host is himself the victim of trickery, and his rival is behind the abduction without having enlisted the aid of demons to achieve it.'

HAILING A HANSOM cab outside our hotel, we were speedily delivered to the North Terrace home of Mr Ling's associate, Master Xian. The residence was an imposing, high-gabled mansion of two storeys with wide verandahs designed to fend off the fierce depredations of the antipodean sun. A manservant conveyed us to an elegant parlour where the house's master awaited us. Chang Xian was an imposing figure. Of middle height, he seemed powerfully built as far as his physique could be discerned beneath the flowing robes of the Mandarin which he wore. His age was hard to gauge. His skin was largely smooth and glowing and his hair and whip-like moustaches were a lustrous black. Yet, despite this appearance of youthful vitality, he had the air of a much older man about him, and one long used to command at that. He greeted us cordially and assured us that we had full access to every part of the house and grounds upon request.

The daughter's room had not yet been cleaned, and Holmes began his inspection there. He studied everything including the ceiling and the floor, looking for trapdoors and manholes and hidden passageways, but there seemed no such way out of the room. Not only was the window locked, but it was also secured by an extra screw, apparently due to a rash of burglaries over the preceding years. The only way out of the room, it seemed, was the door by which we had entered.

Our host remained outside the chamber, at our disposal, as he put it, but did not pry into our investigations.

'You keep a commendably clean house,' Holmes said, upon encountering Xian in the hall.

'Of course,' the regal fellow said. 'I am a man of means and take pains to ensure that my home is maintained in a pristine condition. This is not merely good hygiene and a matter of aesthetics, it is part of *feng shui* which is an essential aspect of the creation of wealth.'

'I beg your pardon?' I could not refrain from saying, amazed at the degree to which such arrant superstition had invaded the daily lives of such apparently sophisticated men. Yet at the same time I couldn't help but think how much this underlined Ling's assertion that the East and West were two distinct worlds.

'*Feng shui*,' Holmes said, for my benefit. 'The Chinese art of arranging the environment to conduct the most serendipitous and beneficial energies.'

'Ah,' I said, hoping the response was sufficiently noncommittal so as to provoke neither controversy nor insult.

Next, Holmes examined the ground below the window. Here among the flowers of the neatly tended beds he found traces of blood. One large drop had a fibre of silk in it which matched the ravaged dressing-gown in the room above. There were also some traces of unidentified powder that left a lingering scent of sulphur. There were no impressions of footmarks or machinery in the few feet of flowerbed and lawn edging that surrounded the flagstones that covered most of the courtyard. This paved area was some twenty yards wide and somewhat over thirty yards deep, and approximately halfway across it we discovered another few spatters of blood and a gory footprint which did not seem quite human. Only the impression of the ball of the foot and three unnaturally long toes could be discerned, yet the entire print was as broad as a complete human foot and at the tip of each toe was what looked like the silhouette of a talon. I confess my blood ran cold at the sight of this uncanny-looking stain, before I told myself that whoever had planned this affair had gone to extreme lengths to plant their false evidence. What disconcerted me even more was the look I thought I saw flash across Holmes's face, which led me to believe he was also somewhat out of his depth.

The barn was next. It was here that I was certain we would find a trapdoor or some other sign of how the 'demon' had carried our friend's daughter away. In the middle of the somewhat cavernous outbuilding was a circle decorated with various characters that looked Chinese, but also held a number of occult sigils, we were informed. More blood was found there and another of those damnable toeprints. I found the device unaccountably chilling and wondered at how deep the impulse towards superstition ran, even within myself. Shrugging the feeling off, I gathered my wits and joined Holmes in a minute examination of the structure, which seemed completely solid and without any means of escape.

Retreating from the stable, we were conducted to a kitchen where the master of the house had arranged for the dishevelled pair who had been seen quitting the barn to be summoned. Though their clothes were now decorously arranged they seemed sheepish and fearful.

'They are servants and do not speak English,' Xian said apologetically. 'I have already questioned them. Their story is that they had crept into the stable for amorous purposes, and not for the first time. They were not long at their occupation when they heard the screams from the house. These rascals were pondering how to respond to those frightful sounds when, shortly thereafter, the demon ran into the barn carrying Mah Ling. The demon reached the centre of the barn and disappeared in a cloud of smoke. Terrified, they ran away, not realising that they had been spied from the window.'

Holmes made a speculative murmur before requesting that the pair be asked whether the presence of the circle had not deterred them. Questions were conveyed in a Chinese dialect and Mr Ling translated. 'They did not see it.'

'Well, the barn is quite big and the circle was far from the entrance,' Holmes conceded. 'I suppose that if they were intent on sneaking into a corner they need not have seen the design.'

'Yes,' I protested, 'but it is somewhat luminous. Were they so in the throes of lust that it escaped them?'

'That seems entirely possible,' Holmes said. 'Nonetheless, I wonder if I might examine the hands of the servants?'

Our host seemed taken aback by the request, yet ordered that his menials cooperate, despite their reluctance and obvious anxiety about the matter. This was in no way assuaged when Holmes produced a penknife and attempted to remove matter from under the fingernails of the man, who immediately withdrew his palm. There was quite a to-do for some minutes as Holmes insisted the procedure be carried out and that it was harmless. Some furious negotiations were conducted among the Chinese members of the party in their own tongue before the manservant was convinced he must comply.

His hands were exceedingly clean, and I did not see what Holmes hoped to gain from this intrusion as there was very little matter to be removed and what was produced, I suspected, was largely part of the nether surface of the nails. Yet Holmes seemed well satisfied.

'Is there a room in which we may experience relative darkness?' Holmes asked.

Refraining from any questioning, though clearly puzzled, Master Xian conducted us to a nearby parlour equipped with heavy drapes that allowed the bright Australian sunshine to be largely kept at bay. Holmes had collected his meagre fingernail scrapings in an envelope he had produced from his pocket. In the gloomy room, under the lens of a large magnifying glass, a few specks of luminescence glowed clearly. Holmes directed our attention to them.

'What does this mean?' the master of the house demanded.

'Very simply,' Holmes explained, 'that far from being unaware of the design on the floor of the barn, this fellow painted it there. Despite the fact that he has gone to some pains since to remove any traces of his villainy from his hands, as usual, a few grains have remained to betray his culpability.'

A sound escaped our host's lips that could only have been an oriental curse. Throwing the curtains open, he took an ornamental sword which hung above the mantelpiece and, grasping the menial by the front of his jacket, threatened him fearfully. I moved to intervene, scared for the man's life and the loss of a valuable witness, but Mr Ling stood in my way and assured me that Master Xian was intent on frightening a confession out of the man rather than taking his life.

Master Xian and Mah Ling's father seemed astounded by the hapless servant's revelations, and I could barely contain my curiosity as I waited for them to be translated into a tongue meaningful to me. Holmes stood by, watching impassively, as if what unfolded before us were a piece of theatre that failed to engage him. Truly, I thought, the man has ice in his veins.

The interrogation over, the scoundrel was thrust into a low armchair where, it seemed, he was consigned to remain unless he wished to risk his master's sword. Ling had become pale and slumped in another chair. Xian also seemed shaken.

'My servant has betrayed us,' he announced. 'My rival offered him much money to paint the device on the floor from which the demon came. He was told, also, to be a witness, in the barn, just in case no one managed to see the demon themselves.'

'Why?' I demanded. 'If your rival wanted your daughter, his goal is accomplished. Why does he require you to know the means, though the device itself and the lack of other explanations would be sufficient evidence for those already predisposed to believing a supernatural explanation?'

'You do not understand.' Xian shook his head. 'This is not so much about the theft of a woman as it is about intimidation. Having a pair of terrified witnesses to my rival's ability to summon dark powers is most potent in that regard.'

'But it is all a trick!' I fulminated. 'They are part of the plot.'

'Even so,' Xian muttered, 'they are genuinely terrified. They have both seen the demon appear and disappear with a bloody body in tow.'

'Preposterous!' I cried.

'Enough, Watson,' Holmes said. 'It has been relatively easy to establish in what way the circle was produced. Yet I can find no explanation for the appearance and disappearance of the demon... unless it was via the device.'

'But, Holmes...'

'Watson, I said I could not find it; two possibilities remain. The first is that my powers fail me. The second, I know, requires a rethinking of our entire world view.'

Holmes seemed shaken. I could hardly contemplate it but it looked to me that he was suggesting that the latter option was to be seriously contemplated.

'Well, as much as I have faith in your powers, Holmes, I am unwilling to abandon reason yet.'

'Sir,' Xian said, 'I know you mean well but you insult us. The Chinese have maintained a civilisation for longer than any has survived in the West. We have our own systems of philosophy and medicine, and have engineered some of the greatest marvels in the world. Gunpowder was used by us centuries before it was known in the West. We invented paper, and more... All of this has not been achieved without the use of reason.

'Let us suppose that this spiritual realm you find so hard to believe in does exist and presents us with a dilemma. Logic demands that we recognise it. For if that is the source of the problem we must deal with it accordingly. No solution can be found by going down the wrong road, no matter how much distance is travelled along it.

'I am greatly saddened by this tragedy, but I am not intimidated. And I will have revenge for my friend. Rest assured.'

'What will you do?' I asked our host, who gripped his sword in a determined fashion.

'That is no concern of yours,' Xian said. 'But we are accustomed to settling our differences among ourselves in this community. My enemy doubtless thinks I am intimidated by this display; he will not be expecting reprisals so soon. You must excuse me. I must finalise the details of our retaliation while the opportunity is still fresh. I will let you see your own way out.'

I was far from satisfied and made to protest, yet, to my surprise, Holmes took me firmly by the arm and ushered me from the room while Mr Ling walked ahead, leading the way.

I could barely contain myself. Yet I felt further remonstrations at this time would distress our friend, Mr Ling, who seemed resolved that a demon had taken his daughter and the only comfort he would receive was that his friend, the powerful warlord – for in a sense that is what Xian was, among other things – would take revenge on his behalf.

'HOLMES, CAN YOU please tell me what is going on?' I demanded, when we were once more ensconced in our suite, having left Mr Ling to rest in his hotel.

'Watson,' Holmes said. 'I have examined the site where the disappearance took place and there is no alternate explanation for the statements of the witnesses, including the girl's father who saw the demon disappear from the middle of the courtyard. The window is too high for a mere human to have leapt from, burdened with a body, without breaking his legs, even if we could explain how he got through a sealed pane. Yet traces of blood and the smoke created in its passing are evident on the frame and sill, showing that it appeared there before appearing again in the middle of the courtyard. There it left more traces of blood and a footprint, and then a final footprint in the circle.'

'I fail to see the difficulty,' I confessed.

'Watson, if the creature was not moving by supernatural means, how did it get between the three places it left a trace upon without leaving any trail whatsoever in between? Add to that its mysterious appearance and disappearance…'

'Perhaps there was a hot-air balloon involved?' I suggested. 'Or a kite? The Chinese are great ones for kites. The villain could have been assisted with a line that would have deposited him in the garden bed and the middle of the courtyard…'

'And the middle of the barn?' Holmes sighed. 'Yet that is not the most pertinent consideration, my friend. You see, even if such remarkable evidence could be manufactured, why go to all of the trouble? Mr Ling is not a detective.

That evidence, in fact, was not presented to him, nor did Master Xian appear to be aware of it. Mr Ling was unlikely to have involved the police, and if he had – and I say this without impugning the expertise of the local authorities – I doubt they would have brought a level of observation to their investigations to have uncovered it.'

Holmes's reasoning made a great amount of sense. Yet what it pointed at seemed too ridiculous to ponder. My friend's state of despondency suggested, however, that he did not think so.

'Holmes,' I urged him. 'You can't give up on reason. I'm sure, given sufficient time to ponder this case, the true solution will be found.'

'My dear Watson,' Holmes retorted. 'Do not upbraid me with abandoning reason. On the contrary, I have always worshipped at her altar alone, and I shall never abandon my faith in her, even now when she points me in a direction I am loath to go.' He sighed heavily. 'I must confess that there have been a number of cases over the years which have defied easy solution. Apparent anomalies that I believed must have an explanation, though it eluded me.'

'So you will look no further into this?' I said with some annoyance. 'An innocent girl has been abducted and possibly murdered and you are willing to let the matter rest, even while there is a shred of possibility that you are wrong about this "supernatural" aspect. Even if you are stumped, shouldn't we inform the police?'

'I see no point in expending my energies in a useless endeavour,' Holmes said coldly. The calculating machine seemed once more to be ascendant. 'I am more than a little familiar with how things work in the communities of the Chinese worldwide. Without their cooperation nothing can be achieved. If they have outwitted us, the local authorities will make no headway.'

I will never be sure that I made the right decision in letting the matter rest there. Holmes would not be moved, of that I was certain. It was in my power, however, to involve the local authorities, though I suspected that Holmes was entirely correct in how fruitless that would prove. I feared that there would be no solution. The girl was lost, almost certainly dead. My main concern was for her father. What persuaded me in the end was the fact that I expected he would have to endure more questioning from the police, possibly becoming the object of suspicion himself, perhaps having his hopes raised again only to have them dashed – all of this seemed too uncertain, as opposed to him having to become reconciled to his current belief that his beloved daughter was lost. Therefore, I decided to let the matter lie.

Holmes suggested we take some exercise to help throw off the funk we had both fallen into, and so we determined that some perambulation was in order. Wandering through the pleasant streets of the South Australian capital, we soon came to Elder Park and continued on to the bank of the Torrens River. I must confess that my attention was mainly directed inwards and I took little notice of the charms of our surroundings though the sky was blue and the water sparkled enchantingly.

'Really, Holmes,' I said at last. 'Are you genuinely contemplating that there might be a supernatural force at work here?'

'I know it is surprising,' Holmes admitted. 'Yet except for the past hundred years, such a belief was as common in Europe as anywhere else in the world. And while scepticism in the extramundane has grown apace in many circles, you must be aware that not just your Dr Doyle remains unconverted to a materialistic worldview. Many of the best brains in Britain are dedicated members of the Society of Psychical Research. And they certainly have plenty of opportunity to follow their studies in our own green and pleasant land, which is said to be the most haunted country in the world.'

'Well, in the West at least,' I observed. 'If Mr Ling is to be believed, it seems that the Chinese all walk about with a coterie of spirits and ancestors in tow.'

'Yes, that much I know to be true, in their perception at least. Now I suspect we have fallen prey to the white man's common assumption of his own superiority by regarding this as a mere superstition or impressionability that the people of the East are yet to grow out of.'

I struggled to answer, wishing to protest at the direction our conversation was taking, but I was somehow unable to find the words. Perhaps because the chauvinism to which he alluded was something that I would have to admit *mea culpa* to if it were indeed a vice.

'You must confess, Watson,' Holmes continued, 'that to prove the nonexistence of anything is impossible.'

'How so?'

Holmes pointed to the waters before us.

'What do you see there?'

'Swans?'

'Black swans. Yet for hundreds of years in Europe the exemplar of syllogistic truth was, *"all swans are white, this is a swan, therefore it is white"*.'

'I see: the logic is correct, yet the facts are wrong.'

'Precisely. Logic only works when we operate from correct premises. But to return to my original point, we cannot prove the nonexistence of things. For centuries, as far as Europeans were convinced, there was no such thing as a black swan. The idea of such a thing was an absurdity and anyone who claimed to have seen it must be a madman or a liar. And yet…'

Holmes gestured at the majestic birds bobbing upon the water.

'You see, Watson, your mind struggles with this case because you are thinking syllogistically: there are no such things as demons, therefore a demon cannot be involved in this case. Perfect logic so far as the premise is correct. However, change the premise: a demon was witnessed to be the perpetrator of this crime, ergo demons, whatever we may have thought, do exist.'

I pondered this for more than a minute while Holmes continued to watch the light sparkling on the water and the seabirds bobbing on the ripples.

'Nonetheless, Holmes, I can scarcely believe it.'

'Yes,' Holmes agreed, gesturing again at the swans. 'I would imagine that the first European to set his eyes on one of these creatures must have felt the same way.'

THE NEXT TWENTY-FOUR hours were among the most miserable in my life. I had been so strongly affected by the disappearance of Mr Ling's charming daughter that I could not put it out of my mind. What relief I did find from this obsession came in the form of contemplating the very nature of existence and that was hardly comforting, given recent indications. Nonetheless, however disturbing these considerations were, I must confess they were intriguing.

I pondered my acquaintance with a number of prominent intellectuals in London who were devoted members of the Society of Psychical Research and were convinced that some famous mediums were genuine and claimed to have had experiences with a shade or apparition on at least one occasion. I had always assumed that this belief was merely an odd blindspot in these fellows' minds and yet, now, I was no longer so sure.

We dined with Mr Ling, who was determined to return to Melbourne as soon as possible. He had no appetite for business and wished to be home while he recovered from the loss of his daughter. The meal was a sad affair, and I was relieved that our friend did not wish to linger and soon retired.

Holmes once again went on one of his rambles and I was left with the comfort of brandy and books, which was scarcely adequate to gift me with any level of sanguinity. The following day the papers were full of reports of troubles in the Chinese community. Despite their desire to keep a low profile, it seemed more than likely that Mr Ling's formidable friend had stuck to his vow to seek revenge, and the conflict had been of sufficient magnitude not to be kept entirely out of the public eye.

While the papers had much to say about the violence, there was nothing more than wild speculation about its nature beyond rivalry among criminal factions. There were also several highly prejudiced articles, critical of the Chinese community, which suggested that its members were in some way more prone to vice than were other sectors of the populace.

ADELAIDE WAS A place forever cursed in my mind due to recent events, and it was with relief that we boarded our ship the following day. There is always a sense of adventure on the water and I felt better for the first time once our clipper left the docks and began to make her way through the harbour towards the open sea. While my spirits had lifted, Holmes remained morose and I suspected that the current shift in his thinking sat ill with him. He seemed tired at dinner and complained of a gripe which had him almost doubled over for a moment as we left the dining table. I settled him in his bed and he was soon asleep. As for myself, I was fairly exhausted by the time I retired. There is something about the sea air that I find always ensures a solid night's sleep, and my head had barely touched the pillow before I became insensible.

I HAD NOT been long asleep, so it transpired, when I awakened to find a dark figure standing over me. Much alarmed, I made to cry out and rise when a strong hand pressed against my mouth and a voice hissed, 'Quiet, Watson, it's me!'

'Holmes!' I whispered.

'Who were you expecting?' Holmes said with a chuckle. 'A demon?'

'Really, Holmes,' I remonstrated. 'Is this some sort of joke?'

'My dear friend,' Holmes said. 'Not in the least. You must be as silent as possible. You will be relieved to know that there is no demon involved in this case – or not one from hell, at least. A very great villain, however, has clearly selected us to be his dupes. Master Xian has exploited this situation to make use of his countrymen for his own nefarious ends, finding those susceptible to vice and creating a spy network whereby it would be easy to keep an eye on our movements. As our travel plans were made well in advance it would not have been difficult for him to have learned of our journey upon the *Christopher*.

'I am certain we have been watched since leaving the home of Master Xian and that he has an agent aboard this ship. Therefore, I have preferred to keep you in the dark in regard to the true situation lest any explanation be overheard or a change in your demeanour observed.'

'Dear Lord, surely you could have found some way to alert me?' I said, aggrieved.

'I felt the course I took was the safest, although it did pain me to place you in a situation similar to the one I put you in at Baskerville Hall during another case involving outrageous claims,' Holmes said. 'Yet, we must hasten. We draw ever further away from Adelaide and we must return swiftly. There will be no more explanation until we disembark from this ship. We will leave our things aboard and recover them at a later date. It would be good, however, if you brought your service revolver. Put these on.'

Holmes was dressed all in black and he offered me similar garb. Obeying reluctantly, I rose and drew on the strange apparel, which included a pair of soft shoes. Within minutes we were on the deck and Holmes ushered me to the rail where a rope awaited. Slipping over the side, I found a small boat alongside us, its mast collapsed. When we were safely aboard, the sloop slipped into the wash, and once well clear of our ship, the mast was raised and the sails let out, and we began to speed back towards the city. As luck would have it, the wind was with us.

'Who are these men?' I asked, nodding at the crew of six who were clad similarly to ourselves.

'Ah, they are cohorts of Master Xian's rival, whom I have made contact with. In return for his help in rescuing Mr Ling's daughter I have offered to help him against the villain who has kidnapped her. Hopefully Xian believes we have left Adelaide in defeat and that his fortress is impregnable.'

'So she's alive!' I exclaimed, much relieved.

'I should think so,' Holmes murmured. 'A man like Xian would never murder Miss Ling when he can connive to keep her in subjugation instead.'

'But tell me, if this fellow has such an elaborate spy network, how could you go to his enemy confident that you would not be observed? How, in fact, can you be sure that these men who accompany us are indeed faithful to the rival?'

'I took all due caution.' Holmes smiled. 'I ensured I was not followed to the lair of Xian's rival, Master Wing, and I entered undetected and disguised, ensuring that I confronted him alone.'

'Good Lord, that seems a risky tactic!' I exclaimed.

'It was not without its moments of intensity,' Holmes admitted. 'Yet all went well and Master Wing has been sworn to secrecy and only his most entrusted men of the longest association have been let into the plot, none of whom has been allowed to leave the company of the others.'

'Very thorough,' I said.

Then I fell into silence as our boat sped towards Adelaide and Holmes advised me how we would effect a rescue.

IT WAS A mere two hours before dawn by the time we were in position at the house. Forming a human pyramid with the crewmen as the foundation, we had scaled the walls and made our way to the roof, three of the crew following behind, silent as cats. Holmes had scouted out the terrain alone the night before and was therefore secure in regard to the way. Taking out his watch, he looked at it briefly. Everything was impeccably timed. He had hardly tucked it away when the first explosion struck. Windows crashed in, doors splintered. There was no need for the stealth Holmes had employed on his previous reconnoitre.

As the assault by Master Wing's minions progressed we threw aside the tiles Holmes had removed on his previous visit and, entering the roof space, traced our way to the area above the room where Miss Ling was held captive, being careful to step on the beams. Confident he was above the right room, Holmes leapt between two beams. The lathe and plaster gave way beneath his feet and he dropped through. Catching hold of the beams, he lowered himself the rest of the way, having ensured that the young lady was not directly below him. Peering down, I saw Holmes bolt the door from the inside so that he was not surprised in his rescue, though judging from the sounds of mayhem that continued to echo about the house, it seemed likely that its master would be preoccupied with other matters.

Miss Ling did not move. A glance at her eyes told me that she had been drugged with opium and Armageddon itself would not have roused her. One of our dark-clad companions threw down a rope with a loop in its end to Holmes, who already had the girl on his shoulder in the manner of a fireman. Putting one foot in the loop, Holmes grasped the rope and we four in the ceiling hauled the pair easily into the roof space where we retraced our steps.

WE STAYED SEQUESTERED in a hotel for twenty-four hours while Miss Ling recovered. Then Holmes applied his somewhat amazing powers of disguise to alter our appearance and that of Miss Ling, so that we were able to leave Adelaide without anyone knowing our identities. The nature of the disguises was such that I do not care to detail them due to some embarrassment on the matter. Let it suffice to say that, of the three of us, Miss Ling was still the prettiest and conveyed the impression of holiness requisite of the role with the most conviction.

And so we left Adelaide with Miss Ling and her father secure. Holmes thought it safer for them to leave the antipodes altogether. The measure seemed extreme to me, yet he assured me that Xian would not easily be thwarted and that he retained considerable power. It would be best for Mr Ling to quit Australia and set up elsewhere, creating a new identity for himself. Luckily he had the financial means to do so.

What with all of the practical matters we had to deal with in arranging our escape from Adelaide, it was not until we were aboard the ship to Melbourne that it occurred to me to demand of Holmes an explanation as to how Master Xian had managed to pull off his hoax to the degree that I myself had begun to accept the possibility of the involvement of demons in the affair.

There was a look of considerable satisfaction on Holmes's face as he sat back in his chair and took a good pull on his pipe before he began to hold forth.

'I can only guess to what degree the situation has been orchestrated from the outset, Watson, and whether or not some favourable circumstances have merely been capitalised upon by our opportunistic and fiendishly clever foe. Yet I can surmise that for some time Xian had been aware of Mah Ling and her beauty, which is almost legendary among the local community. Given his power and wealth, despite the disparity between their ages, he may well have been able to arrange to marry the girl, though from our brief acquaintance with her, I did not see her as one likely to enter into such an arrangement willingly, nor her father the type to compel her. Furthermore, a man such as Xian would rather have several concubines than a wife with whom he might have to share some social power.

'Whether he was aware of our movements and somehow connived to have the Lings encounter us on the boat or whether he simply found out about it is one of the mysteries, though it hardly matters. What does seem sure is that, at some point, he became aware of our having met and befriended the Lings on our voyage, and rather than seeing this as an obstacle to his success he chose to make of it an opportunity. It seems possible that the greatest part of the scheme to abduct Mah Ling had long been concocted. However, it seems certain that the most startling bits of evidence were manufactured specifically for me to find, though they could have been late additions to the scheme. Xian would not have relied on the local authorities finding them. He would have considered the possibility that Mr Ling would not bother to seek help at all, taking the demonic explanation as *fait accompli*. However, should he not, Xian relied upon me reading the evidence as he expected and confirming our Chinese friend's suspicion that further investigation was pointless.

'Of course, I was never in doubt that trickery was involved, and it seemed almost from the start that it had to have been perpetrated by the host. Such a resourceful individual would leave nothing to chance and I suspected that we would be under constant scrutiny, so I played my role of dupe with as much conviction as possible. Keeping the true situation to myself relieved you from the task of playing any role but that of yourself. It was clear from the onset that our foe was exceptionally intelligent, ingenious and totally without scruples. Therefore, I could not take the slightest risk of any slip-up that might cause Mah Ling to come to harm.'

'Yes, yes,' I said, still annoyed at being allowed to believe the worst for so long. 'That's all very well, but how was the fraud accomplished?'

'Oh, that's simple, Watson,' Holmes said smugly. 'I thought you would have figured it out yourself.'

I remained steadfastly silent until Holmes resumed.

'This is the only part of the situation I feel confident I understand fully. It was done in the following manner. Once the house was silent and Mah Ling slept, intruders removed her from her room and sequestered her away. Blood was sprinkled about – we need not speculate upon its source – and, when all else was in readiness, a female lackey left behind in the locked room began to scream. As soon as she heard that the door was about to be attacked she hid in the cupboard or under the bed. Upon entering, Mr Ling had no reason to look for anyone hidden and was soon distracted by Xian's gasp to come to the window. Here the "demon", cunningly costumed, stood looking up at the window in the middle of the courtyard as if pausing for a moment to glance back, an impersonator of Mah Ling hoisted upon his shoulder – her long hair provided a feature easy enough to copy that it instantly misled her father from a distance. Mr Ling's face appearing at the window was the demon's cue to use his smoke bomb to cover his final sprint to the barn.

'Once inside, the girl who was taken to be Mah Ling slipped from his shoulder, and the two swiftly transformed themselves into the fleeing dishevelled servants, the "lovers", their costumes hidden within their robes. All quite obvious, really.'

'What about the bloody toeprints, spaced at such impossible intervals?' I asked. 'I found that particularly confounding.'

'A cast of the sculpted "demon's foot" covered with some porous material which could be partially soaked in blood, held in a hand hidden within the folds of the supposed hostage's dress, pressed upon the ground at intervals.' Holmes shrugged. 'Something of the like. So you see, the entire case is quite straightforward.'

'They always are, once you explain them,' I said gruffly.

Holmes merely grinned and puffed all the more contentedly.

The Mystery of the Miner's Wife

Narrelle M. Harris

'WATSON, THE DELAY can't be helped. Take a walk to exorcise your frustration, if you must.'

I scowled my ill temper over the top of the newspaper at my friend, Mr Sherlock Holmes, and told an outright lie as we sat in the Melbourne coffee palace that brisk, sunny day.

'I don't know what you mean, Holmes.'

'You're throttling that broadsheet as though it's done you personal injury,' he said. 'I can't imagine the reported discussions on federating the southern colonies are at fault. Therefore, your mood relates to this morning's letter from England, which contains no worse news than that your practice is performing perfectly well without you, and that your wife is happily taking the waters in Bath with her friend, Mrs Forrester.'

I glanced at the ragged state to which I had reduced the edges of the Melbourne *Argus* and ruefully conceded the point. 'I hate to sit idle in Australia while Mary remains in England.'

'Ah, you long for the comforts of pipe, slippers and a home-cooked meal.'

'As I recall, you're fond of my wife's cooking,' I said, more acidly than I intended. It wasn't merely a good English roast that I missed. Mary's good-natured acceptance of the way in which my adventures with Holmes could take me far from home was part of the reason I held her so dear. Yet there comes a time when a man longs to be in his own house, in his own bed, and in the company of his own dear wife.

'There's a cutter leaving for Plymouth in three days, if you're so keen to return to an English winter and its deleterious effect on your old wound.'

'No, no, my dear fellow,' I assured him, chagrined by the coolness in his tone. 'I promised I would stick with you till the end of this business. It's clear, in any case, that I'm of no more use at home than I am here.'

That pronouncement betrayed the truth of my forlorn mood. Holmes, rather than attempting to bolster my sense of self-regard, merely laughed. 'For a man who declared himself extremely lazy when we first met, idleness does not agree with you at all. But look, here comes a damsel in distress to liven up your morning.'

A woman was speaking with great animation to our waiter. Her skirts were speckled in dust, and strands of her dark hair were flying loose from the hat that sat askew on her head. Her cheeks were blotched red with distress and exertion. I'd have taken Holmes to task for his teasing at the lady's expense, except that her eyes lit upon mine at that very moment, and she came towards us, hand outstretched.

'Oh, please say you're the Dr John Watson who wrote this week to Everett Gilbert. You're so like his description of you, and we're in sore need of your assistance!'

I rose rapidly to guide her to a seat, though her grip on my fingers told me she was far from fragile.

'I am Dr Watson,' I told her. 'And Everett was very kind to me when we shipped home from Peshawar on board the *Orontes*.'

'And you to him,' she said, plucking anxiously at her gloves. She removed them and continued to tug at the fabric of them in her lap. I ordered her a cup of coffee.

'I am Everett's wife, Ellie Gilbert,' she proceeded, her straightforward manner and flat accent proclaiming her a native-born Australian. 'And you,' she said to my companion, 'must be Mr Sherlock Holmes, the great detective. Dr Watson has written much about you to Everett. I hope this is acquaintance enough, for Everett desperately needs the help of a friend!'

'Of course we'll help,' I said, as alert as Holmes to the untold story. 'Tell us what's happened. Everett has not responded to my last letter.'

'We've not been at home,' Mrs Gilbert said, rising, 'and we should be on our way to Ballarat!'

'The train doesn't return to the goldfields until after two o'clock,' Holmes replied. 'Tell us what you can now.'

Mrs Gilbert steadied her nerves and resumed her seat with admirable calm.

'Everett and I manage a prosperous business, importing fabrics and other haberdashery from Europe. Last night we returned to our home in Ballarat after attending to business here in Melbourne, to find our home practically overturned by the local constables and the body of our housekeeper, Mrs Cusack, being carried out on a stretcher. A terrible ending to a difficult life.' Mrs Gilbert's fingers clutched at the gloves in her lap. 'Naturally, we were astonished and Everett immediately asked the cause of this accident, when that idiot Constable Ryan arrested Everett for Mrs Cusack's murder!'

'You leave out half the story,' said Holmes irritably. 'If Mr Gilbert was in Melbourne with you, why should he be a suspect? Why was the constable so certain the lady was murdered?'

Mrs Everett Gilbert's frank, clear gaze held Holmes's imperiously.

'My understanding is that Mrs Cusack had not been seen since our departure, and finding no sign of her elsewhere, Constable Ryan was persuaded to investigate our home. This led to his breaking down the cellar door and finding her dead there. We arrived as they carried her out, and anyone could see the spike driven through her temple.' She said this unflinchingly, although her fingers quivered, as though held into anxious fists by her willpower alone.

'Was anything stolen from the house?'

'Only a silver salt and pepper set, which wasn't even the best we owned. Most of my jewellery was lodged in the bank before we left.'

'And why does suspicion attach to your husband?'

'Everett and I were to have left for the city together last week. We were seeing to our luggage on the platform in Ballarat when Mr Gallo – Everett had contracted him to dig a new well in our yard – arrived to report a difficulty, as the markers had been moved without consultation. Everett went back to address the issue, while I went on ahead to settle our luggage in the hotel. Everett followed the next day. After the police found the wretched woman in our cellar, and with Everett having been at home alone with her that one night, he was, so said the constable, the most likely suspect.

'Then this morning I noticed Dr Watson's postcard to Everett, asking if he and his friend the detective Sherlock Holmes might visit. I thought you might help to rectify this horrible error. You weren't at your hotel, but the concierge said you often come here of a morning, and so here I am.'

'What does your husband say of the night he was at home alone?'

'That he conferred with Mr Gallo on the re-pegging of the ground and concluded it was a mystery. Mrs Cusack made him a cold collation for his dinner. He left early the next morning and had to content himself with once more making his own breakfast when she didn't respond to his call.'

'Once more?'

'Mrs Cusack was a heavy sleeper and disinclined to early rising,' said Mrs Gilbert with such dour crispness that it was clearly a matter of longstanding contention.

'So he didn't see her before he left for his morning train?'

'Everett swears she came out in her gown and nightcap as he was leaving to ask if the digging of the well would continue as planned. He assured her on this matter and left her alive and well in the hall.'

Holmes drummed his fingers against his thigh. 'Did your housekeeper have any enemies who would wish her dead? An estranged husband, perhaps?'

'Far from it. Mrs Cusack was alone in the world, her husband having died a year ago, and having had no children. He left her impoverished. Out of kindness, Everett offered her a position in our new home, and she had been with us for five months.'

'Was the late Mr Cusack a well-regarded man?'

Disapproval flashed in Mrs Gilbert's fine eyes. 'One shouldn't speak ill of the dead,' she said, 'but it must be said that Mrs Cusack was generally considered better off without him. He was known as a fossicker and a thief.'

At Holmes's puzzled look, I elaborated. 'In gold-town parlance, "fossicker" refers to a man who steals gold from unattended claims.'

'He'd just returned from a ten-year prison term for his thievery,' said Mrs Gilbert. 'Within a week, he was up to no good, digging out an old mining tunnel in the neighbourhood. It collapsed on him and he died before the neighbours could be roused to dig him out.'

'Dangerous things, those old shafts and tunnels,' I recalled. 'The fringes of Ballarat where the old digs were abandoned must be riddled with them.'

'Most have been filled in to eradicate the danger to livestock,' said Mrs Gilbert. 'But Cusack had a habit of visiting old claims to see what leavings he might find. It was also rumoured he'd hidden stolen gold and goods in an old shaft, as much of it was never recovered.'

'Your husband was kind indeed for giving employment to the wife of this man.'

'Mrs Cusack was dull but decent, Mr Holmes. It was known that Cusack knocked her about. Otherwise, I can't imagine anyone, let alone Everett, would wish her harm. In truth, he was very lenient with her lackadaisical ways.'

I could see that the facts of the case were failing to excite Holmes's interest, and I determined that I would travel to Ballarat with Mrs Gilbert on my own account if he declined the case. Gilbert's good-humoured kindness, even in the face of his own injuries, had kept my spirits buoyant on that lonely ship home from my disastrous war. He deserved at least that much.

'You say the constable had to knock down the cellar door,' Holmes said suddenly. 'Where was the key?'

'It was normally kept on a hook by the door, but Constable Ryan told me it couldn't be found at the time.'

'Perhaps the killer took it away with him,' I suggested.

'Oh no,' was Mrs Gilbert's surprising reply. 'The doctor who examined the body found it tied around Mrs Cusack's neck on its string.'

Holmes sat straight-backed and alert, his cheeks tinted with excited colour, indicating that he too found this aspect scintillatingly peculiar.

'How does the constable explain this?' he demanded.

'He insists a second key must exist, though it doesn't. We've only ever had the one, which is why we hung it just outside the door.'

'Well,' said Sherlock Holmes, rising vigorously to his feet, for all the world like a hound set to the hunt. 'We can be packed and on the next train to Ballarat if we pick up our heels, Watson!'

Holmes sent Mrs Gilbert to the station to arrange our tickets and we joined her on the platform only minutes before the departure time. We had a compartment to ourselves, and Holmes wasted no time in seeking further data.

'Tell me more about Mrs Cusack,' he said. 'Her habits, history, demeanour. Anything you can share, and make no allowances for not speaking ill of the dead. Such niceties will only obstruct our inquiries. Assuming your husband is not responsible, we must examine the victim in order to understand the killer.'

Mrs Gilbert pursed her lips, but the primness soon gave way to a very practical streak. 'Oh well, I suppose you're right. Mrs Cusack was not sociable, tended towards slovenliness, and she was not efficient. One would think her constitution very sound, on the face of it, but she often begged off heavy work due to back pain. She was an adequate cook and housekeeper.'

'You didn't like Mrs Cusack?'

'I felt sorry for her, I suppose. Life isn't easy for a miner's wife, and with that man she'd endured harder years than most. She could be taciturn, but she did nothing that would bring me to dismiss her, and she was happy to work for lodgings and a small weekly sum. Everett always treated her with kindness. I think she was fond of him.'

'Your husband was the soul of kindness when I knew him,' I offered. 'I'm sure Mr Holmes will have this matter cleared up soon.'

Mrs Gilbert's expression softened, though Holmes only cast me an exasperated glance.

'And you say she had no relatives and few friends?' he asked.

'None.'

'What other household staff do you maintain?'

'Mr Hutton comes half-days for the garden, but he only came to us two weeks ago,' she said. 'And Mr Gallo was engaged to dig the new well after the old one went dry.'

'And there are no other entrances to this locked cellar?'

'Not even a window, although there is a small grating near the roof, to allow fresh air to circulate.'

Holmes sank into a reverie. When nothing more was said for several minutes, Mrs Gilbert leaned forward. 'Is that all you wish to know?'

'For the time being.' He steepled his fingers and retreated again into thought.

For the remainder of the journey, I engaged Mrs Gilbert in quiet conversation. At first we discussed the landscape; we had left the city far behind and the country was parched. None of the lush greens of England here, but the arid colours of sage and old straw, the way lined with the pale trunks of eucalyptus trees. Melbourne had changed markedly since I had last seen it in my youth, but the countryside was as forbidding as it had ever been.

Mrs Gilbert, a native of this land, was thoughtful on this point. 'It makes you uneasy? Everett says it feels lonely to him, the way the landscapes in India and Afghanistan felt alien to him. Perhaps that's the way when you're not born to the soil you inhabit. I grew up here, Dr Watson, and I've always found the scent of eucalypt and the call of the magpie are as much in my blood as the Thames and the robin are in a Londoner's veins.'

'I am a creature of London,' I confessed, 'though I don't miss the winter sleet, or the noisome fogs.'

'You're of a mind with Everett then. He says his wounded hand doesn't miss the cold at all.'

'It pains my shoulder and my leg a little,' I replied. 'But I endure.'

Her laugh was frank and merry. 'Everett said you had a sense of humour, rather more dry than his. He still tells people he lost those fingers in a card game in Penzance.' A misfiring rifle at the Battle of Kandahar had in fact seen to three fingers of his right hand.

Mrs Gilbert and I spoke then about that long-ago journey her husband and I had taken home on the *Orontes*, nursing our separate wounds and worries for our changed futures. Everett's optimism had meant much to me at that time, and I felt sure in the knowledge that my remarkable friend would clear this dark shadow from his life.

THE CAB WE hailed on arrival in Ballarat took us to the police station, where Mrs Gilbert swept boldly up to the desk. 'I wish to speak with Detective Meredith.'

The grizzled duty sergeant sighed, as though Mrs Gilbert's imperious presence was both commonplace and sadly unavoidable. 'I'll get Constable Ryan for you, Mrs Gilbert, will I?'

'No, you won't,' she said firmly. 'I have brought a London detective, Mr Sherlock Holmes, to see Detective Meredith about my husband's case.'

The sergeant's weary eye lighted first on me and, after an uninterested sniff, on Holmes. He sniffed again. 'This is a London detective, is it?' asked the surly fellow. 'He doesn't look much. I'd bet we've got detectives twice as good even here in Ballarat, let alone Melbourne or Sydney.'

Holmes's fine lips quirked in a swiftly suppressed grin. 'A betting man, are you?' he challenged in good humour. 'What about a wager, then? I'll tell you a secret about yourself and if I'm right, you'll fetch Detective Meredith for us. Does that sound fair, Sergeant –?'

'Clark,' smirked the sergeant. 'And if you're wrong?'

'A sovereign, and the boast that you have bested the London detective, Sherlock Holmes.'

Under the lady's exasperated eye, Sergeant Clark brushed a preening finger along his moustache and strode cockily out from behind the desk. 'Do your best then, Mr Sherlock Holmes.'

'Oh, there was no need to come out on parade,' said Holmes, though his grey eyes were glinting-sharp. 'You're French Canadian. A deserter from the Regiment of Royal Canadians. A failed Klondike prospector who found the cold and the competition too stiff for you.'

Sergeant Clark's wide-eyed stare held a medley of wonder, fright and belligerence. 'How do you know all that?'

Holmes's lazy-eyed smile verged on the beatific. 'Perhaps you could ask one of your excellent Melbourne detectives to explain. Though I'm happy to keep your secret between the four of us.'

'You'd better.'

'Sergeant Clark, I've played the game fairly. I've no interest in revealing your past, only in my client's future.'

The sergeant ducked his head. 'I'll fetch Meredith for you.'

Clark disappeared through a door and Holmes clapped his hands together.

'You observed, Watson, the faded tattoo of a maple leaf overlaid by that of a mermaid on his lower arm: the badge of the Regiment of Royal Canadians which he has tried to obliterate. The attempt to hide it indicates a strong desire not to be associated with them, perhaps through an unhappy experience but more likely because he deserted them for the promise of gold on the far side of the country. Many men in the police and armed forces did the very same thing. The French Canadian patriots use the maple as a symbol, and there's the trace of an accent. I'd bet another sovereign his name was originally Leclerc.'

'And a failed prospector?'

'A successful one would surely not have ended up in this colony as a policeman. He came out to try his luck again, with just as little reward, but his previous military experience has allowed him to take on a more stable career.'

At that moment Detective Meredith arrived, Everett Gilbert in his wake.

'Watson, you came!' Everett strode towards us, the dark circles under his eyes attesting to a restless night, but his bluff good nature and beaming smile were as warm as always.

'Naturally, old fellow,' I responded, shaking his left hand vigorously. 'And this is my friend, Mr Sherlock Holmes.'

'Is this what a great London detective looks like?' boomed Meredith, examining Holmes with a truculent eye. 'My sergeant was impressed though he wouldn't tell me why, and Mr Gilbert's been telling us half the night and most of the day that you perform miracles of deduction.'

'Not miracles,' Holmes demurred, 'but Scotland Yard and some of the royal houses of Europe have found my services useful.'

Detective Meredith's teeth-baring grin wasn't friendly. 'Do you think I'll find your services useful?'

'Anything's possible,' said Holmes, 'though I am here on behalf of Mr Gilbert, who I see has been released.'

'Yes, well, an examination of the body by the local doctor has shown he clearly can't be the culprit.'

Everett Gilbert held up his mutilated right hand, with its thumb and forefinger and the stumps of knuckles adjacent. 'Before the fatal blow was delivered to her temple, poor Mrs Cusack was strangled by a right-handed man – the bruises show four distinct fingers and a thumb. Even Constable Ryan agrees that it's a feat beyond me. Unless, that is, he can prove who stole my missing digits.' Everett's playful wit had changed little, even under these grim circumstances.

'Have you any other suspects?' Holmes asked.

'Hutton the gardener and Gallo the well-digger were last seen two days ago…'

'Long after Everett joined me in Melbourne,' said Mrs Gilbert, with a pointed look at Detective Meredith.

'Just so,' Meredith agreed. 'And the doc thought Mrs Cusack dead no longer than that, so we're looking for them both.'

'Have you any thoughts on how the murderer escaped without use of a key?'

Disgruntled, Meredith glared at Holmes. 'No local locksmith has cast an extra key, though it hasn't been ruled out. Got some ideas have you, Mr London Detective?'

'Without having seen the victim or the cellar, not a one,' Holmes confessed cheerfully. 'Though I might have more to suggest after I've done so.'

'Well, we've got old lady Cusack in a room out the back. You might as well have a poke at her. And this is Dr Watson, who wrote those books about you, is it? You might as well poke, too.'

'If Mr Gilbert feels up to it,' Holmes suggested, 'I may require his opinion on one or two things.'

'I'm right as rain,' Everett Gilbert declared. At his wife's searching look, he said, 'I'm all right, Ellie, but if you want, come with me and be my ministering angel.' His affectionate humour was met with the light of answering affection in her eyes, and she took his elbow.

'I may have opinions of my own to add,' she said staunchly.

'A biased witness, I'd have thought, but whatever you like,' said Meredith. He didn't like us and was daring us to fail.

Mrs Cusack's body was laid out on a table in an empty cell. Meredith gave Holmes a hard look, but my friend was already peering at the markings visible on the corpse's neck and head above the draping cloth. Her throat was mottled with marks of strangulation on one side, and at her temple was a terrible wound. A table had been brought into the room for the local doctor's examination. On one side were the lady's clothes, folded in a neat bundle with her shoes on top. Beside them were two wooden boxes. The first contained small artefacts from her person – a hairpin, a wedding ring, a little notebook filled with numbers and diagrams, and the key on a string.

The second box contained a miner's candle spike, the end of it smeared with blood – the murder weapon. The implement consisted of one long piece of steel leading from the spike, which could be jammed into a tunnel wall, to the loop, which enabled it to be hung from a belt. At the conjunction of loop and spike, a small empty cylinder was fixed.

'Mr Gilbert, is this your candle spike?' Holmes asked.

'No, Mr Holmes. We have ordinary household candlesticks and no need of a spike. It isn't ours, is it, Ellie?'

'No, dear,' replied his wife valiantly, though she was pale as she looked on her late housekeeper with pity and horror.

Holmes lifted the key from the first box. 'And what can you tell me about the key? It's new, very few scratches, not more than a year old.'

'The house is only that old, Mr Holmes,' said Mr Gilbert. 'We built on newly released land, from an area that had been along the edges of the original goldfields. The diggings petered out there a long time ago.'

'And it's the only key to the cellar where the murder was committed?'

'Yes.'

Holmes moved on to the pile of clothes, paying close attention to the shoes and the hems of the skirts and petticoat. Next, he turned to the body, ignoring the mortal injuries at first in favour of an examination under his glass of the woman's hands and fingers. Only then did he inspect the wound in her left temple and bruises on her neck.

He held the spike close to the wound and moved it until he was satisfied that it matched the angle of entry.

'Dr Watson, if I could have your opinion on these marks.'

'A left-handed blow, from the angle, and there is the distinct thumb mark under the jaw and bruises from the fingers of a right hand.'

'Unless the grip and blow came from behind, in which case the opposite is true.'

I almost berated Holmes for suggesting that Everett Gilbert was capable of the deed after all, but Detective Meredith interjected in irritation, 'The bloodstains in the wall made it very clear she was held against the wall with one hand to keep her from fighting back, and stabbed through the head on the left. Clear as daylight. We don't need a London detective to tell us that.'

'Quite so,' said Holmes mildly. 'With your permission, Mr Gilbert, let's take a look at this cellar and see what more can be deduced.'

I SAT BESIDE Everett and Ellie Gilbert on the carriage ride out to their home, while opposite us were ranged Sherlock Holmes, Detective Meredith and a constable named Fletcher. With a ruddy face and an open expression, he seemed very much a son of this sunburnt and rugged country. Everett Gilbert held his wife's right hand in his left and thanked Holmes keenly for his assistance before seeking his wife's reassurances on the state of their business interests.

For my part, I noted the changes wrought on the landscape since those few hungry months spent here in my childhood. In the town, we passed a newly built and grand hotel and other signs that Ballarat was a prosperous and growing city, even after the end of the gold fever of decades ago. Working gold mines still dressed this place in tall buildings, paved roads and decorative iron lace.

But Ballarat had never offered her riches to all. As we passed out of the main roads we came to new houses and shops, built on what had once been barren mounds of displaced earth where men had thrown away modest certainties for the nebulous promise of future riches. The pickings in these outskirts had been even less certain and much less rich. Some hardy men had burrowed entire tunnels seeking that elusive vein, finding death instead of fortunes when the walls collapsed on them.

My melancholy thoughts were arrested on arrival at the Gilbert home.

The sizeable house was flanked by a large block supporting a shed, flowerbeds, kitchen garden and the newly dug well. It was also dry, coming several feet short of the groundwater, and the pump remained in pieces beside the pit.

'Salvatore Gallo came with the highest recommendations,' said Everett ruefully. 'I can't believe he killed Mrs Cusack, but I've no idea why he should abandon his work so suddenly either.'

Holmes leaned over the freshly dug well. 'Your unreliable digger has left his tools in the well,' he observed.

'Gallo hasn't been found yet,' admitted Meredith, 'though he's known to take off to see his wife in Bendigo and ask her for money. He was last seen on Wednesday morning, two days before the Gilberts' return.'

'And five after their departure.' Holmes abandoned the well to examine a new plant bed outside the kitchen door. The bed was recently turned; two tones of rich soil, red-brown and a darker loam, rose some inches above the path.

'Did Mrs Cusack work the garden?' he asked.

'Nothing heavy, but she tended to it,' Mrs Gilbert said. 'Hutton did the main work.'

'Did he know Salvatore Gallo?'

'They're not known associates,' supplied Meredith. 'Gallo's record is clear, too.'

'And Hutton's?'

'Fencing stolen goods, some years ago. He and old Mr Cusack moved in the same circles.'

Mrs Gilbert retired to the kitchen to make tea while her husband led Holmes, myself and the two Ballarat policemen downstairs. The cellar door hung low on its hinges, the lock twisted awry where it had been forced open. Holmes inspected the lock briefly.

'No scratch marks. The lock doesn't seem to have been picked.'

Within the cellar, shelves on the flanking walls were lined with preserved fruits and meat, baskets of vegetables, bottles of wine and other domestic paraphernalia. The opposite wall was of bare brick. The table that had stood against it was askew, and beneath it was a pool of dried blood. The floor showed that the poor woman had been dragged from where she fell to a position by the left-hand shelving.

'Odd,' observed Holmes. 'Why move the body?'

'I wondered that,' responded the detective. 'This is where Mrs Cusack received her fatal blow.' Meredith gestured towards the bloodstained bare wall. 'You see here the smears on the bricks.'

'Curious,' said Holmes, inspecting the bricks and mortar.

'The pattern of the stain?' asked Meredith. 'This section in the middle was shielded by her body as the blow fell, which is why the marks are only on the left.'

'But that's not the most interesting thing. I draw your attention to the mortar in that central section of the wall. The floor is very telling, as well.'

Meredith peered at the lines of discoloured lime mortar and at the floor where dirt and dried blood co-mingled. He and I were none the wiser for the scrutiny, until Meredith exclaimed, 'Why is the floor here so dirty when the rest of the cellar is swept so clean?'

'Why should Mrs Cusack bring garden soil into the larder?' I wondered.

'Why indeed.' Holmes's eyes were alight. 'And you say that the only key to the room was found about Mrs Cusack's neck?'

'Yes,' Everett replied. 'Though generally she was the only one who came here. Ellie complained some mornings she couldn't get in because Mrs Cusack had the key.'

Holmes went to the corner of the room and tapped on the wall, an action he repeated from one corner of the bared wall to the other. When he at last seemed to hear something of note, he re-examined the bloodstained brickwork.

'Watson, would you be good enough to take that tin cup and strike these bricks like so,' he said, repeating his sharp tapping, 'until you see me again?'

I took the cup and struck a smart blow to the bricks as requested, then another.

'How long do you expect to be?' I asked as he darted out the door.

'No more than ten minutes, though it may be longer. Constable, if I may have your assistance, we will leave Detective Meredith and Mr Gilbert here with the doctor.'

Meredith seemed inclined to protest, but Holmes was gone, the eager Fletcher at his heels.

I continued to beat the wall as instructed, in spite of the detective's sour expression.

'This is foolishness,' he scowled.

'I have often seen Sherlock Holmes's foolishness lead murderers to the gallows,' I said, and struck another blow.

'Have you any notion of what this is about?' asked Everett.

'None. Although the bricks sound hollow, don't they?' *Tap.*

'But how could someone disappear through a brick wall?' *Tap.*

'I don't know,' I admitted. 'But neither could they disappear through a locked door.' *Tap.*

Meredith fidgeted uncomfortably. 'I won't put up with this Holmes fellow making the local constabulary look ridiculous.'

I was reminded of times when Holmes, exasperated, had claimed that many constabularies needed no help from him to appear ridiculous. I only tapped the wall again and said, 'In London, he'll more often give credit to the police than not.'

Our discussion was interrupted by a sound that made the hairs stand up on the back of our necks, so unexpected was it: the sound of metal on brick coming from the other side of the wall.

I tapped the wall twice. Twice, the sound tapped back.

'Holmes!' I shouted.

The faint sound became stronger and more rhythmic and the bricks began to shake and tremble in place.

Suddenly, two bricks bulged where they met. At the next sound of metal on brick, they gave way and the tip of a hand shovel appeared in the gap. We witnessed the instrument carving away at soft mortar until the bricks fell on the floor at our feet. A moment later, there was my friend's face, grimed with earth and perspiration, less triumphant than I had expected.

With a mighty heave, he dislocated an entire section of the wall, the bricks bound by discoloured and unset mortar tumbling to the cellar floor. I helped to remove the bricks until Holmes was able to squeeze through the gap.

As he entered, his feet tracked horrible prints of loamy soil turned to mud by congealed blood from beyond the wall. He held in his hand a mucky hessian bag.

'I've sent your constable for more men to retrieve Gallo's body and begin the hunt for Hutton,' said Holmes grimly. 'I hope we're not too late to catch him.'

Detective Meredith's protests died in his throat at the bloody tracks. He leaned into the cavity Holmes had made. In the direction leading back towards the unfinished well, the huddled and unmoving shape of the unfortunate Salvatore Gallo could be seen by the faint light spilling in from an opening.

Holmes removed his ruined boots and in his stockinged feet led the cellar's inhabitants to the parlour where Mrs Gilbert had set out tea. One look at Holmes's begrimed features and she fetched a basin and cloth. Everett took the opportunity to pour small measures of brandy for us all.

'But where does the tunnel come from?' asked Everett helplessly, his ebullient humour overtaken by horror and puzzlement. 'We built this house a year ago. Why didn't we discover it then?'

'Sheer good fortune, or bad,' Holmes said, washing and drying his hands and face. 'The tunnel has been there for a decade or more, one of the many dug by early goldminers. Its entrance either caved in or was filled in some time ago, but not before our late Mr Cusack made use of it.' He took the dirty bag from the floor and placed it on the towel in deference to Mrs Gilbert's polished table. From it he withdrew a salt shaker.

'That's ours!' declared Mrs Gilbert.

Holmes removed its lid and shook out three gold nuggets each the size of a lady's fingernail. Mrs Gilbert pressed her fingers to her mouth in astonishment.

'My business is good,' said Everett faintly, attempting humour, 'but not so good as we season our food with gold.'

'These nuggets are part of the late Mr Cusack's stash of stolen gold, which he hid in the tunnel before his incarceration,' said Holmes. 'I found signs that other goods had been partially buried in an older collapse at the end of the tunnel. Those have been dug out – you can see the holes and wax leavings against the tunnel wall where the candle spike was driven in to illuminate the work.'

'No doubt you think our colonial police service quite dull,' said Meredith brusquely, 'but as we wait, perhaps you could explain this strange chain of events.'

In Mrs Gilbert's kitchen, Holmes drew the threads together for us.

'My experience is that, regardless of the violence between husbands and wives, the latter always know more than they say. Mrs Cusack was likely to know at least some of the details of her husband's cache of stolen goods. The notebook among her effects was full of diagrams and notes in a masculine hand, and if we re-examine it I'm certain it will correlate to the position of this house and the tunnel that runs alongside it. Mrs Cusack clearly knew the tunnel was in this vicinity when she came to you seeking a position.'

'But how could she find it?' protested Mrs Gilbert.

'It's easier to find a thing when you know it must be there,' said Holmes. 'Given how the rear wall of the cellar had been cleared of shelves, I expect Mrs Cusack found it by hearing the difference in the sound between one wall and the next. Most would dismiss the disparity, but Mrs Cusack was looking for a tunnel. She would have heard the hollowness and known what it meant, just as I did.'

'But how on earth did you know to look for it?' demanded Meredith.

'Because if there was no second key, the only explanation for the deceased's presence in a locked cellar was a second entry that had been disguised. I came into the cellar alert for alternative entries, and the unadorned brick wall in an otherwise well-used cellar was the most obvious place to look for them.'

Detective Meredith conceded the method in Holmes's apparent madness. 'You pointed out the mortar to me.'

'The discolouration of the mortar in those bricks indicated that they had been laid at a different time to the rest of the wall. The floor was also sprinkled with dark soil of the kind we had seen mixed with the redder surface earth in the garden bed. Clearly, something unusual had happened there. You recall the secret room in the Sholto business, Dr Watson?'

'Of course.'

'I wondered if something similar might be afoot here and proceeded to sound the wall. When I heard the hollowness behind the bricks, the first pillar of my theory was in place. Mrs Cusack believed she had found the tunnel in which her husband had hidden his stolen gold and over the past five months of employment took her time during the nights to remove the bricks and dig through the few feet until she reached it, replacing the bricks and covering the section with the table.'

'She did all this without us knowing?' Everett was plaintive.

'There were signs. Mrs Cusack was sluggish and dishevelled of a morning for very good reasons, and the slovenliness Mrs Gilbert noted was the result of the digging. The signs of her labours were in her grimy hems, the calluses on her hands and the dirt embedded under her nails. Mrs Cusack also kept hold of the key and dissuaded the Gilberts from entering when she could. The excess soil she raked into the kitchen garden.'

Detective Meredith's disgruntlement was still plain. 'But then you left the cellar instead of breaking through the wall!'

'Doctor Watson will tell you that I like to have my hypothesis complete before sharing the results. The business with the well struck me as significant. The pegs to mark the digging site had been moved by persons unknown. The presence of a hollow behind the wall implied that either the housekeeper or her ally, Hutton, must have moved the markers to deflect the well site from their tunnel. Since the cellar door was locked, escape had to have been through the tunnel. Logic dictated the exit must be in the unfinished well. Constable Fletcher helped to lower me into the pit, and behind the digging tools I found where the well had broken into the tunnel. The second pillar of my case thus proven, I entered the tunnel only to find Hutton's second victim.'

'Was Salvatore part of it?' asked Everett.

'No. He wouldn't have fetched you back from the station if that was the case.'

'Bad luck for Gallo,' muttered Meredith. 'Stumbling across the tunnel meant the end for him.'

'Sadly, yes. He may have been compelled by curiosity when he broke through, but it's more likely he overheard the struggle between Hutton and Mrs Cusack. He followed the ruckus only to be confronted by Hutton, who killed him with a single blow to the head with a shovel.'

'But why was Hutton even there?' protested Everett Gilbert as his wife placed soothing fingers over the wrist of his ruined hand.

'Hutton and the late thief Cusack were certainly confederates. When Mrs Cusack found the digging burdensome due to her own poor health, I expect she contacted Hutton for help. She would have needed his assistance to turn goods into cash eventually. He became the gardener and she let him in the house at night so they could continue digging until they reached the tunnel. The Gilberts' departure for a week of business allowed them to make faster work of it, and they were able to enter the cavity and find the cache. I expect Mrs Cusack fetched the salt and pepper shakers from the shelf to hide some nuggets in, hoping to cheat Hutton of an equal share of the proceeds.'

'Then he discovered her trick, they argued, and he killed her,' I suggested.

'Isn't division of the spoils what thieves usually argue about?'

'And then poor Salvatore was caught up in it,' said Everett.

'Yes. The timing was unfortunate. Having a new exit to the tunnel gave Hutton his idea to replace the bricks with fresh mortar and then escape via the well. Hutton concealed the entrance crudely, but it was sufficient to allow him time to escape.'

'Not for long,' promised Detective Meredith darkly as he rose to his feet. 'I have my case now, Mr Holmes, and I intend to find Hutton and see him hanged. I'll take this as evidence.' He gathered up the hessian bag, salt shaker and gold nuggets. 'And I'll return for your statements, Mr and Mrs Gilbert.'

He stuck out a large hand, shook Holmes's with grudging respect, and left to direct the manhunt. In the event, despite two days' headstart, Hutton was intercepted in Ararat on his way to Adelaide. His capture salved the pride of the Victorian police force who, as Detective Meredith noted in his later letter to Holmes, had the brains and legwork the equal of any London detective after all.

Everett and Ellie Gilbert sat at their table side by side. Mrs Gilbert's hand rested over Everett's wrist, both seeking and offering comfort. Everett patted her fingers.

'Well, Ellie, that'll be another story for the memoirs, won't it?'

Mrs Gilbert smiled fondly at her husband, then turned her clear gaze onto us. 'Thanks to these good gentlemen.'

'Yes! Thank you, John, my dear friend, for coming to our aid and bringing your esteemed friend with you.'

I clasped his hand. 'As one old fighting comrade to another, it was my honour.'

'Even though it has cost me a pair of good boots,' Holmes added ruefully, staring at his stockinged feet. 'I shall have to beg a pair from you to get back to Melbourne.'

Everett Gilbert insisted on gifting his best kangaroo-leather boots to Holmes. 'They'll put a spring in your step,' Everett insisted with an unrepentant chortle.

'One day you'll "roo" your sense of humour,' riposted Ellie Gilbert, eyes sparkling.

Everett burst out laughing. 'You see how well-matched Ellie and I are, John? I trust your fortune has been as good as mine in marriage.'

AS THE TRAIN took us back to Melbourne, I contemplated Everett's obvious contentment with his life, the recent tragedy notwithstanding. Holmes left me to my introspection to read a book on the history of apiology in Australia, and its stingless native bees. He glanced up while turning a page.

'Content at last, I see.'

'My expression gives me away,' I declared amiably. 'But yes. I have been fortunate in my marriage, which allows me both home comforts and adventures. I'm the luckiest of men.'

Holmes returned to his reading, humming a refrain from one of Mozart's Haydn quartets. We would return to England, and I to my wife, soon enough. In the meantime, I had the company of my good friend and the honour to witness the exercise of his great powers to the benefit of even the farthest reaches of Her Majesty's empire.

THE PROBLEM OF THE BIGGEST MAN IN AUSTRALIA

Jason Franks

A CONSTABLE WAS WAITING to meet us when we stepped off the SS *Burrumbeet*. The journey from Sydney aboard the 300-foot screw steamer had not been a gentle one, and Holmes was looking gaunt by the time we arrived in Hobart.

The constable approached us and proffered a handshake. 'Mr Holmes, Dr Watson. I'm Constable Lang, here to see you to the alderman, if you please.'

'How do you do, Constable?' I shook his hand first, since Holmes had lagged some paces behind me while descending the gangway.

'How, indeed,' said Holmes, looking rather queasy. I wondered if it was indeed seasickness that had stolen some of his vigour, and not the side effect of some other substance the great detective might have taken. Since I had chastised him about his habits he had become more secretive about his indulgences.

Constable Lang directed us into a waiting hansom cab, and we climbed aboard with him.

From the window of the cab Hobart seemed a rough place, though it was well favoured by the nearby mountain and the harbour. The Derwent River was equally pleasing and I considered this territory as scenic a place as any that I had visited.

As I was watching the countryside, Holmes was watching Constable Lang, who was nattering nervously about the weather. Perhaps growing weary of the talk, Holmes fixed him with a stare and said, 'How long have you been a policeman, Mr Lang?'

'Coming up to eight year now, Mr Holmes.' Lang seemed uncomfortable.

'And how long since you were transported here?'

'Twenty-three, sir.' The constable was rather more certain of the second number. 'Out west for nine. Then I came down here to get away from the heat.'

Holmes turned to me and said, 'Watson, are you aware that most of the men in the municipal police forces are former convicts?'

'I was not,' I admitted.

Holmes sniffed and turned his attention back to Lang. 'I suppose it makes them rather better trained than their contemporaries in Scotland Yard.'

Lang did not know how to react, and so said nothing.

'It is my understanding that the municipal police forces here have done rather a good job of improving public safety and discouraging crime, if not corruption,' said Holmes. 'And so I wonder at the magnitude of the matter that would have an alderman send for the likes of me and you, Watson, all the way from the mainland.'

'Magnitude is about right, Mr Holmes,' said Lang. 'He wants you to investigate the death of old Tom Jennings.'

I wondered at the importance of this 'Tom Jennings'. I did not recognise the name, and it was given without any indication of rank or title. Lang obliged my musing with a grin.

'Tom Jennings, publican of the Harvest Home Inn,' said the convict-turned-constable. 'And until his recent demise, known to be the biggest man in Australia.'

SITTING IN A leather-upholstered chair in the alderman's office with his pipe between his teeth, Holmes was beginning to look his usual self again. 'Tell me, Mr Fowles,' he said, 'how old was this Thomas Jennings when he died?'

'Sixty-six, Mr Holmes,' said the alderman, frowning at Holmes's tone. It was clear that my colleague did not find the matter as serious as Fowles himself did.

'And he died in his own bed, with his loved ones in attendance. What exactly strikes you as unnatural about this situation?'

'A man like that might have lived another ten years,' said the alderman. 'He was healthy as an ox, until he fell ill. Never took a drink. He was poisoned, I am sure of it.'

'To what purpose?' said Holmes. 'This man was a simple publican, as I understand it.'

'He was that,' replied Fowles. 'But he was not without a degree of celebrity. Appeared in the newspapers, you know. We've had numerous visitors to the town wanting to see him for themselves, some all the way from New Zealand.'

'And you think Mr Jennings had a secret that cost him his life?'

'That, Mr Holmes… Dr Watson… is what I am paying you to find out.'

LAID OUT ON a slab in the mortuary, Thomas Dewhurst Jennings was indeed one of the largest humans I have ever laid eyes upon. Five feet ten and thirty-two stone, he was a barrel-chested man with bushy white mutton-chop sideburns and a rounded face that showed the lines of good temperament, even in its final repose.

'I wouldn't exactly say that his health took a turn,' said Thistlewaite, who had been Jennings' physician when he had been alive. 'But it did rather slowly and steadily erode over the last year, until… well, you see the results reclining here before you.'

'In what way did he decline, Dr Thistlewaite?' I asked. Holmes was prowling restlessly about the room. Here in the presence of death he had apparently regained his equilibrium.

'He showed many symptoms.' Thistlewaite consulted his notes. 'Elevated blood pressure – that was the first of them. Complained of pins and needles. Anaemia. Irritability – which was most unlike him, everyone will tell you. Went off his food – that in particular was when we came to believe he was unwell.'

Thistlewaite had a precise but warm manner about him and I was confident that his observations were accurate. Holmes, meanwhile, had begun to punctuate his restless prowling with the occasional grunt of annoyance, and I knew that he was losing patience. I bit back my embarrassment and said, 'In your opinion, Dr Thistlewaite, what was the cause of Mr Jennings' demise?'

Thistlewaite did not hesitate. 'Renal failure.'

Holmes turned about suddenly, both hands behind his back, and thrust his face towards the deceased man's physician. 'Dr Thistlewaite, do you believe that your patient was poisoned?'

To his credit, Thistlewaite merely shrugged and said, 'There are many factors that can cause dysfunction of the kidneys, Mr Holmes, and poison is certainly one of them. As of yet I have seen no evidence for or against it.'

THE HARVEST HOME INN, where Thomas Dewhurst Jennings had been the publican, was indeed a homely place. The common room was a long chamber with wood-panelled walls and bare dirt floors. The furniture was rough-grained but the bar was polished mahogany with a scuffed brass foot-rail. Here the cosy civilisation of Europe and the raw frontier of the colonies met and made peace.

It was easy enough to discern the place at the main table that Jennings had once occupied. The chair was twice the size of the others, reinforced with leather straps and heavily cushioned. The place setting on the table before this throne was similarly outsized and gleamed yellow in the waning afternoon light. I picked up a golden stein and was surprised by the weight of it – but I could see dull metal shining through the surface coat. 'Gilt,' I said. 'A fancy vessel for a man who took no liquor.'

Holmes, who had already executed a circuit of the room, took the stein from me, gave it a cursory glance, and set it back in its place without saying a word.

Alderman Fowles sat down in Jennings' chair and spread his bowed arms to indicate the dead man's imagined girth. 'A big fellow, wasn't he?' said Fowles. 'And proud of his appetite. I suppose it bespeaks a lack of intellect.'

'Do you, now?' said Holmes.

'Certainly,' said Fowles. I think he was trying to impress Holmes with his own deductive abilities. 'To allow oneself to become so large, knowing full well that the world is engineered for people half one's own size. To require special chairs, special doors. I wonder, did it perhaps make a small-brained individual like the late Mr Jennings feel special, to be stared upon so?'

'The man with the most powerful intellect that I have ever met, Mr Fowles, is larger yet than Mr Jennings.'

Fowles pursed his lips and nodded. 'I see, I see,' he said. 'Perhaps a man of such an intellect may overlook the health of the body while over-nourishing the mind, especially if he is predisposed to obesity by vice.' He gave a little smile and added, 'Poor breeding, I expect.'

Holmes allowed a moment of silence after this pronouncement. His expression did not change when he did at last speak. 'I am speaking, of course, of Mycroft Holmes. My brother.'

Fowles blinked, coughed and rose rather hastily from the chair. 'I beg your pardon.'

Holmes did not bother to reply.

Fowles cleared his throat and took another step away from the large seat. 'Well, Mr Holmes? Dr Watson?' Fowles gestured about the room as if introducing a theatrical production. 'Do you believe, as I do, that Mr Jennings was poisoned?'

I could see some acerbic comment on Holmes's lips, and I sought to pre-empt him for the sake of diplomacy. 'It is possible, from a medical sense, but like Dr Thistlewaite, I have seen no evidence. Further, we have yet to learn of any enemy, any secret, any reason that might have motivated someone to murder poor Mr Jennings.'

Fowles began to splutter a protest, but Holmes raised one hand. 'Mr Fowles, I do indeed believe that Mr Jennings was poisoned, but I would not go so far as to name it murder. As for motive... I believe that, too, is not what it seems.'

Fowles grinned. 'Do tell, Mr Holmes.'

Holmes turned to me. 'Watson, what was the matter that you were discussing with that physician in Brisbane? Turner, wasn't it?'

I frowned. 'Dr Turner has been investigating health syndromes in children with developmental difficulties. His contention to me was that exposure to lead was the cause of it.'

'Lead is known to be toxic to adults, is it not?' said Holmes.

'In London, I have treated many ladies who work in the lead mills,' I replied. 'Not to mention painters, typesetters and other working men who are exposed to the substance in the pursuit of their professions. There most certainly does appear to be a connection between exposure to the metal and a certain pattern of health problems.'

Holmes knew all of this already, of course. 'I am no doctor,' he said, 'but I am a detective, and I do make a study of criminal matters – including poisons. Just last year I read an abstract in the *Utah Journal* that claimed that continued, cumulative exposure to lead can indeed be deleterious to one's health… or even fatal.' In two strides Holmes was back at the common table. He hefted Jennings' tankard as if to weigh it in his hands. 'Lead,' he said. 'Beneath the gilt, it is lead. Mr Jennings was indeed poisoned – by the cup from which he drank and the plate from which he ate.'

Fowles stroked his moustaches. 'Indeed. And now, Mr Holmes, tell us who had motive to undertake such a deed?'

'As I said before, I do not believe this was murder,' said Holmes. 'Simple vanity, perhaps. The man merely wished to sit upon his throne, and eat and drink like a king.' He turned that gaze of his upon the alderman. 'No, Mr Fowles, the motive I spoke of was not the motive of a killer, it was that of a different sort of man altogether. A motive that is gilt with public concern, but which reveals a baser metal under close inspection.'

Fowles gave an audible sigh of relief when Holmes returned his attention to me. 'Watson, did you perchance observe how many volumes of your doggerel Alderman Fowles had upon the shelves in his office?'

I looked at my shoes. 'I did notice one or two. I thought he was merely being polite.'

'You are far too modest, Watson,' replied Holmes. 'Mr Fowles didn't have one or two of your books, he had all of them. Every one, including the volume published only last year.'

'Holmes,' I said, trying to turn the conversation away from my embarrassment, 'what is the point you are making?'

Holmes sighed and shook his head. 'Only that here we have a high-ranking member of society who has brought us here to investigate a celebrity death… not because he truly suspects foul play, but merely so that he can observe us in the flesh.' Holmes rounded on the alderman, who quailed before him. 'Alderman Fowles, we are abroad in this country on serious business, and you have called us from our task to perform for you as if we are travelling players.'

' I… Mr Holmes,' the alderman pleaded. 'I did truly believe…'

Holmes cut him off with a flinty stare. 'I do not care how you would justify this to yourself, alderman,' he said, 'but I do not wish to hear tales return to us about how Dr Watson and I solved the poisoning of the unfortunate Mr Jennings for you. Am I clear?'

Fowles backed out of the room, mumbling apologies and keeping his eyes downcast.

'Do you really think that was wise, Holmes?' I asked, when I was certain we were alone in the empty common room. 'Fowles is a powerful man.'

Holmes showed no particular concern. 'He abused us, and yet we solved his mystery just the same. He has had his amusement. I do not think the alderman has grounds for complaint.' He straightened his collar and turned towards the door. 'But if he does complain, Watson, perhaps you can put him in one of your little books.'

The Murder at Mrs Macquarie's Chair

Robert Veld

T HE ADVENTURE TO which I have given the title 'The Murder at Mrs Macquarie's Chair' was one of several that Sherlock Holmes investigated when we made the great journey by sea to the southern continent of Australia in the year 1890. On one of the occasions when we were in the city of Sydney during our travels that year, we took rooms in an establishment called the Hotel Metropole and it was upon the morning of our second day there in the city that my friend was asked to assist in a new matter.

Sherlock Holmes had pulled open our hotel room door to allow the porter to deliver a letter, and Holmes then issued a message for the man and dismissed him.

'What is it, Holmes?' I asked, having returned from my morning ablutions.

'Can you be ready in ten minutes, Watson?'

'Certainly, I am as good as ready now,' I said.

'Excellent, then we shall waste little time. The author of this letter awaits us in the foyer.' He tossed the letter at me, which ran thusly:

MY DEAR MR SHERLOCK HOLMES,

It is with considerable interest that I have become aware of your most recent arrival into Sydney and it is my hope that I may be able to call upon you at a time that is convenient to ask your opinion regarding a case of the most serious nature that has come my way.

At this moment, I am unaware of what other activities place a burden on your time but I can only appeal to you that the matter is something that appears quite in your line.

Yours faithfully,
DETECTIVE GREGORY MURRAY
Criminal Investigation Branch
No. 4 Police Station
127 George Street, Sydney

In the foyer we were warmly greeted by a tall, well-built individual. His tanned, weathered face was framed by a head of thick, dark hair and a full dark beard that conveyed an air of great authority and confidence.

'Mr Holmes, Dr Watson,' said he, 'my name is Detective Gregory Murray of the Criminal Investigation Branch. I am so delighted that you have agreed to meet with me so promptly. It is a great honour to meet you both.'

'Your letter indicated a matter of a most serious nature, Detective Murray,' said Holmes. 'Perhaps, as Watson and I have yet to partake in any breakfast, you could join us and recount your tale? I am sure that it would not be difficult to find a table away from many a prying ear.'

'I shall be delighted,' replied the detective.

Not long after, we were seated in one of the hotel's dining rooms. Detective Murray sat opposite us, a great grin on his face.

'Mr Holmes,' said the Australian detective, 'I have read much about you and can I just say that I consider your handling of the Lauriston Gardens murder a few years back as a brilliant demonstration. I am fortunate to own a copy of Dr Watson's account of the case, and it has served as something of a textbook on scene-of-the-crime procedure for me ever since. A number of us at the CIB first thought it to be a work of fiction, but one of our detectives who immigrated from the mother country a few years back made mention of you by name. So I must apologise to you for believing you to have been a figment of some writer's imagination!'

'Well,' Holmes laughed, 'Watson's narratives of my cases are styled like melodramatic fiction at times.' Anticipating my protest, he added, 'Easy my dear fellow, a small jest.'

'Now, Detective Murray, to the matter upon which you wish me to assist you. Please present your account and omit nothing.'

'There are two related incidents that have occurred over recent days, Mr Holmes,' Murray replied, drawing a small notebook from his right coat pocket. 'Three days ago on the Tuesday just past, at about five o'clock in the morning, the body of an elderly man was found on a popular walking path at the base of a large sandstone cut feature called Mrs Macquarie's Chair. It is only a short journey east of here down by the waters of the harbour. The body lay facedown with the arms out and the back area of the head severely beaten in, obviously by a blow from some heavy object. It was clear, however, that the victim had tried to defend himself vigorously against his attackers as there was bruising to his forearms as well as his wrists. Despite the immediate area around where the attack took place giving up few clues, a search of the wider grounds was conducted. Two vagrants, both of them partial cripples, were located not far from the scene of the crime with marks of blood upon their arms and hands and, crucially, in possession of the dead man's clothes and belongings. They were both immediately arrested and taken into custody.'

'And I gather that both men have denied any guilt in regards to the murder of this man, otherwise you would not be here,' said Holmes.

'Their only admission has been to the stealing of the dead man's clothes and belongings after happening across his body, nothing more.'

'Were you able to establish how long the unfortunate individual had been deceased?'

'Not more than three hours before the body was found.'

'Has any murder weapon been discovered?'

'No.'

'This path upon which the man's body was found,' said Holmes. 'You found no other clues?'

'No, Mr Holmes,' replied the detective, drawing a folded sheet of paper from his left coat pocket. 'The ground around where the body was found is very hard and not very impressionable.

'The walking path in question circumnavigates a peninsula of our harbour known as Mrs Macquarie's Point that is bordered by Farm Cove to the west and Woolloomooloo Bay to the east. The peninsula is primarily north-east facing, and looking out from Mrs Macquarie's Chair affords excellent views straight across the harbour to an old convict-built defensive facility called Fort Denison, as well as the opportunity to observe the heavy shipping traffic entering and leaving the harbour. The peninsula is itself a part of a large expanse of open public parkland called the Domain, accessible to the public at all hours via Mrs Macquarie's Road, though access is restricted to foot traffic after nightfall. It is a very popular recreational area amongst the local population and is utilised on a regular basis for official functions. Unfortunately, it is also often the scene of vulgar and mischievous deeds at night.'

Sherlock Holmes sat for a time without a word. 'I trust that you have succeeded in identifying the victim?' he asked.

'Yes, I have, his name was Henry Cross. My inquiries have so far put his age at about sixty. He was a widower who had lost his wife some years ago and since that time he had become quite partial to drink. He was a well-known patron of the many public hotels about the town. He lived in a small terrace house in Woolloomooloo, which is not far from the Domain. He has no criminal record that I could find and despite his drinking seemed to lead quite a simple life and he stayed clear of trouble.'

'Had he any family?'

'Two sons, Mr Holmes: Samuel and William. Samuel is married and lives in Redfern. He is a hansom-cab driver and although the family appears to have no real money to speak of, he is the one who seems to have made good from his lot in life. William, on the other hand, is a bachelor who has an eye for the ladies, if you know what I mean, and he, like his father, is no stranger to the drink. His income is meagre by all accounts and he appears to always be in want of money to feed his rather loose habits. He finds employment at Kelly's Boatshed at Darling Harbour on a regular basis. He lives in the same suburb as his father. Unfortunately, he has not been seen for about a week and now, in light of events that occurred late on Tuesday night, I fear that a similar fate to that of his father has befallen him.'

Holmes's eyes filled with excitement as he leaned forward, his focus set on Detective Murray seated opposite him.

'You see, sometime late on Tuesday night, Mr Holmes, Samuel Cross and his wife, Emily, were viciously attacked in their own home by some unknown assailant! It was only Samuel's desperate efforts that drove the attacker from the house.

'What had transpired beforehand was that both husband and wife retired to bed at around ten o'clock. They were roused sometime later in the night by noises coming from the rear of the house. Samuel struck a match and in turn lit a bedside candle, but before either of them could exit from their bed, the unknown brute was upon them. It was Emily who was set upon first with a strong hand catching her about the throat and then a great savage blow to the face which rendered her unconscious. It was then that Samuel struck the intruder in the face with the lit candle, which immediately gave him the advantage. He struck at the intruder a number of times before the attacker fled the house.'

'Did you get a description of this intruder?'

'He was wearing a mask, Mr Holmes, like a great piece of cloth that covered his face with two holes cut out of it for eyes. The only description that I have been able to obtain is that he was at least six feet in height and was of a heavy build, and that he bore a large beard of some kind. He made neither demand nor sound as he set upon the couple. A full search of the house was conducted at first light and there appeared to be nothing taken, so I am convinced that robbery was not the motive.'

'Have you formed an opinion as to a motive then, Detective Murray?'

'No sir, I have not. All I can think is that the family may have enemies of which we do not yet know, though Samuel Cross denies such a suggestion strenuously. There is very little to go on at this stage.'

'And you have yet to locate the whereabouts of the brother, William?'

'That is correct, Mr Holmes. So far there has been no sign of him.'

'Your case is of interest to me,' said Holmes. 'Let us define our position. In the first instance I am not prepared to accept that the two matters, and possibly a third, have occurred as a result of some coincidence. Now, to consider the incidents in their known order, let us first consider the murder of this man Henry Cross. He is found bludgeoned to death and no murder weapon discovered. The body has been stripped of its clothing and anything of value has been taken. The grounds are searched and two men, homeless and cripples both, are found with the dead man's clothes and possessions and taken into custody. A strong case could be made against these two men. To the casual observer this portion of the case would appear to be at an end, would it not?'

'Yes,' I replied.

'And yet the occurrence of the second incident would seem to indicate that it is not. On this occasion a husband and wife, the son and daughter-in-law of the deceased, are attacked in their home by some unknown assailant. Robbery does not appear to be the motive. The other unknown element in this case is the brother and what has become of him. Has he too met with foul play? Is he the man whom we are seeking over this whole affair? There are many questions to which we must find the answers. I should think a visit to this Mrs Macquarie's Chair is where I ought to begin my investigations.'

OUR FOUR-WHEELER RATTLED north-east along Mrs Macquarie's Road out towards the end of the peninsula known as Mrs Macquarie's Point before pulling to a stop at Detective Murray's order. Disembarking from the carriage, Murray led us to a set of stone-cut stairs that wound their way down in a semicircular fashion to a pathway below. At the base of the stairs sat a stone ledge that had been carved into the natural sandstone. On the large vertical rockface above the crude creation there featured the following inscription:

BE IT THUS RECORDED THAT THE ROAD
Round the inside of the Government Domain Called
MRS MACQUARIE'S ROAD
So Named by the Governor on account of her having Originally
Planned it Measuring 3 Miles, and 377 Yards
Was finally Completed on the 13th Day of June 1816

Detective Murray led Holmes over in front of Mrs Macquarie's Chair and pointed, indicating a spot on the ground.

'That was where the body was found, Mr Holmes. That darkened area was where a large pool of blood lay.'

'This ground is indeed hard and most unimpressionable,' said Holmes. 'Little can be seen. Additionally, many people have also passed over it since the murder, probably disturbing whatever traces there may have been.'

Holmes produced his lens from his coat pocket and stretched himself out upon the ground. For a long time he examined the bloodstained area before returning to his feet.

'There is nothing more to be learned here,' said he.

'Our men did make a thorough examination of the area, Mr Holmes.'

'I don't doubt it, Detective,' Holmes replied, looking about the place.

It was then that I saw my friend train an intense gaze upon a large tree that sat atop the ground situated behind Mrs Macquarie's Chair. I could tell that something had struck his interest.

'What is it, Holmes?' I inquired.

Holmes had hurried off up the stairs and was now standing on the grass-covered area above us that was shaded by the large tree. I could see him again produce his lens and proceed to examine its trunk.

'What is it Mr Holmes, have you found something?' asked the detective.

'There is a bullet in the trunk of this tree, and it very likely was fired into the trunk only recently as the damage to the bark around the hole is still relatively fresh.'

'But the man wasn't shot, Mr Holmes. What are we to make of that then?'

'Let us remember it. We do not yet possess all of the data,' Holmes replied. 'We may discover something later that may come to bear upon this.'

'I shall have it removed, Mr Holmes, so that we might have it as evidence should we need it.'

'Very good,' said Holmes, placing his lens back into his coat pocket. 'Now, might I ask you both to leave me to my own devices for a time? I shall be taking a little walk about this place to satisfy my curiosity.'

With his face bent downward and his shoulders bowed, Sherlock Holmes raced off and disappeared from view. The detective and I ascended the stairs so that we might catch sight of where Holmes had run to. The sight that greeted us was one that was familiar to me when Holmes's senses were engaged upon the hunt. Swiftly and silently, he ran about like a foxhound, following some pattern we could not see.

After roughly twenty minutes Sherlock Holmes returned; the nervous, erratic behaviour that we had just witnessed was all but gone.

'Have you managed to find anything, Holmes?' I asked.

'Very little, I am afraid, Watson. I should think it now wise that we attend to the scene of the more recent incident and give the dead man's son our full attention.'

Our trip by hansom took us south to Turner Street in a suburb called Redfern. The dead man's son lived in a small brick house, well kept in appearance and bordered by a low-cut hedge at the front and a timber paling fence on either side. The man who greeted us at the front door introduced himself as Samuel Cross. He was a rather tall individual of about six feet in height, of a thin build with sharp features and a heavy moustache, from under which a cigarette protruded. We were shown into the house and directed to the sitting room where a young woman lay upon a couch draped in a red dressing-gown, her head resting on a cushion. She had an attractive face complete with a pair of beautiful brown eyes and a head of long brown hair. Unfortunately, her recent experiences had resulted in some heavy bruising and swelling evident above her right eye as well as some most grotesque bruise marks about her neck.

'Gentlemen, this is my wife, Emily,' said Samuel Cross. 'If we can keep this interview short I would appreciate it. Emily has been through quite an ordeal, as you can understand, and the death of my father has placed a great strain upon me.'

'We understand, Mr Cross,' said Detective Murray. 'We only wish to take a few moments of your time. Mrs Cross, these two gentlemen are Mr Sherlock Holmes and Dr Watson, from London in England. Mr Holmes is a detective and he has agreed to help me in investigating this matter. It was his wish that he could speak to you and your husband in person.'

'I assure you both that I will not impose upon you more than necessary. However, before we get to the events of the other night I was wondering, Mr Cross, if you might permit me to ask you some questions about your father?'

'Certainly, Mr Holmes, I will answer to the best of my knowledge.'

'Can you think of any reason why anyone would want to bring harm to your father?'

'No, since the death of my mother several years ago he led a very solitary existence. It was no secret about the place that he was one for the drink, but he wasn't one for getting into too much trouble. If he did have a quarrel with someone, I was not aware of it.'

'Do you have any idea why your father would be out at Mrs Macquarie's Point in the early hours of the morning?'

'No, I don't. All I can think is that he may have had a heavy night on the drink and wandered off into the Domain in some drunken stupor and spent the night there. He has done such things before. That is all I can think of to explain where he was found.'

'Thank you, Mr Cross. Now, if we may turn our attention to the events of the other night. Can you provide me with a full account of what occurred here in this house?'

'Well, Mr Holmes, there is really very little to tell you. My wife and I retired to bed at our normal hour of ten o'clock that night. I don't know the hour at which we were awoken by the noise of someone in the house but I struck a match and lit the candle at my bedside. I had barely completed the task when there appeared on the right side of the bed, my wife's side, a great brute of a man, his face covered by a full mask with only holes cut out of it for his eyes. In an instant he had the neck of my wife in his grasp and he delivered a powerful blow to her head, rendering her unconscious. I lunged at him, driving my lit candle into his masked face. I hit him so hard that the candle broke from its holder and was immediately extinguished. He let out a cry of pain and I at once took the advantage in the darkness, delivering a number of blows about his head. It was during my retaliation that I became aware that the man possessed a large beard under his mask that I must have partially exposed during my attack.'

'And you became aware of no other features of your attacker?'

'No, Mr Holmes. The whole affair happened so quickly and in such total darkness.'

'What did you do then?'

'After our attacker retreated I retrieved what remained of the candle, relit it and tended to my wife's injuries. She remained unconscious for some minutes before she came to. I was reluctant to leave her on her own at first so I stayed with her for a time until I thought it necessary to seek the assistance of some of my neighbours. It was a while after this that I notified the police.'

Mrs Cross now spoke. 'I can add very little to what my husband has just told you, Mr Holmes. I really do not recall much of that night.'

'I understand completely, madam, and I do so wish you a quick recovery from your ordeal. Do you not have family of your own on whom you may call at such a traumatic time as this?' Holmes said.

'I have a sister but she lives in Melbourne and I dare not draw her into this, especially as we do not yet know if all of the danger has passed.'

'Your concern for your sister's welfare is well founded. I have one question for you, Mr Cross, regarding your brother,' said Holmes, turning back to Samuel Cross. 'Were relations between your brother and yourself amicable?'

'We have never been the closest of brothers, Mr Holmes. William is a man of loose habits, fond of the bottle. He is also quite poor in the management of his own financial affairs. I know of a number of occasions when he sought money from our father, and can recall at least two occasions when he approached me. So I hope that you can understand that matters were not always pleasant between us. Do you suspect that he has something to do with all of this?'

'It is still too early to say whom I suspect in regards to this business, but may I now ask if I might be permitted the opportunity to take a brief look over the bedroom in which this most unfortunate incident occurred?'

'Certainly Mr Holmes, if you will follow me.'

Following Samuel Cross down a narrow hall, we were permitted into the bedroom. It was a surprisingly large room that was well lit courtesy of a window that faced west. A wide bed placed against one wall ran lengthways across the room with a gaping fireplace opposite it. A simple dressing table was situated over in a corner well clear of the fireplace and two small brown chests of drawers could be found at the head of the bed on either side. A much larger brown chest of drawers completed the room's furniture.

'So this is the side of the bed upon which you sleep, Mr Cross, and your wife the opposite side, closest to the window?' asked Holmes, approaching the bed and looking about the room.

'Yes, Mr Holmes.'

'I see. Thank you. If I may, one final question of you before we leave?'

'Certainly,' said Samuel Cross.

'Is your brother of about your height, of a heavy build and possessing a beard?'

'Yes.'

'Thank you for your time, Mr Cross, I bid you farewell.'

As we left the house Holmes stood at the side of our four-wheeler before stepping into the carriage. I could tell from the intent expression on his face that his calculating mind was already heavily engaged upon some new development.

'Detective Murray,' he said, 'I believe that little time should be wasted in conducting a search of the brother's house.'

'Mr Holmes, there are legal formalities to comply with in regards to such matters. I cannot simply obtain a key and enter the house.'

'I am aware of such things, Detective, but might I suggest that you act without delay? I believe that there may be much depending upon it.'

'Very well, Mr Holmes. I shall make every effort to do so.'

'We can do no more until you have that key, Detective.'

'Can I ask, Mr Holmes, if you have already formed any theories in regards to this matter?'

'I can hardly answer that question at the moment. I think that for the time being Watson and myself might make our way back to our hotel. Nothing more can be done today and the hour is getting on. There is much to consider, and I should think that a pipe or two of the appropriate tobacco will help me in setting my mind upon the right path.'

THE FOLLOWING MORNING a telegram from the detective reached us before breakfast with the news that there had been success in obtaining the warrant to conduct a search of William Cross's house and a key obtained from the landlord. After being picked up by Detective Murray in a hansom the address was but a short drive from our hotel, with our four-wheeler pulling up at the corner of Judge Lane and Forbes Street in Woolloomooloo. Judge Lane was bordered on its north and south sides by a continuous line of narrow two-storey terraced houses, each small dwelling a facsimile of the next.

'The one belonging to William Cross is here on the corner, Mr Holmes,' said Detective Murray as we exited the cab. 'All of these houses have two points of access: a front door, of course, and a rear gate that gives entry into the back yard. The rear-entry gates for all of these dwellings are accessible from a lane that runs off Forbes Street just down there. However, this corner residence differs from the rest. Being on the corner as it is, the gate that gives access to the rear of the house is instead located at the side of the boundary wall. Standing here on the corner and looking down along the side of the house, you can see it there.'

Approaching the front door of the dwelling, Murray drew a key from his pocket and proceeded to unlock the door. Upon entering into the narrow hall I could see a sudden change come over Holmes. With his eyes shining and his features alert, he set off through the house and at once up the narrow stairs to the floor above us, leaving myself and Detective Murray to ponder his activities.

From one end of the house to the next the two of us looked up and wondered in amazement at the sound of Holmes's frantic movements. It was only a minute or two before he emerged with the same red-hot energy still evident in his face as he dashed again from room to room and out through the back door and into the yard. It wasn't long before Holmes reappeared in the back doorway, shutting the door and reopening it before entering and immediately dropping to the floor with his lens to examine it. On more than one occasion I could see him scratching at the floor with his fingernail. Then he abruptly got to his feet.

'What have you found, Mr Holmes?' asked Murray.

'I am glad to say that my investigation of this house has not been without some significant interest,' replied Holmes, leading us towards the back door. 'The upstairs bed has not been slept in for some days. Also, I might direct your attention to the back yard and the two cigarette butts that you will see upon the unkempt lawn; this clothesline to our left; and this most remarkable build-up of dried wax here on the ground outside the back door which precedes smaller intermittent drops that lead into the kitchen. The kitchen, as you can see, is also of great interest. Wouldn't you agree?'

'Mr Holmes, I am yet to grasp the full meaning of all that you have said.'

'Imagination, Detective. It is the one quality that you must embrace if you are to succeed in our profession. There is data here to stimulate the mind. It does not yet provide us with our solution but I fancy that if you can give me all but a day or two, I may be able to give you some end to this business. Please leave this house as we found it and do not alert anyone to what we have discovered here today. And now, Watson, we had best be on our way.'

Returning to our hotel, Holmes sat opposite me in the four-wheeler in perfect stillness. His face was one of deep concentration with his eyes fixed in a vacant stare. I could tell that he was much consumed by something. It was only when we were at last a short distance from our hotel that he broke from his trance-like state.

'There is much still to do, my dear Watson.'

'If I can be of assistance, Holmes?'

'I have little doubt, my dear fellow, that before this business is concluded I shall be much in need of your assistance. However, for what I must accomplish this afternoon it would be best if I go about matters alone. I should be gone no more than three or four hours.'

'But where are you going?'

'There are points upon which I require clarification. I shall drop you at the hotel where you may partake in some lunch if you require it.'

SHERLOCK HOLMES RETURNED to the Hotel Metropole shortly after four o'clock. Without so much as a word he pulled a chair into the centre of the room, loaded his pipe with tobacco and curled himself up into the chair. There he remained, motionless and deep in thought for over an hour, the smoke from his pipe curling upwards before he suddenly sprang up.

'We have progressed some way.'

'You have had some success then?'

'I have.'

'Where have you been?'

'To Kelly's Boatshed, William Cross's employer. It was a most enlightening visit. Its proprietor, Norman Kelly, is an elderly gentleman, though I suspect he would have been a most formidable opponent in his youth. He is not an overly talkative individual but I did learn one most remarkable fact about our missing person.'

'And what is that?'

'William Cross is right-handed. Do you not find that significant?'

'Not particularly.'

'I mark it as a point of interest. Anyway, are you game for a late-night expedition?'

'Most certainly, but where?'

'Back to Woolloomooloo. I have already arranged for Detective Murray to collect us at eight o'clock.'

The detective indeed arrived shortly before eight. As we stepped into the cab I could see a look of great excitement upon his face. It was clear to me that whatever plan Holmes had set in motion was now well advanced and that he had already taken the detective into his confidence.

'Are your men in position, Murray?' said Holmes.

'Yes, Mr Holmes. I have three constables already there, keeping well out of sight. They were given strict instructions and will do their job when called upon. I could hardly believe it when I got your note. I acted on it immediately.'

'And you have a lantern?'

'Yes.'

'Excellent. However, I must confess that I cannot guarantee a favourable outcome tonight. While I have baited the trap, I cannot be certain that our quarry has become curious enough to enter it.'

'You have high hopes though?'

'Yes, it is my hope that we shall see the murderer tonight. But our man must be allowed to complete his transaction.'

'Stop here please driver,' called Holmes, knocking at the roof of the cab. 'From here we will be making the rest of our journey on foot. I will now ask the both of you to refrain from any further questions, and if you must speak it is to be no more than a whisper. Now come, we have some way to go.'

Exiting our cab, Sherlock Holmes led us through a maze of narrow streets and back alleyways not unlike those of London's East End until he stopped in a street bordered on both sides by the great collections of narrow two-storey terraced houses that we had seen earlier that day.

'Where are we, Holmes?' I whispered.

'We are only a short distance from William Cross's residence; it is there, in that next block of dwellings. We must make our way down there and conceal ourselves in the alley across from the side of the house, and hope that our man shows.'

Our night-time vigil grew into a long one, with the air growing ever more bitter with each passing hour. On more than one occasion I saw Holmes produce his pocket watch and angle it towards the available moonlight to check the time.

'How much longer is this to last?' asked Murray at one point.

'I have no more of an idea than you,' Holmes replied. 'I will confess it is something of a long shot. Perhaps our quarry suspects a trap and will not come.'

At that moment the faint sound of a hansom cab could be heard approaching our location, growing ever slightly louder before coming to an abrupt stop some way distant.

Holmes gestured for us to maintain complete silence as he pointed out a man making his way up the street from the direction in which we had come.

'Now pay attention,' whispered Holmes.

The man, who appeared to be wearing a hard felt hat and a long frockcoat, stopped at the side rear gate and then lit a cigarette. There he stood smoking for a minute or two, casting an occasional glance up and down the street, then unlatching the gate and entering the yard before closing it behind him.

'Now, watch and pay attention. There, do you see it? Do you see it?'

'It's a faint glow of light of some kind on the other side of the wall. It's only very dim but it's a light none the less.'

'A candle.'

'Detective, stay alert and be prepared to act. I must now leave you both, otherwise a significant opportunity will be lost to us. Keep an eye out and stay out of sight.'

Sherlock Holmes slipped away silently. Murray and I remained crouched, our bones chilled and our limbs stiffened, concealed in the darkness of the narrow alley. From our vantage point we could observe little, save the faint glow from the lit candle that moved about the house, its light visible only on the occasions that it passed by the few side windows that the small, two-story residence possessed.

Finally Holmes rejoined us. 'Where have you been, Holmes?' I asked.

'I have been looking for something, and I succeeded in finding it. That is our man in there. When he exits the house, Detective, have your men ready.'

We did not have to wait more than a few minutes before our mysterious visitor appeared at the side gate in preparation to leave. At that moment Detective Murray emerged from the alley and gave a low-pitched whistle, its sound bringing in his men from different directions towards their quarry. In an instant they were upon him with handcuffs on his wrists.

'Detective Murray,' said Holmes, approaching the prisoner, 'may I present to you Samuel Cross. His hansom cab is parked two blocks south of here if one of your men might care to retrieve it. I was convinced through his narrative concerning a bearded intruder and references to his brother's loose ways that he was attempting to incriminate his brother. No one had seen or heard from William for a number of days, so this served his purpose well. I thought that if I could convince him that we had fallen for his subterfuge and believed William was the likely suspect in the murder of their father, he might try and complete the incrimination in order to remove any possible suspicions from himself. I set the scene for this earlier today simply by telling him that we intended to make a thorough search of his brother's residence. However, I also informed him that a plain-clothes police officer had been stationed near the front of the house, ensuring that he would make any entrance via the side gate. I have no doubt that if I take your lantern and the key and make a quick search of the house I will find something of interest that wasn't there earlier today. If you should wish to come with me we shall see if I am correct.'

Sherlock Holmes disappeared at once beyond the side gate and into the house in company with Detective Murray. In their absence our prisoner sat in perfect silence with his head bowed and his chin buried deep into his chest. More than once without a word he tested his restraints, but his efforts soon subsided. He seemed resigned to his fate. It was only when Holmes and Detective Murray reappeared after some ten minutes that he lifted his head and fixed his gaze upon Holmes.

'A cloth mask, if I am not mistaken, Mr Cross,' said Holmes, holding the artefact out. 'We found it towards the back of the fireplace. I must confess that I was somewhat disappointed by your lack of effort in attempting to even conceal it.'

'I didn't want to make it too difficult for you, Mr Sherlock Holmes,' snarled the prisoner.

'I knew almost immediately that your story concerning a late-night intruder was a falsehood, Mr Cross, and the questions I asked you concerning your brother were most deliberate. Under normal circumstances, a right-handed person would grasp at someone's neck with their lesser hand, being their left, and strike at them with their dominant right hand. The result being that the point of contact would be primarily upon the left-hand side of the face. The opposite, of course, would be true of a left-handed person, and yet upon seeing your wife I observed the heavy bruising that was visible on the right side of her face, meaning that it was most likely that her attacker was left-handed, just as you are. I did, of course, confirm through your brother's employer this afternoon that he was right-handed, and thus unlikely to have delivered the blow that rendered your wife unconscious.

'I also considered it unlikely that an intruder wanting to attack a couple in their bed would look to subdue the wife on the far side of the bed first when the greatest danger to them would surely come from the husband once he awoke to any commotion. You might also remember that when we called upon you at your home you greeted us while smoking a cigarette. Tobacco ash is a subject close to my heart, Watson could tell you! I observed your cigarette closely and I found when we called at this house for the first time yesterday two matching stubs lying about in the grass of the blend you smoke. I am sure we will also find they will be a match for the specimen that you dropped outside the gate here tonight. Not a unique tobacco blend, but together with the other evidence not at all an unhelpful find.'

'Well done, English detective,' Cross growled. 'So far though, all I think you have got me for is hitting my wife.'

'You brute! It is shameful what you have done, to treat a woman in such a manner! How long has she been living in fear of you?' I protested, and found myself starting forward.

'Easy, Watson,' said Holmes, clutching at my arm.

'Have no fear, Dr Watson, we will make sure that this man can no longer harm his wife. I will visit the house in the morning and explain what has gone on here tonight. She will now be free of this devil.'

'Yes, a domestic devil indeed, Detective Murray, and I believe I can partially imagine the scenario that led to his evil acts. Let me see if I can go some way to describing the events as I believe they occurred,' said Holmes, looking at Cross.

'About a week ago you killed your brother in the kitchen of this very house, quite possibly with a knife, as a result of some family quarrel I suspect. It was most likely still daylight so you took his keys with the intention of returning later in the night to dispose of his body. You returned with your hansom, entered into the back yard of the house via the side gate and made your way towards the back door. You had difficulty finding the keyhole in the dark, so you lit a candle that you had brought with you for just such a purpose and entered the house. Making your way into the kitchen you spent some time considering how best to dispose of the body before doing an excellent job of cleaning up the scene of your crime. You wrapped the body in something, perhaps a large blanket, and then found that you needed something with which to secure the blanket to the body and to make it more manageable for loading into your hansom. The only thing that you could find suitable for this purpose was the outside clothesline. Before leaving you spent some time considering your plan and pacing about the yard, smoking at least two cigarettes in the process.'

Our prisoner once again lowered his head and for a time he said nothing. He then began to gently rock back and forth and his breathing became heavier and somewhat irregular. When he again lifted his head there was an expression of great anger on his face.

'Very good. He did take some time to die. I can see that it is clearly to you that I owe the privilege of having these bracelets upon my wrists. I was warned about you, but I didn't listen. He did tell me that it could be a trap.'

'Who? Who warned you about me?' asked Holmes.

'You are close Mr Sherlock Holmes, but you are only halfway there…'

'Right,' interrupted Murray, turning to his constables. 'I want this man taken back to the station immediately. Perhaps a long night in a small, cold cell might make him change his mind. Transport him in his own four-wheeler and send the first cab you come across to collect us.'

Samuel Cross offered no resistance as he was put into his own vehicle with a constable at the reins and two in the carriage accompanying him, and it soon disappeared into the darkness leaving Holmes, Murray and myself alone. However, it was only a couple of minutes later when the sound of multiple intermittent gunshots broke the silence! We ran into the street, and we raced off in the direction of the sounds.

'I counted five gunshots, Watson!' cried Holmes, as the three of us ran. 'If it is a single gunman, he will have one shot remaining.'

No sooner had the words passed from Holmes's lips than a sixth gunshot rang out from the direction in which we were headed, its sound causing each of us to increase our speed.

'It's cold-blooded deliberate murder, Watson! It can be nothing less!'

A small number of curious onlookers were already gathered by the time we arrived. The scene that greeted us was one that filled me with absolute horror. The four-wheeler had come to a complete stop not even a mile from where it had left us, its carriage door open. The driver and two of its occupants, one being the prisoner, were slumped forward in their seats with gunshots to their chests. A fourth lay upon his back on the road some ten yards from the cab. As I pushed through the people and mounted the hansom I checked each of them for any signs of life.

'They are dead,' I said, turning to Holmes and Detective Murray. 'Each has been shot in the chest at point blank range. The prisoner has been shot twice. The gunman obviously wanted to make sure that he didn't survive.'

'They were ambushed,' said Holmes.

'This poor chap,' I said, kneeling down by the body of the constable on the road. 'He must have survived for a time and put up a fight.'

'Quite so,' said Holmes, as he too knelt down.

As I stood up Detective Murray took out his police whistle, put it to his lips and produced three long bursts of high-pitched sound. He then proceeded to walk back towards the small crowd that had gathered. I could see great distress upon his face.

'I am Detective Murray of the CIB!' he called out to the crowd. 'Did any of you see anything? Anything at all?'

There was no response, and even in the darkness I could see tears forming in Murray's eyes. He lashed out with his right fist at the side of the carriage in a fit of rage that delivered a heavy thud. My efforts to console him did little to calm his mood.

'These were good young men, Dr Watson, each of them! They were all new to the force, not one of them had yet seen out two years' service.'

At that moment four police constables arrived at the scene from different directions, having heard the whistle. Stepping away from me, Murray called them to him. One was issued with instructions to return to the station and summon reinforcements while the other three were tasked with keeping the ever-growing crowd at a distance. It was then that Murray returned to me.

'We shall have more men here on their way to us shortly,' he said.

'Watson!' called Holmes, lifting the right side of the body of the young constable on the street. 'Our man's death has not been in vain. In his struggle with the gunman he succeeded in removing this.'

From beneath the body Holmes pulled a piece of cloth and brought it towards us. He held it out and Detective Murray raised his lantern, its small glow illuminating the find.

'Good Lord,' I said, 'it's another one of those cloth masks, similar to the one you found in the house earlier.'

'It has a faint but peculiar odour,' said Holmes. 'One I do believe I am familiar with – linseed oil, if I am not mistaken.'

'And what are we to make of that, Holmes?'

Holmes did not answer. I could see even in the darkness that his face had taken on the distant expression that I so commonly associate with him when his mind is in turmoil. For a brief moment he stood before us making neither movement nor sound. It was then that he came to with a frantic nervous energy and extended his left arm and placed his hand upon my shoulder.

'Watson, you are sure that in examining the bodies you could only account for five gunshot wounds?'

'Yes, Holmes.'

'Are you certain?'

'Yes, I am.'

'And yet we heard six shots. Of that I have no doubt.'

'Then where did the sixth bullet end up, Mr Holmes?'

'Would you mind, Detective Murray, if I were to borrow your lantern?'

With the lantern in his right hand Holmes at once ran off in the direction of the body upon the ground and within an instant he let out a great cry of satisfaction.

'Come here at once!'

'What is it, Mr Holmes?' said Murray.

'Two small drops of blood, Detective. You can see them most clearly. In his struggle our gunman himself appears to have been shot by his own gun – the sixth gunshot! Depending on the seriousness of his wound I should think that we stand a good chance of chasing down our man, especially given his advanced years.'

Having uttered this bizarre remark, Holmes set off like a ravenous dog in pursuit of its prey with Murray and me desperately trying to keep up. We traversed myriad close streets until at last Holmes slowed his pace and turned into a small alleyway. In the glow of the latern light was the figure of an elderly man huddled against the side wall of a house, clutching at his left leg.

'Gentleman,' said Holmes, 'may I present to you Mr Norman Kelly, the proprietor of Kelly's Boatshed.'

'You knew it was him, Holmes?'

'I thought it not unlikely, Watson. The reference that Samuel Cross made to being warned about me earlier tonight did, as you possibly observed, surprise me. However, the thought then immediately occurred to me that this might not be a reference to my reputation with criminals as articulated in the press, which could have been relayed to Cross by another scoundrel who had read a newspaper report or one of your tales, but actually a first-hand encounter being reported. The only person to whom I spoke about this affair outside of Samuel Cross and his wife was Norman Kelly. When I visited him at his business the stench of boiled linseed oil was very much in the air as that oil is, of course, used in the building and repair of boats and ships to prevent the timbers from absorbing water and rotting.'

'I'm done,' our prisoner said, placing a revolver down on the ground and raising his hands in surrender. 'I haven't got anything left in me. It's over, the whole thing is over. The father is dead, the two sons are dead, and now you've got me. What has become of the wife?'

'Emily Cross,' Holmes said, unsurprised.

'Yes, young Samuel's wife, Emily. She is the most evil woman that I have encountered in all of my life.'

'She was a willing participant in the whole affair?' I asked.

'She had an influence over her weak-minded husband unlike anything that I have seen. I am guilty of murder tonight and I have been guilty of it before tonight. But I didn't kill the other brother, or the father, that was her doing. If she suspects that anything has happened to her husband tonight, she may have already flown.'

With a sense of urgency Detective Murray placed a pair of handcuffs upon

Kelly's wrists as I administered what medical assistance I could to our prisoner, while Holmes waved down a four-wheeler. At speed we were taken back to the scene of the shootings where Murray was met by a larger contingent of police officers who had arrived in our absence. Murray immediately despatched some officers to apprehend Emily Cross.

It was sometime in the very early hours of the morning before we arrived back at the George Street police station where a note was waiting – informing us that Emily Cross had indeed apparently fled.

Norman Kelly confessed a full account of the affair. With two constables dragging him into a room and giving him a chair opposite us, he sat slumped and motionless, the set of handcuffs still clamped upon his wrists. Then he buried his face into his hands for a time before raising his head and looking about at all of us, finally fixing his gaze solely on Holmes.

'I should have shot the thief thirty years ago,' he said. 'He never deserved my help and he deserved what he got.'

'You must remember,' said Holmes, 'that we have come in only at the end of this drama and know nothing of its origins. If at some time you have been wronged, we are not in any position yet to know that.'

'Very well. I will put the story straight. For who I am and for what I have done in my life I have probably lived too long already. My real name is Walter Thacker. By all accounts I was born in 1830. I never had it easy in my younger years so I guess that it wasn't a surprise when I started to associate with those who lived outside of the law. Small robberies were my thing. I used to wear an old cloth mask, like the one you found tonight. By the time I was in my early twenties I had pretty much been in contact with every major outlaw of the day in New South Wales, and my reputation had spread. They all knew who I was but the authorities didn't. They all wanted me in their gangs but I stayed clear of all that. Being part of a major gang usually didn't turn out too well for those involved.

'By early '65 I was approached by a bushranger named Ben Hall. I'd known him since about '63 and I must have made an impression on him. Things were becoming quite desperate for him, and he wanted my help as I was someone he believed he could trust. He had a large cash and gold bounty hidden away and I was to act as its caretaker in his absence. New South Wales was becoming too dangerous for him and his plan was to head north and leave the state. I was to keep the bounty safe and provide him some cash whenever he needed it. In return I would get an amount of my own for my troubles. I agreed and a plan was worked out to maintain communications. You would probably question why I didn't just take off with the lot and disappear once he had left. To be honest, I did think about it but I had no doubt that even if it had meant capture, Hall would have hunted me down and put a bullet in me, and in any case he had set me up very nicely. However, in May of '65 Hall was killed north-west of Forbes and I suddenly found myself in sole possession of a small fortune that no one else in this world even knew about. I kept its whereabouts a closely guarded secret and only took what I needed when I needed it. I never told another living soul, except one.'

'Henry Cross,' replied Holmes.

'Yes. Sometime after '67 I had settled out at Taralga, near Goulburn, on my own. I didn't bother with marriage or children. It was there that I first met Harold Granger, who you all know as Henry Cross. He seemed a quiet kind of fellow and a hard worker. However, like me he had crossed over onto the other side of the law in the years previous but was now trying to make an honest go of it. I came to believe that I could trust him. I helped him out with money on a number of occasions and he became like a brother to me, something that I had never had. Unfortunately, I trusted him a little too much.'

'You revealed the location of the bounty to him and he betrayed your trust,' said Holmes.

'Yes. In April '71 Harold up and disappeared in the night and it didn't take me long to suspect why. I set off in the hope that I would be able to catch up to him but I didn't, and by the time I arrived it was all gone, all the money. I gave up all hope of finding it or Harold ever again. A year ago, I changed my name and came to Sydney and used what I had left of my own cash reserves to buy a small house and the boat-hire business. It was then that fate dealt me a favourable hand.

'William Cross – Granger his real name – came asking for work at my boat shed one day about six months ago and I took him on. He was handy despite being unreliable at times. About three weeks ago, he came in late to work after having had a big argument with his father over wanting to borrow money. He told me that his father always seemed to have plenty of it but that he had no idea where he used to get it. Then his father came into the shed wanting to talk to him. He was drunk and a little worse for wear, but I recognised him straight away, though he didn't immediately recognise me. However, it did not take long before he did and an almighty argument followed.'

'I would imagine,' asked Holmes, 'that this roused curiosity in his son?'

'It did. I felt that I had nothing to lose, so I told William that I once knew his father and that he owed me a cash debt. I said no more.

'The next day both brothers, in company with young Samuel's wife, came to me and questioned me about their father's past and the debt. At first, I believed that they were trying to act in defence of their father; however, it soon became obvious to me that their intentions were something quite different. They knew that their father always seemed to have money but none of them knew where it came from. They had previously laughed off as wild tales the accounts of their father being the town drunk who lived like a homeless man but would pay for a loaf of bread with a ten-pound note, but now they realised the truth. It filled them with greed and anger.'

'So you told them of the bounty, how it had been stolen from you, and how you wanted to get back what you believed to be rightfully yours,' said Holmes.

'Yes, we were going to use young Samuel's cab to abduct his father and drive him out of the city and threaten to kill him if he didn't tell us what we wanted to know. But a few days before we carried out the plan, William told us that he didn't want any part of it. His conscience had got the better of him. He even threatened to go to the police. And that Emily Cross, that woman, she got in our brains like a worm in an apple. We went to his house the next day and Emily killed William with a knife straight into the chest, she must have stabbed him seven or eight times without a single ounce of emotion. I'd never seen anything like it, and for a time I even feared for my own life. We returned during the night to clean up the mess and get rid of the body. It was my idea to weigh it down and dump it in the harbour.'

'So what happened out at Mrs Macquarie's Chair?'

'It all went wrong. We got the old man late at night as he left one of his drinking establishments. I threw a coat over his head and bundled him into the cab and we drove off as fast as the horses would take us. Never have I seen a man so desperately fight for his life. He broke free of my attempts to restrain him and succeeded in opening the carriage door and jumping free of it. He sprang to his feet and ran off into the Domain at speed. We immediately went off in pursuit and it was only when we reached Mrs Macquarie's Chair that we caught up to him. It took me some time to regain my breath but it was Samuel's wife who struck at him repeatedly and knocked him to the ground. As he regained his feet Samuel pulled a revolver on him and asked him where he had hidden the money and gold but he refused to answer and he managed to grab the gun from his son. Before I had a chance to intervene Samuel's wife struck him across the back of the head with a rock and as he fell to the ground the gun fired. She threw the rock out into the water, picked up the revolver and we all fled. The plan had failed and everything that we had done up to then had all been for nothing.'

Holmes spoke through lidded eyes. 'So, in order to remove suspicion from Samuel Cross and the rest of you, a tale involving a masked night-time intruder was devised and you fixed your stories so that the brother William would look to be the guilty party.'

'I suggested the idea but it was Samuel's wife who insisted on being hit and wounded so that it looked genuine. After that was done we agreed to keep our distance from one another so as not to bring suspicion upon ourselves.'

'But you have failed,' said Holmes, with no note of triumph.

'When you came into my place and started asking all of those questions about his brother I thought that there might have been some trouble coming. The police had already been in to see me but I knew straight away that you were different to our home-grown coppers. So, after you left me I headed over to young Samuel's place to warn him about you. But, as I came walking up his street I saw you already there talking to him in his front yard! I kept out of sight and waited for you to leave. The young fool told me everything about your first visit to see him the day before, and of what you had told him about believing his brother to be the main suspect in the murder of his father. He believed that he had you fooled with the whole masked intruder story. I thought differently: you seemed no man to dance like a puppet.

'When Samuel told me about you wanting to search his brother's house the next day I knew that it had to be a trap, but he wouldn't listen, he thought it was the perfect opportunity to plant something that would frame his brother good and proper – I now see it was the she-devil leading him. We argued over it for an hour before I left. He told me that he was going to do it and that would be an end to it. I knew that his downfall would also mean mine, so at sunset I headed out to Woolloomooloo and waited to see what would eventuate. From my vantage point I saw the three of you arrive but as the night drew on I fell asleep, the first time I've slept in almost two weeks.

'It was actually the sound of Samuel's cab as it drove past that woke me. I left my hiding place and went out after him but he got too far away for me to intercept him. After he stopped and exited I stayed close by his cab, waiting to see if he would make it back, and that was when you came running up looking for it. I crouched down in the shadow of the alley across from the cab. You were there, only yards from me. I wanted to kill you there and then but I knew that it would draw attention in my direction; knew only more of the police would be set against me, and young Samuel would still be alive. If he had been questioned over this whole business there is no way that he would have kept his mouth shut about me. Maybe I should have killed you, and maybe I wouldn't be sitting here now.'

'You are an animal!' Detective Murray yelled, rising from his chair.

'Maybe so, but only an animal wanting to survive,' Kelly replied, then continued his tale. 'After you left I made my way towards the house that you were watching and I saw the whole thing unfold. When I saw that the young fool had been caught, I hesitated. For one calm moment I placed my revolver against my own temple. But I am that animal that does all it can to survive, as I said.

'I set off back down the main street and waited off to one side. When I saw the cab approaching I threw my mask on and stepped out into its path. The driver slowed right down and I put a single shot straight into his chest. He was dead instantly. I then stepped around to the side of the carriage and pulled its door open. I put a single bullet into the young fellow on the far side and two straight into Samuel. It was then that the second young fellow grabbed my arm. I still managed to get a shot into him but he kept at me. We ended up out in the street and he pulled my mask from my head. I could tell that he was weakening but he still wrestled my gun back towards me and pull the trigger. We both fell to the ground but I struggled back to my feet and took off. The rest you know.'

'I think we've heard what you need,' Holmes said quietly to Murray, and we left the room while Kelly was taken to a cell.

The first rays of the morning sun appeared as we sat in Murray's office. Despite a look of satisfaction upon his face it was evident that the burden of the night's unfortunate events lay heavily on his shoulders.

'I would like to thank the two of you gentlemen for your help in this matter,' he said. 'While it has been a terrible loss of life, at the very least we've ensured that vengeance will be carried out in the name of our men who have lost their lives in the line of duty. We will track down the woman. She will not escape justice.'

'Yes, that is some small consolation, Detective, but one we must be content with. I am so very sorry for the loss of your men.'

'As am I, sir,' I added.

'Thank you, I appreciate your kind words. Let us call this farewell then.'

As Holmes and I left the station my mood was grim, and Holmes soon confirmed his mind was also troubled. 'Watson,' he said, 'I fear I failed Detective Murray and his men. Such savagery, such greed, I did not anticipate it, even though I consider myself an expert on the criminal mind. I solved the puzzle that the evidence yielded to reveal what had taken place, but in this case did not foresee the ugly immediate future acts of desperate and evil people.'

Our stroll had somehow brought us back to Mrs Macquarie's Chair as the sun rose above the tranquil Sydney Harbour. 'Holmes,' I said, 'that may or may not be fair on yourself, but consider this: you have opposed villainy all over the world, and sought to bring justice where there is only obscurity. Tonight your actions were able to identify a culprit, but not forestall other evil actions. You, old friend, must remember that this has to be enough sometimes.'

Holmes dug his cherrywood pipe out of a pocket and absently sucked on the well-chewed end, not looking at me, but nodding as he surveyed the water.

'Perhaps,' he said, 'the inevitable capture of Emily Cross might be our only comfort in this affair.'

I clasped him on the shoulder and we walked on. 'Yes, indeed it will be,' I said.

Never once did I imagine that a day would come when we would both be proven so horribly wrong.

The Mysterious Drowning at St Kilda

Steve Cameron

IT SHOULD HAVE come as no surprise that Holmes's fame had extended well beyond English shores and into the distant colonies, however even I, who had spent so much time in the presence of my friend, was astounded at the stream of callers to our Fitzroy lodgings with all manner of requests for assistance. It seemed that every evening our landlady, Mrs Withers, would present another visitor: a young man in search of a missing family heirloom or an older woman whose cat had wandered from home, or even a young lady who could not recall her reason for calling upon us but merely stared at Holmes with adoring eyes. Holmes showed little interest in any of these cases and it fell to me to politely but firmly show them the door.

It was a fine evening in late May when the events of which I now write occurred. We had shared a late supper, and I was seated at an oak bureau documenting our most recent antipodean adventure in my journals. The gaslight burned steadily as I wrote while Holmes sat easily in an armchair, eyes distant and hands steepled.

'Watson, get the door, would you?'

I glanced at Holmes, his eyes still staring into the distance, seated as before and apparently unmoved. There had been no knock, but I knew better than to ask.

I sighed, placed my pen on the bureau, rose and opened the door to find a rather portly middle-aged gentleman on the landing, fist raised as though about to knock. He had red hair that was beginning to grey, a moustache on his lip and ruddy cheeks that seemed to bulge. He wore a dark suit that had once fitted him better than it did now and carried an attaché case. Mrs Withers, of course, would have taken his coat and hat.

I bid him enter, which he did, and was surprised to see Holmes already standing with his long thin arm extended.

'Inspector?'

Our visitor seemed somewhat taken aback. 'Inspector Webb,' he offered.

'Delightful to meet you,' said Holmes.

The visitor nodded and took his hand. 'And to meet you also,' he said. 'How in heaven's name did you know my rank?'

'It has gone nine o'clock, and Mrs Withers would not admit a visitor at this late hour unless he were on some official errand. Your shoes are sturdy yet scuffed. It is likely you spend more time in the alleys and laneways of Melbourne than you do on the more fashionable streets. A policeman. But you are not a junior member of the force, since I would estimate you to be in your middle forties. I would presume you to be an inspector as those of lower ranks would not dare to approach me thus, fearing the wrath of their superiors.'

Webb leaned forward. 'Wrath?'

'Calling upon an "independent agent" like myself.'

'Your deductive skills would appear to be even more impressive than I was led to believe. You are everything they say you are.'

'I know,' said Holmes.

Webb turned to me and shook my hand. 'Dr Watson, I presume?'

'Inspector.' I indicated an armchair and said, 'Please.' Holmes returned to his own armchair as Webb sat. I took my place upon the settee.

Holmes offered a cigarette to Webb, who declined. He then lit his own.

'I would like to confer with you on the matter of…' said Webb.

'…the matter of the mysterious drowning at St Kilda,' interjected Holmes.

Our visitor threw up his hands as Holmes gazed at him coolly and continued to smoke.

'Good Lord!' declared Webb. 'How on earth could you possibly deduce that?'

'I followed this case with interest as it unfolded in the newspaper reports,' stated Holmes. 'A most peculiar series of events. Quite puzzling. No other recent case would warrant a late visit from an inspector, despite being declared as solved. Your attendance here indicates that you believe it to be nothing less than murder.'

Webb leaned back in his chair. It was a moment before he finally spoke.

'Mr Holmes. I would certainly appreciate any assistance you might offer. Would you be prepared to take a look at the case file?'

'Of course,' said Holmes. 'I knew I would as soon as you set foot in this room. Had I not been interested, I would have had Watson shove you out the door upon your arrival.'

THERE WAS LITTLE information in the file Holmes and I had not already obtained from the accounts in the press. On the 23rd of the previous month, the body of a young woman was found in the water near the St Kilda pier. She was well dressed, wore gold and silver jewellery, and had a bunch of keys and a purse containing English farthings upon her person. A wedding ring suggested she was married. No documents were discovered that would have assisted in her identification. There were no marks of violence upon her body, and despite a steady stream of visitors to the morgue her identity remained unknown. An inquest was finally held which returned a verdict of 'found drowned'.

The day after the unfortunate woman was buried, two men visited the morgue and identified the clothing and possessions as belonging to Miss Pauline Levi, the betrothed of one of the men, Mr Lightman. He had known Miss Levi as a child and, upon her reaching age, had paid her passage out from Leeds with the agreement they would be married. Upon arrival, arrangements were made for the wedding. On the eve of the occasion, Miss Levi disappeared with her luggage, informing her landlady that she was moving to her future home. The landlady, being called upon, also positively identified the young woman's possessions.

Since her arrival in Melbourne, Miss Levi had spoken favourably of a young man she had met upon the ship, and so Mr Lightman had simply presumed his betrothed had eloped with this young man. He had been unwilling to pursue the matter further as he had already been humiliated after having to dismiss his wedding guests on the day of the intended marriage.

Regular readers of *The Argus* would have knowledge of these events, and their later disproval when Miss Levi was found alive and well. She had, as Mr Lightman had originally inferred, departed Melbourne in company with the young man from the ship and was now married and living in Mildura. Her clothing and possessions had coincidentally been extremely similar to those of the victim. She had also matched the physical appearance.

A most strange event occurred a week later. A dentist in Launceston, Mr Sicklemore, had read of the drowning and telegraphed to the police his suspicions that the deceased was Mrs J E Roberts of Tasmania. Her false teeth were sent to him whereupon he confirmed it so, while her sister identified the clothing. It seemed Mrs Roberts's husband had developed symptoms of insanity and had been committed to the Kew Asylum. She had apparently become increasingly despondent during the previous months. The file contained varying reports from witnesses as to her pecuniary situation. Some claimed she was destitute, while others believed her to be in possession of sufficient finances.

A fresh inquest was then held, and there seemed no doubt Mrs Roberts had, indeed, suicided.

'THIS ALL SEEMS quite straightforward, Inspector. What makes you believe this is a matter of murder?'

Webb leaned forward in his chair. 'Coincidences do occur, Mr Holmes. One, sometimes two. In this matter, however, there are too many coincidences for my liking.'

'Are you suggesting Lightman may have been involved in the demise of Mrs Roberts?'

'No,' said Webb. 'I mean, I don't think so. I believe his identification of the deceased was as it appears, a simple error. As for the rest? I cannot explain in any meaningful manner, but there is a point where too many supposed coincidences cannot be tolerated. I spend my nights sleepless, considering every facet and piece of evidence, and I cannot convince myself this conclusion can be the truth.'

'I agree,' smiled Holmes. 'You are indeed astute. There are indeed too many coincidences.'

'And how many coincidences are too many?' I asked.

'In this matter,' said Holmes, 'precisely one.'

THE FOLLOWING MORNING found us on the banks of the Yarra, a muddy river which the local residents love with affection far beyond its deserve. Opposite the water sat the modern, red-brick building that housed Melbourne's brand-new morgue.

Inside we met Constable Davidson. He was tall and thin, and had a long beaklike nose. As Holmes introduced us, he squinted at us from behind his desk. The office smelled of formaldehyde.

'Ah, yes. Inspector Webb informed me that you may be attending. Wait here,' he snuffled, before leaving his office and closing the door behind him.

Holmes and I sat in silence for the very few minutes he was gone. He soon returned with a large bag, which he deposited on his desk.

'It's all here,' he said, and carefully removed the late Mrs Roberts's possessions from the bag. A black stuff dress, an imitation sealskin jacket, an improver and petticoat, under-linens and stockings. These were all somewhat weathered, having been in the water for several days. The constable then produced a smaller bag from the larger, from which he produced a purse containing about 21s in coins, a small bunch of keys, and her jewellery; a brooch, a couple of bangles and a wedding ring.

Holmes was examining the purse. I had reached for the jacket when the constable muttered, 'Hello, what's this then?' and pulled a small penknife from the wire improver. 'Now why didn't anyone notice this before now?' he asked.

He passed the knife to Holmes. It had four blades, which he opened one at a time and closely inspected. 'New,' he said. 'It's never been used.'

'Why would a married woman be secreting a knife in her bustle?' asked the constable.

'It does seem odd,' I said. 'And not particularly convenient. Should one wish to draw the blade, I mean.'

'Where was it precisely?' asked Holmes.

'It was right here,' said Davidson, and indicated the wire frame at the foot of the petticoat. 'Part of the hem has been unpicked.'

'It is far more accessible than if it were in her purse,' suggested Holmes. 'And suitably concealed on her person should her purse be out of reach.'

'What does it mean?' I asked. 'Was she in fear of an assault?'

'We shall see, Watson,' was all he said before he returned to inspecting the items. Nothing further of any interest was found. We thanked the constable and departed.

THE TRAIN JOURNEY from Melbourne to Kew was pleasant enough. From the station we engaged a hansom cab which deposited us at the Kew Asylum. The buildings were magnificent, of the French style, and surrounded by sweeping, manicured lawns.

Inside we were met by a middle-aged matron. Holmes identified himself and asked for Mr Roberts's attending physician.

'Dr Henry Parker is not currently in attendance,' she said.

'In that case, I wonder whether it would be possible to visit Mr John Edgar Roberts?'

She frowned. 'I'm afraid you will have to confer with Dr Parker,' she said.

'My colleague here, Watson, is a medical doctor,' said Holmes.

She shook her head. 'I must apologise, but you would be best speaking with the doctor.'

The matron gave us Dr Parker's address, and wished us well.

As we travelled by cab to the doctor's address in East Melbourne, I broached the possibility that the Tasmanian dentist might somehow be involved. Holmes waved the suggestion away with a snort of contempt.

'But doesn't it seem rather odd that Mr Sicklemore was able to identify a woman merely from a newspaper article?' I asked. 'Surely the published description could pertain to many women. Offhand, I could suggest three or more names who would match quite adequately.'

'Watson, you read Webb's file. The police in Tasmania made inquiries, and Sicklemore was able to account for himself during the entire month.'

'Perhaps,' I countered, 'Sicklemore employed another to carry out this nefarious deed?'

'Next you will be suggesting Sicklemore is an evil genius, a cunning mastermind.' Holmes smiled and grasped my shoulder. 'I admire your zeal, Watson, but we must always search for the simplest, most obvious explanation.'

'Which does not include a mere suicide, despite the coroner ruling it as such?'

'Not in this matter, no,' said Holmes.

DR PARKER'S HOME was quite lovely: a modest terrace house in a quiet street. I knocked, and shortly thereafter a tall middle-aged man with dark hair and a dark suit answered the door and enquired as to who we were. Holmes introduced us, and the man in turn introduced himself and bid us enter.

He took our coats, and led us down a hallway towards the rear of the house. To the left was a finely furnished drawing room. Above the fireplace were several framed photographs. One showed a young boy seated alone; Dr Parker with a woman and the boy gazed at us from another.

A woman, seated on a settee with her head bowed, was dressed in black. Although I presumed she was the doctor's wife, I could not see her clearly for she was facing away from us. She held in her hand a framed photograph of three people, identical to the one on the wall.

'That is Mrs Parker.' The doctor nodded as we passed. 'Please forgive her, she suffers from melancholia.'

'Of course,' said Holmes.

Dr Parker led us into his timbered study and we were seated across from him, his imposing desk between us.

'So,' the doctor started. 'The famous Mr Holmes. How may I be of service?'

'It is necessary for me to consult you regarding the drowning of Mrs Roberts at St Kilda. I am led to understand that her husband is in your care. I would very much like to speak to him regarding this matter.'

'I'm afraid that is impossible,' said the doctor.

Holmes smiled. 'I have dealt with insane men before, Doctor, and I can assure you I would say nothing that would retard your patient's convalescence.'

'I have no doubt that is true,' sighed the doctor, 'but it is still impossible. Mr Roberts tragically suicided not one week ago.'

Even Holmes was taken aback by this. 'That is, indeed, unfortunate. How did this occur?'

The doctor leaned back. 'I did not inform him of his wife's drowning immediately as I felt this would not be beneficial to his cure. After a few weeks without a visit from Mrs Roberts, he grew understandably confused and upset. In the end I had no alternative but to inform him. He took the news rather well, at first, but then he began to believe she had become despondent because of his condition and so the guilt became too much for him to bear. He managed to obtain a pruning knife in the gardens while taking in the air, and slashed his own throat later that night. His body was discovered by an attendant the following morning.' Dr Parker sighed, and shook his head. 'Tragic. Completely tragic.'

'Indeed it is,' offered Holmes. 'How was Mr Roberts progressing with his treatment?'

'It was slow. He had short periods of normality, which suggested an improvement, and then he would suddenly revert and display all the symptoms of insanity once more.'

'Obviously you knew Mrs Roberts?'

'Obviously,' smiled the doctor. 'I met her when her husband was committed, and then occasionally after that. I have many patients at the asylum and I seldom saw her when she visited as the attendants handle such matters. Mrs Roberts was a fine woman, but she became increasingly depressed as her husband's confinement continued.' He shrugged. 'She was also short of finances, and was planning to return to her relations in Launceston.'

'Was Mr Roberts free to leave the asylum?'

'No, he was confined and can be accounted for at all times.' The doctor laughed. 'You don't seriously believe he played a hand in this tragic death, do you? What possible reason could you have for suggesting Mrs Roberts was murdered?'

'None,' said Holmes. 'And it was you who suggested that particular scenario, not I.'

'Mrs Roberts was morose.' He shook his head. 'I should have paid more attention to her behaviours.'

I was aware that Holmes had further questions he wished to put, but they were to remain unasked as the doctor suddenly rose, his hand outstretched.

'I apologise, Mr Holmes, but I have other matters to which I must attend.'

Holmes grasped his hand and they shook. 'Thank you for your time.'

'Should you have any further enquiries, please do not hesitate to call upon me again,' said the doctor, 'limited though my assistance may be.' He gave Holmes his calling card. We were then shown out.

'Interesting,' said Holmes, as we walked through the gardens towards the street.

'The doctor was certainly distracted,' I said.

Holmes' eyes sparkled, as they do when his mind is working. 'And he was in a hurry for us to leave.'

'Is it possible that Dr Parker is responsible for the death of Mrs Roberts?'

Holmes glanced at me and shook his head. 'He is not the murderer. His manner did not suggest he bears the burden of guilt. Although he was distracted, I suspect he has much on his mind: a melancholic wife, a deceased son, some guilt towards not recognising Mrs Roberts's state of mind, and a patient in his care who, although apparently improving, took his own life.'

'A deceased son?' I cried. 'However did you ascertain that?'

'You observed the same domestic situation that I did,' said Holmes. 'It should be obvious.'

WE SUPPED IN a café on Collins Street that evening. A fine dinner, sirloin steak *à la jardinière* with a glass of rich burgundy. Afterwards we smoked cigars and discussed the case thus far.

'So,' started Holmes, 'what do you make of this curious matter?'

I leaned back on my chair, and thought for a moment. 'Not much,' I admitted. 'Apart from the doctor's reluctance to converse, all I see at the moment are a great many coincidences.' I paused. 'A young woman is discovered drowned. Despite the papers publishing her description, no person identifies her while she lies in the morgue. Within days of her burial, two men come forward and identify her as Miss Levi based on her clothing, her undergarments, her jewellery and her physical appearance. Although betrothed, her fiancé waits some days before making his approach to the authorities. The police conduct further enquiries, and so her landlady confirms the clothing belongs to Miss Levi. In the meantime nobody makes a report regarding the now missing Mrs Roberts. Then, of course, Miss Levi returns from the apparent dead, having married.'

Holmes nodded, and puffed his cigar.

'Then,' I continued, 'a dentist in Tasmania reads of the drowning in the paper and for some unknown reason believes the deceased may be one of his patients, Mrs Roberts. He writes to the police in Melbourne, and identity is confirmed by comparing her false teeth. The two women left their lodgings on the same day, wearing identical clothing, possessing English currency and similar jewellery, and seemingly vanished. No person reports either as missing, and Mrs Roberts's luggage remains undiscovered to this day. Then a week ago, the husband of Mrs Roberts, who is confined to a lunatic asylum, also suicides. As far as I can fathom, a series of coincidences. Incredible coincidences, and yet only you and Inspector Webb believe there is more to this case than it appears.'

'It is indeed puzzling,' said my friend. 'But the pieces are beginning to come together.'

'Pieces? What pieces? We have learned nothing other than that with which we commenced,' I exclaimed.

'You still cannot see that which is not completely obvious,' said Holmes. 'Tell me what I am missing.'

'All in good time, Watson. All in good time. But first we have the theatre to attend.'

J. L. TOOLE, the supposed prince of English comedians, was appearing in *Uncle Dick's Darling*. I must admit I found the performance rather amusing. Holmes, on the other hand, snorted his displeasure during much of the second act, slumped in his seat with his arms crossed, and remained in that posture until the final curtain call. 'Idiotic and puerile,' he sneered, while I applauded enthusiastically.

We exited among the throng of theatregoers, Holmes stern and not speaking. It was a mild evening, and so we refused all offers from the waiting drivers and instead casually strolled to our lodgings in Fitzroy, arriving as the clocks were striking ten.

THE FOLLOWING MORNING we ventured down to St Kilda, where the body had been discovered floating in the water the previous month. The day was grey and overcast, and I could smell the promise of distant rain on the air. A row of white mansions, which had recently been divided into holiday accommodations and boarding rooms, faced the sea. I could well imagine children running, laughing, sipping lemonade on the sands and wading in the gentle waves on a hot summer's day. Here at the onset of winter the beach felt glum.

Holmes and I walked from Fitzroy Street to the gymnasium baths, and back to the pier. When I asked my friend what he hoped to discover by visiting this site, so long after the demise of the unfortunate woman, he merely said, 'Nothing. Nothing at all. But it never hurts to become familiar with all locales connected to an investigation. It puts a perspective on things, don't you think?'

We ambled along the pier, not talking, just enjoying each other's company.

When we could walk no further, we stopped. Holmes turned and faced back towards the land, his arms folded, his brow furrowed. He then spent some time scanning the shoreline north from the port of Melbourne to the southern horizon where Brighton lay. It appeared as though he was attempting to discern the precise point Mrs Roberts had entered the water.

After lunch, Holmes and I separated. He wished to locate the boatman who had discovered the body, and to go thence to speak to Inspector Webb at the police barracks on St Kilda Road. I, on the other hand, was tasked with visiting the coffee palace in South Yarra where Mrs Roberts had resided, and then onward to Carlton. A short time before her disappearance Mrs Roberts had applied for a position as a lady-help to a Mrs Bowers of Rathdowne Street in response to an advertisement. She had, however, ultimately rejected the position.

'These inquiries need to be made. In an investigation, one must follow every lead, be sure of every detail, otherwise how is one able to encompass the larger picture?' Holmes declared with that cold efficiency he possesses. 'It is somewhat curious that a woman in supposed monetary distress would suddenly decline the opportunity of a regular income. Perhaps it is nothing, Watson, but you just never know.'

THE MANAGER OF the coffee palace was unable to provide any details I had not previously read in the police reports. Mrs Roberts had been in a dejected frame of mind, due to her husband's circumstances. One morning, she had suddenly appeared from her room with her luggage in tow, settled her account and departed. The manager had not seen or heard from her since. He had been shocked when he had read the reports of her demise in the newspapers. An employee of the establishment who had been present at Mrs Roberts's departure was able to corroborate the manager's witness in every detail. I decided to sit for a while before venturing to Carlton. I smoked a cigar and ordered a cup of coffee which arrived forthwith, its aroma and taste pleasing my senses.

MRS BOWERS'S HOUSE was large and set well back from the road, and I inspected it carefully as I strode up the short, winding gravel drive. I was almost at the front door when my thoughts were broken by a gruff voice calling to me.

'She's out, mate, and she's unlikely to return before it's gone three.'

I turned and saw an older man, in working clothes and cap, tending to the garden. The man's eyes were narrow, his features weathered. His accent had been quite strong, and I had hardly registered what he had said.

'Pardon?' I offered.

'Mrs Bowers. She's gone out, and won't be back till three o'clock.'

'And you are?' I asked.

He held his shears high in his left hand, explaining to me. 'Harold Peters. I come in once a week and do some gardening for Mrs Bowers.' And with that he turned away from me and recommenced his clipping.

For the next couple of hours I wandered aimlessly around Carlton. There were houses of all manner, from rows of modest terrace houses to larger homes like that owned by Mrs Bowers. Carlton's residents appeared to be a curious mix of the affluent, artisans and clerks. The streets held a number of small textile workshops, several flour mills and a brewery. There was a hotel on almost every corner, and I must admit I was tempted to enter one, but I did not know Mrs Bowers and could not know her reaction should I arrive smelling of ale.

I determined to arrive at quarter past three, which I managed to do, and was met at the door by Mrs Bowers. She was a tiny woman with a swirl of grey hair piled high atop her head.

'Ah,' she said, after I had introduced myself. 'Peters informed me I should be expecting a return visit from a plain-clothes constable.'

'Constable?' I said. 'I'm not a policeman, I'm a medical doctor, although I do assist my friend, Sherlock Holmes, in many of his investigations. I wonder why Mr Peters should have suspected I was a policeman.'

'Do not concern yourself over it,' she laughed. 'Constable Fleming and

Inspector Webb twice attended here regarding Mrs Roberts, although I cannot fathom what assistance I could offer. I only met her the once, and our brief conversation at that time centred on her possible employment.' She leant in towards me, as though about to divulge a secret. 'Perhaps he simply recognised your investigative air. I've always suspected Peters of having a less than savoury past, although I must say he has never caused me any alarm.'

Mrs Bowers then invited me into her sitting room, and offered me tea. We sat opposite each other as we spoke.

'It's a sad unfolding of events,' she said. 'Poor Mrs Roberts.'

'Sad indeed,' I offered. I opened my notebook before continuing. 'So Mrs Roberts applied for the position of lady-help in reply to an advertisement you placed?'

'Yes,' she nodded. 'She appeared to be highly accomplished and gave every satisfaction, and so we agreed that she should give me an answer the following day. Contrary to this arrangement, she did not call upon me, but sent me a postcard.'

'Do you still possess this postcard?' I asked.

Mrs Bowers retrieved the postcard from a sideboard. 'Constable Fleming copied the message previously,' she said as she passed it to me.

I took the card and read it. The message, written in a fine hand, was brief.

Dear Madam,
Suited with nice place. I return you many thanks for your trouble.
Yours respectfully,
A MARRIED LADY.

After copying the message into my notebook, I returned the postcard to Mrs Bowers.

'And what was her demeanour when you interviewed her?' I asked.

'Morose.' She sighed. 'She told me of her troubles, her poor husband confined in a lunatic asylum, her dire financial situation. I was quite taken aback when she rejected my offer. I was certain she would accept.' Mrs Bowers drained her teacup and placed it on the table. She picked up the postcard.

'Suited with nice place, she wrote. I presume she was offered another position. Do you happen to know?'

'No. I have no idea at all,' I conceded.

'Very sad,' she said. 'To be so filled with such despair as to take her own life.' I nodded my agreement.

'Peters,' I said. 'How long has he been in your employ?'

'You're not still concerned that he thinks you are a policeman, are you?' She smiled. 'About a year. I engage him once a week.'

'Was he present on the day Mrs Roberts visited here?' I asked.

'Why yes,' she said. 'I do believe he was.'

DUSK WAS FALLING as I hurried through the streets of Fitzroy towards our lodgings. I had resolved to meet Holmes there, and to share all that we had learned. Mrs Bowers' earlier absence meant I was later than intended, but that was of minor importance.

As I arrived at Mrs Withers's boarding house, I saw light in the upstairs window. Holmes was waiting for me. I was at the gateway when I heard a soft footfall behind me. I started to turn and caught the image of a shadowy figure to my right with an arm upraised. I was about to call out, when I was struck by a blow to the back of my head. As I fell forward, I managed to see the figure holding an iron bar. He was wearing an overcoat and his broad-brimmed hat was pulled low over his face, so I could not discern any other features. I hit the ground, hard, and saw the feet of the figure as he stood over me. In my mind, I could picture him raising the bar again, ready to strike. From somewhere I heard Holmes shouting, then saw my assailant turn and run as I lapsed into unconsciousness.

'YOU WERE FORTUNATE,' declared Holmes. 'Here, drink this.'

I was sitting upright in bed, having woken a few minutes earlier. My head pounded like a train, and I could barely think. I sipped the proffered brandy and felt the colour return to my cheeks.

'The doctor shall be here shortly,' said Holmes.

'Don't be ridiculous,' I muttered. 'I am a doctor. I don't need another.'

But Holmes wasn't listening. He seemed excited by this development, and was almost dancing around the room as he spoke.

'We're onto something, Watson,' he grinned. 'I always knew it, but now this proves it. We now have evidence. An eyewitness.'

'Eyewitness? Me? I didn't see anything, Holmes. I cannot even describe my assailant's features.'

'Not you,' he snorted. 'I don't expect you to have seen anything. I mean me. I witnessed the attack from the window.'

'And can you identify my attacker?' I asked.

'No,' conceded Holmes. 'It was dark. I merely saw a shadowy figure behind you. But we have evidence. Look!' Holmes showed me a broad-brimmed hat. Felt, and light brown in colour. 'He dropped this as he ran.'

I took the hat from Holmes and inspected it. 'There are initials inside the band,' I said.

'Yes,' said Holmes. 'H.P.'

'Henry Parker,' I offered.

Holmes shook his head. 'No,' he said. 'It wasn't the doctor.'

'How can you be so sure?'

'When the doctor gave me his calling card, he did so with his right hand. Your attacker was left-handed. The doctor is tall, far taller than your assailant was. And I am certain he was not responsible for the murder of Mrs Roberts. His manner when we interviewed him did not suggest any involvement in that particular crime.'

I shook my head, trying to clear it, trying to think. Something, a small thought, an idea was dancing around the periphery. Suddenly it came to me.

'Harold Peters,' I cried. 'And he was left-handed. He was holding his shears in his left hand when I met him.'

'Who's Harold Peters?' asked Holmes.

'He's a gardener, in the employ of Mrs Bowers.'

'Wait,' said Holmes. 'This needs logic and order. Tell me of your day, of all your enquiries from this morning until this afternoon. Then I shall tell you of mine.'

Holmes sat and smoked, listening intently as I detailed my enquiries. I only paused when the doctor arrived; he examined me, told me I was lucky and declared I needed rest.

'Yes, yes,' said Holmes, who rushed the poor chap out the door. 'I shall ensure he stays in bed and does nothing.' My friend was genuinely frustrated that we had been interrupted while I was telling my tale. With the departure of the doctor, I continued my story. When I was finished, Holmes told of his day.

As expected, the boatman had been unable to add anything further. Holmes had then spent time conversing with Inspector Webb and reading files. He had enquired about Dr Parker and learned he was a well-respected and compassionate doctor. His son had passed six months earlier from consumption. Holmes had then left the barracks for the morgue. He had managed to speak to the physician who had conducted the autopsy; the man informed Holmes the examination had been straightforward. Holmes had then decided to visit the port of Melbourne.

'I have located Mrs Roberts's luggage,' he said proudly. 'It was simple really. Since I last met the inspector, the police have been able to ascertain her maiden name. I enquired at a shipping agent and discovered she had placed her luggage in storage under the name of Miss Clayton. She had stated her intention to purchase passage to Tasmania within a few days and said she would return to claim her luggage. Of course that never occurred, and the agent did not connect the luggage owned by Miss Clayton with the deceased Mrs Roberts.'

'How did you determine at which shipping agent to enquire?'

'We are creatures of habit. I was able to determine which agent she had booked when she first travelled to the Colony of Victoria. As I expected, she had visited the same agent on this occasion.'

'Surely the agent was concerned by unclaimed luggage and notified the police,' I said.

Holmes shook his head. 'Apparently luggage is deposited for extended occasions quite frequently,' he said. 'Miss Clayton, or Mrs Roberts, had mentioned in passing she was waiting on some financial assistance from her sister before purchasing the ticket. As she did not soon return, the agent presumed the money had not yet arrived. He expected her to call again when she was ready.'

'And?' I asked. 'What did you discover in the luggage?'

'Nothing that a woman travelling would not usually pack in a trunk. I'm afraid its contents were of no assistance at all.'

'So, what do you think?' I asked.

'About what?'

'About Harold Peters, the left-handed gardener with a possibly nefarious past, being the murderer?'

Holmes waved the suggestion away. 'Poppycock. Absolute poppycock and wishful imagination. Not a scrap of evidence. And there's the matter of your assault. How could he have been responsible for that? He did not even know who you were this afternoon. He presumed you were a policeman. There's no way he could have ascertained your lodgings so quickly and managed to lay in wait for you.'

'He could have followed me,' I suggested.

'At the last minute he would have had to run to catch up with you, and yet you barely heard a single footstep before he hit you. And as for murdering Mrs Roberts, what possible motive could he have? Apart from having the same initials, there's no evidence.'

'But it is one more coincidence,' I said. 'In a case where there are too many coincidences already. It fits the pattern.'

'There are coincidences and there are coincidences. This is not one that matters.' He reached out and grasped my shoulder, his eyes bright. 'But we're close, dear Watson, so very close. I believe we have enough pieces now. All we have to do is make them fit!'

I FELT REFRESHED when I woke the following morning. My head was clear, although my neck still ached when I tried to move it. I do not know if Holmes had spent the entire night sitting in the chair by the window, but he was dressed in the same clothes; although in itself that was not unusual. He must have been downstairs at some time, for he was reading the newspaper.

'Ah, Watson,' he said, when he finally saw I had awoken. 'I'm glad you're awake as I was just about to rouse you.'

'Good morning,' I said weakly.

'Yes, yes,' he said, and waved my salutation away. 'We have it! The final piece! I now know who murdered Mrs Roberts.'

'I thought you had all the pieces last night.'

'Well, yes. But this is the real final piece that brings the picture into focus.' He brandished the newspaper like a sabre. 'There's been another drowning at St Kilda.'

'Another coincidence?' I asked. 'Why does this one fit the case while mine didn't?'

Holmes ignored this. 'Listen,' he said, and started to read.

DROWNING AT ST KILDA.

Promenaders on the St Kilda pier late last night were alerted to a disturbance when they heard strange noises near the end of the pier. Upon investigation, it was found they were being made by a woman who was struggling in the water. A man jumped in to save the drowning woman, and succeeded in bringing her from the water.

Efforts were made by bystanders to restore animation, but all these were in vain. These efforts were ultimately abandoned as hopeless. Constable Cutler removed the body to the morgue, where it was identified as Mrs Henry Parker of East Melbourne.

'The doctor's wife,' I cried.

'Indeed,' said Holmes. 'And she, I'm afraid, is our murderess.'

'A woman? A woman is responsible for the killing of Mrs Roberts? How in the good Lord's name did you reach that conclusion?'

Holmes smiled, and his eyes narrowed as he focused on organising the logical processes that had brought him thus. 'Mrs Parker became morose after the death of her young son. She certainly never recovered from it. Dr Parker, also unable to cope, withdrew from her and concentrated on his patients, becoming absorbed in his work. I suspect their marital relations were not what they once were. Mrs Parker was grieving more than just the loss of her son, she was also grieving the loss of her husband and their marriage.'

'How did you reach that conclusion?' I asked.

'Do you remember we saw her sitting in her drawing room?'

'Of course,' I nodded.

'Tell me about it.'

'She was dressed in black, holding a photograph of her husband and son in her left hand.'

'Exactly!' declared Holmes. 'There were other photographs in that room of her son sitting alone, and yet she chose to hold one of her family. She was grieving the loss of both her son and her husband. And you will notice she was left-handed.'

'Yes,' I said. 'Which means it was likely she who assailed me last night, disguised in her husband's coat and hat. But why did she attack me?'

Holmes shrugged. 'Once she learned we were investigating, I can only presume she decided to attempt to throw us off the scent. Perhaps she thought she was attacking me. Perhaps she didn't care which of us she attacked, so long as we thought we were chasing a man.'

'So why did she then kill herself?'

'I suspect once she realised she had lost her husband's hat, we would be able to trace it back to him, and then to her.'

'But motive, Holmes. What is her motive? Surely she didn't kill Mrs Roberts because her marriage was not what it was?'

'No,' said Holmes. 'But when we spoke to Dr Parker, he appeared distracted. I knew he wasn't responsible for the murder, but I knew he was hiding something. He told us he had barely seen Mrs Roberts, and yet was able to provide us with information regarding her financial concerns and her plans to return to Tasmania. He knew her better than he let on.'

'An affair of the heart?' I cried.

'No, I am convinced the doctor is nothing more than a compassionate man who sympathised with Mrs Roberts regarding her husband's condition.'

'And he didn't inform us he knew her well?'

'I am sure it was a matter of embarrassment to him that a married woman was misreading his intentions, which is why he was so desperate for us to depart. He had no desire for us to explore that avenue of enquiry.' Holmes paused. 'And we cannot blame her either. She was alone, confused and almost destitute. The doctor was simply being kind to her, and she was in need of comfort.'

'Why did she reject the employment with Mrs Bowers, then?'

'Mrs Roberts was mercurial, fickle in matters of the heart. Some witnesses stated she seemed dejected, others stated she was content. She applied for a position as a lady-help, a role usually undertaken by unmarried women. She was also feeling affection for the doctor. The manner in which she rejected Mrs Bowers's offer of employment, the emphasis placed on the closing "a married lady", suggests she had an epiphany, and realised she should remain faithful to her husband and be true to her vows of marriage. She also wrote that she was "suited with a nice place". I believe this is when she decided to return to her family in Tasmania.'

'I cannot fathom why the dentist in Tasmania would have contacted the police in Melbourne, believing the victim to be Mrs Roberts, purely acting upon a report he read in a newspaper.'

'Mrs Roberts is from a small town. No doubt she sent a telegram to her sister regarding her impending return. Sicklemore heard of this, but when she did not arrive on the advised date and read of the false teeth and the victim's description, he took action. It was good luck he did so. I shall, however, ask Webb to make further enquiries regarding this, if only for your satisfaction.'

'And so it had to have been Mrs Parker, fearing she was losing her husband and in a jealous rage, who alone murdered Mrs Roberts,' I said.

'We must confirm this with the doctor, but I suspect Mrs Roberts visited him one last time, in order to close the affair. At least in her own mind.'

'And Mrs Parker discovered they had met, suspected they were having a liaison, and so killed her in order to save her marriage.'

Holmes nodded. 'It was most certainly something like that.'

'But how did she manage to commit the murder?'

'Mrs Parker lured Mrs Roberts to St Kilda. Perhaps she forged a note from the doctor arranging a meeting. Once there, Mrs Parker overpowered her and threw her into the water.'

'Overpowered her?' I asked. 'She wasn't a particularly large woman.'

'No,' said Holmes, 'but there is no doubt she was strong. She managed to knock you out. As a doctor's wife, she had access to chloroform, or perhaps ether, which would have rendered Mrs Roberts unconscious. The autopsy did not show any signs of violence, no marks or injuries.'

'And so, unconscious, she drowned.'

Holmes nodded.

'But the autopsy?'

'The autopsy was perfunctory. As there were no marks or other evidence of an assault, the physician had no reason to believe it was anything other than suicide.'

'What about the knife found in her bustle?'

'She obviously felt as though she needed some form of protection. I don't believe the doctor even now has any idea his wife was a threat, so it is unlikely he warned Mrs Roberts. She had departed the coffee palace and her luggage was in storage. She had little money left, and so her accommodations at this time must have been less than salubrious. As a married woman without a husband, a knife offered her some comfort of defence.'

Neither of us said anything, as we were both lost in our own thoughts.

'There's only one thing that I cannot understand,' I said at last.

'What's that?' Holmes frowned, as though surprised he had missed something.

'Where does Harold Peters fit into the grand scheme of things?'

'He doesn't! He's a gardener.' Holmes shrugged.

'There is very little evidence for your theory. This is mostly supposition,' I said. 'What if you're wrong?'

Holmes looked shocked. 'Wrong? In a matter like this?' He laughed. 'I don't think so.' He reached for his coat and hat. 'I shall return shortly.'

'Where are you going?' I asked.

'To inform Inspector Webb the case has been solved, and thence to pay a visit to Dr Parker.'

'Surely you don't intend to tell him, do you?'

'Of course,' said my friend. 'He needs to know his wife was a murderess.'

'Holmes,' I said. 'Think about it. The poor man bears no liability for Mrs Roberts's death. His wife alone was the cause. She is no longer in a position to be prosecuted, and as she was suffering from melancholia would probably have been diagnosed as insane anyway. Dr Parker is likely grieving the death of his wife and does not need to be disturbed.'

'What is your point?' asked Holmes.

'My point is that nothing can be gained by informing him. The case has been officially closed. There has already been far too much tragedy in the doctor's life. Maybe it's best to let sleeping dogs lie.'

Holmes paused for a moment. I could see he was considering all I had said. 'Perhaps you're right,' he said at last.

'I am,' I said. 'Inform Inspector Webb of your deductions. Ask him about informing Dr Parker, but I'm sure he will see it the same way.'

'Well,' said Holmes. 'No one will ever learn the truth.'

'We'll know,' I said.

He grinned, and opened the door. 'Watson, rest up. I think perhaps what we need is an evening at the theatre.'

'Really, Holmes?'

'Certainly,' he said. 'I read that J L Toole, that godawful comedian we saw, is performing a different show almost nightly.'

'But you hated him when we saw him,' I said.

'True,' said Holmes. 'But perhaps he'll be funny and I shall enjoy him this time.'

'Unlikely,' I muttered, 'but stranger things have occurred, such as the series of coincidences that diverged to thwart the police in this matter.'

But Holmes did not hear me. He was already through the door and down the stairs.

The Adventure of the Lazarus Child

Dr L. J. M. Owen

THE TRAIN IN which we travelled had screamed thrice, its piercing whistle echoing across a desiccated valley, then slowed to cross a bridge as we eased toward Queanbeyan Station. I had lured Mr Sherlock Holmes there, to a remote mill-and-mine town in New South Wales as far distant from Sydney as York is from London, ostensibly to investigate reports of a child risen from the dead.

In truth, however, by that stage our Sydney lodgings had grown so malodourous and damaged that I had sought means of escape. My patience with Holmes's relentless experimentations had ended two days previously with crashing glass and our pious landlady's cries of 'Oh, Dr Watson!'

Holmes, it emerged, was determined to analyse the murderous potential of the Australian flying 'boomerang'. His attempts to fling the wooden object about his room had resulted in one shattered casement. Not content with this level of devastation, Holmes had then hung through the broken pane and thrown the device again, only to have it return through the adjacent closed window. After providing reparations to our scandalised hostess I had searched for a distraction from Holmes's incessant research – anything but the categorisation of cigarette ash, testing of indigenous venoms and manufacture of exploding powders.

Thankfully, just that morning I had read of a most sensational phenomenon: the Lazarus Child. A boy, the broadsheet relayed, had been pulled from a watery grave after three days, blackened and decomposing, only to spontaneously return to life while under medical supervision. The re-animation was attributed by the attending physician to the prayers of the child's parents.

In the hope that a tale of divine intervention would incense Holmes, catch at his mind and demand logical explanation, I had folded my newspaper to an article on the expansionist ambitions of New South Wales' richest mine owner and left it at our table, with the Lazarus headline peeking from below.

Later that day, at Holmes's insistence, we had booked rail tickets to Queanbeyan.

As we alighted from the train I held high hopes that the dusty, sun-beaten town would provide at least one week's reprieve from Holmes's more destructive attempts to flee boredom.

FOLLOWING AN UNEXPECTEDLY salubrious evening in the reception rooms of the town's Globe Hotel, I had awoken to find my companion returning from his toilette. As Holmes rarely emerges from his chambers before mid-morning I was most pleased, for this deviation in routine indicated his full engagement in the planned distraction.

'Shall we?' Holmes said.

'Shall we what?' I japed.

'Really, Watson, do come along.'

'We have some time yet, Holmes, for we arranged to interview the doctor at nine of the clock and it is not yet gone seven.'

As the appointed hour approached Holmes and I struck out for our target: the town's red-brick hospital sprawled atop a nearby hill. Two long blasts from an arriving train had assaulted our ears as we entered the sanatorium and searched for a member of the hospital staff, eventually locating a most winsome nurse. So immersed in her reading was she that, when I spoke, she jumped. After regaining her composure she guided us to the door of one Dr John William Morton.

The doctor, a medium-sized man with an impressively large office, greeted us effusively. 'Dr Watson, Mr Holmes, so very pleased to meet you. Please come in. And Miss Morgan, tea for our guests? Four cups please.'

'Yes, Dr Morton.' The young nurse bobbed stiffly and, in a swirl of starched linen, turned to stride down the hall.

The doctor indicated where Holmes and I were to be seated. 'You've come to inquire after Billy Lyons, I understand, referred to by the papers as the Lazarus Child?'

I was intrigued by the lack of animosity in the doctor's demeanour, when he might reasonably have been expected to display resentment at interrogation by strangers.

'Anticipating that you may wish to speak to others involved in the matter, I've asked Sergeant Beard to join us,' the doctor continued. 'The sergeant was in charge of searching for Billy during the days he was missing.'

Any response I may have made was superseded by Holmes. 'Tell me, Doctor, do you believe in miracles?'

At Holmes's taunt, Dr Morton threw his head back with a guffaw. 'Goodness no. I was asked by a reporter if the rumours were true, if the boy had truly been revived by the hand of God. I answered only that I had no other explanation, without giving consideration to how that might be interpreted by someone seeking a sensational headline.'

There was a knock at the door.

'Ah, Sergeant Beard,' said the doctor, moving aside to allow a large man in a fraying police uniform into the room. 'So pleased you could join us. May I introduce you?'

As we completed the obligatory rounds of polite exchanges there was another rap at the office entrance.

Dr Morton admitted Miss Morgan, who set down a tea service, bobbed once again and exited.

'And how fares your brother's campaign, Sergeant?' the doctor asked as he poured milk into bone china cups.

'I'm optimistic, though his rival is gaining momentum.'

'The sergeant's family was amongst those who founded Queanbeyan,' Dr Morton said.

The sergeant explained further. 'My father was one of the first settlers, you see, back in the thirties. He's insisted my whole life that one of his sons must become mayor of Queanbeyan. As I'm a copper, it must be my brother.'

'Riveting,' Holmes responded, his usual tactful self.

The doctor then lowered his tea cup. 'Very well, how may we be of service? Please understand that I spoke the truth when I answered the reporter. I don't know how Billy Lyons returned to life.'

I saw that Holmes had assumed his hound-on-the-hunt countenance and almost pitied the doctor. 'I see,' he said. 'To begin with, how long ago did events take place?'

'One week gone yesterday,' said Dr Morton.

'And before that, precisely how long had the boy been missing?'

'Three nights,' said Sergeant Beard. 'His mother raised the alarm one evening after he failed to return from play. I led a search of the riverbanks and nearby bush, but there was no trace of him. By the third night it seemed hopeless, so I was most relieved to hear of his discovery the following morning.'

'Where exactly was the boy located?' asked Holmes.

Sergeant Beard pointed out the window, to the foot of the hill. 'See the fifth cottage to the right? That's the Lyonses'. The boy was found at the bottom of a drainage channel from the mill that runs behind the house.'

Holmes pressed on. 'How did he arrive in your care, Dr Morton?'

'My quarters are here on the hospital grounds. His parents brought him to me at first light, screaming at me to help.' I noticed the doctor wince at the memory. 'One glance told me it was hopeless, yet I was bound to confirm that via examination.'

'And?' Holmes prompted.

Dr Morton indicated a table that stood at the other end of the room. 'I brought him in here and removed his outer shirt. He was cold to the touch, his flesh spongy. Moreover his body emitted an odour most foul, reeking and putrescent. I examined him for signs of animation and pressed on his chest, but there was no breath, only water. He held all the signs of having left this life quite some time ago. There was naught to be done.'

'Were the parents present during your examination?' asked Holmes.

The doctor shook his head. 'They were making such a din, yelling at me to help their son, that I asked a nurse to escort them to a waiting room some distance away before I began my examination.'

I watched Holmes's countenance as he set down his cup and shifted his body towards the doctor. 'And then?'

'And then, Mr Holmes, I went to console the Lyonses.'

Holmes's eyes had narrowed. 'So the boy remained here unattended?'

'Yes, but the Lyonses insisted on viewing their son's body so we returned here… to a most shocking sight. Billy Lyons was alive!'

'It was obvious immediately?' I asked.

'Yes! He was coughing, gasping for breath.'

'And there was no one else in the room? No signs of interference with the body?'

'Nothing, except…'

'Yes?'

'Water. There was water everywhere, on the table and in a puddle beneath it.'

I was then completely taken aback when in one swift movement Holmes lunged from his chair to grab the doctor's collar and shout, 'Tell the truth!'

Dr Morton wrenched himself from Holmes's grip, sending his cup flying, then screamed back, 'I am!'

Sergeant Beard half stood up, his own uniform dripping with spilled tea. I, however, saw Holmes's expression and realised he was playing a trick, one of his more explosive interview techniques. 'Steady on Holmes,' I said, sipping from my cup.

Holmes chuckled roughly at my response then retook his seat. 'I must apologise, Doctor, Sergeant: an old trick of mine, used in cases sometimes where an outrageous claim is made. Merely checking if the good doctor is withholding information. And he is…'

'I am not!'

'Though he doesn't know it.'

I saw that the doctor and Sergeant Beard shared my confusion. 'Don't be obscure, Holmes,' I admonished.

'The nurse who served us tea just now, Dr Morton. Was that the same nurse who escorted the Lyonses to the waiting room the morning Billy Lyons apparently returned himself from the dead?'

The doctor nodded.

'Would you please ask her to join us?'

Appearing sightly dazed, as so many of Holmes's victims do, Dr Morton complied and walked once more to his office door. 'Miss Morgan?'

The nurse arrived moments later with an armful of bandages. I noticed her eyes sweep the room as she entered. 'Would you like another tray of tea, Dr Morton?'

Holmes answered before the doctor could speak. 'No thank you, Nurse Morgan. We were instead hoping you could tell us how you revived the drowned boy.'

I saw Miss Morgan's eyes widen as the rolls of gauze slipped from her arms. 'I beg your pardon sir, I…'

'You like to read, Miss Morgan? Medical notices and so forth?' Holmes asked.

Nurse Morgan had bent to retrieve the bandages, causing her voice to be muffled. 'Yes, sir, but how did you…'

'Just now, you were reading a notice from the Royal Humane Society of Australasia.'

'Yes, but…'

'It looked rather worn. Possibly from having been carried continuously in a pocket for, say, a week or so?'

Miss Morgan patted at her skirt pockets, almost by reflex.

'It describes a means of artificial resuscitation, does it not?'

'How did you…'

I saw by Holmes's face that he was enjoying himself immensely. 'Reading upside down. A most useful talent.'

I understood what Holmes was intimating, of course. I had heard of this method, long taught on the Continent, of reviving the recently drowned. 'But why would anyone attempt the technique on a rotting corpse?' I asked.

The nurse's answering expression was flinty. 'As certain medical privileges are the exclusive reserve of doctors, sir, and given that I am a mere nurse, poor

Billy's body presented a rare opportunity to rehearse artificial resuscitation without fear of causing damage.'

At this, the intently quiet Sergeant Beard frowned. 'You interfered with a corpse?'

The nurse seemed caught between deference and defiance. 'I thought that practising artificial resuscitation on Billy might one day allow me to save a life. Although I had no thought of reviving him, my intentions were pure. I followed the instructions in the notice by applying pressure to his abdomen until water flowed from his mouth. Once liquid ceased to be expelled I moved to simulating respiration. I was beyond shocked when he drew breath of his own accord!'

'But how is this possible?' Dr Morton had echoed the very question that rose to my lips.

Holmes, however, had his own hypothesis. 'Miss Morgan, how long after drowning can your technique be successfully applied?'

'The notice suggests just two or three minutes; even then there is no certainty. The longest-known lapse in time between drowning and resuscitation is forty-five minutes.'

Holmes then spun on his heel and faced me. 'And so, Watson, how long was it since the boy had ceased to breathe?'

'You believe he drowned less than forty-five minutes before he was found?'

'Far less. I calculate that it would have taken his parents approximately four minutes to run his body up the hill to your accommodations, Doctor, and a further two minutes for you to transport him here. After dismissing the Lyonses you inspected the body for all of, let's say, one minute? Two further minutes elapsed before Miss Morgan returned here to revive the boy, meaning that it was, in total, a mere ten minutes since he was pulled from the water.'

'But he was decomposing, the doctor said so.' This came from Sergeant Beard.

'Nurse Morgan, is that true?'

Miss Morgan looked hesitantly from Holmes to the doctor. 'He was foul-smelling and blackened, certainly. Though…'

'Yes?'

'His flesh, while spongy and discoloured, didn't hold the usual feel of a corpse that has passed through rigour mortis.'

Sergeant Beard's frown then returned. 'Are you saying that this… this woman is able to raise the dead?'

Miss Morgan pinned him with a steely gaze. 'Are you saying that women are not capable of following written instructions?'

Dr Morton held out a conciliatory hand to the nurse. 'It was a most admirable undertaking on your part, Miss Morgan, and resulted in the saving of a life. I have long regretted that you are of the wrong sex to study medicine. Apart from that one deficiency you would have made a most excellent doctor.'

I moved to correct this misguided sentiment but at that point an insensible utterance emerged from the nurse's mouth, after which she slapped at the doctor's hand, dropped her supplies and stormed from the office. I was only a little shocked by her behaviour, having witnessed such displays from intelligent young women before.

'Your nurse needs to be married off, Doctor, and soon. My father always said the best remedy for a spirited woman was children,' said Sergeant Beard.

'I'll speak to her at a later time,' said Dr Morton.

'Perhaps not too harshly,' I suggested, with some irony. 'I might not have been able to save that boy myself, and you certainly did not, Dr Morton.'

'Indeed, and testimony about her actions has provided ample explanation as to how our so-called Lazarus Child returned to life,' said Holmes.

Despite further insistence from the sergeant that only divine intervention, and not female interference, could have been responsible for returning Billy Lyons to the land of the living, I had to agree with Holmes. The case had been solved, and all too quickly, meaning Holmes would now wish to depart for Sydney and his damned experiments.

It eventuated, happily, that I was quite wrong. For Holmes then said, 'And in doing so, the good nurse has brought us to the heart of this matter.'

I was certain I recognised his expression. 'And that is?' I asked.

'Where was he? In a town of this size, with such limited places to hide, where was the boy?'

I was most relieved when Holmes then dashed from the office, calling for both Sergeant Beard and myself to follow. The hunt, apparently, was on.

BLINKING AS WE emerged into the prickling heat of the colony's intense sun, the sergeant and I marched down the hill in Holmes's wake. As we approached our destination, a boy of possibly seven years looked up from his play to dash inside.

A beaming and befreckled woman appeared at the cottage door. 'Sergeant Beard! Good day!'

The sergeant brushed at the tea stains forming on his uniform. 'G'd-day, Mrs Lyons. I've brought visitors, gentlemen from England, who've heard of young Billy's adventures.'

Mrs Lyons smiled more broadly. 'How wonderful! You're most welcome. Come in, I'll fetch Mr Lyons.'

I was thankful to enter the cooler interior of the tiny stone building. Once all parties had settled around the home's much-used table, Mr and Mrs Lyons confirmed the sergeant and the doctor's account of losing then regaining their son. The boy himself sat quietly beside his father, occasionally coughing.

'Thank the Lord our prayers were answered and Billy was returned to us,' said Mr Lyons, squeezing a proprietary arm about his son's shoulders.

'It was the Lord revisiting his miracle of Lazarus on us,' said Mrs Lyons.

The sergeant looked hard at Holmes as he said, 'Indeed. He arose after three days and three nights, as the Good Book says.'

If at first I was surprised by how stubbornly the sergeant denied the means by which the boy was resuscitated, I was astonished that Holmes refrained from comment. He returned, instead, to the question he found most fascinating.

'It's still not clear to me where your son was for the three nights that he was missing.'

Billy, I noticed, froze.

His mother's breath caught with a sob before she answered, 'In the mill drain.'

But Holmes was not to be deterred. 'Are you certain? Why did you not search the drain before?'

Mr Lyons had patted his offspring's back. 'We did! A number of times, though I can't explain how we missed him.'

Holmes was silent. I noticed my companion's gaze had fixed on a bowl at the table's edge. He leant forward and dipped his fingers in its grey ash, then rubbed them together beneath his nose. 'Marijuana and tobacco? *Cigares de Joy?*'

Mrs Lyons nodded. 'Only the best for our Billy! But they're so expensive. I wonder that the apothecary is allowed to keep prices so high. It's not right, not right at all.'

I held my own opinion on the perils of tobacco consumption, particularly by children, but forbore to comment. I wondered, instead, how the Lyonses could afford them. 'Is Billy your only child?'

'He has an older brother who works at the local mine,' said Mr Lyons.

Mrs Lyons sucked in her breath. 'That mine is in trouble, though. God punishes those who cause others pain.'

Holmes's countenance indicated that he, too, had lost the thread of the conversation. 'I beg your pardon?' he asked.

'Like the apothecary, the mine owner opposes marijuana and laudanum use by the workers. Even when they can afford it they have to hide it.'

'And did you have any difficulty learning to smoke?' Holmes then asked Billy directly.

'Of course not,' said Mrs Lyons.

Holmes ignored her. 'Had you smoked before?'

'No, Mr Holmes, he hadn't as there was no need for him to do so before… before he was returned to us,' said Mr Lyons.

I then noticed, as I was certain Holmes did, that the boy turned his head away, indicating his father was in some way mistaken. 'Mr Lyons, I'm sure you realise that it takes practice to smoke, especially when one is young, and especially when one's lungs are as damaged as your son's must now be.'

'Indeed, Watson.' Holmes leant toward the boy. 'You had smoked before, hadn't you?'

Billy shook his head most violently.

'Can you tell us where you were before you awoke in the hospital? I know you weren't in the water all that time.'

The boy was now trembling.

'Holmes, perhaps that's enough.' As I spoke, Billy sprang from his chair and ran out of the cottage.

'I'm sorry. He used to be happy as Larry, but since, well... he refuses to talk about it,' said Mr Lyons.

Holmes stood abruptly. 'Thank you, then, Mr and Mrs Lyons, for your hospitality. Sergeant, if you would be so good as to escort us to the apothecary? I believe he may have information pertinent to the case.'

IT WAS NOW approaching mid-morning and the streets of Queanbeyan were baking. I wondered, then, if it were possible to become accustomed to such piercing light. My eyes had not yet adjusted during our journey to the apothecary, one Mr Matthews, who was defiant in his stance on *Cigares de Joy*, opium and alcohol for laudanum. 'I set high prices to dissuade my customers from purchasing them. While I am bound to stock them, I believe they should be used in limited circumstances. I especially discourage their use amongst children.'

Holmes struggled to understand this attitude. 'This policy must cost you dearly, given the popularity of the treatments. What businessman would place morality ahead of profit? You are not to be believed, sir!'

The apothecary stared at Holmes in shock.

I attempted to soften my friend's interrogation. 'Perhaps Mr Matthews places a higher value on the health of children than on increasing his bank account.'

I watched as understanding slowly dawned on Holmes's face. 'Oh, of course. Yet you do sell *Cigares de Joy* to the Lyonses, Mr Matthews, in the knowledge their young son smokes them?'

'Regretfully, yes.'

'And did you sell those same cigarettes to the Lyonses before their son's much-feted adventure?'

'No.'

'Then why not refuse them service now?'

'Despite my discouragement, Mrs Lyons insists on treating Billy's lungs with *Cigares de Joy*. If I decline to provide them, the Lyonses may seek an inferior supply, one with additional, unwelcome side effects.'

'What do you mean?' said Holmes.

'Dr Morton has reported a number of mine workers presenting at the hospital with laudanum poisoning. Some of them also have *Cigares de Joy* of an inferior quality, with unidentified and possibly dangerous ingredients. They aren't my customers, although this is the only apothecary within thirty miles of the mine.'

I had wondered instantly at the very same possibility that Holmes then suggested. 'An illegal trade?'

Mr Matthews nodded. 'Despite my best efforts, and those of the put-upon mine owner, the workers continue to purchase these substances, convinced it helps them heal faster and work longer, despite all evidence to the contrary.'

Our religious town guide, Sergeant Beard, then broke his characteristic silence by clearing his throat. 'As I told you previously, Mr Matthews, that is a matter of police concern and I am working tirelessly to root out any such trade.'

'*"If anyone destroys God's temple, God will destroy him."* From the Book of Proverbs, I believe, Sergeant?'

'Indeed, yes, Mr Holmes,' said Sergeant Beard.

I was perplexed, for although Holmes held the same knowledge of the Good Book that any man educated in England might possess, he had once boasted to me that he purposefully shunted details of the scriptures from the 'lumber room' of his brain, as they were as of little use in solving cases as knowledge of current politics and philosophy. In our years of acquaintance he had shown no particular attention to religious texts; quite the opposite, in fact.

Holmes then clapped his hands together, indicating an ending to the meeting. 'Thank you, Mr Matthews, Sergeant Beard. I believe Watson and I shall retire to our lodgings for a spot of lunch.'

'What have you inferred thus far?' I asked my friend as we traversed sweltering streets, certain he must have arrived at some conclusion.

Holmes merely smiled in that infuriatingly superior manner he sometimes adopts. 'None, Watson, I merely require sustenance.'

I knew better than to believe him, though at that moment I was gladdened to see him so thoroughly embroiled in the case.

THE FOLLOWING MORNING I awoke to discover Holmes was absent. Eager for breakfast, I strolled the warming streets and from there the riverbanks in search of my missing companion. As I neared the eastern edge of the town, but half a mile from the train station, I spotted a body lying across the tracks. My heart rose to become a thrumming in my ears, suddenly drowned by three short, piercing whistles. A train approached!

I ran into the blinding sun, screaming at the prone figure to move. I was mere steps away before I realised it was Sherlock Holmes lying in the path of an oncoming locomotive. My feet moved faster than I had thought possible. I prepared to reach down and save my dearest friend by pulling him from the tracks, but to my great surprise he reached up to grab my arm and roll us both from harm's way as the train thundered past.

'Watson, what have you done?' he cried.

I lay heaving, struggling to catch my breath. 'Holmes, Holmes, are you well?'

'Apart from you springing my trap! Whatever possessed you?'

I was most confused. Holmes was vexed with me, after I had just saved his life?

As the train receded I looked up from my position on the ground into the shocked face of a man standing in the doorway of the end carriage.

Holmes then jumped to his feet, shouted, 'See you at our lodgings!' and leapt toward the bushes beside the tracks.

Peering after him, I could vaguely perceive inverted legs fleeing into the trees. Stowaways, no doubt, who had jumped from the back of the train to avoid detection, only to be chased by Holmes for some obscure and deeply irritating reason of his own.

Mopping at my brow, I determined to return to the Globe and partake of an excellent breakfast followed by a long, cool bath. It was late in the afternoon before Holmes flung open the door to our rooms with a look of deep satisfaction, apparently oblivious to the distress he had caused me earlier.

'Watson, you're here! Let's go.'

'Where?'

'The police station. We have matters of import with the local constabulary.'

'We do?'

I grudgingly left the cool recesses of the Globe for the dusty streets of Queanbeyan, accompanying Holmes to the station where he then spoke with Sergeant Beard. Two constables stood attentively behind their superior.

'As discussed with Mr Matthews, Sergeant, there does indeed appear to be a black market in laudanum and marijuana cigarettes operating at your local mine.'

Sergeant Beard's patience was apparently exhausted at that point. 'Mr Holmes, enough! I am in charge. My constables are under instruction to search cargo wagons headed to the mine.' Here, one of the constables nodded slightly. The sergeant continued. 'As a well-respected member of the community I have made inquiries at all levels, and with the goodwill of my many sources I will find any smugglers and bring them to justice.' Sergeant Beard snorted. 'Without your help!'

'But I've come to advise you of an opportunity of which you may not be aware. I have reason to believe that a consignment may even now be making its way to the mine.'

That, at least, had given me a hint as to Holmes's activities earlier in the day. 'To whom have you been speaking, Holmes?'

My friend would not divulge details, however. 'No-one I care to name at present, Watson.'

Sergeant Beard stared hard at Holmes, tugging at his threadbare collar. 'This bears looking into.'

'Should we saddle up, Sergeant?' one of his constables asked.

The sergeant shook his head. 'I don't wish to alert anyone involved. I'll go alone. If anyone inquires, say I've gone to investigate reports of a sheep thief on the road to the mine.'

Not to be deterred, Holmes chimed in again. 'Shall we all meet back here tomorrow afternoon, say, at three of the clock?'

The sergeant merely grunted.

As we turned to exit the room Holmes hesitated, his eyes lingering on a nearby desk.

'What is it, Mr. Holmes?'

'Nothing, Sergeant. I was merely contemplating this evening's meal.'

'Truly?' I asked, as we stepped into a rather glorious sunset.

'Truly, Watson. I'm famished.'

THE FOLLOWING AFTERNOON Holmes and I braved the blistering sun once more to return to the police station and be greeted by an expanded gathering. Sergeant Beard and his two constables stood with Dr Morton and Mr Matthews next to a deeply tanned, middle-aged woman whose demeanour indicated a pressing desire to be elsewhere.

Sergeant Beard began with introductions. 'Mr Holmes, Dr Watson, this is Mrs Burns, the current owner of the local mine.'

Holmes had transformed, with an alchemy akin to magic, into his bloodhound persona. 'You own the mine, Mrs Burns?'

'My husband passed away last year after an accident in the furnace, leaving the business to me.'

'And the mine is in financial trouble.'

'Excuse me? How dare you ask such a question!'

'It wasn't a question, Mrs Burns, but a statement. You are in significant debt, so you have turned to an illegal trade in *Cigares de Joy* and laudanum to both invigorate your workforce and fend off your creditors. Is that not so?'

If Holmes was at his pompous best, Mrs Burns was disdainful in return. 'You are mistaken. As I have explained to the sergeant, and previously discussed with both Dr Morton and Mr Matthews, I have banned all such substances from my camp.'

'Mrs Burns has indeed spoken to me, Mr Holmes, requesting that I limit the supply of euphorics to her workers,' said Mr Matthews.

'I, too, have discussed the matter with Mrs Burns,' Dr Morton chimed in.

Sergeant Beard shifted his large frame, clearly uncomfortable with the direction of the conversation. 'I'm afraid you've been deceived, gentlemen. I have long suspected Mrs Burns of being the overseer of the drug trade at the mine. And finally, I have evidence.'

Though she was still dwarfed by the men in the room, I was impressed when the mine owner drew herself to her full height. 'Your evidence is false then, Sergeant. I admit that my finances are… pinched… at present. However, I would make little profit from running an illicit trade in the very substances that cripple my workforce. Laudanum and marijuana impair my workers, making them ill, unfit and accident-prone. They don't improve a person's health, no matter what the papers say. Since my husband's death I've worked like a drover's dog to get them out of my camp.'

'You're lying, Mrs Burns.' Sergeant Beard pulled packets of what appeared to be cigarettes and opium powder from his pockets, almost with a swagger. 'I found these last night in the drawers of your paymaster's desk at the mine, Mrs Burns, in your own offices! Whether you admit your involvement or not, I now have enough evidence to arrest you.'

Mrs Burns frowned. 'I doubt my paymaster would be involved in any illegal activity. But if he is I will ensure he is brought to face you.'

'It's not your paymaster, Mrs Burns, but you!'

'You have no proof!'

'I'm afraid, Mrs Burns, the sergeant is indeed holding proof of who is running the black market at your mine,' said Holmes, stepping to the room's window and drawing the curtains as wide as possible. 'If you would be so good as to stand here, Sergeant Beard? Ensure the packages are in full sunlight, please.'

Confusion swept the policeman's face, but he complied.

'And constables, if you could stand on either side of Mrs Burns? Watson, if you, Dr Morton and Mr Matthews could stand behind her?'

I understood that Holmes was closing off Mrs Burns's means of escape, but I failed to see how a woman so slight could overpower seven men. Nonetheless, I did Holmes's bidding.

Holmes then began to pace. 'As I said, you hold the solution in your hands, Sergeant.'

I groaned in recognition of Holmes's self-satisfied tone. I knew he was about to be unutterably clever, and therefore smug for days after.

'Something amiss, Watson?'

'Nothing, Holmes, please continue.'

'With pleasure. Allow me to explain. Firstly, after our visit with the Lyonses it was clear young Billy had smoked *Cigares de Joy* before his disappearance, but not with his parents' knowledge. Given how expensive they are I doubted he had come to them by honest means. Secondly, following our discussion with Mr Matthews, it seemed most likely that there was indeed a black market operating at the mine, an undertaking requiring significant deceit. And so I perceived a possible connection between these two sets of dishonest acts. I deduced further that the illicit trade might, in fact, be linked to the boy's three-day disappearance. And, I reasoned, the most likely source of contraband items would be Sydney, as it is the nearest large port. And the most efficient means of transporting goods from Sydney to Queanbeyan?'

I took my cue. 'By train.'

'Indeed. By train. I noticed the morning of our arrival that the engineer gave three short blasts on his whistle, then slowed the train a significant distance from the station. On the day after our arrival he gave, instead, two long blasts and then slowed only as he reached the station. This change in behaviour could be, I concluded, the sending of a signal. If indeed the three blasts heralded the arrival of contraband, they might alert waiting smugglers to ready themselves to catch items thrown from the train. And so I laid a trap, using myself as bait, in the expectation that at least one racketeer would be sufficiently curious to investigate whether I was killed by the train or not. That would have afforded me an opportunity to detain them.'

Holmes's explanation filled me with anxiety. 'But what if the engineer had given two long blasts yesterday?'

'I would have regained my footing with alacrity, of course.'

'I don't see how this relates to me,' said Mrs Burns.

'All in good time.' Holmes paused to draw a long breath. 'Despite your interference yesterday in my plan, Watson, I managed to capture the slowest runner. It was none other than young Billy, forced into partaking in the trade.'

'Billy is part of this?' asked Dr Morton.

'Not by choice. After adequate persuasion, the boy confessed.'

Sergeant Beard shifted his weight. 'This is all well and good, Mr Holmes, but hardly necessary, given the evidence against Mrs Burns.'

At this the mine owner harrumphed and glanced from the men surrounding her to the room's only door.

'Patience, Sergeant. And please do keep your hands in the sunlight. Where was I?'

'The boy's confession,' I answered.

'Ah, yes. In short, I was correct. Billy admitted that, three evenings before being discovered at the bottom of the mill drain by his mother, he was loitering in one of the town's alleyways and pried his way into a storeroom. Inside he discovered many boxes, some of which contained *Cigares de Joy*. Attempting to imitate his elder brother, he tried to smoke one but, predictably, coughed until he was ill. The noise alerted the owner of the contraband, who then locked the boy in, threatening to kill him if he made a sound.'

'Well, that wasn't me, so who was it?' Mrs Burns demanded.

'He heard only their voice.'

'Surely, Mr Holmes, the boy could at least tell if the speaker was a man or a woman.'

Holmes declined to answer. 'Locked away without food or water, with naught at his disposal but cigarettes, he practised smoking, growing increasingly delirious and dehydrated.'

I then recalled Miss Morgan's comment at the hospital. 'That's why his flesh was spongy upon examination!'

'Indeed, Watson. He reports having lost all sense of time. Growing increasingly desperate, he decided to pile the room's contents in one corner and attempt escape. He forced a shingle from the ceiling and made it onto the roof, but then fell into a vat of night dirt.'

'Ah, the source of the putrid smell?'

'Correct again, Watson. He then struck out for home, and almost reached it, but stumbled in the dark and fell into the mill drain behind his parents' cottage. Unable to stand, exhaustion overcame him and he succumbed to a watery grave. His mother, however, was preternaturally alert to sounds that might herald the return of her son and was woken by the splash and drawn outside to the source of the sound. The boy's final moments of struggle would have disturbed the surface of the water, catching dawn's first rays, pinpointing where he lay.'

'So he had only just drowned when his parents found him, and that's why it was possible for Miss Morgan to revive him,' said Dr Morton.

'But Holmes, none of this tells us who imprisoned the boy.'

'Ah, Watson, but it does!' In one swift movement Holmes whipped the room's only set of curtains closed.

As we were enveloped by darkness, my own shocked gasp joined a chorus of exclamations: in the middle of the room floated two green, disembodied hands clutching glowing packages.

'For here is our culprit,' said Holmes's voice. With that he ripped the curtains apart.

Standing in the centre of the room, frozen like an animal hunted, was Sergeant Beard.

'What is this trickery?' The sergeant examined his own hands from all sides. 'And how dare you imply that I am involved? I'm a godfearing man, a man of the law, not a criminal.'

'Wrong!' Holmes said with glee. 'On every count! To begin with, you are not the religious man you claim to be, Sergeant. For Lazarus arose how many days after his death?'

Sergeant Beard stared at Holmes as though he had gone mad, a familiar expression on those who encountered Holmes in full flight.

'Your answer, sergeant, at the Lyonses' home, was three, was it not? When the correct answer is four.'

'So?'

'And where, Sergeant, does it say *If anyone destroys God's temple, God will destroy him?*'

'Proverbs, as you said.'

'Wrong! Corinthians. First Corinthians, chapter three, verse seventeen, in fact.'

I was perplexed by this revelation. 'Holmes, when did you read a Bible sufficiently to quote chapter and verse in such a fashion?'

'When we were in Sydney, Watson, on a day when you visited a member of your old regiment. There was a distinct lack of suitable reading material in our rooms, forcing me to inspect the landlady's copy. You had already berated me rather severely that morning for incidental wear and tear on our lodgings, so I sought an alternate occupation to my experiments. As you know, the Book had previously failed to interest me, in that it has only the briefest relevance to the modern study of criminology and in that I cannot reconcile with the commands to grovel, apologise and self-loathe contained therein. On this occasion, however, I persevered and chanced upon verses describing a most novel means of torture and execution. I determined immediately to read it from cover to cover and, as a result, have retained multiple interesting and instructive passages.'

Sergeant Beard shrugged at Holmes's explanation. 'So, you've memorised the Bible and I haven't. So what?'

'It is significant, Sergeant, for it establishes a pattern.'

I have to admit Holmes had lost me again. 'A pattern?'

'A pattern of deceit. I realised during our conversation with Mr Matthews that I had made an assumption, an erroneous one. I had unconsciously placed the sergeant in the same category as our lesser Scotland Yard friends: inept, resentful of my talents, but ultimately harmless. A man as pious as you purport to be, Sergeant, should have known those Biblical references; if not he would hardly commit the 'fresh sin' of lying about his knowledge of the Good Book. Once I realised you were dissembling in that regard I was forced to re-evaluate my entire perception of you.'

The sergeant's face darkened. 'As the senior representative of the Crown in this town, Mr Holmes, I refuse to listen to any more of your nonsense. I have evidence that Mrs Burns is behind the drug trade and, as all can attest, under no circumstances would I engage in criminal activities myself. I have no reason to.'

'Oh, but you do, as you told me the very moment we met. For what stronger motive is there than filial piety? You seek to make your father happy by supporting your brother's election campaign, is that not so? But elections are an expensive business, and you are in short supply of funds, as evidenced by your shabby single uniform and its tea stains from two days ago.'

Sergeant Beard's neck flushed rosily under the combined gaze of all in the room.

'And so, realising that you were a man in need of money, a man with a propensity to dissemble, and a man – as you yourself boasted – with extensive connections at all levels of local society, I reasoned that you were the perfect candidate to conduct a regional black market – though not as its instigator, because that requires capital investment, of which you are fiscally incapable. Running a black market on behalf of, say, a mining magnate eager to acquire Mrs Burns's holdings, however, could prove most lucrative for you. How large a reward have you been promised for crippling Mrs Burns's workforce with drugs, forcing her to sell her mine to your backer? Enough, surely, to finance your brother's election campaign and perhaps realise your father's lifelong dream. Isn't that right, Sergeant?'

'No more! All you have is the word of a lying boy. Leave. Now!'

'Not just yet, Sergeant. I'm not relying on the boy, but rather the proof of your own hands.'

I was, by this point, wondering when Holmes would finally provide an explanation. 'So what was that glow? And what does it mean?'

'Don't you see, Watson?' Holmes said. 'After the Lyons boy guided me to the storage room in which he had been trapped I added a little something of my own to the contraband, a sprinkling of one of the powders I developed in Sydney made from zinc sulphide and copper. Once exposed to light it emits phosphorescence, that greenish glow on the packages and the sergeant's hands.'

The sergeant rallied. 'No judge will be interested in that kind of jiggery-pokery.'

'Perhaps not, but a judge will listen to witness statements.'

Sergeant Beard straightened. 'Statements? From whom? The boy?'

'Two of Queanbeyan's finest citizens, Dr Morton and Mr Matthews.'

Holmes glanced at the doctor, who nodded ferociously. 'Mr Holmes explained the situation and asked me to watch the storage room yesterday. It is true that you were the only person to enter, Sergeant. You went in just before dusk and came out with bulging pockets.'

'I was with the doctor and I saw the sergeant as well,' said Mr Matthews.

'You.' Mrs Burns stepped forward and shook a finger in the sergeant's face. 'You would seek to destroy my livelihood, force me to sell my mine, then falsely accuse me of crimes you yourself committed? How dare you!'

I was aware that in that moment the sergeant abandoned his protestations, although he could not quit without one last barb. 'You have only yourself to blame, Mrs Burns. You should have sold the mine when you were first approached. Women have no place in the world of men, as everyone knows.'

Mrs Burns slapped Sergeant Beard across the face. Apparently unsatisfied, she then brought her skirted knee sharply upon his person. 'Interesting that you should speak so firmly against women, yet fail to defend yourself against one,' she said.

'Father insisted we never raise a hand against a woman,' the sergeant croaked as he crumpled to the floor.

Holmes then directed Beard's men in a manner that left them in no doubt as to what might occur if they didn't comply with his requests. As a result the two silent, shocked constables hesitantly stepped forward to pick up and restrain their disgraced superior.

Holmes drew the room's attention back to himself. 'Please, accept my apology for the subterfuge, Mrs Burns. I deemed it necessary.'

The remarkable businesswoman shook her head. 'No apologies necessary.

In fact I should be thanking you. I will return to the mine and clear out any remaining contraband. I'm not losing my mine without a fight, believe you me.'

'At your service, then,' said Holmes, with an inclination of his head.

In that moment I noted a particular tone in my companion's voice, one that I had previously come to dread, for usually it heralded the end of a case and his spiralling into boredom. Bracing myself against the inevitable destructive experiments and their damage upon my purse, I asked, 'We're to return to Sydney, then?'

'Not just yet, Watson.'

'Oh? For what reason?'

'A report I noticed on the sergeant's desk yesterday.' Holmes lunged for a piece of paper. 'It's from a town called Yass, some thirty miles away. Two days ago the wife of the bank manager was abducted in broad daylight.'

'And?'

Holmes flourished the piece of paper. 'In front of twenty witnesses. By a band of Japanese samurai warriors. Who then vanished into thin air.'

'I see.'

Holmes grinned. 'I've arranged horses.'

I made an attempt to stop it, but was utterly unable to prevent an answering smile from sweeping across my own face.

THE ADVENTURE OF THE FLASH OF SILVER

Doug Elliott

EW OF OUR adventures in the great southern land of Australia in 1890 were as curious as the case that came to the attention of Sherlock Holmes soon after we had settled into rooms at Petty's Hotel in Sydney. That comfortable hostelry became our home for a time and we were able to secure a private sitting room where we often took our breakfasts, engrossed in the morning's newspapers.

On one such morning, as a feeble winter sun cast its pale sheen across the dark patterned carpet, I was curled up in a spacious armchair perusing the *Sydney Morning Herald* when Holmes dropped his own paper onto his lap.

'I am in complete agreement, Watson,' he said. 'The Players have indeed distinguished themselves.'

'Yes,' I said. 'A decisive win. But I never spoke a word. How in heaven's name did you know what I was just thinking?'

'A moment ago you raised your eyes from your paper to gaze out the window. Your thoughts were clearly a long way from Australia. You began to absentmindedly rotate the apple in your right hand. I knew that cricket was the subject and you were feeling for the seams. The small grin upon your face confirmed that you had just read of the match between the Players of England and the Australian Eleven in which our team triumphed by an innings and 263 runs.'

'Quite simple when you put it that way,' I said.

'Perhaps I should have remained silent and left you with your mystery,' he replied.

As I contemplated my own obtuseness, the hotel boy arrived to announce that two people wished to see the great Sherlock Holmes. Many of my reports of Holmes's cases had not yet been published, stories that would raise his reputation to its zenith, so Holmes had been confident that his researches in Sydney could be conducted with a degree of anonymity. Nonetheless, his recent efforts in bringing the case of the Nikola Formulae to a satisfactory conclusion had been leaked to the Australian press despite efforts to mask the affair, and the news that the great English detective was stopping in Sydney brought a trickle of appellants to Petty's, each with an earth-stopping problem for the investigator to solve.

Holmes treated these visitors with formal politeness, but in the end turned most of them away. 'The problems of the antipodes are every bit as tedious as those of London, I fear,' he observed to me after one such visitor had departed.

But this particular morning would prove to be very different.

In a few minutes the boy ushered in a tall woman of middle years, who entered the room hesitantly followed by a dark-haired man carrying a bowler and wearing a vicious scowl.

Garbed in mourning in a heavy black dress and broad-brimmed black hat, the woman stood indecisively just inside the door, glancing between the two of us, and then suddenly lifted her veil to reveal one of the most striking visages I have ever seen.

Her pale patrician face was surmounted by a lustrous crown of chestnut hair, and her flashing green eyes quickly fixed upon my companion who, like me, had risen to greet our visitors.

'You are Sherlock Holmes, the English detective,' she announced in a clear, steady voice.

'I have that honour,' said Holmes with a slight bow, 'and this is my colleague, Dr Watson.'

'I am Emma Demears. I read that you were in Sydney. This is my brother, Wallace Greenbriar.' The man bobbed his head in our direction, but his attention remained upon the woman, the scowl fixed on his face.

Holmes waved our guests to two heavy chairs, and we reclaimed our own seats.

'Mr Holmes,' she continued, 'I need your help. My husband Arthur is… was… one of the most successful wool merchants in the country.'

'I have read about him,' I exclaimed. 'In today's paper.' All eyes swung in my direction, and I stammered out what I knew of the poor man's story. 'Your husband, though aged in his sixties, was accustomed to take himself down to the local seaside baths each morning at sunrise for a solitary swim before breakfast.'

Mrs Demears gave a small nod, which I took as permission to continue.

'On Tuesday morning, yesterday, when he had not returned to his home after an hour, Mr Demears' valet proceeded down to the baths where he discovered his master lying dead in shallow water at the beach.' Our visitor gave an anguished gasp as I spoke these words, and I realised that I had been rudely insensitive. I found myself unable to complete my story.

Holmes, of course, had no such compunctions. 'According to the *Daily Telegraph*, it was initially believed that your husband had drowned. But Mr Demears' valet felt that this was unlikely, given his master's considerable swimming abilities, so he examined the surroundings carefully. In a little rocky pool at the tidemark he discovered a small sea creature, a species known to local fishermen and beachgoers as a blue-ringed octopus. This creature is notable for its highly toxic bite, which is invariably fatal. The police have thus concluded that Arthur Demears fell victim to this creature during his morning swim, leading to a verdict of death by misfortune.'

'But it is not true, Mr Holmes,' cried the lady. 'It cannot be true. I know that Arthur was not killed by an octopus. He was murdered.'

Holmes leaned forward, peering intently at the woman's luminous face. 'What makes you so sure that it was murder?'

'It cannot have been an accident,' she said emphatically. 'Arthur knew the Manly Baths intimately. He had been swimming there for five years, summer and winter. He knew all about the jellyfish and the octopuses and the sharks and all of the other hazards of the ocean. By nature he was a cautious man. He never could have simply blundered onto this creature. I do not know how it was done, but I know it was murder.'

'But who would have wanted your husband dead?' asked Holmes. 'Who would have benefited from his demise?'

'Mr Holmes,' she said, 'Arthur was about to conclude a business arrangement by which Demears & Co would absorb Pengelly & Sons, one of its largest and harshest rivals. None of his directors wanted to pursue this path, but Arthur was adamant that it would proceed. There have been in recent weeks a series of bitter meetings with several of those directors, and with the directors of Pengelly. The result of his death is that the merger is now halted. The directors of both companies may now return to their long-standing jobs. They may take Demears & Co to its grave, but as individuals they will remain wealthy and comfortable. Mr Holmes, your recent exploits are well known. I implore you, please investigate this matter. I will not rest until my dear husband's murderer is brought to justice.'

Holmes fell into silent contemplation, an expression of doubt upon his face. 'But surely there is more,' he said at last. 'Suspicion alone does not warrant an investigation.'

Mrs Demears' brother suddenly struck his thigh in exasperation. 'Emma, I told you this was pointless,' he exclaimed. 'This fellow is no more open to your absurd theory than the police are. For God's sake, let this silly obsession of yours drop before people begin to think you're a madwoman.'

Mrs Demears turned her face to her brother and her eyes were bright with defiant tears. For a moment, no one spoke.

Holmes looked at the brother. 'Mr Greenbriar, I take it that you do not share your sister's concerns about Mr Demears' manner of death,' he said mildly.

'She's badly mistaken. Her love for Arthur and her great grief have confused her thinking.'

At this, Emma Demears reddened visibly.

'Sir, there's no chance Arthur's death was murder,' Greenbriar continued. 'It looks like an accident; therefore, it was an accident. However much they may oppose the merger, none of the company directors would stoop to murder.'

'You are familiar with them, then,' said Holmes.

'I manage the daily operations of the Demears office in Sydney. And I have had frequent encounters with the men of Pengelly & Sons. They can be a bit rough – it's a rough business – but they're not killers.'

'Is there no one else who suspects foul play in this matter?' Holmes asked.

'Only Arthur's valet, James,' replied Mrs Demears. 'He believes, as do I, that Arthur was far too familiar with the ocean and too wary to overlook a blue-ring. Mr Holmes, it has been a day filled with horror. I was not even at home when the police came to tell me about… the incident. I had been staying with my aunt, Beatrice, up in Freshwater for several days, and they had to send a constable to me with the news.' Tears welled up in her eyes and her voice broke as she covered her face with her hands.

Abruptly Holmes rose to bring the discussion to a close. 'We will look into this matter. I shall need to speak with the detective assigned to your husband's case.'

'That is Inspector Wade,' she replied. 'His office is in Hunter Street. Our family solicitor will ensure that he is available to you.'

'Very good,' said Holmes quietly, then he turned to her brother. 'Mr Greenbriar, I must also interview the presidents of both companies. Can you arrange it?'

Greenbriar looked intensely unhappy at this turn of events, but reluctantly agreed. 'I will send you a note here in an hour with their names and addresses and will arrange for you to meet with them later today.'

'Oh, thank you, Mr Holmes,' Mrs Demears enthused. 'You will find me at my home, *Guwara*, at Manly. I so look forward to the results of your investigation.' Replacing her veil, she swept out of the room with her sullen brother in tow.

'Manly, again,' I muttered, reminded of a previous incident during our Australian tour.

Holmes smiled. 'Manly again, Watson. But two cases do not a crime epidemic make, particularly in a sea-side suburb as popular with travellers as Manly. I had two murders and a grand larceny in Brighton all in the one year, before your time, and was almost disappointed when they had no connection with one another.'

FROM PETTY'S HOTEL on York Street, with its views of the harbour to the north, Holmes and I walked down to Circular Quay, the central ferry terminus for the port of Sydney. From a row of passenger jetties a truly impressive fleet of small ferries plied the calm waters of Port Jackson, connecting the business centre of the city to the residential suburbs clustered around the extensive harbour.

A payment of three pence each gained us return tickets on the steam ferry *Fairlight* bound for the seaside town of Manly. Soon after leaving the jetty, we slid past the great grey bulk of Fort Macquarie with its imposing battlements and castellated towers, crouching in silent vigilance on Bennelong Point. From there, the harbour opened up before us, low hills rising from the water, crowned with handsome houses overlooking the busy waterway. Just before we reached the two rocky headlands that guarded the entrance to Port Jackson, our ferry veered to the left and made a straight run into Manly Cove.

At Manly Wharf a passerby directed us towards the gentlemen's baths. In response to Holmes's query about a house called *Guwara*, the man pointed across the cove to an imposing structure on the hillside overlooking the water.

After a short walk beside the calm waters of the inner harbour, we found ourselves facing Little Manly Cove, a narrow bay perhaps eight hundred feet long with a small sandy beach at its northern end where we now stood. Flat, rocky platforms marked its eastern and western sides. The rectangular baths were enclosed by timber barriers running south from the beach and west from the rocky shoreline. At the far end of the eastern side sat a low, wooden building which no doubt contained dressing-rooms for bathers. Next to it, rough, stone stairs rose out of the water to the level of the rock platform.

A closer examination of the barrier revealed that it comprised a row of wooden pilings about six feet apart rising to about eight feet above the waterline, which was then at low tide. Between the pilings, timber palisades had been driven down to form an almost continuous barrier, no doubt to keep the dangerous denizens of the sea away from swimmers. At the far corner of this enclosure, the palisades had been replaced by a twenty-foot section of wire netting.

As we walked along the beach it became evident that the baths were in an advanced state of dilapidation: many of the palisades were rotted, broken or missing completely, and great rents could be seen in the wire netting. It was plain that the enclosure would offer protection from only the largest sea creatures.

In fact, a shoal of small fish had apparently taken up residence in the bay, for we occasionally caught a glimpse of one springing into the air after one of the insects with bright, transparent wings that hovered near the surface of the still water.

Holmes strode immediately to the rocky platform along the eastern edge of the baths. The receding tide had left a scattering of shallow pools at the shoreline, where no doubt an errant octopus could become trapped. But Holmes furrowed his brow.

He walked slowly alongside the water for the full length of the enclosure, bent over almost double, often dropping to his knees to peer intently into the little tidal pools.

After perhaps half an hour, Holmes straightened and strode off down the beach, back the way we had come. I followed in some bewilderment, certain that we were about to return to the ferry wharf. But moments later he turned up the path leading to the grand residence that had been pointed out to us earlier.

The three-storey house in its own extensive grounds was solidly built of weathered sandstone blocks and red brick. At the top of a broad flight of steps a stone arch framed a heavy timber door with GUWARA inscribed above it.

Our knock was answered by a housemaid who informed us that Mrs Demears was visiting a friend in the city and would not return until much later.

'Very well,' said Holmes with no evident disappointment. 'May we speak with James, Mr Demears' valet?'

The maid was momentarily nonplussed by this request, but quickly recovered her composure and ushered us into a small drawing room at the front of the dwelling with expansive views across Manly Cove. She curtly asked us to wait, then vanished into the interior of the house. A few moments later we were joined by a slight man in valet's livery. James was in his forties with small, hooded eyes and dark hair beginning to turn grey. He appeared to be much disturbed by our visit, standing stiffly before us, his hands working compulsively, his eyes avoiding ours.

Holmes introduced us. 'You may know,' he said, 'that Mrs Demears has retained us to investigate the manner of your master's death. You were the first to discover his body.'

The man relaxed slightly. 'Mr Holmes, sir, you must excuse my behaviour. I cannot believe that Mr Demears is gone, and it has upset me terribly. I so wish I could have revived him.' Tears rimmed his eyes as he fought to retain his composure.

'And you noticed the blue-ringed octopus nearby?' Holmes asked.

'Yes, sir. I thought I might find a clue to the cause of Mr Demears' death in the tidal pools nearby, and I saw the creature not ten feet from where he was found.'

'Can you describe what you saw?'

'The animal was perhaps six inches in length, light brown in colour. It was covered with irregular black areas, each of which bore a blue ring at its centre.'

'Yet in spite of finding this deadly animal so close to your master's body, you believe his death was not an accident.'

'Mr Demears cannot have been so clumsy as to stumble into the thing. It is one of the well-known dangers of the tidal pools in Sydney, and the master has… had been swimming by the shoreline here for some years. There must be another explanation for his death.'

'As a servant, you have had a long and close association with Mr Demears. How would you describe his manner recently?'

'I have been in service for twelve years, with Mr Demears for the past seven, and I have never had a fairer or more generous master…' Here James hesitated.

'And yet…?' said Holmes.

The valet's gaze flicked back and forth between the two of us. 'And yet, in the past two years his character has undergone a profound change. He has become more impatient, more demanding, more forgetful, and yet more aggressive and, dare I say, cruel. I may tell you this now that he has passed away. He was often rude and unreasonable with the servants, beat his children over the most minor transgressions, and berated poor Mrs Demears terribly over trifles. Life with the master had quite descended into a nightmare.'

'Had you any explanation for this sudden transformation?'

'In the servants' quarters we could only put it down to incipient senility, striking at an early age. Cook told us that one of her aunts had experienced something similar. I overheard Mrs Demears on more than one occasion begging him to consult an alienist, to seek some relief, but he always resisted.'

'Do you think someone killed him in retaliation for some slight or abuse?'

'I cannot say, Mr Holmes,' said the man sadly.

'Who do you think is responsible?'

James pondered the question for a few moments. 'Sir, the master antagonised almost everyone he met in recent months. I fear that the octopus was very low down the list of those who may have wished him harm.'

Our interview completed, we offered our goodbyes and James escorted us out. As he was closing the door, Holmes spun round to face him.

'You are a swimmer yourself, then?' he asked.

'No, sir. I was raised in the country, in South Australia,' said James with a rueful smile. 'I try to stay away from the ocean as much as possible.'

'And yet you immediately identified the blue-ringed octopus when you saw it that morning.'

'Ah, yes, of course,' he said, as if a thought had just come to him. 'Last year the Demearses' eight-year-old son Albert was playing by the harbour, collecting shells. He came home with a blue-ringed octopus in a jar. Mr Demears was horrified and gave the boy a stern lecture on its dangers. I had a good look at the thing and learned about its fatal bite. Mr Demears later placed it in a jar of alcohol which he kept in his office upstairs here. I believe he kept it as a signal warning against complacency about safety in the water.'

WE RETURNED TO Petty's to find that Wallace Greenbriar had been true to his word. A lengthy note addressed to Holmes set out the names and locations of the men whom Holmes wished to interview.

Our first stop was a Sydney police station in Hunter Street, a short walk from our hotel. It was evident that Detective Inspector Wade was meeting us under duress. The influence of the Demears family solicitor apparently extended deep into the ranks of Sydney's public servants. Wade was a bollard of a man with receding blond hair and a broad, florid face with a much-broken nose and tiny, black eyes. We met in his cramped office on the first floor, the detective tapping his blunt fingers on the ancient desktop, impatient to have done with us.

'This case is closed,' he snapped, 'and I don't want any fuss being raised that deflects us from more important work. I'll answer your questions now, but no further meetings will be scheduled and no further information about this case will be forthcoming. You have one chance to get what you want and then get out.'

Holmes was the soul of amiability. 'I do understand your concerns, Inspector,' he said smoothly. 'We will be as brief as possible.'

Wade fixed my friend with an icy glare, waiting for more.

'To begin, then,' said Holmes. 'We have visited the baths at Little Manly Cove. Can you tell us where the body was discovered?'

Wade spoke in a rapid monotone as if reading from his official report. 'Demears' valet discovered the deceased at about eight in the morning, Tuesday, that is to say, yesterday. It was facedown in about one foot of water against the rocks along the eastern side of the cove.'

'How were the police summoned?'

'The valet called out to a passing boy on his way to school, sent him to the Manly police station in Market Lane.'

'And the valet waited with the body until the police arrived?'

Wade nodded. 'He pulled the body up onto the beach and attempted to resuscitate his master, but it was to no avail.'

'How was the body clothed?'

'In Demears' usual bathing costume, which extended from mid-calf to his neck and covered his upper arms. He did not follow the current fashion among Sydney men of swimming in the nude.'

'And you determined that he had not died by drowning.'

'The surgeon found no water in the man's lungs. He had stopped breathing before his face was submerged.'

'Were there any marks upon the body?'

'There were fresh scratches on his palms, which we believe he acquired in his death throes while trying to climb up the rocks out of the water.'

'Did you rule out any other cause of death, such as heart failure?'

'A fatal heart attack leaves certain unmistakable signs upon the heart and its major vessels. The police surgeon observed no such signs during the post-mortem examination.'

'Tell me about the octopus.'

'Demears' valet noticed it as we were examining the body. It appeared that, as Demears climbed up out of the water following his morning swim, he placed his hand into the tide pool and the creature bit him. The sudden sharp pain caused him to fall back into the water, and as the paralysis claimed him he tried to scramble up to the rock platform. Unfortunately, he soon succumbed to the poison, his breathing stopped and he fell back again into the water.'

'Was there no bite mark on the man's hand?'

'The surgeon was not able to identify a particular bite wound amongst all the scratches.'

'Is there any doubt that it was the cause of death?'

The detective raised an eyebrow. 'You are referring to the wife's claims of murder?'

'Do you have any suspicions of your own?'

'Mr Holmes, this is a simple case of accidental death. We have had experience of the blue-ring before. Its venom can result in nausea, respiratory arrest and heart failure, but most commonly we see within minutes a severe and sometimes total body paralysis, including the muscles used for breathing. The victim quickly expires from lack of oxygen. Even if he had fallen back into the water, Demears could not have inhaled any water into his lungs. This is all consistent with the surgeon's findings.'

'Your officers no doubt captured the creature,' said Holmes. 'May I see it?'

Wade stiffened. 'I'm sorry to say it was lost. By the time the detectives arrived at the scene the tide had risen and carried it away.'

Holmes raised an eyebrow. 'Most unfortunate.'

'But this has no bearing upon the case,' Wade quickly assured us. 'The octopus was seen by both the valet and the constable, who will testify to its location at the time.'

Holmes paused to consider this new information. 'One more thing, Inspector,' he said at last. 'Might I view the deceased's body?'

Wade's face reddened and his hands clenched. 'Mate, you've tried my patience enough. Either you're pulling my leg or you're ratty. It's time you left.'

Holmes was unperturbed. 'Mrs Demears has given me quite clear instructions that I should conduct a complete investigation. Granting my request will ensure that there will be no further questions raised. I am an experienced investigator, Inspector, and I will conduct my examination efficiently and without disrupting your endeavours. And I promise that this will be the last you shall see of me.'

Wade glared at Holmes for some moments before relenting. 'Very well. I will send word to the morgue that you are to be admitted. The body will be released to the family later this afternoon, so please do not waste anyone's time.'

'PERHAPS IT WAS an accidental death,' I suggested, as we walked along George Street in the direction of the harbour and the morgue.

'I am convinced otherwise,' said Holmes.

'How do you come to that conclusion?'

'To have come in contact with the octopus, Demears would have had to climb up the sharp, uneven rocky slope and across the tidal pool where the creature was trapped. But no experienced swimmer would have climbed out that way while barefoot. He would have left the water by way of the sandy beach, or swum to the end of the enclosure and climbed the stairs.'

'Perhaps the water level was higher then,' I ventured. 'The platform could have been under water. Demears could have swum over the platform, barely touching the rock at that point.'

'I'm afraid not, Watson. I referred to the local tide tables before we left Petty's this morning. At the time of Demears' death, it was only an hour beyond the low tide.'

THE SYDNEY MORGUE occupied a sandstone building on a narrow lane called Bethel Street near Circular Quay. Inside, the atmosphere was suffused with the stench of death and decay, and only my medical experience permitted me to control my digestive urges as we were led through a warren of dank corridors. Holmes seemed unconcerned by the miasma and actually hummed a strain from Schubert as we descended deeper into the building.

At last the attendant ushered us into a large, dimly lit room lined with wooden shelving that resembled tiers of bunk beds. About half of these were occupied by human forms covered in linen sheets. In spite of the cool temperature of the room, the smell of putrefaction was overpowering.

The attendant approached one of the niches and casually threw aside the sheet to reveal the pale form of Mr Arthur Demears. He was a man in his early sixties, with a tall, sturdy frame and well-developed muscles. He bore a thick thatch of white hair, now in disarray, and his square face was sunken in death's repose. After giving the body a cursory glance, Holmes picked up each hand in turn and examined it closely with his magnifying lens, turning it to catch the feeble light. This completed, he gave the soles of the feet the same rigorous inspection.

After a few minutes, Holmes straightened, apparently satisfied. Grasping the victim's left hand, he waved me closer to the table. 'Have a look at this,' he said.

As Inspector Wade had reported, the palm was covered with a confusion of scratches and cuts. At first I saw nothing remarkable, until Holmes pointed to the base of the index finger. On closer examination I saw a perfect circle of tiny punctures less than half an inch across.

'What kind of sea creature leaves a mark like that?' I asked.

'Rather a denizen of the land, I think,' said Holmes. Turning to the doorway, he nodded to the attendant and strode back the way we had come. I followed gratefully, puzzled by what I had seen but happy to be relieved of the oppressive atmosphere and knowing that I could never have found my way back to the street on my own.

A SECRETARY USHERED us into the palatial office of Roger Ferguson on the top floor of the Demears & Co building at Circular Quay. Its expansive windows afforded a view across the harbour to the north-east and to the wharves immediately below, where five or six sleek clippers were being attended by a cadre of great, chuffing steam cranes that lifted bales of wool in and out of their spacious holds.

Ferguson was a rotund, ponderous man in his late fifties with a bald head fringed with white hair and a formidable silver beard. The company director's handshake was powerful, reflecting a man who was accustomed to taking control.

'Gentlemen, when Emma insisted that I see you today, I have to say I was puzzled. She says you are investigating poor Arthur's death. I cannot say what there might be to investigate. The police believe it was an accident, a bite from a blue-ringed octopus.'

'First of all,' said Holmes in his softest voice, 'let me convey our deepest sympathies on the loss of your friend and colleague.'

'Colleague, that's for sure,' Ferguson replied. 'We've served together on this board for more years than I've got hairs in my beard. But friend? Arthur was too ruthless in business to have any real friends.'

'He made enemies, then?'

'No more than any other man of affairs. But in the past few years, Arthur became more and more scattered in his thinking. His head for business was clearly failing, but he also grew more stubborn and argumentative. He would brook no suggestion that he might be wrong. He was taking the company down the plug-hole with this acquisition of Pengelly's that he'd cooked up. No amount of reasoning could change his mind. We had some mighty rich battles about it, he and I, in the boardroom and at his home. Part of me is happy that he's gone. Now we can return to sanity and do what is necessary to operate this firm.'

'I understood that Wallace Greenbriar manages the daily operation of the company,' Holmes said.

Ferguson gave a snort of derision. 'That man could not manage a mob of schoolboys,' he said, his voice low. 'Look, Arthur always needed to be on top of the international wool markets and our competitors, so he was constantly travelling, his wife with him. He went to America, England, Brazil and everywhere else in between. And as soon as Arthur was on the boat, Wallace would swagger around here as if he owned the place, all the while carefully avoiding doing any real work or making any real decisions. And now that Arthur is gone, he believes he has the right as Emma's brother to a share of the company. The man is insufferable.'

NOT FAR DOWN the quay from Demears & Co stood the squat warehouse of Pengelly & Sons. One of the stevedores pointed out Albert Marks, the managing director, standing at the dockside. Wallace Greenbriar's note had warned us that Marks was 'a vindictive man with a vile temper and a penchant for getting his own way'.

The man we approached was tall and lean, in his mid-forties, with a dark complexion and thick, wavy, black hair. His shirt sleeves were rolled up, revealing the ropy muscles of his forearms. He was accompanied by a thin, shifty-looking fellow wearing rough clothes and a leather apron. As we approached, Marks was slicing open a wool bale with a long, vicious-looking knife. He set the knife aside and plunged his arm into the interior of the bale. Drawing out a fistful of fleece, he pulled the strands apart and subjected them to an intense examination.

As we introduced ourselves, Marks spun around to face us. 'You're working for the Demears family,' he snapped, glaring at Holmes. He retrieved his knife and turned it over in his hand. 'You have no business on this wharf. You'll clear out of here right this minute, mate, or I'll have my lads chuck you in the harbour.'

'We are working with the police, Mr Marks,' said Holmes with authority, 'investigating the death of Arthur Demears. Should you refuse to speak with us, unfounded suspicions might arise. I would hate to inconvenience you any further upon the matter.'

Marks's jaw dropped and he stared at the knife in his hand for a few seconds. Abruptly, he appeared to make up his mind. 'Bloody Pommies!' he said with some feeling. 'All right, then.'

He turned to the other man, who was apparently his foreman, shaking the fleece in the man's face. 'Mick, this year's shear from McAlpine is not up to his usual standard. I don't care if he's had rain or floods or a plague of bloody frogs. He gets paid for the quality of his fleece and he'll get paid twenty per cent less for this year's rubbish.' He flung the fleece dismissively to the ground.

The foreman nodded and strode away towards the warehouse.

'Now then,' Marks snapped, turning squarely to us. 'What do you want with me?'

'You argued with Demears over his proposal to acquire your company,' said Holmes.

Marks exploded with rage. 'Of course I bloody argued with him. The man wanted to buy the company out from under me, put me out in the street. And he wanted to pay ten shillings to the pound for it. Then he threatened, bribed and browbeat my directors to the point where he almost had the votes he needed to do it.'

'Surely Pengelly was experiencing some difficulties, then. No one will attempt to purchase a firm in the bloom of success.'

I kept glancing at the knife flashing in Marks's hand and wondering why Holmes was deliberately antagonising such a powerful and volatile fellow.

But Marks held his temper. 'No denying we've been doing it tough the past few years,' he admitted. 'But there's been a drought in South Australia and Demears has been poaching some of our best graziers. We'll come back. I know it. I just need to pound some sense into our directors.'

'But now that Arthur Demears is dead, the threat of the acquisition vanishes,' Holmes suggested.

Marks allowed himself an evil smile. 'It does. Almost as if that octopus was in the employ of Pengelly, isn't it?'

'Was it?' asked Holmes.

Marks pointed the knife tellingly at Holmes. 'Don't you go spreading the word that this is any different than it is,' he said, his voice heavy with menace. 'Demears' death was an accident, pure and simple. Nark it, Mr Holmes. Let it lie. Ye'll have the johnnies down on us, and for no good reason either.'

He turned and strode off down the quay.

'Marks frightens me, Holmes,' I admitted as we walked back to Petty's. 'He seems eminently capable of causing bodily harm, if not murder. Is it possible that he pushed Demears underwater, drowning him, and then slung him over his shoulder to carry him up to the beach? In that position the water could well have drained out of the man's lungs, confusing the police surgeon.'

'An admirable theory, Watson,' replied Holmes, but would say no more upon the subject.

Back in our sitting room at Petty's, Holmes withdrew to a quiet corner and bent over the tide tables for a few moments, then rose abruptly.

'I have heard about a remarkable restaurant in Market Street,' he said. 'Tomorrow promises to be an eventful day, so we would do well to enjoy a hearty meal tonight. Meanwhile, if you will excuse me, I must acquire a few supplies for tomorrow's investigations.' With that, he departed and did not return for several hours.

Over a fine dinner of roast lamb and steamed vegetables, enlivened by a bottle of Adelaide claret, Holmes directed our meagre conversation to trivial topics and remained tight-lipped about the case at hand until we had returned to our hotel.

'I would much appreciate if you would accompany me on an early-morning journey back to Little Manly Cove,' he said. 'I believe there are still clues to be uncovered there.'

HOLMES SHOOK ME awake early the next morning and we emerged from the hotel to a clear day as the sun rose over the eastern hills. Carrying a well-worn carpet bag, Holmes marched purposefully towards the harbour as I struggled to keep up. The ferry ride was uneventful and a short walk round the Manly foreshore saw us once again on the narrow beach before the baths. Two men in swimming costumes splashed about at the far west side of the watery enclosure but except for them, we were completely alone.

'What have you deduced about our case now, Watson?' Holmes asked.

'I admit to being completely baffled,' I replied. 'Demears had no shortage of enemies, but I can make no headway as to the culprit or the method, if it was indeed murder.'

'Oh, it was murder,' said Holmes. 'The fresh circular wound upon Demears' hand is highly suggestive, don't you think? The tiny punctures around the circle were so precisely spaced that they could only have been created by a man-made object, not by the horny and irregular beak of an octopus.'

'But they could have been made at any time prior to Demears' death. They may have no bearing upon the case.'

'Quite true,' he replied, 'but if we assume for the moment that they were made by a sharp object of some kind, dipped in a lethal poison, a number of intriguing possibilities emerge. And the only way we can confirm our assumption is to find the weapon itself.

'The killer would naturally dispose of the weapon as soon as possible after the event, if for no other reason than to avoid being accidentally scratched by it. What would be more natural than to fling it far into the bay? A few hours underwater would wash away the poison, and it is unlikely that anyone would stumble upon it before it was covered by the shifting sand.'

'So it is hopeless,' I cried, gesturing towards the bay. 'The object must be completely lost out there under water.'

'Not necessarily,' he replied, consulting his pocket watch. 'The tide is now at its low mark and the water is quite clear. Conditions are perfect for spotting sunken murder weapons. While I scan the seabed from out there, I suggest you see what you can from the shoreline.'

Holmes strode off towards the changing rooms, from which he appeared a few minutes later wearing a black full-length swimming costume, no doubt the 'supplies' he had purchased the night before.

Handing me his carpet bag, he waded into the water, eyes cast downward, scanning the sandy bottom of the seabed. He began to swim around the bay, following what was evidently a planned pattern, while I peered into the shallows from the comfort of the foreshore, not really certain what I was looking for. All the time I was struggling with the singular notion of Sherlock Holmes swimming, a skill that I had never known him to possess, or even to discuss.

Perhaps an hour later he emerged dripping onto the beach, disappointment written boldly upon his face. 'Nothing, Watson,' he cried. 'I found nothing. And without the murder weapon our case is lost.'

Ten minutes later Holmes had changed back into his street clothes and we turned wearily in the direction of the Manly wharf. 'I assume you found nothing yourself, Watson.' he said.

'Regrettably not,' I replied. 'Merely a handful of small seashells and a dead fish.'

We trudged a few more steps before Holmes suddenly halted and spun round in the direction we had come. 'A dead fish,' he said. 'Only the one?'

'Yes, just one. The shoreline is remarkably pristine for being such a popular place.'

Holmes's eyes lit up with the familiar energy of the sleuth-hound on the track. 'Pray, where was it?'

'In a small tidal pool on the western edge of the baths,' I replied, completely nonplussed. 'About fifty yards off the beach.'

Suddenly Holmes was running back towards the baths, tossing a 'Wait here!' over his shoulder. When he returned a few moments later his entire demeanour had completely altered. There was a decided spring in his step and he whistled as he walked.

'Wonderful observation, Watson,' he chuckled. 'A dead fish, indeed.'

'Holmes, what is this all about?' I asked.

Holmes flashed an enigmatic smile. 'All will be revealed very soon, my friend. All will be revealed.'

THE VALET ANSWERED our knock at the front door of *Guwara* in a state of great agitation. 'What is it, James?' asked Holmes.

'The octopus is missing,' he blurted out. 'I don't understand it,' he exclaimed as he ushered us into the drawing room. 'This afternoon I went up to Mr Demears' office to retrieve some papers for Mrs Demears. As you might understand, the blue-ringed octopus was very much on my mind and I glanced across to the cabinet that held the master's preserved specimen. To my utter astonishment, it was no longer there. I searched the office thoroughly, but it has completely disappeared.'

'When did you last see it?' Holmes asked.

'I cannot be sure, sir,' said James after a moment's thought. 'It is not as if I note its presence every day. I am almost certain it was in place a month ago. The family had just returned from a week down the south coast, and Mr Demears commented to me that he had seen one such creature at the shore near Wollongong.'

'So the jar could have been removed at any time within the past four weeks,' Holmes observed. 'Who had access to the office during that time?'

'A great many people, I fear. In addition to the family members and the servants, Mr Demears had taken to conducting business meetings in his office here. It is a large room with an arrangement of table and chairs suitable for the purpose.'

'And were Mr Ferguson or Mr Marks present at meetings during this period?'

'Why, yes. Each of them attended at least one meeting here in recent weeks.'

'Thank you, James,' said Holmes. 'I believe we can now reveal the conclusion of this case. Is there a telephone here in the house?'

James indicated that there was.

'Then do be good enough to call the police station in Hunter Street in the city and ask Detective Inspector Wade to come round with a constable on an urgent matter. When you have done that, inform your mistress that we wish to speak with her.'

The man departed, evidently puzzled and still very much in a state of nervous excitement.

We were soon joined by Emma Demears, wearing a dark grey house dress. She was followed by her brooding brother, Wallace, who appeared in no better mood than when we had last seen him.

James made to retire, but Holmes called him back. 'With your permission, Mrs Demears, I would prefer if James remained with us. The matter bears on him as well.'

'What have you discovered about my husband's death?' she asked eagerly.

'I believe we can offer a satisfactory explanation,' said Holmes.

'It is as I feared, then,' she said, the tension evident in her voice. 'It was murder.'

'Unhappily, it was,' said Holmes. 'Let me attempt, in my own way, to reconstruct recent events.'

We all took up chairs near the window, while James remained standing by the door. Holmes leaned back and steepled his fingers. 'In the past year, those close to Arthur Demears noted a marked change in his behaviour. His mental faculties began to fail. His judgement faltered and he became more erratic, more arbitrary in his decisions. He developed an *idée fixe*, an ill-considered plan to acquire his rival, Pengelly & Sons. His fellow directors began to question the wisdom of his continued management of Demears & Co.

'At the same time, he lost his habitual even temper. He would fly into fits of rage at the slightest provocation, berate his peers, his servants and his employees. He became cold and harsh with you, Mrs Demears, and your children. Finding the situation intolerable, one of his victims determined that the only solution was to end his life.

'To accomplish this act, the killer needed to confront Demears alone, but there were few opportunities to do so. Demears was a very public man, surrounding himself with business colleagues during the day and evening. At home his family and the servants were always present. His only solitary hours were during his daily swim at Little Manly Cove. There were unlikely to be any witnesses to a confrontation at that early hour, but nevertheless one could not risk a blatant attack upon the man, an act of violence that might draw someone's attention.

'The perfect solution was poison, a silent killer that mimicked the effects of the blue-ringed octopus venom, making his death seem a simple matter of mischance. But how to administer it? The weapon was this.'

With a flourish, Holmes held up a small silver finger-ring. The large, central gem had been removed from its setting and the clasp bent open, forming a circle of sharp points.

'A gaudy but no doubt inexpensive and easily acquired piece of costume jewellery,' he continued. 'After removing the gem, the killer dipped the clasp points into the poison and slipped it carefully onto a finger. The killer approached Demears on Tuesday morning at the baths under some pretext. It was a simple matter of turning the ring around so the points were on the palm side, then pressing Demears' hand in greeting or farewell, piercing it with the poisoned spikes. I need not point out that this could only have been accomplished by someone who was intimate with the victim, someone who could approach him closely without raising alarm.

'Within minutes Demears was paralysed, falling into the water, completely unable to move or even to breathe. The killer scraped the victim's palms with a sharp rock to mask the puncture wounds, then decanted the preserved octopus, which had been brought along as a diversion for the detectives, from its jar into a convenient tidal pool, trusting that the sea water would dilute the odour of the alcohol. Then, as Arthur Demears died in agony, fully awake and alert but completely unable to breathe, the killer calmly walked away.'

'Mr Holmes!' gasped James, staring at the ring. 'How did you know that such an infernal device existed?'

'When we examined Mr Demears' body, Watson and I observed a circle of tiny punctures upon his left hand, a mark that exactly matches the open clasp of this ring.'

Wallace Greenbriar was looking at the ring with an expression of horror upon his face. 'But where in heaven's name did you find it?' he cried.

'I found it where I expected to find it,' Holmes replied. Then turning to me, he added, 'With the able assistance of my good friend, Dr Watson.

'I knew that the killer would most probably try to dispose of the ring by tossing it into the water. So Watson and I returned to Little Manly Cove this morning at low tide, determined to take advantage of the clear, shallow water to search for it. Regrettably, we failed to find any relevant object upon the seabed. I began to fear that the killer had hidden it elsewhere.

'But Watson demonstrated his remarkable powers of observation, spying a small, dead fish in one of the rock pools. This fish, in fact.' Holmes thrust his hand into the pocket of his overcoat, pulling out the fish, about nine inches long, that I had earlier seen by the bay. A distinct marine odour pervaded the room and Holmes's intimate audience recoiled in their seats.

'As you can see, there are no marks of violence upon its body. How could it have died, I wondered, and why was it the only dead fish in the area? I then recalled our first visit to the cove yesterday, watching the fish jumping out of the water to snare the insects that hovered near the surface. That in turn reminded me that fish are attracted to sudden flashes of light in the water, any of which may represent a fortuitous meal. Assuming it was small and metallic, our deadly weapon striking the surface would have appeared to a passing fish to be just such a temptation. And indeed, a few minutes with my jack knife just now revealed this very ring lodged in the belly of this alert but unfortunate creature. In swallowing the ring, it was scratched by the open clasp and killed immediately by the residual poison upon it. The tides did the rest, pushing the body into one of the tidal pools.'

Holmes stood suddenly and turned towards Mrs Demears. 'I fancy you may have seen a flash of silver, madam,' he said, 'as the doomed fish took your bait.'

Mrs Demears paled. 'What are you suggesting?' she cried, rising to confront my friend. 'I loved my husband. I would never have harmed him.'

Holmes faced her squarely. 'Perhaps not the Arthur Demears you once knew and loved. But he had become a fool and a monster. You feared that he would stupidly destroy his long-established company and with it the wealth and the comfort to which you are accustomed.'

'That is ridiculous!' she cried. 'You think I am so mercenary as to kill my husband for money?'

'That and more, I am afraid. You and your family lived in fear of his tempers. He even struck you, Mrs Demears.'

At this, the lady's hand flew to her mouth and a look of horror suffused her face. 'How… can you say such things?' she gasped.

'When you came to us yesterday, you had concealed a recent bruise around your eye with an artful application of cosmetics. Others may perhaps have missed it in the dim light, but I am adept at observing such details. I can see it plainly even now.

'As you watched your husband's irreversible decline, you determined that there was only one course of action open to you. You resolved to kill him. You lacked the strength to overcome him physically and could not risk employing an agent to perform the deed for you.

'On a trip to Brazil with your husband, you learned about an alkaloid that the natives use in hunting, dipping their arrows into the poisonous tar of a local vine. It was curare, viciously effective even in small amounts, paralysing the entire body including the respiratory muscles, killing within minutes. Just as, you recalled from your husband's earlier warning, did the venom of the blue-ringed octopus.

'You acquired a quantity of curare in South America and, upon your return to Australia, devised this method of administering it,' he said, holding up the ring.

Mrs Demears pointed an accusing finger at my friend. 'Your attack on my character is highly offensive, Mr Holmes. You should aim your suspicions at more credible suspects such as the directors of Demears or Pengelly.'

'I had, of course, considered those possibilities. One might point out that the ring is too small for a man's hand. Its use would have been impractical unless the killer could actually slip it onto a finger. But there is a more compelling piece of evidence that points uniquely at you.

'Once I had identified the murder weapon beyond question, I needed to reconstruct the method. If a man had wanted to scratch another man's palm with his ring, he would have put the ring on his right hand and then offered it to shake the victim's hand. This would have left punctures on the victim's right hand. But the little circle of punctures marked the palm of Mr Demears' left hand, as Watson and I observed. There is no natural circumstance in which a man will clasp the left hand of another man, in particular a business associate. So your husband's colleagues and business rivals could not have killed him in this way.

'In bidding her husband farewell, however, a woman will naturally hold out both hands in an affectionate invitation to her husband to grasp them. The ring on her right hand would have thus scratched his left hand. Mrs Demears, your husband's killer could only have been you.'

Impressed as I was with Holmes's deductions, I remained troubled by a small doubt. 'If Mrs Demears was staying with her aunt in… Freshwater,' I asked, 'how could she have done this foul deed? Surely her aunt can account for her movements.'

Holmes turned to James. 'In service the greatest sin is to bear witness against your masters, but I must remind you that if you do not answer my questions truthfully now, it will go badly for you with the police later.'

James gave a small nervous nod, and Holmes continued. 'How long is the walk from Aunt Beatrice's place at Freshwater to Little Manly Cove?'

'About an hour,' replied James, his voice barely above a whisper.

'Does Aunt Beatrice live alone, with no servants?'

'Yes.'

'And does she suffer from profound deafness?'

'Yes.'

'And is she an exceptionally sound and late sleeper?'

'Yes.'

'As I suspected. So then, Watson, I see no impediment to Mrs Demears arising in the pre-dawn hours, walking to the baths to arrive just after seven, killing her husband as I have discussed, and then returning to Freshwater, all without her aunt's knowledge.'

Mrs Demears swayed and dropped heavily back onto the chair. The room was deathly quiet except for her sobs. A knock at the front door echoed through the house.

'That will be Detective Inspector Wade, I expect,' said Holmes brightly. He turned to the open-mouthed, wide-eyed James. 'Best to let them in, I think.'

'I AM STILL puzzled about one thing, Holmes,' I said, relighting my cigar back in our sitting room at Petty's later that evening. 'Wasn't Mrs Demears taking an enormous risk in raising the question of murder with you, practically daring you to catch her? Particularly as the police had considered no other cause of death but happenstance.'

Holmes gazed at the fire and tapped the ashes from his pipe. 'As long as James persisted in questioning the verdict, she could never be at peace. At some time in the future his agitations might give the police pause. The best way to lay all doubts to rest was to set a highly regarded and adept hound upon the trail.' Here he smiled modestly. 'If someone as capable as I were to fail to dislodge the elaborate fiction she had created involving the blue-ringed octopus, then James and his theory could be dismissed for good. And of course she was an impressive woman, a clever actress, and supremely self-confident.'

'A rare compliment from you, indeed. But she was no match for the great Sherlock Holmes,' I replied.

'I seek not greatness, Watson. I seek merely the truth,' he replied, sniffing the air. 'Now if you would, please ring for the boy and have him send my coat out for cleaning.'

THE DIRRANBANDI STATION MYSTERY

Christopher Sequeira

THERE WAS MORE than one matter my good friend Mr Sherlock Holmes was asked to look into in the year 1890, during the time we were in the Australian state of Queensland. These included the hideous affair of the Drowned General, the singular business of the Invisible Machete – where Holmes saved a man's life through a recently acquired knowledge of vulcanology – and the baffling ordeal of the Toowoomba Monster. Additionally, I have made special arrangements to separately secure my notes and ephemera relating to Holmes's examination of the controversial case of the strychnine murder of Albert Hyde and the consequent trial of his wife, Elizabeth, at Ipswich for that crime, and I have stipulated the records of that matter must remain sealed for a period of some decades.

One case, however, which I do believe worthy of public disclosure nearer to the time of my recording it, is an investigation that allowed me to see Holmes deal with some of his own limitations.

Holmes and I had taken up residence for a time at the National Hotel in Queen Street in Queensland's capital city, Brisbane. Weeks earlier the city had experienced catastrophic flooding and storms, yet with incredible industry and organisation the citizenry had worked to set the place to rights, and most services and activities had returned to normal. There was, however, a fairly steady stream of carpenters and repair workers bustling about our hotel, with frequent arrivals of replacement items for water-damaged fittings, so traffic in the hotel was common.

Into this tableau there appeared early one day a thin, loose-limbed gentleman, taller even than Holmes, dressed in the attire of the country farmer or landholder: 'wide-awake' hat, boots, a dusty, creased suit, and a small bag under his arm. He appeared about thirty-five years of age, and was a clean-shaven, sharp-eyed specimen.

'Mr Sherlock Holmes, is it? I am Joseph Patrick McCarthy, of the town of Dirranbandi, and I've come to ask for your help, sir,' he said.

Holmes greeted the man and ushered him to a chair.

'Be seated, Mr McCarthy. You may say anything in front of my associate, Dr John Watson that you would to me. I fancy the demands you face running a livestock station are burdensome enough without having to contend with criminal problems, and the added frustration of an unsupportive local police.'

McCarthy actually started up out of his chair, and stood staring at Holmes with half-clenched fists and an open mouth, as if my friend were a nightmare incarnate sprouted from a fitfully slumbering brain. For the first time in several weeks I also was similarly surprised. I had come to think that my years of exposure to Holmes's extraordinary deductive capabilities had taught me to understand and thus emulate and anticipate his methods to a degree, but faced with the local differences in dress, speech, occupations and other aspects of life I could seldom discern a man's recent history from his appearance here. Holmes had clearly adjusted far more quickly to the newer environment.

'Who told you of my troubles?' stammered McCarthy. 'Was it that blasted, interfering parson, O'Brien?'

'Calm yourself, sir,' said Holmes soothingly. 'I had never heard of Dirranbandi before you uttered the name, nor has any person conversed with me about you or your plight, but your appearance tells me all I need know. Your trousers betray a shiny pattern of wear in patches on the legs that only a man who sits astride a horse for many hours a day sustains. Your complexion and the condition of your hands make plain you have lived and worked years in the outdoors. The fragment of fluff in your right cuff looks very much to me like recently shorn wool. Your arrival at this time suggests a long train trip begun early this morning, long enough for you to have brought the lunch that you carried in your bag. Ergo, a man of the land, not of the city, of an establishment where livestock is kept. My current presence here is largely known of only by law enforcement professionals – and for you to have asked one of them for help means the official forces will not aid you. That you are the man responsible for running the business you work at follows from the rest – who else would feel the need to vacate from the job for several days to resolve a matter, and who else would be permitted to do so?'

McCarthy scratched his head, then grinned and slapped his thigh.

'Well, sir, I can now see why the circuit magistrate at St George had a quiet word and sent me in your direction – one of his legal brethren had heard of your work and said you might be a man to aid me. Your head is certainly fit for far more than keeping your hat on, by Jingo!' said McCarthy.

'Let me explain what my problem is. I'm the head sherang at what was originally named Gillen Station, at Dirranbandi, in the state's south-west near the border with New South Wales, though some just call it Dirranbandi Station nowadays. It's a tiny town, we have, sir, only named five years ago. More folk probably come and go at Gillen or one of the other of several sheep and cattle stations in the district than do in the township itself, as those livestock stations have been in the area a long while. Still, Dirranbandi town has now got a general store, a hotel and a post office, but there's no rail yet any closer than St George at some hours' ride away, so all travel is by horse, bullock or shank's pony, if you're truly game.'

Our guest smiled and continued. 'The notion that there was a criminal element in the area actually began five months back when a Cobb & Co coach with three passengers was held up at gunpoint by a sole masked bandit riding a white horse, on a road up from New South Wales that passes about ten miles out of town. The report was well remarked upon because witnesses spoke of how, after a cursory examination of the customers' meagre valuables, the thief absconded with only the driver's travel schedule and papers.

'There was talk that perhaps the thief planned to impersonate a driver later, but since the route began and ended miles away such matters didn't worry Dirranbandi folk too long.

'But a new criminal problem began when townsfolk started reporting a rash of house burglaries. Someone was sneaking into homes and stealing items;

silverware, jewellery and the like, things too significant to have been misplaced, no question about it. But they were only stealing one or two items at a time, not ransacking a place.

'My wife herself, Genevieve, was out one day and returned to find a large, gilt-framed painting given her by her mother was gone. We were puzzled, because there was a valuable brooch in the same room a thief could have taken, but didn't. Nonetheless that frame was worth more coin, certainly.

'A town meeting was called to take place at the Dirranbandi Hotel, run by Rex Chalmers and his wife, Dorothy. Postmaster Donald Hoff was there; the town clerk, Frederick Simms; our district's parish priest, Father O'Brien, who was in town making his rounds; farmer John Cripps; and my lead stockman, Harry McCulloch, as well as several others. It was agreed to organise a joint appeal to the nearest police station at St George, near sixty mile away.'

Holmes interjected. 'I am assuming no one witnessed a theft personally, or had a description of a thief or thieves, or else you would have already said so, Mr McCarthy?'

'You are correct, sir. No one had seen an intruder, but with so many of these folk busy with work and with normally no need to lock one's house in such a remote habitat, the thieves, regrettably, had easy opportunity to break into a dwelling. The one or two places that had actually been locked had been fairly easy gotten into, via a window.

'I don't mind saying – there was tension in the hotel at the meeting. Some suspicion was levelled at me and my workers, for my crew includes, from time to time, some – well, let's be straight with the talk – itinerant labourers with far from spotless pasts. There was also a little annoyance that the state government had refused previous letters asking that a salaried police constable's position be created in Dirranbandi, and the clerk, Frederick Simms was questioned rather severely, I thought, as to whether he had done his job and supported such requests to the government people. I understood why townspeople were anxious about that, for, with the nearest constable at St George, we often didn't even see him after a burglary for a week or two. We've still been cleaning up after our floods this season, just like the city folk here – though our problem was the Balonne River – so I understand why the St George constable wasn't more prompt. But you can imagine how folk might not think of that when it's their goods that've been nicked – um, stolen, that is.

'I'm a practical man, and not one to waste time when people get their gall up, so I let most of the nonsense-talk at the meeting slide, but I near had to box Chalmers' ears for a smart remark he made about my workers. Truth, there's been many a barny, a fight, at the hotel since the trouble began; hot feelings about the thefts are usually at the bottom of the tussles. I worry a bit that we won't ever become a proper town at this rate, sometimes.'

McCarthy paused then, and squeezed his hat in his long hands.

'There's one more thing, and I do hesitate to mention it. After the line of talk about the bushranger holding up the coach, Mary Davis, a rather… eccentric woman who's long been a local and now also helps out at the hotel, put it about that the district has become a "safe haven for bushrangers and bandits of every stripe", and that this has secretly always been the case, since the Ned Kelly Gang used to hide in the town of Hebel, ten year back and ten mile away! Mary said there'd been sightings of other notorious villains such as Captain Starlight and his colleague Warrigal; and Stingaree, the monocled bandit; and others as well.

'Now, normally one would take anything Mary said with a grain of salt, but my man, Harry McCulloch, was riding back to town four weeks ago and almost collided with a man on a white horse! The fellow turned and Harry swears he was masked. The stranger was not to be trifled with, and like a flash of lightning he snared Harry's arm with a stock-whip lash! Harry was pulled from his horse to the ground, the colt sent running and Harry had to walk to town, very much shaken, whilst the mystery man rode off who knows where.'

'Was your man robbed?' asked Holmes, sharply, although he remained tilted back in his chair, fingers steepled and eyes closed.

'No, sir, and the masked fellow said not a word, apparently, but whistled a jaunty tune as he sped off. Harry's horse came into town on its own ahead of him, and I believe my man, although it is a curious tale, it is.'

Holmes opened his eyes, sat upright and shifted in his chair, then leaned towards McCarthy and gazed at him intently. 'And now, sir, the incident that propelled you here. For thus far we have anecdotes of weeks past, of no pressing urgency, things you and your fellow Dirranbandi residents had come to terms with. What happened to change your priorities?'

McCarthy nodded grimly.

'Mr Holmes, you do fathom things. What happened is that one of my station hands, Douglas Kent, has gone missing two days ago. Douglas was not well liked by the others, I'll admit – he was considered somewhat lazy – but we are not talking about a labourer simply gone and disappeared before his shift and then gossipers speaking ill of him, oh no. For the room the man was sleeping in is splattered with blood, and I feel the man has been injured – nay, likely murdered. It is just a bunkhouse room, with no stick of furniture, but there are signs of a fight, and the blood includes a trail as if a body has been dragged out of that room! Furthermore, I know Douglas had one item of value in the world, a gold watch of his grandfather's, so I wondered if the town thief came after that watch, and perhaps Douglas and he fought, and then, well…' McCarthy's voice trailed off.

The silence was short lived. Holmes was up from his chair and almost pulled McCarthy to his feet with a vigorous handshake.

'Mr McCarthy, I shall take your case, if transportation and lodgings can be provided, and I see little reason to delay. Watson and I can return with you; a couple of carpetbags holding a shirt or two and a large parcel of some of the excellent tobacco I have been able to obtain in Brisbane will be all I require. While the good doctor and I have seen some of your fascinating country, I must admit the south-west of this state has not yet been a part of our excursions.'

As much as I could have chided Holmes for committing me to participate in a long, hot, possibly pointless journey to a remote town, there wasn't the slightest doubt I would also go to Dirranbandi.

THE TRIP WAS, as it turned out, more trying for Holmes than for myself, as my friend always struggled with extremes of heat less easily than with cold; whereas my days on the Asian continent and an earlier period in Australia had made me most familiar with the climate.

The railway took us most of the way, into the state's south, and then it was horse and cart to Gillen, or Dirranbandi Station as it was called, but we passed through the town of Dirranbandi itself in doing so. Holmes insisted we not stop and instead go straight to the sheep station and the missing man's quarters rather than orient ourselves to the village and its few shops and businesses. I agreed with his judgement. On the admittedly very remote chance that after all this time a missing man was perhaps not dead but lying injured in whereabouts unknown, the priority was a sensible enough one.

The property was a vast, largely flat acreage, and a long, single-storey house served as the main residence and office, with various buildings set behind this for stables, dormitories, dining and other functions.

McCarthy introduced us to the lead man, McCulloch, a thick-necked, red-faced fellow of about forty, with a great mass of beard and sandy hair under a hat that seemed jammed to his head. McCulloch eyed us closely, with what I perceived as hostility, but he seemed to relax a trifle when McCarthy gave him a frown and shake of the head.

We were taken along a simple pathway to a dormitory, really only a great shed with the thinnest of wooden walls. Once inside we could see from vacant mattresses that most of the men bunked in one large chamber; but a few corner spaces had their own 'rooms', partitioned off, some with doors. We went to the last one of these, a prized spot that McCarthy told us the missing man had been offered because he snored so atrociously the other men insisted he sleep as far removed from them as possible.

The minute we entered I feared the worst for the vanished man, this Douglas Kent, and could see why McCarthy had decided to get more serious help than wait a week for a constable to find time to come down from the nearest police post.

The humble little room that we walked into through a flimsy door contained a mattress and pillow, and a travelling bag lay on the floor. A small metal biscuit tin was open and empty, save for some spent matches and cigarette fragments in it, and this lay near the head of the mattress.

Splatters of bright red blood, however, overpowered all other impressions of this dully whitewashed chamber.

The blood was predominantly in a large sprayed stain on one wall, at a height of five or so feet from the floor, and drip-marked down. There were lesser splatters and drops here and there in the vicinity of the main mark, and a pool of dried blood was noticeable adjacent to the second door that opened to the outside. There was no mistaking the trail of blood in that door's threshold indeed resembled marks that might have been made by someone dragging a large object or person's body over and out to the exterior of the dormitory.

Holmes studied the room, the walls and the doorframe, and then carefully pushed the door open and followed the stains outside. Here he began that hound-like process I knew well: stooping down to clues, bouncing from trace to trace, examining minor elements with his magnifying lens as he tracked impressions to a dirt pathway that extended back into the exterior of the property. McCarthy, McCulloch and I accompanied my friend's rapid, darting movements as he followed the spoor.

Holmes's efforts halted at a huge, long horse trough of water. He studied this intently and examined the grass and pathways all around it.

Holmes spoke agitatedly. 'Our quarry made use of this; excess blood was washed thoroughly away here. In addition, there is such a random proliferation of very recent horse tracks made by animals brought to drink here – it has been near three days, after all – that they have obliterated what bloodless impressions I might have been able to make use of. Let me return to that room, then, as I fear it is all I have as an indicator of the fate of its missing occupant.'

Back in the room, Holmes now re-examined every square inch of the location, inspected and kept a cigarette end and a loose clump of dirt from the travelling bag, and after a time he simply paused, staring at the grim surroundings.

'Note carefully,' he said to me in a low voice I was sure was not meant to be heard by McCulloch and McCarthy outside. 'Those blood stains on the wall are more significant than these trails on the floor in allowing us to understand what became of our man.'

My initial response was, I must say, confusion; for I could tell nothing other than that some form of violence had caused a man to lose precious blood. Then I studied the marks and was stricken by a feeling of disturbing familiarity; but, as a man who'd seen blood aplenty, including his own on a desert battlefield, I simply could not recall the details of a specific occasion where a scene matched this one.

I indicated my failure to draw further conclusions to Holmes, who nodded then bade me move to the doorway, and then he stood alone in the room a moment or two. Suddenly he stooped and studied a fragment of twisting fluff and cotton that looked similar to the material the mattress was made from, and he then even inspected the piece with his lens. Asking me to check to make completely sure that we were not observed from the doorway, Holmes sprang at the mattress and began to prod and poke it – and then he grinned and waved me over as he slipped a hand into a practically invisible slit made in the mattress's seams. With a small effort he extracted a shining gold watch! He put the timepiece into his pocket and silenced me with a gesture.

We emerged from the room and Holmes advised McCarthy and McCulloch that we would follow the pathways from the dormitory to seek further evidence of the flight of the wounded – or the transport of the dead man – but that we were pessimistic of success. We walked alone into the sprawling acres of the property.

Once we were away from other ears Holmes spoke, a tone of certainty in his voice. 'Watson, I have little doubt that a prone, likely dead if not on the verge of dying, man was carried from that room and then deposited elsewhere. The person possibly sought a pathway via the horse trough purposefully, and may have not only washed the worst of revealing blood away but also transferred the body to a tarpaulin or other device that kept the blood from continuing a trail beyond that point. But there is a more prominent reason the blood splatters do not continue profusely; a reason a medical man like yourself might imagine. And *this* clue might provide you the data you need to complete the conjecture.' So saying, he handed me one of the cigarette ends from Kent's tin, which I studied carefully.

There was a tiny amount of dried blood on the end that would have lain upon a man's lips.

I stared at my friend and memories of hospital wards from my earliest days as a physician flooded into my mind. I recalled blood-sprays such as we had seen in Kent's room, and understanding dawned. I slowly nodded my head and instinctively lowered my voice.

'The man's body was spouting blood, then stopped, which means either a wound was completely staunched, or… there was no wound. My lord, Holmes, the blood spray on that wall; the pattern of that – he was expelling that blood himself, violently coughing!'

'Indeed. A serious lung disease of some kind; tuberculosis, mayhap. I chance Douglas Kent's reputation for laziness may have been related to weakness as his health faded.'

'So, Holmes, the marks on the door threshold, they still look every bit as though a man or large thing was *dragged* out of that room. Was Kent dragging something through his own blood stains, or was someone dragging Kent?'

'Watson, you saw the man's room, and the beds of the others who inhabit the dormitory. These workers own nothing large enough to be dragged across a doorway and leave such marks as we found. No, the presumption that best fits the facts is closest to McCarthy's own: that Kent was carted out of the room after blood was spilt – the difference we theorise is that the blood's origin lies not in assault, but disease.

'Let us suppose, simply, that Kent was one of a group of thieves plaguing Dirranbandi – it might even be that there were only two of them. Thief One goes to meet Thief Two, Kent, and finds him expiring, or expired from the final ordeal of his illness, blood sprayed everywhere. Now, at least three hypotheses as to why Thief One dragged Kent away present themselves to me, including the notion that a dying Kent was seen as a risk of some kind.'

'You don't simply think a thief came looking for Kent's watch and stumbled on the dying man, but the man could now identify him, so had to be silenced?' I ventured.

'No, Watson, then simply killing Kent on the spot would have served Mr Thief sufficiently.' Holmes sighed. 'Motives are… not obvious here,' he muttered. 'We should get Mr McCarthy to run us into the town. If a man is to understand the meaning of a series of crimes carried out against a community, it behoves him to obtain a proper understanding of that community.'

JOSEPH MCCARTHY DROVE us in a cart to the hotel. It was a large, wooden building in the narrow main street. We entered through prominent double doors and immediately appreciated the change in temperature from the dusty warmth of the town outside.

McCarthy had arranged for a few locals to be there, and Holmes was introduced to publican Rex Chalmers and his wife Dorothy, long-standing farmer John Cripps, town clerk Frederick Simms and the locum priest, Father O'Brien.

It was clear there was antipathy between McCarthy and the priest, for the station boss could barely look at the minister, while O'Brien, an animated, wiry man with blinking eyes, constantly grinned at the other man in a manner I thought akin to baiting the fellow until I realised – after O'Brien perched a pince-nez atop his nose – that he was near-sighted.

McCarthy explained himself to us, quietly. 'I've never been partial to parsons, and this one rubs me the wrong way. He covers a massive area and so rides in here once a week and thinks that gives him the right to stick his nose in our business – but I don't think he's been any help at all. I want practical help, like a policeman, not some silly feller mumbling parables out of a book, I'm sorry, Mr Holmes, Dr Watson.'

Holmes nodded and raised an eyebrow. 'I suppose you have considered the fact that Father O'Brien might be your thief, have you not?'

McCarthy nervously agreed. 'There's no hiding anything from you, is there, Mr Holmes? Yes, I did suspect him at first – wondered if he might be some sort of fraud, for he's only been newly appointed to the district. But I know for a fact he's not our thief, because my man Harry McCulloch and he were in town here together visiting a sick friend of Harry's when my own wife's picture frame went missing from our house.'

'Well, I should very much like to converse with this fellow, if he's a newcomer to these environs,' said Holmes, and he and I wandered over to where the parson sat.

'Mr Holmes, Dr Watson, I fancy Mr McCarthy is not fond of me, but I do understand; not all men in these parts put their faith in the spiritual, for the challenges they deal with are very material here. As the son of a country schoolteacher I understand that. But, to the problems that trouble this little town; do you wish to hear the thoughts of an itinerant minister?'

Holmes smiled and urged the man on.

O'Brien put his pince-nez away and spoke. 'I have been visiting Dirranbandi for three months intermittently. The thefts have been going on for close to five months, they say. The greatest problem is the fuel these matters give to suspicions and petty grievances, and this boils over into many a skirmish here in the hotel or in fights amongst workers at Gillen or other stations. And this has one particularly troubling side effect –'

'That's enough!' yelled a voice from the other side of the room, halting our conversation. We turned to the commotion.

McCarthy was standing up to the short, barrel-chested town clerk, Frederick Simms. The two looked poised for a fistfight.

McCarthy growled at Simms. 'You'd best simmer down, townie, or I won't be responsible for what happens. My men are my concern, not yours!'

Simms was not deterred. 'Responsible, aye, you are a one for responsibility! This damn thievery can be lain right at Gillen's door. You employ nothing but the bottom of the barrel, I expect you pay them that!'

'Simms, you try my patience sorely. I've got a man missing and I take it serious. Serious enough to employ a professional inquiry agent like Mr Holmes –'

Simms yelled and swept an arm in our direction. 'Employ professionals? For all I know those two dandies are in cahoots with the danged thieves! You constantly ask us to take your word for things, McCarthy, but never a skerrick of truth. One of your men is missing, yes, missing and run off with our danged valuables. Douglas Kent is a complete no-hoper, like the rest of the strays you take in there – it's a damn breeding ground for scoundrels!'

McCarthy's man, Harry McCulloch, had pushed himself to the side of his boss, and I could see his red eyes smoulder above the bushy beard. Almost in reflection, the farmer, John Cripps, a fit-looking fellow, stood alongside Simms.

'Don't be starting something you can't finish, Harry,' said Cripps. 'Fred here's entitled to speak his mind. We've been patient, but you know your men aren't the most honest of sorts. How many times have you been in here yourself and whinged about having to let one go over the last few years?'

McCarthy reddened. 'Exactly! I sometimes have thirty men, and if one plays up, he's gone! Don't you be twisting things, John Cripps! More than one of my crew has helped you when pickings needed to be done.'

I saw the mood of the room, as I'd seen sometimes in army barracks. There was an appetite for violence here, a desire to witness a physical contest as a distraction from more troubling things. It saddened me and I moved to grab Holmes's shoulder and steer us out of the impending drama.

But like lightning Holmes had moved to the conflict in four long strides, and was now standing between Simms and McCarthy.

'This is not how you solve your problems, gentlemen!' he said authoritatively. 'I have investigated and cleared over three hundred cases of capital importance in England and Europe, and I give you my word that thanks to Mr McCarthy's request, I will pursue all avenues here to resolve your matter, too.'

I was astonished, for Holmes's completely fearless manner actually seemed to soothe things, as Simms shook his head and stared at my friend, a more measured tone in his voice.

'Oh. I did not realise – three hundred, really sir?'

But my hope was short lived. 'Who died and made you mayor, Pommie?' bellowed Harry McCulloch, and I saw McCarthy's face blanch with that look of regret a person has when they have repeated a mistake; he knew he should have left McCulloch back at the station.

McCulloch had pressed his bearded chin right at Holmes. Several of the men in the room began to cluster about and grunts and snickering laughs told me some would have liked to see Holmes embroiled in a fight.

McCarthy spoke up. 'Harry! The man's on our side, for Pete's sake!'

McCulloch didn't take his eyes off Holmes. 'Is he, Joe, is he? Trying to lord it over us, and knows not a cracker about what we do. Sniffs about poor Doug's doss and can't tell us a damn thing. What use is this toffee-nosed Pom?' And McCulloch swung a fist right at Holmes's face.

Holmes darted back and the blow did not touch him, and a couple of men tried to restrain McCulloch.

Holmes raised his arms into a boxing pose. 'McCulloch, this is a misunderstanding. But please, do not test me. When one has eliminated the imp–' he began. McCulloch broke free of his holders and lashed another knotted palm at my friend's face.

The blow just grazed Holmes's cheek. Then he dodged to one side and with blinding speed he threw a curious, loose-wristed, open-palmed strike at McCulloch's throat; it almost seemed more slap than punch! The man collapsed onto the floor, purple-faced and gasping.

I turned to McCarthy. 'About time we took our leave,' I said. 'Bring McCulloch; I'll treat him back at the station. I've patched up Holmes's messes before today, sir.'

I WILL SPARE my readers the discomfort I suffered on that trip back to the station. Holmes said not a word and the worst of it was I occasionally caught him grinning to himself.

AFTER OUR RETURN to Dirranbandi Station Holmes and I ate a quiet and simple evening meal with McCarthy and his wife. After our repast we sat in cane chairs on the verandah outside the McCarthy residence drinking coffee. McCarthy left us on our own so that he might see to beds for us.

Holmes was troubled. 'I shall admit I am baffled to some degree as to why people might take their anger out on someone trying to help them, Watson. I do understand the townspeople are frayed and confused, for clearly they have put all they have to the considerable challenge of making a life in this part of the country. But why treat us as suspects, when we clearly have no objective but to assist in finding the truth? It is quite irrational.'

I offered an insight. 'I suspect, Holmes, that the true irritant here is that these people don't expect existence here to be easy, but it's the land they thought would be tough and treacherous to deal with, not each other.'

Holmes was silent for some time. Then he spoke again.

'Watson, I fear perhaps I have truly experienced more than a failure born of hubris – I am out of my depth!' My friend's tone disturbed me greatly. Holmes had never counted modesty amongst the virtues, but it is plain truth to say there were barely a handful of occasions in which he had been at an impasse. I could not believe the man who had saved royalty from assassination, recovered looted masterpieces and averted international declarations of war could feel stymied by a small, rural burglary case. Why would this disturb his equilibrium so much?

His next words made all clear to me.

'I am trying to solve what I am least adept at, a social mystery. One taking place in a community I neither understand nor, it must be said, plan to reside in long enough to fully comprehend! Given time I could surely unearth sufficient physical evidence to identify the miscreant here; purely from a technical perspective I might resolve this case. But the swifter progress this matter deserves eludes me because the aspirations and motives these people have for living in this hot, isolated place, when they could be living and working in Brisbane even, I do not fathom! Unlike our British brethren who have generations on the land, as even the Holmes family squires understood, I cannot appreciate the desire to make a home in this stark land, and I struggle to see what our criminal seeks if not financial reward, which you and I know he clearly eschews. Rational deduction, confound it, cannot help a man resolve an illogical scenario, or one that seems irrational because I, with my – forgive me, old fellow – soft-bellied upper-class and educated leanings can't properly conceive of it! Pfah!'

Outbursts of this type were uncommon, but not completely unknown to me in the nine years of my friendship with Holmes. He spoke seldom of family, and I had reasoned that at heart his career of delving into the darker side of humanity had made him judge his early life harshly, as being too removed from the trials and tribulations that make great men make great sacrifices. He once opined that the Holmes family intellect had been given to him and his brother too easily: by nature, not effort. I argued that even if that could be proved true, it was what a person did with their talents that was the measure of them.

I was about to try similar soothing words now, but Holmes carried on speaking.

'Yes. This entire matter makes no sense, and I wonder if I have become befuddled by the heat and dust of this locality, and these folk with their bizarre, twanging accents. I do not truly grasp what life is like in these remote communities, how hard it must be. I have origins of privilege, and dabble in my "pretty little drawing-room murders"; this environment is so incompatible with my professional experience, Watson!'

I had had enough of this self-pity and was determined to steer the conversation in a better direction.

'Holmes, we are what we are, and if you are a fish out of water here, well, no man is more capable of learning to walk on land than you, if I may make a terrible hash of a metaphor. Do not give up. I recall I myself struggled in India and Afghanistan at different times, with the alien environments and cultures, the weather. I had my own awakenings there, discovering that even though I was an army man, that a man is just a man in dust and heat – a uniform counts for nothing, it doesn't always get the respect one anticipated. But I know you will persevere.' I concluded my words and did not prod my friend for a response at that moment.

I silently gazed out at the night sky. It was restive and inspiring, that amazing expanse, and as Holmes had made no reply to my comments I assumed he too was lost in self-contemplation. However, when I turned to him I discovered he was staring fixedly at me, not at the night sky, one hand resting on his chin, an unlit pipe twirling in the other.

'What is it, Holmes?' I asked, seeing that I, not our quiet rural surroundings, was the object of his current attention.

'I have formed a hypothesis,' he said. 'In the morning we must return to Brisbane for a few days, and I needs make inquiries with some institutions.'

'Whatever you think is necessary, of course,' I said.

He smiled. 'I shall be frustratingly close-mouthed about my activities, old friend. I dare say you will find that to be annoying, so let me say in advance, by way of recompense, I have you to thank for stimulating my mind to progressive paths in this case.'

It was my turn to demonstrate a sampling of witty badinage.

'Why thank you, Holmes, I am sure you will be proved correct. And that I *will* find this annoying.'

WE RETIRED TO bed in a comfortable guest room. I admit to falling asleep immediately. The last thing I expected was to have Holmes awaken me in the still of the night, a dark lantern in hand. 'Get dressed, quickly and quietly, not a word, not a word,' he said.

I did as he instructed and we noiselessly stepped through the darkened house and out to the verandah and then out to the back of the house.

The expanse of the property was moonlit and clear, and it was warm enough that I scarcely needed a coat. Holmes was following a dirt path away from the dormitories. I saw masses of rusted metal and realised we were entering a portion of the land for disused and broken equipment. A few small lean-to sheds covered in piles of broken wooden barrels and other waste covered the surrounding area. There was the stench of old chemicals; I suspected paints and oils and perhaps sheep-dipping materials might have been disposed of here.

Finally Holmes approached one shed almost completely missing its tin roof, took hold of a large broken barrel blocking its front, and swung the barrel on its base, revealing a door. He opened that door and leading with his lantern he waved me in silently.

The moonlight beamed above us through the half-roof, revealing an old tin travelling trunk dominating a pile of odds and ends somewhat the worse for wear due to the elements being able to get at them. On closer inspection I saw that this was not a pile of refuse, but a cache of the missing items from the town. Here was a gilt frame, there an antique vase, here a gold brooch! I was shocked.

Then Holmes silently pointed to the trunk and opened its lid.

Inside was the pitiably folded body of a small man, the front of his clothes covered in blood.

AT HOLMES'S WHISPERED urgings we left all as it was in that miserable rubbish dump, deciding to proceed with our trip to Brisbane; Holmes assured me it was essential and the evidence here needed to wait. We returned to the house, and if McCarthy or his wife realised we had been out, nought was said the next morning. We were taken to the station and only then, when we were alone, did we discuss the matter.

'Watson, I could not sleep. For I had decided that the crimes were not committed for the profit in the items, but to perhaps cause disquiet in the town, and your words last night inspired new lines of thought around a motive. This in turn led me to a possibility; the disappearance of Kent might be opportunism – the chance to create further unrest and concern by having a person announced as missing, rather than his death being a sad but ordinary passing due to illness.

'If the removal of Kent lay in opportunity, lay in chance, then I formed the view that the body might not have been taken far, and might not even be well concealed. I wandered the property for two hours before I made my discovery then returned and woke you.

'And this made our planned trip back to the capital city more urgent than before. It is my hope that research here will provide all we need to complete our case.'

HOLMES AND I arrived at Brisbane late in the evening and resumed our rooms at the National Hotel. Holmes left early the next day and by some peripheral comments he made about certain tobacconists and men's shirt suppliers, it was clear he'd frequented both the banking district and the government offices of the city. There were further outings by him the next day, but that second evening he returned humming a classical tune that was familiar, although I could not place it, and he announced that we had train tickets already booked to return us to the south-west again. A four-piece was performing in the city that evening and Holmes remarked that we were deserving of a recreational diversion, and I could not disagree. We ate a quick meal at the hotel and attended the concert. I watched Holmes recline in his chair during the show and wave his fingers about and was certain of one thing. He had solved the case.

THE JOURNEY BACK to Dirranbandi was tiring this time and both of us dozed repeatedly on the train at the foremost part of the trip. But once we alighted at St George there was no doubting, by evidence of Holmes's fevered cracking of knuckles and reflexive rubbing of hands, that he was eager for the denouement of this matter.

WHEN WE RETURNED to Dirranbandi it was directly to the Dirranbandi Hotel, where Joseph McCarthy had been wired to meet us. Holmes spoke with Simms, the clerk, as well as Chalmers, the publican, and our client, McCarthy, and he surprised them all with a proclamation that I had no inkling he was able to make.

Holmes advised them to summon all the townsfolk to a public meeting that very evening because Holmes had been told by government officials whom he'd met with in Brisbane that the authorities planned to install a policeman in the town; and Holmes would also announce where the investigation of burglaries and the missing man must next traverse, for he and I were now finished with it, having passed our findings to the government.

HOLMES WAS INFURIATINGLY taciturn as the townsfolk of Dirranbandi assembled at the hotel. He would reveal none of his thoughts and simply studied a local agricultural gazette that was in the hotel. I knew this meant that the gathering of interested parties was part of his plan to criminally implicate a guilty person; for not only could Holmes never resist an opportunity for a theatrical revelation of a case's findings, but also the way his eyes surreptitiously scanned every entrant to the meeting told me he was looking for an exhibition of behaviour that betrayed weakness.

My theories were verified as soon as Holmes began to address the assembly.

'Ladies and gentlemen, I very dearly regret to inform you that the government of the state will not be creating a position of police constable for Dirranbandi, despite my announcement earlier today. For I have persuaded them, personally, *not* to!'

There was an audible gasp and one or two people jumped to their feet. But Holmes waved them back to their chairs.

'No, all of you. I have deemed a police presence in this township unnecessary, and conveyed that view to the government. The missing man, Douglas Kent, is not dead, I am convinced; he is just a foolish, indigent vagrant who has clearly left the district for softer climes. There is no need to investigate his disappearance, nor the petty thefts he undoubtedly was responsible for – that is, responsible for in those instances where the items in fact haven't simply been misplaced,' Holmes said with an acid, grating tone.

I do believe this is the only occasion in which I witnessed an unruly crowd start to foment a view that involved tarring and feathering my friend. Then a loud, calm voice intervened.

'You must have good reason for that action, sir, surely!' said Simms, the town clerk. 'I have been over to Joe McCarthy's place, and there was blood in that room, a lot of it! Sure looks like something awful happened to Doug Kent!'

'A virulent nosebleed is what the unfortunate Douglas Kent probably experienced, I dare say,' said Holmes. 'Not a cause deserving of having constables charge down from St George, nor the government allocate precious monies to inquiry.'

Now the farmer, Cripps, stood forth and waved a finger at Holmes. Where Simms was measured, Cripps was furious.

'Are you mad, sir? This town is suffering; we've had the floods, we've had the worst yields, and now the thefts and this man, Kent! Not to mention the dashed bushrangers – maybe one of them took Kent, perhaps in a fight for spoils! No, you haven't solved anything, Mr High-and-Mighty-Detective. Charlatan! We're not going to stand for this, sir, we are not!'

'AYE! The bushrangers!' roared a loud raspy voice I thought for a few seconds was the product of one of the more leathery men in the room, and was instead astounded to discern the words came from a tiny, grey-haired woman helping behind the bar. 'I warned ye all 'bout 'em, I did, ye fools, ye flamin' fools!' Suffice I say a muttered whisper in the room confirmed for me that this was the famed Mary Davis.

Holmes ignored the interruption and glanced at Cripps, then continued in the languid, uncaring manner that was raising hackles. 'Really, sir, despite your... supporter's *enthusiasm,* I do appreciate your, let's be kind and deem them... *alternative criminal theories*... but I must assert again, there is no cause for alarm; calm should be the order of the day. All the thefts were... inconsequential.'

'You selfish toff!' said Cripps. 'People here have lost things – it might not all be worth thousands and thousands of pounds, but it means much to them!'

A huge chorus of approval went up from a corner of the room closest to the bar, mostly from attendees who had managed to obtain beverages before the meeting started, I noticed. Elsewhere there were voices of disagreement to Mary Davis's rantings, so I felt some measure of sanity prevailed, but I wondered how long this would last. Holmes seemed to deliberate inwardly, then he spoke; a sharper tone in his voice.

'And how, Mr Cripps, could you so confidently claim knowledge of the total, cumulative value of the thief's takings?'

The room actually went still for a few seconds. Sherlock Holmes strolled over to Cripps, who stared at him, confused. 'I never said – I mean I was just guessing, from what folk said, is what I mean...' stammered Cripps.

Holmes directed his words at everyone but his eyes never left Cripps's face.

'This was a case where the items that were stolen were not the *object*, which I suspected from the start once I was told felons took heavy paintings rather than brooches. I knew the thefts were for a reason: to be *noticed*. Watson and I have since verified this by discovering that the place where the stolen items were secreted is not protected against the elements; some of the valuables would suffer damage if kept there long. So there was another motive, and it was one that eluded me until my friend the good doctor's reminiscences of his Afghan campaign reminded me of the importance to some people of wearing a uniform, of being a figure of authority.

'And that in turn made me imagine an economic motive for crime perhaps unique in my investigative career. I was suitably humbled that I had failed to appreciate the issues facing you good people in your developing communities and towns in this gigantic country, its population so at the mercy of the tyranny of weather, of distance.

'In an isolated town, a *salaried* police constable position is a rare and valuable form of *income*, especially if one is not successful at other occupations, like farming.

'My first inquiries were to the offices of the state's police commission in Brisbane and I was able to look at the history of proposals and applications to establish a constable in Dirranbandi. No fewer than eight letters in recent months have been written supporting this by persons lobbied by Mr John Cripps, and his own name is mentioned in most of them. He has, it seems, some military and civil experience and a short stint as a contract police officer, and so was promised by a friend in government that he could have the job of Dirranbandi's police constable, if only the population increased – but this is to a level it was not expected to reach for twenty years!

'My next investigation was to Mr Cripps's own bank in Brisbane, and there I learned that his farm has failed, and he will be forced to vacate within the year.

'So, his farm foreclosed. His hopes of an alternative salary via a government post in Dirranbandi soundly rebuffed. Unless, a compelling, mayhap political matter requires that police presence be increased in the district…'

'I posit that Mr Cripps latched on to Mary Davis's tales of bushrangers and thought to create a threat that would move government. He colluded with the ailing Douglas Kent to thieve items and this went swimmingly, and then a snag caught his line – one night when he went to meet Kent the man collapsed in his room and died, his lung disease overtaking him. Cripps cleverly – fiendishly cleverly, I would say – was actually inspired on the spot to make the death appear to be murder so as to ensure a need for a permanent police presence in Dirranbandi. But he knew an examination of the body would reveal death by disease – so he had to hide it. He then went back and made the room look like the scene of a fight and an attack, and Kent's terrible expectorated blood on the walls aided him in doing so. The gold watch was pure unhappy fortune, it confused the issue. It wasn't on Kent's person as he routinely slit the mattress of wherever he slept and secreted it there, unbeknownst to anyone. Because people knew he owned it, and it was missing, they subsumed it into the bigger story of stolen valuables that obsessed this town. Thus it provided a false motive for Kent's "murder"; my finding of it early in my investigation did not assist me.'

Holmes's voice now had a new tone. Triumph. He stared at Cripps, whose mouth was a tight line. 'I must congratulate you, Mr Cripps. An ability to improvise. But I wonder, if this ploy had not worked, how far would you have gone? Would actual murder be beyond you, sir? Would the region have experienced multiple killings, if the burglaries had not generated a police officer position?'

Cripps wiped his mouth with his hand, and muttered to himself. I could actually see the black looks of anger being transferred by the people in the room from Holmes to Cripps. The man lifted his head and shook it as if waking from a dream.

Then Cripps straightened up, and with a face a mask of hatred he calmly reached into his inside coat. He withdrew a shiny pistol and in less time than I had to register it, he cocked it and pointed it at Holmes's face.

To this day I know not whether Holmes could have done anything in time to save himself, for he did not have to. There was a blur of motion and a sound like a pistol shot, and Cripps' gun flew from his hand and the man screamed!

He fell to the floor clutching his wounded hand and McCarthy scooped up the fallen weapon. All eyes turned to see who had knocked the gun from his hand with a flick of a stock-whip.

It was Father O'Brien.

Seeing that Holmes was safe and no one else was in danger I finally reacted, perhaps without too much thought. I punched the confused Cripps under the chin and he fell backwards and knocked his head on the floorboards and slumped unconscious. I turned to O'Brien but was checked – the parson had coiled his whip in his left hand even as he produced a pistol of his own in his right!

Holmes broke the silence.

'I must thank you for saving my life, Father O'Brien. Or would you prefer we use your more famous pseudonym: Stingaree, the Bushranger?'

Stingaree made an almost imperceptible bow, and deftly tucked his whip in his belt, then used the same hand to pull from his breast pocket a shiny monocle which he screwed into his eye socket, never wavering with his pistol; it remained levelled at a height that comfortably targeted a standing person's heart.

'Mr Holmes, please, I would be honoured if you would address me as "Stingaree". For you to be acquainted with my humble little career in extra-legal activity is quite flattering.'

Holmes replied, 'Not at all, sir, not at all. Your exploits are in fact instructive in the chronicles of crime, not just because you have never been apprehended, or because nobody knows your real name, or for the way you have effected some of your greatest thefts, but because you are reportedly the only professional criminal at large today capable of expertly performing Bach's *Sonata in G Minor* on the harpsichord, if the tales of the way you entertained your hostages at the Prince of Wales Opera House in Melbourne a few years ago are accurate.'

'Such kind words, from the man whose violin solo is famed to have impressed the great Madame Norman-Neruda herself. I really do regret I must hasten to leave – I suspect we would have much to talk about of musical matters. But, that is an occupational… limitation I long adapted myself to. However, do indulge me – how did you identify me?'

'There were seven indications, but in particular I noticed one side of your pince-nez was not prescription lens, just glass, which reminded me of the talk of the monocled bushranger. Then also your coat had retained several hairs from a white horse, as the mystery man who stopped McCulloch rode.'

Stingaree chuckled. 'You teach me a lesson! I take great pains to hide my white mare, and ride into town on a second, less conspicuous beast to obscure my plans. Didn't think to brush my clothes, though!'

'If you were a liar, and a bushranger, but not the town thief – for McCulloch alibied you – then I reasoned you were here for other purposes. As I had already reasoned that there was a potential real connection between the stories of the Cobb & Co coach robbery and Mr McCulloch's encounter with a masked man, it seemed the presence of a false preacher and these other events fitted together much better. In Brisbane a few cables provided me with facts to complete a theory. You held up the coach to obtain confidential documents in its manifest that would allow you to pinpoint the coach company's secret new routes around the Dirranbandi area, including one particular route from Lightning Ridge, just the other side of the state border, that is due next week. A valuable shipment of opals is to be transported; this is the prize you were planning to win.

'All this conjecture made sense to me; it is a clever, long-range plan to make a significant heist of valuable gems, and would not be carried out by someone drawing attention to themselves with petty little thefts in Dirranbandi. I then knew I unfortunately had two separate felons in the area to deal with: one a clever, scheming professional bushranger, and one a sneak-thief with an obscure agenda. The latter, I decided, was the case my client had engaged me to resolve, but also one that a community of decent, aspiring men and women needed me to act upon.'

Stingaree laughed loudly. 'Oh, sir, that is well done, by the Lord Harry it is! Perfectly correct, you are! But why shall we call my happening here "unfortunate"? I have in fact just saved your skull from being perforated.'

'I might have evaded a bullet on my own,' said Holmes, eyes a-twinkle. 'I have knowledge of an obscure combative art known as *baritsu* – you may recall seeing me demonstrate it upon Mr McCulloch – and I fancy I might have kicked the pistol from Mr Cripps's hand. But then I would not have seen you reveal yourself, would I?'

Stingaree actually winked at Holmes. 'Really, well, that would have been a thing to see, Mr Holmes. I might *almost* believe you capable of that. But I must take my leave. I do hope you shan't pursue me, and I hope we shan't meet again, sir – I rarely deal with a foeman as bright as you, and I might have cause to make sure you mightn't put me down, and be rather final about doing so.'

Holmes nodded. 'I understand the sentiment. If we do cross paths again we shall start with a clean slate, which is no advantage to you. Good day, sir.'

Stingaree touched the brim of his hat and moved quickly backwards out of the room.

If there was a moment I felt my emotions jumbled it was when I raced outside after Stingaree to see him leap upon a white horse tethered outside and gallop away. Holmes sauntered from the hotel with almost infuriating slowness and I was not amused to witness my friend casually wave a farewell in the bushranger's direction. Holmes looked at me and saw my frown.

'Watson, the man just saved my life, or close enough to. Let us allow him this one moment of surcease, as it were. I must admit, there have been times that I have regretted coming to Australia, and have maintained a pessimism about its towns and cities. But a fellow whose hands can do justice to Bach and also use a stock-whip with such accuracy; I stand corrected: this country truly does allow for the development of individuals of *culture*.'

BUSHELL PHILPOT and CHELLEW

CURIOSITIES STORE

BUNYIP

PHIL CORNELL after PAGET '13

The Adventure of the Purloined Bunyip

Philip Cornell

My celebrated friend Mr Sherlock Holmes and I now found ourselves in the colony of South Australia which, unlike the other Australian colonies, was not founded as a penal colony but was rather established by free settlers. The city of Adelaide felt refreshingly relaxed compared with those cities that had to overcome the stigma of a convict past, though I fancy my friend may have found the criminous past of the other colonies rather more to his taste.

Holmes and I alighted at Adelaide and, as we loaded our luggage onto a hansom cab, our attention was arrested by an urchin selling the local newspaper, *The Advertiser*. 'Famous detective in Adelaide!' he cried.

'Over here, my lad,' called Holmes, tossing the lad a couple of ha'pennies. 'It would seem our fame has preceded us,' he observed, as I read the article.

The Advertiser has learned that the celebrated Mr Sherlock Holmes, the British private consulting detective, and his biographer Dr J. H. Watson, are currently visiting Adelaide. Mr Holmes's successes have become well known in law enforcement circles but are now becoming more familiar to the general public due to Dr Watson's efforts to put them before readers. We await to learn whether his services will be sought by any of our citizens.' I could not suppress a smile at the word 'celebrated', and the description of myself as Holmes's biographer, but Holmes merely let out a *'Pshaw'* and slumped into irritated silence.

Having passed a mounted policeman waving his arms to direct the late-afternoon traffic, our cab drew to a halt at the Botanic Hotel in East Terrace.

As the cabby passed down our bags, Holmes mused aloud when we passed the doors of the saloon bar that occupied the ground floor. 'Perhaps this is the very place where that unscrupulous rascal Henry Peters had his ear bitten.'

The relevance of my companion's remark escaped me but this was not an unusual occurrence, as Holmes would often expound on the subject of some obscure criminal and his misdeeds when he chanced to visit a site related to an incident he had studied.

Our rooms were comfortable, if unpretentious. We unpacked that portion of our luggage that we were likely to require while in Adelaide. As Holmes placed his pipe on the mantle I noticed that it was the cherrywood rather than his favourite briar, which did not bode well for his mood.

'You seem annoyed by the newspaper report of our visit,' I observed.

'I am not anxious to be bothered by every Adelaide inhabitant who wants to tell his grandchildren that he engaged "the celebrated Sherlock Holmes".'

I restrained the temptation to express doubt that the name of Sherlock Holmes would be remembered by anybody's grandchildren. Humility is not one of Sherlock Holmes's virtues.

After breakfast Holmes and I prepared to see a little more of Adelaide but, before we could do so, a knock on the door heralded a lad I had noticed at the front desk, bearing a telegram. Holmes read it and, with a grim expression, passed it across to me. It was from one J. Ross-Philpot of Bushell, Ross-Philpot and Chellew – Curiosities Store.

Wish to retain you to investigate the theft of rare curiosities. May we see you tomorrow morning at eleven?

'I understand,' I said, 'that you do not relish being approached about a case, but doesn't this arouse your… curiosity?'

Holmes fixed me with a baleful glare, but I could tell he was somewhat intrigued. My friend dashed off a terse reply, *Will consult you at eleven – Holmes*, and handed the form to the boy.

'I wonder,' I mused, 'how they knew where to contact us?'

'The cabby, I expect,' said Holmes.

IT WAS AN odd quirk of my friend's character that he found inactivity totally enervating while the prospect of an interesting case filled him with energy. At the appointed hour we met Mr Chellew, a fellow with intelligent, penetrating dark eyes and a small neatly trimmed beard; Mr John Bushell, whose humorous twinkling eyes looked out from beneath bushy brows; and a professorial-looking fellow who introduced himself as Mr Joshua Ross-Philpot. They presented themselves and explained that they were three of the partners in a store that sold curiosities.

'Mr Holmes,' declared Mr Chellew, 'some villain has stolen the preserved remains of a bunyip!'

'A bunyip?'

'The bunyip,' explained Mr Ross-Philpot, 'is a creature which has never been seen, but whose blood-chilling cries have been reported by the Aboriginals.'

'And by other plausible witnesses,' added Mr Bushell, whose white beard made him rather resemble the popular conception of Father Christmas.

'So... a *supposed* bunyip,' scoffed my friend.

'This island continent is the home to many creatures whose existence was scoffed at at first,' explained Mr Chellew, with a hint of reproof for my friend's tone of scepticism.

'When the first duck-billed platypus was sent back to Britain from the newly discovered Australia, it was dismissed by zoologists as a clumsy fraud constructed from an otter's body to which a duck's beak had been affixed. Yet that turned out to be a genuine creature,' he pointed out.

'Might the bunyip's cry be an unknown species of bird?' I suggested. 'An Australian bittern booming, perhaps?'

I ventured to wonder if the preserved remains of the creature might have been stolen by a circus or sideshow. 'Such dubious establishments are known to exploit the gullible with spurious exhibits.'

'Perhaps,' said Chellew.

'Or maybe,' I continued, 'it has been sold as genuine to some lesser museum.'

'Not necessarily a *lesser* museum, Watson,' replied Holmes. 'The Sydney Museum in College Street has an exhibit purporting to be a bunyip skull.'

'Holmes, the out-of-the-way facts that your magpie mind accumulates never cease to astound me.'

'If you have a fault, my dear Watson, it is that you are rather too readily astounded.'

'Have you not seen me avidly consuming the local reportage and magazines since our arrival? More trivia has adhered to my mind than I would like.'

I sensed that our guests were rather bemused by our banter, and Holmes reverted to a more businesslike tone.

'There are indeed aspects of your case that interest me. I will accept your commission.'

Our clients seemed relieved by Holmes's decision.

'Thank you Mr Holmes,' said Mr Chellew.

'Might I then visit your store to learn more about the items in question?'

There was just enough room for us to share their cab and we were soon drawing up outside the curio store. Introductions were made to Mr Bushell's charming wife, Vivienne, who had been minding the shop in the absence of the other owners.

Holmes and I murmured appreciation as we were shown some of the contents, including fossils of the strange creatures of the antipodes. There were also Aboriginal paintings on sheets of eucalyptus-tree bark, masks and other curios of the same type that one might find in a similar London shop, odd statuettes, butterfly cases (though the butterflies displayed were unfamiliar to me), examples of the taxidermist's art and an elaborately carved walrus tusk.

'There are other items kept in boxes stored behind the shop,' added Mr Chellew, 'which we rotate at intervals with those on display and in the window.'

'And there are also certain items,' said Mr Ross-Philpot, 'not really suitable for the eyes of the ladies or those of delicate sensibilities. Those are only retrieved when specifically requested.'

Holmes and I were occupied looking at these additional curios when Mr Chellew let out a 'hullo' of surprise.

'There seem to be other items missing as well! Plaster-of-Paris-casts of a pair of yowie prints,' he said. Noticing my expression, he explained that the yowie was the Australian equivalent of the yeti of the Himalayan peaks or North America's sasquatch. 'We had best conduct a full inventory.'

'And I shall be in touch when I have made further enquiries,' said Holmes as he shook hands with our clients.

When we were back in our cab, rattling along North Terrace, Holmes asked me an odd question.

'Are you familiar, Watson, with the term "cryptozoology"?'

'My Greek is a trifle rusty,' I replied, 'but I imagine it has something to do with hidden or obscure animals.'

'It is a pseudoscience devoted to the very type of mysterious or legendary creatures that we have been discussing and, like any field of interest, it has its avid adherents, particularly in America.'

'Crackpots,' I said, 'is the description that springs to mind.'

'Perhaps,' said my companion drily, 'yet I think a trip to the library may be in order. Can you occupy yourself for the next few hours? We shall meet again for dinner at the hotel.'

I amused myself with a stroll around the botanical gardens, which lay immediately across the road from the hotel. The variety of plants and trees were so different to the ones in Kew Gardens that I almost lost track of time.

'Have your researches yielded fruit?' I asked when I rejoined Holmes.

'Yes indeed,' replied my friend as we tucked into some of the local roast lamb.

'Holmes, I have been thinking. It seems to me that you may be a little hasty in dismissing these strange creatures out of hand. Didn't we have some experience of a creature unknown to science in the Persano case?'

'I hardly think that the remarkable worm is in the same category as Abominable Snowmen or unicorns,' retorted my friend. 'But I have learned something of interest. It seems that a prominent "cryptozoologist" lives here in Adelaide.'

Holmes pronounced the word so that I could almost hear the inverted commas, but despite my best efforts he would say no more.

It was a warm day so I left Holmes deep in thought in our room and went down to the public bar for a soothing glass of ale. As I nursed my pint glass I became aware that the group of young men seated at a nearby table were medical students, joking together about their professors and discussing their lectures. I was immediately back at Bart's in my imagination, recalling that my fellows and I used to jest about our professors in exactly the same way and try to guess what form our examination questions would take. I mused that when my young dresser Stamford had introduced me to Sherlock Holmes, he could hardly have imagined that we would both find ourselves on the other side of the world investigating the theft of so strange a thing as a preserved bunyip. I could scarcely have imagined it myself.

When I returned to our room, Sherlock Holmes did not seem to have noticed my absence, but resumed the conversation we had been having about the Adelaide authority on such strange creatures.

Accordingly, the following morning my companion and I caught the train to Port Adelaide where we were met by this Dr Dunwich, who explained that he had originally graduated as a true biologist until his interest in obscure and controversial branches of the animal kingdom replaced the more conventional ones.

'You are familiar, I take it,' he explained, 'with the science of cryptozoology. The scientific study of anomalous animals such as the yeti, bigfoot, the yowie, the wendigo, the South American chupacabra, the jackalope, the so-called Jersey Devil…'

'I'd query the term "scientific study" when the very existence of such creatures is no more than speculation.'

'There are more things, Mr Holmes,' said Dr Dunwich, with the gentle patience of one used to dealing with sceptics, 'than are dreamt of in your philosophy.'

'Well, we can certainly agree that there seems to be a good deal of interest in such matters. Do such enthusiasts have organisations to which they belong?'

'Or do they subscribe to magazines on the subject?' I asked.

'In England,' replied Dr Dunwich, 'there is the Society of Cryptozoology and a much larger organisation in the United States which is called The American Cryptozoologists' Club. They do publish a bi-annual journal.'

'Do you have a recent issue I might look over?' asked my companion.

'Yes, here is the January number.'

Holmes made a couple of other remarks, then thanked the doctor and, on promising to return the journal, we caught the next train back to Adelaide. Holmes said nothing as he pored over the journal and I knew better than to interrupt him when he was so focused. After ten or fifteen minutes, his eyes glinted.

'Ha!' he ejaculated. 'An American collector is offering to purchase any examples of obscure cryptozoological esoterica on generous terms!'

'So somebody might stand to make a good deal of money by selling the stolen specimens.'

'Precisely.'

'But who?'

'I fancy a telegram or two might answer that question,' said Holmes thoughtfully, 'for which I'll need the cooperation of the Adelaide police.'

'I HAVE HEARD of you, gentlemen,' said Inspector Matthias Mitchell of the South Australian police force as we shook hands. 'An edition of *Beeton's Christmas Annual* with your solution to the Lauriston Gardens murder from a few years ago was passed around amongst my colleagues.'

'I need to ascertain who in Adelaide might have responded to this classified advertisement,' explained Holmes, indicating the journal. 'An official wire would carry more weight than one from a private individual like myself.'

'Leave it with me, Mr Holmes,' Inspector Mitchell replied, clearly pleased to help the detective about whom he had read.

Sherlock Holmes had brought one of his violins with him to Australia. It was not his precious Stradivarius, which he had purchased from a pawnbroker unaware of its value for a very modest sum, but rather another instrument once given to him by a thankful client whom Holmes had absolved from serious charges of fraud. He whiled away the time extemporising an air of his own devising while I occupied myself making notes about our current investigation.

The following morning saw Inspector Mitchell bring the reply to Holmes's enquiry. Holmes read the telegram with a smile playing round his lips, as one who sees his conclusions confirmed.

'Did I ever acquaint you with the case of Derham Groves, in the colony of Victoria?' asked Holmes.

'I don't believe so.'

'I suppose not. You had, as I recall, forsaken me for married life…'

'Now, Holmes,' I began, sensing the thread of my friend's comments, but he continued unabated.

'It involved a pair of pearl-handled revolvers, once the property of a noted figure in the American western frontier. I must relate the details to you one day. The case was not without some remarkable points.'

I knew my friend well enough to know these remarks were intended to distract me from pressing Holmes about the contents of the telegram. His next suggestion confirmed this.

'Do you fancy a stroll, Watson?' asked Sherlock Holmes suddenly. 'I wish to ruminate, and on a delightful afternoon like this I fancy I can do that more pleasantly outside than in this hotel room.'

'Yes, certainly,' I replied. There was a clear blue sky of the kind we rarely saw in London, and the thought of some fresh air and sunshine was most agreeable.

We ambled together down East Terrace, taking detours down side streets and venturing sometimes into back alleys. I soon became a little unsure of where I was, but I knew Holmes to have an unerring sense of direction and an insatiable curiosity about the geography of any city where he found himself. After numerous turnings we stood opposite the public library and I wondered whether Holmes intended again to look through the newspapers or consult some volume but instead he indicated the second-hand bookshop opposite, behind an imposing statue of the poet Burns. We entered and while I browsed amongst some volumes of militaria, Holmes seemed to be struck by a small, chocolate-coloured leather-bound volume with pages that appeared to have once been gilt, though that had largely worn off. He looked thoughtful and I wondered if he had found something that related to our case, so I moved to join him. I saw that the book was an old volume of Pepys' *Diary*.

'It is the belief of my brother Mycroft that he and I are descended from Sir Richard Holmes, who was the assistant administrator of the navy in the days of King Charles the Second. He is mentioned in no very flattering terms by Samuel Pepys, who was himself a valued aide to King Charles, with duties that included naval matters.'

I wasn't sure whether I should congratulate Holmes on his family connection if the ancestor in question had not been very highly regarded by the eminent diarist, so I muttered some vague sounds of finding the matter interesting. Before I could say more, Holmes glanced at his pocket watch and indicated to me that we should wend our way back to our hotel, where he left our book purchases before we returned to see our clients.

'Well, Mr Holmes, what have you been able to discover?' asked Mr Chellew when Holmes and I re-entered the curio store.

'A great deal,' answered the detective. 'My investigation has provided a motive for the theft and I am very hopeful of recovering the abstracted items.'

'That is splendid!' exclaimed Mrs Bushell, to which her husband added, 'But who is responsible?'

'Yes, have you any ideas?' asked Mr Ross-Philpot. 'One of our customers perhaps, or we have a boy who works in the stock-room.'

'All things in their proper order,' said my friend. 'It struck me immediately that only an enthusiast in the field would see any real value in what one might categorise as *cryptozoologica*, a very specific variety of curio. A simple burglary could be ruled out, and I could eliminate the stock-room boy, who would not be so discriminating.'

Holmes lit his briar, drew in a lungful of smoke and paused for a moment before continuing.

'There is however a ready market for this very type of curiosity in America.'

'Am I to infer that you suspect one of us?' asked Mr Bushell.

Ignoring the interruption, Holmes continued. 'One amongst you has answered an advertisement by a collector offering to pay generously for Australian curiosities of this sort.'

The partners looked at each other in amazement, and then all turned to Sherlock Holmes.

'Am I not correct, *Mr Ross-Philpot*?'

The man glared at Sherlock Holmes, while the others gasped in disbelief. A long moment passed before Mr Ross-Philpot spoke.

'You can't arrest someone for stealing his own property!' he said.

'The joint property of *all* the partners, you unscrupulous rascal,' corrected Mr Chellew coldly.

'Inspector Mitchell of the South Australian police is waiting outside. I'm sure he can be trusted to bring the appropriate charges,' said Sherlock Holmes drily.

A SEARCH OF Mr Ross-Philpot's home, Bush Villa, revealed the stolen curiosities concealed in the attic. Holmes examined the strange collection.

'This "bunyip" would appear to be a naturally mummified body…'

'Naturally mummified?' I asked.

'By being buried in dry earth and sand,' explained Holmes. 'It would seem to be the body of a juvenile, either of an Aboriginal or the child of an early settler, which would appear to be somewhat deformed.'

My medical interest was aroused.

'There seems to be marked scoliosis. Curvature of the spine,' I pointed out.

'And see here,' remarked my friend. 'These would appear to be *webbed* fingers. The skin between the fingers has been largely preserved in the drying process.'

This last observation sparked an almost forgotten memory from my childhood.

'As I understand it, the "bunyip" was believed to be an aquatic creature…'

'… which lived in the naturally occurring ponds or watering holes,' said Holmes, finishing my thoughts.

'Billabongs.'

'Quite,' said Sherlock Holmes. 'It seemed to me understandable that this grotesque specimen should be thought by the credulous to be such a creature, though a sad commentary on how those looking for the outré will ignore more likely possibilities.'

Later, as Sherlock Holmes and I rattled back by cab along East Terrace to our hotel, I ventured to suggest that it was no bad thing the newspaper report had led to Holmes being bothered by clients and that he had, perhaps, found their case not without its interesting aspects.

Holmes permitted himself a dry chuckle.

'Perhaps the end result was worthwhile, but the case afforded less chance to apply ratiocination to a problem than it did to my capacity to expend energy running to ground obscure resources. I had decided Ross-Philpot was guilty on our first visit to their establishment.'

'How?' I wondered.

'The original note he sent to us described the theft of 'curiosities', *plural*, Watson! Yet, the fact that more than that one specimen, a bunyip body, was stolen did not emerge until the day we first visited the store and the inventory was thoroughly checked. Only Ross-Philpot knew of multiple thefts because he was responsible! My sole concern then became not simply proving it but also finding impartial evidence that would clearly demonstrate his guilt to his partners. For I knew that they would no more believe the truth than those who see a "bunyip" when all I saw was a sadly deformed infant.'

'People persist in seeing what they wish to see rather than observing the truth. It is an eternal weakness in mankind,' I said.

'Very true, Watson. Our visit to Adelaide has brought several rewards. An interesting commission, this little volume of Pliny's *Natural History*, which I found in Treloar's antiquarian bookshop opposite the public library, and *this*.'

From his satchel, Sherlock Holmes produced the handsome scrimshaw walrus tusk, which his grateful clients had given him in appreciation.

'It will make a nice addition to my gallery of trophies in Baker Street, will it not?'

THE CASE OF THE VANISHING FRATERY

T. S. P. Sweeney

IT WAS WITH thoughts of Afghanistan, rather than the case at hand, that I rode on my ancient, swaybacked mule under the Australian sun burning us through the too-sparse tree cover.

It was not the terrain, nor even the heat that brought to mind the place I had served in battle. No, it was my companion who kept my thoughts placed firmly in the past. Not Sherlock Holmes, of course – the detective rode upon his own mule, seemingly oblivious, sweating and shaking. He had claimed to have fallen prey to a severe influenza-like malady, but as he refused to let me examine him I must admit I suspected the very worst: that he was withdrawing from a boredom-induced lapse into cocaine or morphine use.

It was my other companion who took me back to my army days, and unpleasant recollections.

'Only a few miles to go, my friends,' said Brother Colton Hanlon of the Fratery of Saint Dymphna as he peered over his shoulder at me. His face – as red and sunburnt as his bald pate – wore a smile intended to be disarming, though in truth it had the opposite effect upon me.

He had not always been Brother Colton Hanlon. Once, a long time ago, he had been a wayward soldier by the name of Sergeant Hanlon, a thief and rapscallion who had somehow coasted through the majority of his service to queen and country as a provost, punishing those whose crimes were often no worse than his own.

It was near the end of my own time, however, that young Hanlon's crimes caught up to him, in the form of two bottles of the postmaster-general's finest burgundy discovered in his quarters. Hanlon went to the flogging post, and soon afterwards found himself in my care. He had sworn then to all and sundry that he had found God and would become a changed man. I had, I must admit, assumed he would fail, and thought I'd never see him again.

And yet here he was, having joined a lay brotherhood of the Catholic church and working as a missionary of sorts to the antipodes.

Though it appeared he had found a new path in life, a part of me could not help but hold some further misgivings.

'He is a man conflicted,' came Holmes's voice. I started; I had not noticed his approach, distracted as I was in my observations of Hanlon. These were, I believed, the first words Holmes had spoken in more than a day.

'He is obviously concerned about the goings-on at this monastery of theirs,' I said.

'That is not the conflict to which I refer,' he said, glancing quickly at the back of our guide. 'He, personally, is a man experiencing something of a crisis of identity.'

'Holmes, how on earth do you come to such a conclusion when you have barely said two words to the man?'

'There are many points to indicate as such, for he who is willing to look.' The good detective smiled slightly, seeming to come more alive as he spoke. 'Take, for example, his name.'

'His name?'

'Hanlon is of Irish origin, though more often expressed as O'Hanlon. Yet he bears the first name Colton, which is of quite ancient etymology within England. Add to that his lacking the distinctive Irish drawl, and what are your conclusions, Doctor?'

I frowned; in truth, I had little considered the former sergeant's origins. 'He is born of England, but comes from Irish stock?'

'Correct, Watson, but what else does his name tell you?'

I found that I hadn't the foggiest notion and indicated as such.

'The name tells of a conflict moving through generations! The bastardised Irish surname, perhaps an ill-fated attempt at disguise that does not quite go far enough to hide the Celtic roots or the pride therein. A name and pattern of speech intended to disguise this pride, and yet the following of the Catholic faith remains – a true sign of Irish pride if ever there was one when you consider the troubles such beliefs have caused them.'

'What else do you deduce, Holmes?' I asked.

'He joined the army – the military police, no less! – and yet was a criminal, you said. He has taken holy orders, and yet remains a lay brother, unbound by any oaths truly enforceable by the Church he serves.' He nodded, as if in punctuation of his point. 'Conflicted.'

We both held our tongues a moment. The sun beat down upon us, and Holmes seemed to wilt beneath its glare, sweating anew.

'What does that all mean to our case, my friend?' I whispered, suddenly concerned Brother Hanlon might overhear us.

'Nothing whatsoever to the case as it has been laid out thus far, Watson.' Holmes dabbed at his face with a handkerchief, squinting against the glare. 'But it may prove crucial to remember that we have been brought here by a man steeped in inner turmoil.'

He turned away from me then, his eyes locked upon the back of our guide.

'And such a man is not to be entirely trusted.'

I HAD BEEN seated at a table in the Fortune of War – an inn of remarkable age for the relatively young Sydney – playing cards with a group of army officers who frequented the establishment, when Hanlon walked in.

I recognised him immediately despite his bald head and the other unkindnesses of age.

Hanlon approached the publican, sweat pouring from his sunburnt brow. It may have been autumn outside, but given the heat one would hardly have recognised it as such, compared to the autumns back home, even within the darkened space of the Fortune.

'I am looking for a pair of gentlemen, fresh come from England.' Hanlon's voice was still a harsh, gravelly thing, at odds with his plump, almost jovial face.

'Lots of men come through here,' replied Arthur, the bartender, his voice defined by that most unusual Australian twang that seemed a corruption of many of the Empire's accents. 'Few of 'em could be called gentle, though.'

His remark was greeted by laughter from the scattered patrons, current or former soldiers all.

'Yes, yes.' Hanlon clamped his fingers around the edge of the bar, knuckles turning white. 'But these two are unique: a self-described detective and his associate, an army doctor.'

I tensed immediately. Our 'adventures' since arriving in Australia had not been kept as secretive as one might have liked, but I hardly expected to be so well known as to have old acquaintances look me up.

Arthur's eyes flickered very briefly towards me, but Hanlon appeared to miss it, being too lost in his own frustration.

'If you will excuse me, gentlemen,' I said to my companions, laying down my cards and leaving the chips where they lay. My exit was met with some amount of good-natured grumbling; I am afraid my luck had run rather poorly, and my companions would no doubt miss my company as a result.

'Sergeant Hanlon.' I stepped towards him, right hand extended. My left was in the pocket of my coat, grasping the revolver I kept there. I remembered well the former provost's unsavoury reputation, and liked not at all the fact that he knew Holmes and I were in Sydney.

'Captain Watson, sir!' Hanlon jumped near a foot in the air, hand raising for a salute before settling instead into a shake, with a large, gap-toothed grin on his face. 'It is wonderful to see you, sir. I have been tramping up and down these streets to every public house and lodging I came across, in the hope I should find you.'

'Not that I am unhappy to see you, old boy,' I said, smiling around the lie; though I was uncomfortable, I did not seek to offend. 'But why should you be looking for Holmes and me, or indeed, even know we are in the colony at all?'

He stepped in beside me, his hand closing, vice-like, around my own. My finger tensed upon the trigger in my pocket.

'Not here, not here.' He looked around, his happiness at locating me now forgotten. 'Where is the good detective? I must speak with both of you.'

'Upstairs.' I removed my hand from my pocket; whatever was going on,

I sensed now that Hanlon presented no danger. 'In our rooms, or in the commons perhaps.'

'We must go there then, please. Sir.' He headed towards the stairs, still leading me by the arm. I allowed myself to be dragged, not a little bemused by it all.

'Why?' I asked, halting my momentum. Though he was a big man, and strong, he let go immediately when I asked.

'Why?' His eyes were wide and his lip trembled, as though he were on the verge of tears. It put me in mind, then, of the last time I had seen him, sitting before me on the table as I applied soothing unguents to the dozen lashes upon his raw, bloodied back. 'Because it is a matter of life and death, Captain. A matter of life and death!'

HANLON HAD SPOKEN correctly when he said we were not far from our destination. Soon after Holmes had issued his mule-back warning, Hanlon led us through the gates of the old monastery. We had travelled some sixty miles from our lodgings in Sydney, meandering south and west, stopping for frequent breaks to allow for our guide to purchase various odds and ends or simply converse with the inhabitants of the small communities along the way. It had been an easy journey, but a slow one, and I must admit I was quite eager to arrive, even with the portents of danger.

''Twas a manor originally.' Brother Hanlon had dropped his mule back between Holmes and myself. 'Built upon this site by the Revan family around the time the government officially recognised the township of Wollongong, some thirty years ago.'

'Quite older than that, I should say,' said Holmes, pointing at the tall, rough-cut stone wall we rode past, stained with the rusty trails of rain that no amount of scrubbing could quite clean off. 'The style, not to mention the wear, indicates this wall to be nearer a half-century than not, built here by a lord who was obviously interested in his privacy.'

Hanlon looked somewhat crestfallen at being corrected, but soon perked up as he continued his description. 'The male line of the family died out, with no suitors for the sole daughter – barren, so the rumours say – and thus the property was ceded to the Church upon his death.'

'Revan, you say?' I spoke up; I'd known a Major Revan, once. 'A Catholic Scottish lord building a manor deep in the woods of Australia? Most peculiar.'

'But not unheard of,' Holmes replied, staring now at the monastery itself.

'The Church, in its wisdom, gifted the manor to a holy order of monks travelling here from Spain.' The lay brother harrumphed, though whether at this latest aspect of his tale or at our interruptions, I could not say. 'The lands were prepared for their use, the buildings converted to be more suitable. But the Spaniard vessel bearing them never arrived, and soon enough the land fell once more into disuse.'

The path turned from hard-packed dirt to cobble as we rode closer to the house, passing outbuildings and stables. Several brothers in their black smocks stood in the gardens, tending crops or weeding flowerbeds. All turned to stare as we passed, some offering smiles or polite waves, others merely watching.

'Concurrently, Brother Rickaby – the founder of our Fratery – was already living with the miners at Mount Keira, and had petitioned the Church for a dedicated home.' He smiled then, his eyes upon the great manor as we drew to a stop. 'And, as I am sure you have guessed, the Church was happy to agree.'

I handed my reins to a young boy, winking at him as he doffed his cap and held the beast still to allow my dismount.

'You take in orphans?' I whispered to Hanlon as he dismounted beside me. I did not wish to be overheard, lest I cause offense to the child.

'Dymphna is the patron of orphans and runaways, is she not?' Holmes had got down from his own mule, far less gracefully than usual. I prayed the damnable drugs would flee his system sooner rather than later.

'She is indeed, Mr Holmes, and it is our mission to care for those children who have no one else.' Hanlon turned back to me, ruddy face scowling as Holmes wandered to the windows of the great home. 'Tell me, Captain Watson: is he always like this?'

'Honestly, Brother, he is sometimes better and oftentimes much worse,'

I replied with a gentle smile. 'And I am "Captain Watson" no longer! Please, call me Doctor, or Watson, or even John, should you so choose.'

'Come, then, Dr Watson and Mr Holmes!' Hanlon smiled, opening his arms to take in the expanse of the building; one could almost forget the circumstances that had brought us here, seeing that beaming pride upon his face. 'Let me show you our home and then we shall discuss the matter at hand.'

OUR TOUR OF the premises was an interesting one from a historical perspective, but I found it unusual that the dire circumstances that had brought us here seemed to be all but forgotten by our host.

However, Hanlon excused himself from playing the tour guide after a few minutes, the nervousness he had shown upon our meeting in Sydney returning twofold when he was summoned to see the leader of his order.

Holmes and I removed ourselves from other company, slipping away to view the property unfettered by escort. A pair of brothers, burlier than the rest, appeared about to object as we walked away, but we were nonetheless left to our own devices.

We had begun with the outbuildings, though Holmes expressed little interest in the designs of the stables or kilns, instead busying himself with examining the local flora and talking to the occasional orphan tending to the maintenance of the vast property.

I myself was quite taken with the tiny chapel built behind the manor, all made from locally cut wood, whitewashed and lovingly maintained. There was even a plate-glass panel depicting Calvary that was quite beautiful, and which surely would have cost more than the entire chapel.

Eventually, and with Holmes looking mildly faint under the autumnal sun, we stepped into the manor house itself. It smelled vaguely of dust and smoke, and felt strangely abandoned despite now housing an entire religious order.

The ground floor was arranged into a simple grid: kitchens, dining hall, larder and staff quarters bordered and bisected by corridors.

'I saw similar to these whilst travelling to Aberdeen,' I said to Holmes, indicating the intricate black iron coverings over the window I stood before, angled and perforated to allow light through but still adding a gloomy air for all that. 'I must admit that I find them a rather unappealing feature for a house such as this.'

'Archers, my dear Watson.' Holmes placed a book he had been thumbing through back upon the shelf. Its cover indicated a history of the Spanish royal family, and it was leather-bound and obviously valuable – intended for the ill-fated occupants of the house, perhaps? 'Such defensive methods are common in older manors throughout Europe.'

'Archers?'

'I imagine that when this house was built, there was a certain concern in that direction, and such lattices will defend against a thrown spear as well as an arrow.' Holmes stepped to the window, produced his pipe and lit it. 'Considering the apparent reason we are here, perhaps such defences are justified.'

We walked further into the building, silently but for our footsteps upon the slate floor and the steady puffing of Holmes upon his pipe, past paintings of saints in outdated style and rich furniture covered in a skein of dust.

'You said "apparent reason" earlier, Holmes,' I opined after a long while. 'You believe us to be here under false pretences?'

'I believe this place to be something of a fortress, old boy, even if it is defended by children and men of the cloth.' He waved his pipe around, indicating the thick stone and the heavy timber door leading from the atrium to outside. 'Beyond that and my earlier misgivings about your acquaintance Hanlon, I say –'

He was interrupted from speaking any further as a panting brother found us, his fiery red hair and freckled features giving the appearance of youth despite the crow's feet around his eyes and the muscles bulging on his forearms.

'Sirs, please follow me. Brother O'Rourke shall see you now,' he said in a thick Irish brogue, turning towards the stairs before we could formulate a reply.

'Shall we?' I said to Holmes, with a certain tenseness. I deeply wished to hear his further thoughts on the matter, but it appeared that such discussions would have to wait.

'We shall, my friend.' Holmes extinguished his pipe and tucked it away, clasping his hands behind his back. 'We shall indeed.'

HOLMES, HANLON AND I were in the office of the leader of the order, Brother O'Rourke. 'You must understand that it was not my idea to bring you here, gentlemen,' said the brother – a thin, hard-looking fellow with eyes as black as his hair and the bearing of a military man for all his priestly dressings – with little in the way of fanfare. 'And I will not have you here any longer than the night.'

'I say, that is hardly –' I began, but O'Rourke cut me off, smacking his fist against his battered wooden desk.

'You will not interrupt me!' Spittle flew as he spoke, his cheeks flushed. 'I will not have heathen Englishmen here interfering in matters of this Fratery!'

'But, Brother –' Hanlon spoke this time, wringing his hands like a child.

'Silence!'

'This is hardly necessary, Brother O'Rourke.' Holmes leaned back in his chair, quite at ease despite the hostility from our host. 'We "heathen Englishmen" are not here to interfere, and find no issue with members of your Church or Brotherhood at all.'

'Then why are you here?' The tone was still venomous, but at least the head of the Fratery was no longer yelling.

'Why, because Hanlon here told us what was going on, of course.' I could hardly hide my own outrage, at O'Rourke for his manner, but also at Hanlon for leading us here under what appeared to be false pretences.

'And what exactly has our illustrious brother told you?'

Hanlon wilted as his superior spoke.

'That there have been attacks upon your walls and your people these past weeks,' said Holmes. 'Members of your order disappearing without a trace…'

'That about sums it up, yes,' Hanlon cut in. O'Rourke cast a fiery look in his direction.

'I know not if you read the news from outside this part of the Empire, but Sherlock Holmes is the foremost investigator in the northern hemisphere, and, I dare say, in the southern as well.' I leaned forward, resting my arms upon the stubborn man's desk. 'Allow us to help you, and perhaps we can get to the bottom of this matter before more of your people up and vanish.'

Silence fell, the only sound the crackling of the fire. The heat was almost unbearable, though I appeared to be the only one to notice it.

After a long moment, O'Rourke spoke again, biting off every word. 'I neither need, nor want, your help or that of the illustrious Sherlock Holmes. This matter is one to be handled internally by the Fratery, and I will brook no interference from the likes of you.'

He stood up so quickly that his rickety old chair almost toppled into the fireplace behind him.

'I acknowledge that you were brought here wrongly by one of my brothers, and that you may even have the best of intentions. Thusly, you may stay the night in one of the outbuildings and depart on the morrow.' He winced as he said it, as though even such a slight concession physically pained him. 'Know this, however: any further interference on your behalf shall lead to you being ejected from these grounds, and we shall then see how you enjoy the long walk back to Sydney. Do I make myself clear?'

'Quite,' I replied, placing my hat atop my head, rudeness be damned.

'Undoubtedly,' said Holmes, turning away.

'Brother Hanlon, stay!' O'Rourke's voice cracked like a whip as he spoke, dark eyes flashing. 'I fear we need to speak once more about the boundaries of your authority within this order!'

I closed the door behind me, leaving the former sergeant to his fate.

'It appears our journey has been for nought,' I said to Holmes as we descended the stairs. I enjoyed the blessed cool now that we had escaped that stuffy office with its unnecessary fire.

'I would not say that, my good Doctor,' said Holmes, stepping through the door into the cool night air. The stars danced above us in the bleak sky, combining with the moon to provide an almost eerie, ethereal glow to the manor house and its surrounds. 'The night is still young, and who knows what mysteries it may yet bring?'

And without another word he strode off towards our lodgings for the night. Muttering to myself, I followed.

'DISAPPEARING, YOU SAY?' Seated in our upstairs rooms in Sydney, Holmes had puffed upon his pipe as he spoke, his manner growing ever sharper as the potential for diversion overcame his malaise.

'As though into thin air, Mr Holmes.' Hanlon sat opposite the detective, still red-faced and puffing, as if the mere act of relaying his story were enough to exhaust him all over again. I stood against the wall, watching them both from the side, still unsure of what to make of my old wastrel acquaintance.

'You did not think to set a watch?' I asked.

'Of course we did! I suggested it, in fact, as did several of the others, former Company men all.' He looked affronted, as though I impugned upon his reputation as a soldier. Perhaps I did, at that.

'But they saw nothing?' Holmes said, ignoring Hanlon's indignation.

'Not only did they see nothing, sirs, but they remembered nothing either.'

'Asleep at their posts?' I could not keep the scorn from my voice; it was near the worst crime a soldier could commit against his fellows, and one often met with far worse punishments than the flogging Hanlon had once received.

'No, sir.' He hesitated, as though ashamed. 'At least, not so as we can remember.'

'What can you tell us, Hanlon?' I said after a long silence, voice quiet. It seemed a moment, then, for whispers.

'None can recall anything that has happened.' The former soldier's face seemed to crumple in upon itself as he spoke. 'Even with the best will in the world to stand guard, all within the manor recall nothing but darkness until the following morn.'

'And when you awake?' Holmes and I asked simultaneously.

'A brother or two has vanished with nary a trace nor sign of struggle. If it was not for their belongings and our recollections, why, it would be as though they had never existed at all.'

'How then can you be sure they are not deserting your Fratery of their own free will?' Holmes clutched a piece of sandstone in his hand, tumbling it haphazardly through his fingers, always seeming on the verge of dropping it. His other hand held his pipe, pointing it at the brother as he spoke. 'If none of you are awake to see it, perhaps they themselves are orchestrating an escape from the confines of religious order?'

Hanlon shook his head vigorously, putting me in mind of a bulldog with his jowls flapping. 'No sir, Mr Holmes, and I know that for a fact.'

'How is that, Colton?' I asked, puffing at my own pipe.

'Because the brothers that go missing are the most pious of us, Captain Watson, and –' Hanlon cut himself off, sucking at his teeth in frustration.

'For God's sake man, spit it out!' I stepped towards him, angry in spite of myself. 'You people are the ones seeking our help, after all.'

'I heard them, Captain,' Hanlon whispered, looking down at his hands. His pudgy fingers worried at each other upon the surface of the table, writhing like worms. 'One night, I told Brother O'Rourke that I was going to fast and say prayers in my cell. Instead, I went to the kilns with a flagon of Brother Kenny's beer.'

Holmes and I both stared.

'I only wanted a wee tipple,' he said, raising his hands defensively. 'It was my ma's birthday, God rest her soul, and I wanted to drink to her.'

'What did you hear while in the kilns?' Holmes glared at the man, though whether with anger or mere concentration I could not tell.

'I was frightened, you understand? I was breaking my vows, and it weren't a natural thing to be hearing, besides, out there in the dark.'

'Who did you hear while in the kilns?' There was no mistaking the anger in my good friend's voice this time.

'I don't know who they were, sirs, but I do know one thing.' Hanlon took a deep, gulping breath. 'They were singing, like nothing I ever did hear. A song of the dead, it was, and no mistake.'

'Singing?' I could hardly keep the astonishment from my voice.

'Aye, singing, Captain.' Hanlon closed his eyes, face pale at the terror he had experienced. 'And when they were finally done with that savage song, the sun was up and three of our most beloved members were gone from their beds.'

Holmes toyed with his piece of sandstone, lithe fingers tracing the designs painted upon it, and did not respond.

'WATSON, WAKE UP!' Holmes's voice was a whispered hiss in the darkness.

I would like to say that I returned to wakefulness with the kind of alacrity I enjoyed in my youth, but truthfully it was a struggle and necessitated my good friend covering my mouth with his hand to muffle my drowsy questioning.

'Listen,' he said, so soft that I could barely hear his words.

A faint drumming came to me then, drifting in through cracks in the rough-hewn timber walls of the old servants' quarters we lodged in. The sound was a sharp, high-pitched one, like two pieces of wood crashing together instead of leather drum-skins, accompanied by a fierce, deep droning noise.

A low song was taken up, voices joined together, rising and falling in pitch. I knew not the words, of course, but I recognised immediately the source.

'It appears we meddling Englishmen might have some work ahead of us after all,' I said to Holmes. I drew my coat and boots on as quickly and quietly as I could and then loaded my revolver. Holmes clasped his own pistol in hand.

We made our way to the door, the bunkhouse silent but for our footsteps. I checked on a few of the boys as we walked past them, but not a one stirred.

The night was dark as pitch when we exited the building, the pale autumn moon and accompanying constellations completely obscured. We stood frozen in the doorway a long moment, listening to the sound of the drumming and the chant, louder now. I waited for my eyes to adjust to the near total darkness, but they refused.

'Watson.' Holmes grasped my shoulder, making me jump with surprise.

The circumstances we found ourselves in threatened to unman me! 'Head to the manor house and check on the brothers, see if any have been attacked.'

'Wait,' I said, grabbing his arm as he began to set off away from me, the darkness threatening to swallow him whole. 'What will you be doing?'

'Paying a visit to our mysterious watchers in the dark!' he said, disappearing.

Steeling my nerves, I moved in a crouch, zigging and zagging in the direction of the largest blank space in my eyeline. I expected, perhaps irrationally, to feel the bite of spear or arrow or bullet between my shoulders at any moment, but I passed unscathed. The droning song continued to accompany me, smothering the clearing that held the monastery in a way that even the all-encompassing darkness could not manage.

I pressed my back to the wall of the old house, my initial attempts to peer through a window rendered fruitless by the damned iron screens. I checked the main doors in turn, but found these locked. Instead, I made my way around the side of the house, hand trailing along the stone to keep my bearing, stepping as gingerly as possible upon the creaky boards.

At last I came to a small side door – a servant's entrance into the kitchen. It stood not just unlocked but open, the dim light inside both inviting and alarming.

I edged my revolver around the frame, keeping to my crouch to throw off any would-be attackers. There was nothing, just the dancing light of a few candles sitting upon the kitchen table.

My heart continued to pound in my chest as I entered the corridor inside the house, easing the kitchen door closed and enveloping myself in total darkness once again.

Keeping my hand on the wall as I moved – and I would be damned if I should rush considering the sheer amount of rickety furniture and groaning bookshelves lining the corridors – I made my way slowly to the grand staircase. I encountered no one along the way, and indeed heard no noise beyond my own soft breath and the now-muted droning song from, as Holmes had put it, the 'watchers in the dark' outside.

I climbed, being careful to keep to the long rug dividing the centre of the sweeping staircase. When I reached the top, I heard a whisper from my right.

My revolver snapped up immediately, any logical thoughts about this being one of the Fratery brothers overridden by that instinctual part of the brain that had kept me alive all these years.

As I peered round the corner, my eyes fell upon the dim light of a shuttered lantern, clasped in the hand of a black-robed man wielding a wooden spear. As I watched, another identical figure exited one of the rooms, grunting softly as a heavy weight settled across his shoulders. It only took me a moment to spot the feet dangling from the load he bore.

Unfortunately, in that same moment the shadowy figure holding the lantern spotted me and threw the spear.

With a curse, I ducked behind the wall, the deadly missile sticking, quivering, from the painted face of the patron saint of the Fratery where I had been standing a moment before.

I sprang back around the corner, revolver raised, but the men had already retreated from sight. I pursued them, shouting for the inhabitants to awaken and arm themselves.

Alas, no help came, and I launched myself down a servants' stair only to find myself back at the kitchen, where the door stood agape once more. I ran to the doorway and could just make out the two figures fleeing into the night, their still-living cargo bouncing on the shoulders of the one and stopping me from taking aim with my weapon.

I heard a commotion behind me. Assuming that the brothers had finally awoken, I turned to find another robed figure standing over me, seemingly half again my height. His face was obscured by a deep hood, but I saw the trace of crooked yellow teeth before his fist caught me in the side of the head.

I fell, still clasping my revolver, and tried to take aim even as I hit the ground. The heavy blow had rocked me and I struggled to clear my sight.

My attacker had no such difficulty, and my last recollection was of a hideous grin before his boot caught my temple and I knew nothing more.

FOR THE SECOND time that night, I was shaken back to consciousness with a man looming over me. Unlike the previous occasion, however, this time Sherlock Holmes was nowhere to be found.

'Are you all right, Dr Watson?' Hanlon sat next to me, half his face a livid bruise, his nose a bloody smear bordered by blackened, swollen eyes.

'You look worse than I feel, Hanlon,' I managed to groan as I drew myself into a seated position. I had been dragged onto a chaise in one of the downstairs living areas, and dust puffed into the air as I disturbed it with my movement.

'Oh, I'll be fine, sir, had far worse than this, as you'd know!' Hanlon reached a hand toward my face, as though to touch the bruise that was no doubt forming in parallel to his own, but seemed to think better of it.

'How long was I unconscious, Hanlon?' I asked. I felt quite groggy and the room was spinning.

'I can't be certain, sir, but it has been some time since the singing first started.' He shrugged apologetically. 'I encountered one of the big brutes outside, and I'm afraid I lost track of the time in the ensuing scuffle.'

'Hanlon, where is Holmes?'

'I don't know, sir. I only came across you, knocked unconscious.'

'What about the other members of your order?' I asked, frowning. 'Why did no one but yourself awaken?'

'I wasn't asleep,' Hanlon replied, looking sheepish. 'After Brother O'Rourke spoke to me, I was ordered to the penitent cell to "fast and consider my transgressions", as he put it. As for the others, I couldn't rightly comment.'

I stood up, a tad wobbly on my legs. I gingerly felt the side of my head and determined that there was no serious damage there, but I did wonder if I might be experiencing a swelling of the brain due to trauma.

'Come with me, Hanlon,' I muttered as I headed to the main staircase and ascended two steps at a time, hand gripping the railing lest I take a tumble in my dizziness. The former sergeant trailed behind me.

I held my revolver once more. In truth, I did not expect that any of the attackers would still be present, but I had already had one lesson in making assumptions this night.

The 'cells', such as they were, appeared as anything but when compared to the dark, dank lodgings Holmes and I had enjoyed in the servants' building; instead, the quarters of the brothers were made up in the old bedrooms of the house. Though the furnishings were austere and the beds simple things, it was still far more plush than one would expect, and put me in mind of more than one inn that I had stayed at back home.

In the first of the rooms we found a pair of cots, each inhabited by the snoring form of a brother of the Fratery. I shook first one and then the other, but neither would awaken. Even a jug of water poured by an eager Hanlon accomplished nothing more than rendering the sleeping man and his bedsheets sodden.

'Drugged, I should say, and unlikely to wake soon, if the depths of their slumber should be any indication.'

I lurched my way to the next room, Hanlon still trailing behind me and muttering about why someone would drug his brothers.

This room contained a pair of bunks, one of which was occupied by a rotund member of the Fratery – Brother Kenny the brewer, so Hanlon informed me – who also could not be roused. The other bunk was empty, the covers thrown to the floor.

One of our victims.

The next room down was the one where I had disturbed our erstwhile kidnappers, and thus I was not surprised to find both cots empty, one tipped over in the haste of the villains to remove the occupants.

Hanlon paused outside the room, fingers tracing the length of the wooden spear that stuck out from the wall and which had so narrowly missed ending my life. I heard him mutter under his breath – something about 'savages' – before he turned back toward me and we continued with our search.

The next two rooms were also empty, though the bunks here were neatly made up.

'Are these rooms unoccupied, Hanlon?'

'No, sir,' the former sergeant shook his head, his battered face perturbed. 'I know all four of the men who sleep here, all ex-soldiers like ourselves. Good, solid members of the Fratery, and all of whom should be sleeping here right now, sir, or on watch.'

I opened my mouth to reply, but was interrupted by a great cacophony from outside.

'Was that…?' Hanlon let the words hang.

'Gunfire,' I confirmed, my mouth set in a grim line.

THE DOORS TO the manor burst open as Hanlon and I raced down the stairs. I gripped my revolver, ready to shoot, but held my fire at the last second when I recognised the first of the men running inside.

'Brother O'Rourke?' Hanlon was equally dumbfounded.

'No time for questions, Brother Hanlon – we are under attack!'

Two others came inside after their leader, robes muddy and torn. Both carried muzzle-loaders of an archaic design and were returning fire with remarkable precision.

I stepped to the right side of the door frame and peered out into the gloom, but could see little. There was no return fire so far as I could tell, though I could hear a shot or two off in the distance.

'How is it that you are awake, Brother O'Rourke?' I looked to the head of the Fratery as I spoke, but he pointedly ignored me, glaring instead at poor Hanlon.

'What are you doing with him, Hanlon?' O'Rourke held a heavy revolver resembling one of the models the Americans like so much, and was gesticulating wildly as he spoke. 'You should be abed asleep, as should they.'

'He is not asleep because you made him undergo penance,' came a familiar voice from behind me. 'As for us, well, we both decided to retire to our rooms early since I suspected trouble might be afoot before first light.'

'Holmes!' I gasped. My old friend sat on the foot of the stairs I had just walked down, clad only in shirt and trousers, and in his stockinged feet. He was as covered in filth as the brothers, but that was not what stood out most.

His own pistol was pointed at O'Rourke.

'Watson, if you would be so kind as to disarm our dear members of the Fratery there, I would be most appreciative.'

Muskets and revolver swung to point at Holmes and I both.

'You will do no such thing.' Brother O'Rourke's heavy gun was aimed directly at Holmes, long barrel unwavering. 'In fact, Hanlon, retrieve their weapons. Now.'

Hanlon stepped between us all, looking genuinely confused and more than a little frightened at the sudden hostilities. At that range, with weapons pointed towards me, I certainly sympathised.

'I do not understand.' Hanlon had his hands raised, palms out, one facing Holmes and me, the other his brethren and leader. 'If we are under attack from outside, why are you pointing guns at each other?'

'They're working with the damned tribes, Hanlon!' O'Rourke paused, letting the faint dirge from outside wash over us. 'They're helping them kidnap and murder the members of the Fratery!'

'But there has been no record of conflict with the Tharawal tribespeople in more than fifty years, Brother O'Rourke. Most say they don't even exist anymore.' Hanlon shook his head as he spoke, forehead glistening with sweat. 'And Captain Watson and Mr Holmes have only just arrived; they couldn't be involved in this.'

'Not the whole time, you idiot, but tonight!' O'Rourke stepped forward, fist clenched, white-knuckled at his side as he approached the old sergeant. 'Now listen to me and disarm them.'

Hanlon turned to face me, a pleading look on his face. I shook my head, my own revolver aimed squarely at the brothers-cum-riflemen.

'The esteemed Brother O'Rourke is right about one thing, Hanlon,' said Holmes, a very slight smile playing about his lips. 'We are, in fact, working with the peoples of the Tharawal tribe. Or at least I am – I dare say the good doctor has not the slightest idea of who the Tharawal are.'

I spared him a glance, eyebrow cocked; though I did not know the name, I could hazard a guess.

'There, you see, Hanlon, he admits as much.'

Hanlon took another step forward, face firming at his superior's words.

'But they,' continued Holmes, 'are not behind the spate of kidnappings. Stop a moment, Hanlon, and listen to the interesting things I have learned about the Fratery of Saint Dymphna this night.'

'I HAD SEPARATED from Watson upon exiting the bunkhouse, sending him to the manor in the hope of catching the kidnappers in the act – something he appears to have managed, judging by the bruises upon his face, though not quite as effectively as I had anticipated.

'I myself stepped into the darkness of the night, making my way through the fields in the hopes of coming up behind our mysterious singers. I suspected at first they were a distraction, designed to disguise their attack and confuse any defenders.

'However, the more I considered what had been happening here at Revan Manor – the mysterious kidnappings and even more mysterious memory lapses in those who remained – I began to wonder at the point of creating quite so much ruckus when the attacks were taking place with such effortless secrecy.

'Hanlon's story of hearing the haunting song while secretly drinking in the kilns made me further question the veracity of the theory that the singers and the kidnappers were one and the same. Why had he only heard them once, when the kidnappings had been occurring for weeks?

'Upon hearing tell of what had been going on – guards who had seen nothing, valued brothers disappearing with their roommates never even stirring – I began to suspect that a type of poison or other such substance was being used. I confirmed this suspicion – one I am sure the good doctor also held – by not allowing us to share in the meal presented to us before bed. Sure enough, all the boys in the bunkhouse had soon lapsed into unconsciousness and were unable to be awoken.

'It was with these thoughts swirling around in my head that I came across our mysterious musicians. They were indeed members of the Tharawal people – a dozen of them, all young men, unarmed but for their instruments.

'I called out to them, my pistol tucked into the waistband of my trews, and they initially assumed I was hostile. We spoke and I explained who I was and why we had come to the area. Though at first reluctant to trust me, their leader – a lad named Warran – warned me that we had stumbled into a most dangerous situation.

'Further discussion was unfortunately curtailed when our actual kidnappers came upon us. Seven men, all armed with crude approximations of spears – designed to shift attention away from their own crimes when the constabulary inevitably came knocking – with their victims draped across their shoulders.

'On previous occasions, the kidnappers had not been quite so harried and had thus never directly encountered my new friends. The Tharawal youth had been reluctant to advance any closer, bound by their own, complex, views on honour and what was occurring.

'This time, however, they clashed directly, and never let it be said that the indigenous people of this continent are not as fiercely brave as those of the Americas or Africa! Despite lacking armament and fighting against experienced warriors, the boys attacked, their song never wavering. I myself managed to wing one of the foes before darting in, fighting a large beast of a man with yellowed teeth. Truly, my fists have still not recovered – his bones were like steel! – and my ribs feel as though they are cracked in a half-dozen places.

'In the end, we were triumphant, albeit not without cost. We bound and gagged the kidnappers with strips of their own robes, except for those few who managed to escape.

'I left one man's mouth ungagged, of course, and it was then that we made our discovery.'

'WHAT DISCOVERY WAS that, old boy?' I asked, enthralled by Holmes's tale, and also somewhat gratified that my own thoughts on the drugging of the inhabitants of the manor had been confirmed by the great detective.

'Yes, what is going on, Mr Holmes?' Hanlon's voice held a note of pleading.

'Perhaps Brother O'Rourke wishes to complete the tale?' O'Rourke and his fellows said nothing as Holmes spoke.

After a long pause, he continued.

'The big brute we bound, but did not gag. At first, he refused to talk – what good soldier would, after all? – but in the end we got him to speak about all manner of things.'

'That's quite enough.' O'Rourke had gradually gone paler as Holmes had spoken, but his gun had never wavered. 'Step aside, Hanlon, and let me finish this.'

'What?' Hanlon did not move, turning back toward the leader of his order. 'Finish this how?'

'He means to murder us, do you not, O'Rourke?' Holmes's voice was even, as though he were discussing the weather. 'Much like you've had your men murder the kidnapping victims, no?'

Hanlon stood, frozen.

'Jesus, Danny, you've been killing them all?' One of the brothers who had held a rifle trained on me this whole time stepped back, a look of horror on his face. 'They're all good Irishmen, good Catholics.'

'This isn't what we signed up for, O'Rourke.' The other threw his weapon down, freckled face contorted by rage.

'They're living here in this English colony taking in English strays and doing nothing to help our struggle, and you call them good Irishmen?' O'Rourke spun on his erstwhile brothers, thumb cocking the hammer on his gun. 'They are all traitors to our cause, and now so are you!'

I watched, bewildered, as Brother O'Rourke, or whoever he was, prepared to fire.

A heartbeat later, Brother Hanlon slammed into O'Rourke's back, shoulder driving into his spine and smashing him to the ground. The old provost pinned the man down, throwing his gun away, hand raised to strike.

'Tell me the truth, O'Rourke.' No subservience in Hanlon now; I dare say he had reached his breaking point some time ago. 'Tell me the truth of what is going on here or I will beat it out of you.'

'Yes, Danny O'Rourke.' Holmes had stepped forward from the stairs and crouched beside the pinned man. I myself had stepped forward as well, resting a hand upon Hanlon's shoulder. 'It is time to confess your sins.'

'SO YOU WISH me to confess? Very well then, Englishman, if that is what you want, then you can hear tell of my mission.

'I suppose you know all about the Fratery of Saint Dymphna now, thanks to Hanlon? Well, I knew old Brother Rickaby, the founder of the Fratery, quite well. He took me in back in Dublin, cared for me when my ma and pa were killed by your queen's soldiers.

'Rickaby was a good man, in his own way. Kind hearted, caring. He loved the Irish, but he loved all others as well, and it was there that we had our first disagreement. He would not hate the English for what they had done to us. Would not fight to take back our land. Would not even support those who fought on his behalf.

'I left him when I turned fifteen, making my way across Europe, as keen to get away from his hypocrisy as an Irishman as I was to be away from the English. I joined the army in Spain, fighting in one of the Irish Guard regiments, and made something of a name for myself. It was there, while our regiment was being rested in the south, that I heard about a group of monks being sent to Australia to settle in the hinterlands.

'You must understand that I had spent years – years – attempting to rouse support amongst my fellow Irishmen to return home and fight the English. Many expressed interest, of course, but few showed any true fire for the plan, being far too downtrodden by centuries of oppression. Ireland, it seemed, was a challenge too great to surmount.

'So I made a plan. Myself and a handpicked group of volunteers – including Brother Swain, the big fellow who should know to keep his mouth shut! – absconded from our barracks and seized the vessel of the monks. We had the crew sail us to Australia as planned, but we stopped away from any major ports. I had the majority of my men row ashore and then used my most trusted few to scuttle the vessel with the crew and the monks still aboard.

'It had been my initial plan merely to roam the countryside, recruiting members to our band as we went. In the back of my mind, however, had been the thought of this isolated manor to which the monks had been bound. As we made our way from the coast around Wollongong and up into the hills, I heard that old Brother Rickaby – ancient now – had moved to the colonies with the few remaining members of his old Fratery, tending to the orphans and the vagrants of Wollongong and the surrounding mines.

'It was simplicity itself to find the brother and discuss old times, and to encourage him to petition the Catholic church for a new, permanent home at Revan Manor, what with the inexplicable disappearance of the Spanish monks. Simpler, still, to suffocate him while he slept once the request had been granted.

'He never felt a thing; I felt as though I owed him that much.

'I introduced myself to the remaining members of the Fratery, many of whom remembered me as being like a son to the old man. I explained how I had founded my own order in Spain, inspired by my upbringing. They were incredibly eager to induct us all post haste into their own brotherhood, and from there it was even simpler to rig the votes to make me the leader…'

'BUT WHY?' THE look of horror on Hanlon's face was no doubt matched by my own. It was almost impossible to comprehend the sheer callousness that O'Rourke was expressing.

'Because when Danny O'Rourke realised that he was not going to take back Ireland, he determined instead to build an army to take a different land.' Holmes looked unwaveringly at the prone revolutionary as he spoke, though my own eyes were also focused upon the man's former allies, still standing, stunned, their weapons dropped and forgotten.

'Where better to build a paradise away from the damned English than on the other side of the world, especially one where so many of our brothers and sisters had already been wrongly sent?' O'Rourke smiled wistfully as he spoke. 'We started out small, carefully removing the traitors and those too weak or unfaithful to the cause from our ranks. Soon, we would have begun sending our brothers out into the communities of downtrodden Irish to preach of freedom from English tyranny, not through peace, but through the sword.'

'You'd have gotten even more innocent people killed in this madness?' I asked, aghast.

'Innocent? If you are unwilling to raise arms to fight oppression, you are not innocent – you are a collaborator!' O'Rourke spat. 'We'd appeal to their spirit, put fire in their bellies. Soon we'd have more fighting men than could be stopped, supported by good Irish folk across the entire continent. I was so very close.'

'Why me?' Hanlon's fingers knotted themselves into the front of O'Rourke's robe, tightening it around his neck like a noose. 'Why did you seek me out to join the Fratery?'

'Because you were lost,' I said, before O'Rourke could respond. 'He needed men of Irish and Catholic stock for his mad quest, and he needed those who could be trained to fight – or better yet, already could – but most of all, he needed men looking for a cause.'

'You were conflicted, Colton,' said O'Rourke, almost kindly. 'I knew the type of man you could be, if only you got away from the bad choices they had forced upon you, conscripting you into the army and –'

Brother Colton Hanlon hammered his fist into O'Rourke's mouth, hard enough to knock teeth free.

'You do not know me, O'Rourke,' said he, voice rough. 'But I've known bastards like you my whole life.'

'I STILL DO not understand,' I said, some time later, as Holmes and I stood on the outside deck of the great manor, smoking our pipes and watching Hanlon work.

Colton Hanlon, for all his faults, had nevertheless been a sergeant and a military policeman. Such training and experience does not leave you – believe me, I am more than ample proof – but it was still interesting, and even slightly amusing, to watch him bark orders at the bewildered brothers of the Fratery as they dragged the restrained revolutionaries from within the house out onto the lawn.

'What is it you do not comprehend about this little adventure, Watson?' Holmes had a mischievous twinkle in his eye, though whether from preparing to espouse his knowledge of the case to me or due to amusement at the scene before us, I was not entirely certain.

I paused a long moment, framing my thoughts in my mind. The coterie of brothers – all older, original members of the Fratery from before O'Rourke's coup, or brand-new ones who had yet to be approached with whatever twisted semblance of the truth the revolutionary had been espousing – had been awakened with the antidote carried by the kidnappers about their person. Though their minds were foggy from the drug, they were quick enough to act once talk of murder and conspiracy was brought to their attention. The revolutionaries – those who had not been drugged themselves in O'Rourke's paranoia, or those already captured by Holmes and his allies – had given up easily, drained of their will to fight with the knowledge of the true horrors their master had been unleashing.

'The Tharawal youths – why did they help you? Indeed, why were they here at all?'

Holmes drew deeply upon his pipe before he responded. 'Hanlon was right earlier. At least, partially.'

'What do you mean?' said I.

'When he said that there had been no record of conflict with the Tharawal in at least fifty years, he was mostly correct, barring the odd bit of racial violence or occasional murder in the mining towns.' Holmes did not look at me as he spoke. 'The Tharawal do still exist, as is clearly evident, though not in the way one might expect.'

'What does that mean, Holmes?'

'Those boys were not "savage tribesmen" as Danny O'Rourke might have put it; no, they were merely youths from settlements in the area, working in the mines or on the land. All of them, however, are descendants of the Tharawal people, and they maintain their traditions and the knowledge of their ancestors, even as their lands and history are irreversibly altered around them.'

Another silence fell upon us at that thought. Many back home could not understand why it was that the bright light of European – especially British – settlement was not welcomed by the native peoples of their respective continents. Holmes and I had, through all our various travels, seen firsthand the kind of destruction such settlement could bring, even with the noblest of intentions.

Apparently we were seeing another example, albeit indirectly.

'But what made them decide to interfere?'

'A simple thing, compared to such grandiose goals as revolution, but one that Mr O'Rourke should have kept well in mind.' Holmes emphasised the title 'Mister' slightly as he spoke.

'And what "simple thing" was that, Holmes?'

'Those boys were all taken in and cared for by Brother John Rickaby and his Fratery of Saint Dymphna. Warran was travelling through this area when he spied some of O'Rourke's henchmen carting their kidnap victims – those who were of the old order, or who had failed some sort of ideological test – to the cliffs above the river and throwing them in, still unconscious.'

'God above!' I interrupted the great detective's dispassionate retelling, I had known, of course, that O'Rourke had been murdering his fellow brothers, but I nonetheless found myself stunned once again by his callous disregard for life.

'Warran happened to recognise one of the victims, but was unable to save him due to the number of so-called brothers and their weapons. He tried the constabulary, but none would hear a word from him. So instead he gathered some friends and they did what they could, despite the danger to their own lives.'

'Remarkable. Their plan was to awaken the manor with their song, wasn't it? They could sing and play their instruments from within the woods, ensuring they could provide their warning without being seen.'

'It was indeed, Watson.' Holmes smiled as he puffed on his pipe, obviously impressed by their ingenuity. 'But they had no way of knowing that O'Rourke had access to such a powerful drugging agent, nor that he would be so ruthless as to use it to drug every person, including children, on the property.'

Hanlon walked up to us then, his face set in a determined mien. It was the first time I had seen him looking so sure, so confident. Behind him, the pile of tied-up revolutionaries wriggled and groaned, half of them only now starting to awaken, the rest faced with the prospect of prison for sedition against the Crown.

'Thank you both for your help,' Hanlon said, shaking Holmes's hand and then my own. 'Though it was hardly the mystery I had imagined when I engaged your services, I am nonetheless glad that you were here to solve it.'

'Saying it was our pleasure would, perhaps, not be entirely accurate,' I chuckled, 'but I can assure you we are glad we came as well.'

Hanlon stood beside me, the three of us peering out over the grounds as the sun slowly crested the trees.

'It is hard to believe that one man could have caused so much horror.' Hanlon spoke softly, as though to himself. 'Such a sinister plan, so many years in the making.'

'Wanton murder and destruction,' I said.

'Revolution.' Holmes almost seemed to relish the word. 'Truly, one must admire his ambition, if not his methods.'

'What will you do now, Hanlon?' I asked, after a long while.

'The Fratery is in disarray, of course,' he said, frowning as some of his fellow brothers roused the children from the bunkhouse Holmes and I had stayed in. They came out, one by one, bleary eyed. 'There has been much damage done, and perhaps the order shall never recover.'

I glanced at him, unable to hide my smile.

'But,' he continued. 'We will try. The Fratery of Saint Dymphna does far too much good in this world to be brought down by a lunatic like O'Rourke.'

'I believe that is the right and noble choice, Colton.' I clapped him on his shoulder. 'You have come a long way from the man whose back I once stitched up in Afghanistan.'

'Perhaps I've come further than I myself realised, John.' He smiled, shook our hands once more, and took his leave.

We watched his back as he departed, again shouting orders and whipping the Fratery into shape. A call was made for riders to head to town and contact the constabulary there, and for someone to pack a meal – not poisoned, mind! – for our journey back to Sydney.

We mounted our mules and followed our guide – one of the boys, this time – through the gates of Revan Manor. It was hard to believe in many ways that we had only spent a day there.

Holmes spoke as we approached the road, the sun once again surprisingly warm upon our backs. 'Watson, I dare say that your friend Colton is a man who has resolved his –'

'Inner conflict,' I interrupted with a grin, to make it clear our years of long friendship had also left me with some capacity to anticipate another man's thoughts. 'Yes, inner conflict. I dare say you are right.'

THE STORY OF THE REMARKABLE WOMAN

Lucy Sussex

THE TALE I relate now was garnered by chance, during the steamship passage when we travelled from Australia to New Zealand. I must admit that the remarkable lady whose story it was first caught Holmes's attention. Being then younger, and rather more romantic, I saw little in a woman not in her first youth, and clad in widow's black. My devotion was all for the young damsel passengers, who being shrewd colonials quickly ascertained my means and marital status, which did not prevent some harmless shipboard flirtation. Thus I had pleasantly but fruitlessly occupied myself when not attending upon Holmes, or watching the vistas of rolling waves and the occasional whale.

On this trip we had fraternised with the first-class passengers: apart from the aforementioned young ladies and their mammas, we had a colonial politician and his entourage (dreary boasters), missionaries (even drearier), an ex-opera singer (who talked scandal and food), some mining speculators (monomaniacs about minerals) and a colonial touring cricket team (splendid fellows, but rather limited in conversation). Holmes had tired of them all quickly, taking his meals in his cabin, citing ill-health, albeit a hearty appetite, from all the sea air.

Arrival in Hobart saw the disembarkation of some passengers, and new arrivals. We two sat in our deckchairs idly smoking and watching their progress up the gangplank. The lady concerned waved goodbye to a family group, dominated by an enormous perambulator, containing twins. She passed the politician on his way down, with a curt nod, then ascended to our vantage point. With an evident air of relief, she saw her luggage stowed and settled

337

in a deckchair not far from us. We overheard her ask the steward, in a voice well bred but with a northern English burr, for the latest London newspapers. Additionally – and I nudged Holmes – she specifically requested new detective stories.

Holmes made no immediate response, his keen gaze appraising, as she sat down with her neat pile of newspapers, opening not *The Strand* first, but *The Times*.

'Observe, Watson,' he said, 'how she is reading the papers.'

I did so, puzzled.

'Those colonial lasses,' he said, 'who have been so diverting you, they would have begun with the fashion page, the latest hats for their feathery little pates. The politician, why, the politics; and the missionaries, the church news. The mining speculators, the stock market. This lady, why, she glanced thoroughly at all these columns, with the eye of a professional, but showed most interest in the great trials of the day. And see how she has followed the coverage from *The Times* to the *Daily Express,* and lesser papers. I will hazard it is the Bermondsey poisoning that has her attention. An enigmatic case… and the lady is likewise an enigma. What do you see, Watson?'

I saw we would soon be treated to one of his deductive lists; he was like a novelist depicting character traits. Although my abilities in that line had been honed by time spent in his company, I would never pin his subjects as precisely as he did, like butterflies in a collecting box.

'Why, a colonial widow, in her black.'

'Not once but twice. She wears two rings, one silver, a starveling band, donned with love. It is battered, showing physical work, such as few women of her English class perform, having servants. The second is thicker, fine gold, unmarked. She has learned frugal habits, her clothes chosen to wear well rather than be fashionable. In a hard school, I would warrant – perhaps in actuality, as she has the schoolma'am air. Those times have passed, for now she can afford a first-class passage, and the small pleasures of life. She savours both her fine tea and her reading.'

'Including our own detective tales, perhaps?' We had already had several amusing conversations on this trip with admiring readers of our rivals –

Gaboriau, or Fergus Hume. I had tried not to giggle when Holmes denounced them as sensational, criminous rubbish! Now I eyed the lady again, as a prospective reader. Try as I might, I could not perceive anything except an unexceptional matron.

'What interest could there be, Holmes, in a woman visiting her grandchildren?'

'Step-grandchildren. That family looked nothing like her.'

At the dinner table, as the mail-steamer wended its way out the harbour and towards New Zealand, we found the lady at the place of the departed politician, and Holmes sat himself beside her. I was quickly diverted by a colonial miss who had clearly had a contretemps with one of the cricketers and so sought to pretend fascination with my humble self, in full sight of the gentleman concerned. Thus I heard little of the conversation between the lady and Holmes, except that Bermondsey was clearly mentioned several times, and at one stage the pair arranged their cutlery and glasses to represent the murder scene – to some disapproving glances from the one remaining missionary. I was too busy trying to offend neither the young miss, nor her beau; charming though she was, I wanted to avoid a thrashing from the muscular young man.

After dinner, we made our escape to the lee side, which, since the night was balmy, formed a pleasant spot for postprandial drinks and conversation. Holmes introduced me to the lady, a Mrs Maxwelton.

'And have you two solved the Bermondsey case over dinner?' I asked.

'That will wait for the cables from the trial,' she said. 'We merely compared opinions, and politely differed.'

'An unusual interest for a lady,' I commented.

'Hardly,' said Holmes. 'Have you never noticed the well-dressed females who attend sensational Old Bailey trials, eyes gleaming with excitement beneath their veils?'

'In my case it was professional and familial,' she said. 'My father was a criminal lawyer, and when he went blind, he had me take notes in court for him. Thus I developed the skill of reportage and the love of an intricate case.'

She smiled, stroking her first wedding ring.

'He would never have done so had he known I would meet a young court reporter, and marry him. My poor father was wrathful at losing his amanuensis, and cut me off without a shilling. So, hearing of the gold strikes in the colonies, we emigrated… and I have never regretted it, not even when my dear husband died of a fever, leaving me alone, in a strange land, and a lawless one too.'

Holmes met my eye: *I told you so.*

'What did you do then, ma'am?'

'I taught, and while my charges were asleep, wrote for the colonial press. Sketches mostly… some even about crime, since I knew a bit about it.'

Did I mistake it, or did she glance significantly at me?

'I have observed,' said Holmes, 'during my time in the colonies, that crimes seem much the same as in England.'

'Now, yes, but during the gold era there was great incentive for evil. People went from rags to rich silks with a single nugget find. Not necessarily theirs.'

'Perhaps you could elaborate?' he said.

'I can tell you of a truly remarkable case, since you have an interest in the subject. And perhaps we could see if you agree or disagree with my reading of it – I do not say solution.'

'Proceed!' said Holmes, and I gave up all thought of the young ladies for the evening. We ordered some sherries, and sat watching the lights of receding Hobart.

'It happened over thirty years ago, in the wildest of the goldfields days. I shall not specify the locale, nor where I placed my poor relation of the events, save that it was in a publication for a different colony, for which I changed the setting.'

'As is tactful for writers,' I said, 'when dealing with contentious matter, drawn from life.'

'True,' she said. 'I did not want the original to be recognised. As a lawyer's daughter, I knew all about the danger of libel.'

'So,' said Holmes, 'just as we are on a steamer travelling between Australia and New Zealand, you took an Australian tale, and set it in Maoriland, or vice versa.'

'It began,' she said, 'with a corpse pulled from a river…'

THE CORPSE IN THE RIVER

Two men trudged up the muddy main street of a goldfields settlement, which I will call Whispering Flat. They carried a shutter, upon it a shrouded form, trailing a faint but fearful stench, and behind also a motley collection of children, dogs, and the local curious. On the hotel verandah, as the cortege neared, a constable argued with the landlady.

'An inquest in my hotel? Haven't I enough work with these blessed floods?'

'Missus, your hotel is high and dry, unlike so much else here!'

The arrival of the dead on the doorstep forced the issue: the landlady gave way, crossing herself. With a few sharp orders, a back room got prepared for the deceased.

'Poor thing, he'll make no difficult requests,' she said. 'Except for justice.'

The pallbearers wiped their muddy feet on the doormat, not well, and carried the dead to his penultimate rest. A small crowd followed, now including a hotel guest, an unobtrusive woman, young-old, in widow's black, slipping a sensational novel underneath her shawl. An inquest was much more exciting!

'That was you, madam?' said Holmes.

'Of course!'

On a table, the dead burden was laid: a half-decayed body, pulled out of the river, in what looked like a flour bag, but at closer view proved to be tent canvas, of good quality. Through a rip in the canvas could be clearly seen discoloured, bloodless flesh, with protruding from a gash a sawn-off branch.

The onlookers insinuated themselves into the room, commenting heartlessly.

'Who would treat a man like a litter of pups?'

'Someone as knows that if you throw a body in water, as he rots, he bloats with his own gas and bobs to the surface.'

'Even in a sack?'

'See there? Those be rocks sewn in with the poor devil, holding him down.'

'What's with the branch impalin' him?'

A shutterbearer held forth: 'I can tell you all about that. See, this rata…'

'A New Zealand tree, I have read,' said Holmes.

'Did I say that? Perhaps I meant the Australian eucalypt. Whatever the species, the tree had uprooted with the rain and rolled down the flooded river, to sweep the dead from his sandy grave. Then it snagged, corpse and all, in the bridge. When the water receded, there he remained, a silent witness to murder.'

'Continue, madam,' said Holmes.

'As the inquest began, I sat quietly in a corner, as I had with my father, hearing the evidence. A doctor testified to a fatal blow to the head, delivered with force and an axe-blade. The verdict: Wilful Murder, of a person unknown, by a person or persons unknown. The dead man was not particularly remarkable, in form or in what remained of his face: indeed little was distinctive except that in the selvedge of the canvas were striped threads, red and blue, of a good, lasting dye, despite the immersion.'

Mrs Maxwelton shrugged, taking a sip of sherry. 'And one further thing. I have been gifted with sharp hearing, and also eyesight, which have not diminished with the years. I could not help noticing that the sewing of the poor man into his shroud was uncommonly neat. A tailor's work, or a woman's.'

Holmes eyed her quietly.

'And what happened afterwards?'

'Oh the usual procedure: interment of the dead, a report in the colonial newspaper, which I cut out and saved, along with my own notes on the case, a reward offered… and nothing. With the flood's ebb, so likewise did the interest in the case. I, like so many others, moved on, to new rushes, or in my case to the position of governess at a sheep station. A very remote place it was, with no chance of newspapers. At night, when writing my little sketches, I would get out the clipping and worry at it. There was a story in it, but it lacked all conclusion – it puzzled me mightily.'

'Indeed something with which I am familiar,' I laughed.

She continued, with a small smile. 'Several years passed: the alluvial rushes became mining operations, with quartz crushers, and more settled townships. I left my position for something less lonely: a denominational school in a growing town, with the blessing of a tri-weekly newspaper. I did make friends there, the closest the wife of the newspaper editor, whose daughters I taught. Her husband was assiduous in covering all the news he could: local, from Home in old England, and also correspondence from throughout the Austral colonies. One day in his paper I read a story: a body found in a river some fifty miles away, inside a canvas shroud, dead from an axe blow. I got out my cuttings, and placed the newsprint, the yellowed and the fresh, side by side on my school desk. The devilry was in the detail: the mention of selvedge threads, red and blue. I could still envisage them.

'A murderer, striking twice, miles and years apart? I spoke to the editor, now also an employer. He and his wife were the only ones in the town who knew I wrote, since he had pirated a sketch of mine from another paper, all unthinking. I had half-seriously asked for a reprint fee. Instead he offered me proof-reading, much-needed extra revenue, for my stipend was stingy: I hewed my own wood for the school stove, and scrubbed the floor. He also spoke with the parson, my main employer, arguing I should be given leave to be a witness. Not much good did it do, for that man of the church was hard and narrow. Until…'

She glanced at me. 'If you are a writer you will be familiar with the urge, in telling a story, to exaggerate, even when you are depicting the truth. It might not be strictly accurate, but it makes a better story.'

I nodded.

'I blurted out to the parson: "I saw him in a dream, the poor murdered man, and he stretched out his hands towards me, seeking help."'

She gave that slight smile again.

'I will tell you two gentlemen now that the dream had occurred several years earlier, dismissed then as being caused by too much burning the midnight oil, or bad cheese. But the parson had a superstitious side: I had seen, hidden behind his tracts, Spiritualist journals.'

Holmes raised his eyebrows, almost imperceptibly.

'As I had hoped, it tipped the argument in my favour. And so I took the mail coach, a long and weary journey over the dirt roads, to the town where the report had originated: it was older, more settled, nearer to the colonial capital. There I presented to the town justice letters of recommendation, from the parson, the editor and our town policeman, whose son I taught. For I was but a petticoat, and I needed the borrowed authority of the male.

'He was a brisk man, who made me feel his busyness, in manner if not words: "A sorry business! It was gazetted months ago that the engineers would turn the river's inconvenient course. And so they did, to find in the drained riverbed a corpse, with the flesh still on him."

'I replied: "So I read in your *Chronicle*."

'He said, "We held an inquest, and buried the deceased, the weather being warm. But without his canvas shroud, in case of further evidence, of which we had no great hope. People scatter from rush to rush, leaving only ghost towns behind. Like Whispering Flat, where these letters say you saw the similarly clad corpse."

'Silently I handed him my prized newsprint, in an envelope. While he read I glanced outside, to see a fine carriage, open to the sunny day, and visible within was a bell-topper, and a bonnet topped with nodding ostrich plumes. It swept past, to a grimace from a man in a shabby hat. He was in the act of tying a horse, attached to an equally shabby cart, to the rail outside the police office. The justice continued reading while I stood in front of him like an errant schoolgirl. Finally he returned his attention to me and said, "I will require your deposition, on oath."

'A knock on the door; a constable, who conferred with him in whispers. With that something changed, as at a ball, when the belle arrives and throws all the other girls into shade.

'He said, "We have a second witness, it seems! I will empanel another inquest. You will wait, ma'am, until we call you."

'And so I did, escorted by the constable to the front parlour of the inn, where I had weak tea, bread rolls, and nothing to read except the Newgate Calendar. Finally the constable returned to escort me across the road to the courthouse.

'As we did, we passed a man leaning up against its wall and addressing himself to a wedge of pie. From his battered hat I recognised he who had grimaced at the carriage – although I had an odd sense that I might have seen him somewhere before. But I forgot about him for the moment, because the coronial jurors awaited me. Confounded nuisance, said their faces, and an old petticoat too! I gave my testimony, facing the justice, and at the end was taken to a table, where lay a length of canvas, dirty and stained. Even without the smell of death-rot, I could identify the striped selvedge. Then, dismissed, I sat in a corner again, unnoticed.

'The call came: "Timothy Atwoode!"

'Enter the pieman, hat in hand: broad and strong from manual labour, his ruddy face amiable, expressive of no great intelligence. As he swore his oath I saw the jurors' mood change – such was the power of bonhomie.

'The justice said, "State for the jury your occupation."

'Sometimes storekeeper, sometimes carter, sometimes miner, at Fairfax Town.' The lady's accent altered, from Yorkshire to the Midlands, as she spoke Atwoode's words. 'I stock the newspaper, and read it, too. And when I saw your *Chronicle*, I came as fast as I could, though slowed by my old horse goin' lame.'

She spoke in her own voice again. 'He gazed around, and with two steps confronted the canvas on the table. Almost immediately he slapped his hand down in a hard, identifying thump and said, "I swear that striped stuff is what I got from Sly Joe Seccombe."

'The justice said, "Mr Seccombe, if you please."

'"*Mister*, though none on Whispering Flat called him that, and he was no rich man either then. Just landlord of the Welcome Stranger, afore the flood half washed it away, and a poor shanty it was too…"

'I still could not place Atwoode, yet I recalled the name of the inn. When that flood had receded, a driver and gig had been sent to fetch me to the sheep station. Several miles upstream from Whispering Flat we had passed a drab roadside shanty, where a woman swept flotsam and jetsam from the verandah. The sign, Welcome Stranger, had remained in my mind, for indeed it looked most unwelcoming. At the sight the driver had spat, flicking his whip. The horse sped up, the woman's white face a blur behind us.

'As the man Atwoode spoke, I closed my eyes, to concentrate better. Against the backdrop of my eyelids, the storyteller's fancy painted pictures. He spoke, and I created a magic-lantern slide: of a stormy night and a man with the goldminer's swag, nearing the Welcome Stranger. He jangled the few coins in his pocket – enough for a night's rest? Inside, a fire, the smell of grog and boiled beef, and two men clasping hands in recognition.

'Atwoode said, "Back home Seccombe and I, we was brother weavers at t'mill."'

She continued with her magic-lantern slides. 'A hearty plain meal, gratis from old friendship, at a table with other guests flitting between the rushes. The Welcome Stranger being crowded, Atwoode got billeted in the garret, lying on piles of tenting. He stroked the fabric, with a weaver's eye for quality.'

She returned to the courtroom scene. 'Atwoode turned and eyed the jury. "And then," he said, "that night, came the barghest, arising from the canvas and wringing his ghostly hands, all dripping water and blood he was."'

'The justice asked, "A dream?"'

'He said, "It were gone in candlelight."'

She paused, wrapping her shawl around her, for the sea air grew chill. 'When he said that my magic-lantern show came to an end. I found I could not envisage the scene at all.'

'Too much of a story,' I ventured.

She nodded. 'I thought to Atwoode: you have over-egged your tale and though these gentlemen do not notice, I do.'

We fell silent, contemplating the dark sea. Holmes rubbed his hands together. 'Shall we go inside, and continue?'

We resumed in the saloon, in a corner farthest from the piano, at which one of the young ladies was trilling a music-hall song.

'Where was I?' Mrs Maxwelton said, settling herself. 'Ah, in the courtroom, listening intently to a testimony about which I was beginning to have doubts. But the next details did convince, as when a writer draws from memory rather than fancy, the authenticity unmistakeable: Atwoode said that he rose with the dawn, and in the dim light absently donned a hat, not his own, and too good to be forgotten in a garret.

'In his own words, which I transcribed: "I asked Sly – Mr Seccombe – I could have it. Though it faded, there was a stain in the linin' that never did.

As per-sis-tent as old blood, and the colour of it, too." He held out the hat to the jurors, who took it and passed it around.

'And that was not all Atwoode asked for: he wanted supplies, especially tenting: the stuff in the garret, surely no use to a man with a roof over his head?'

'What, when Atwoode had seen a ghost arise from it?' I said.

'Precisely,' said Holmes, signalling to the steward for refreshment. 'Thus betraying his unreliability, though not to the jurors, it seems.'

I thought a moment. 'Did Atwoode perceive he had something to give him a hold over Seccombe, more than old friendship?'

'The hat,' said Holmes. 'That is obvious.'

Mrs Maxwelton nodded. 'I underlined it in my notes.'

'Go on,' said Holmes.

'Atwoode's evidence continued. "Though Mr Seccombe wrung his hands, he could not tell me nay."'

'Nor explain, no doubt,' I interjected.

The lady spoke in Atwoode's voice again. 'His missus, she went even more whey-faced than before, and when I left I heard her cuss at him, call him a fool. I lingered, listening on the verandah, and heard him say: "Hush now. A few more quiet nights, a few more lucky diggers, and we'll have gold nuggets for all the carriages and finery you want."'

She eyed us again. 'The justice asked Atwoode if he had any witnesses to support his evidence. And he replied: "I remember from there only the Seccombes, and a German miner called Hans. He had an injured hand, which Missus bound up for him. She made him posset, too. A handsome lad he was."'

'Was,' said Holmes.

'Indeed, he used the past tense.'

'Handsome no more?' I queried.

'Or simply… no more?' said Holmes. I saw that he was enjoying himself, though he tried not to show it.

'What happened then?'

'Atwoode continued his evidence, that he, together with Hans, had followed the river road down from the Welcome Stranger to the rush at Whispering Flat. He pitched his new tent, staked a claim and had some minor success, better than Hans. And then came the flood, bringing with it a poor dead soul, transfixed by an uprooted tree, and sewn into...'

'Striped tenting!' said Holmes.

'Just like Atwoode's,' she replied. 'And somebody reported that interesting coincidence to the police.'

'Atwoode surely found himself in a pickle,' I commented.

'He told the inquest: "Though it be agin' decency to cast 'spersions on a brother weaver, I said where the tenting came from.'"

The steward returned, with coffee. At the other end of the saloon the piano started up again: hymns, with even more trills.

Holmes sipped at his cup fastidiously. 'The Australians have an expression, to "dob", a heinous crime, I imagine dating from the convict days. But Atwoode did it to Seccombe, to save himself from the gallows.'

'A habit in which he continued,' I added.

She nodded, sipping her own coffee.

'But you, madam,' said Holmes, 'must do your own narrating. Tell us what happened next.'

'What happened? Why, suddenly, as if their ears burnt from the bad report, appeared the Seccombes in the courtroom. No shantykeepers now, for I recognised the couple from the fine carriage, he burly and well dressed, wearing a bell-topper, leading by the gloved hand a woman, her face wan underneath a bonnet decked with ostrich plumes. The feathers agitated, though inside the court the air was still. I saw Atwoode purse his lips, as if about to spit, but then he smoothed them into an amiable smile, directed at the jurors.

'His next words were uttered in a tone mild, as if reading a story to a schoolroom. "My neighbour Hans, he had no need to tell the police how well Missus Seccombe looked after him at the Welcome Stranger, but he did. Mind you that was arter she came visiting him at Whispering Flat. Later that day he had a lucky strike, he said, gold nuggets enow for baccy and beef, and more too. Even though he had a *scheisse* claim.'"

'That is German,' said Holmes.

'Meaning ordure,' she replied, without a blush.

'But what was Atwoode insinuating?' I asked. 'A bribe?'

'The jury, from their faces, surely made that interpretation.'

Her voice slipped into the accent of Atwoode again as she continued. 'Hans being a fine young fellow, and testifying from his own good will, Mr Seccombe got cleared of any wrongdoing.'

'At that the man in the topper burst out, traces of Atwoode's brogue in his voice. "I told the police at Whispering Flat that the tenting went to those as asked me for it, and what they did afterwards was not my concern. Nobody saw the dead man at my inn, nobody knew who he was, God rest his soul."

'"Mr Seccombe," said the justice. "I am taking testimony here, and I ask you to keep your peace."

'The feathers shook violently, and the woman suddenly collapsed into hysterics. Seccombe pulled her from the floor, she striking blindly at his chest, and swearing at him, softly but like a fishwife.

'The justice said, "Please absent yourself, sir, and your good lady with you."

'Seccombe and the constable near dragged her outside, leaving the inquest in a state of simmering, *sotto voce* unrest. I overhead various insinuations, of which the loudest was a carrying whisper: *Good lady indeed!*

'But Atwoode stood still, genial as ever.

'The justice said, "That all happened several years ago. Do you still have your striped tent?"

'"Gone in a campfire, sir," said Atwoode.'

Holmes interjected. 'How convenient!'

'Truth again bent to fit a narrative?' I said.

'Or an outright lie,' she replied.

At the other end of the saloon the damsels and their swains at the piano were putting aside the music for the night.

'Go on,' said Holmes.

'The justice addressed Atwoode: "Years have passed since Mr Seccombe was at Whispering Flat and kept a lowly inn. Dare you accuse a man amongst the wealthiest in this locality?"

'The remark had the effect of setting off the courtroom buzz again: *Just how did Seccombe achieve that?... His Missus inherited, he sez... A likely story! That drab an heiress?*

'There was laughter, before the justice called for silence, and for Atwoode to answer the question.

'Atwoode replied: "I must speak truth, as God is my witness, sir. Even if I were to end up dead and in the river, for the telling of my tale."'

Holmes bent forward. 'Simple and courageous words, yet at the same time hinting at much.'

She eyed him levelly. 'Certainly the observers at the inquest understood them perfectly, to gauge from their buzzing. The justice made a speech then, about similarity – the cloth, the river-grave and the blows to the head – being suggestive, but not strong evidence. But I thought: *modus operandi*. My father always said evildoers are creatures of habit.'

I said, 'But to kill again, after the wealth gained, even if it were by a slow process of robbery and murder?'

Holmes said, 'Which leads one to speculate as to the motive.'

She clasped her hands in her black-clad lap. 'As I wondered myself. Just then Atwoode created a sensation by announcing he might be able to identify this corpse, and suggesting that he was not the only one who could. "His young wife begged me to, the poor creature, she being too near her confinement to travel," he said.'

'Whose young wife?' I said.

'Those were the justice's very words, to which Atwoode replied, "Why Hans, my fellow miner at Whispering Flat, whom chance and the news of gold brung to Fairfax town. Lucky again he was, with a monster nugget this time. Though his Gretchen begged him to take care, he would take it secretly to the capital to be assayed. He left, and we've heard nowt of him since."'

Holmes said nothing, but his face said, *Aha!*

'The justice sent the constable for the police gazette, and then read to the court: "Missing persons, January 31. Hans Eckhardt, twenty-two years of age, flaxen hair of a tight curl, five foot four, slender build." I saw the constable nod, ever so slightly, and a man beside me murmured to his neighbour: "I dug the grave, I seen that corpse. Fair curly hair and short of stature, like he says."

'The justice frowned at Atwoode. "Men desert their wives all the time, particularly on the goldfields."

'"Not one as pretty as she," he replied.'

She added, 'And I saw in his face for a moment pure covetousness.'

We were alone in the saloon now, with even the night owls gone yawning to their rest. Holmes and Mrs Maxwelton met each other's gaze, in complete silence.

'Let us consider the evidence,' said Holmes. 'Two corpses, dead years apart, but by similar means. We would guess that the first was a lucky miner, unlucky when he fell into bad company. It was only the chance of a flood that revealed him. How many more mouldered into bones, sand below them, river water above them, killed for the same base reason: the element gold?'

Modus operandi,' I repeated. 'A positive Penny Dreadful serial of murders.'

'But two murders did come to light. Were they as identical as it seemed?' Holmes mused.

'I am coming to that,' she said.

'Then I will endeavour not to interrupt again! What happened next?'

'The justice asked if Atwoode suggested the corpse be disinterred. He replied, "Aye, so I can set poor Gretchen's heart at rest, she not knowing if she be widow nor wed. She has charged me to identify him, and I will too, by the break in his thumb-bone, which Mrs Seccombe bandaged up, when they were all good chums."'

'More insinuations,' I said.

She sighed. 'The court well-nigh cheered at his words, though the justice tried to keep order. I sat in my corner as the order for disinterment was made, for first thing the next morning. Atwoode stood down, and I saw men in the courtroom shake his hand, offer to buy him nobblers. What a fine fellow he was, for doing his duty! But he protested that he must keep his head clear, for he had a hard and gory task tomorrow.'

She fell silent for a moment.

'And indeed he did identify the corpse. I had returned to my classroom by then, my usefulness as witness over. But I read in the paper of the coronial verdict, and of the Seccombes being committed for trial. I read also of police digging up the yard of the derelict Welcome Stranger and finding more striped cloth, and objects – broken pipes, boots, belts, even a prayerbook – that could be identified as the possessions of missing miners. Had they done that job properly at the time, Hans the miner would not have died.'

'He doomed himself,' I said, 'when he testified for the Seccombes with the first corpse, clearing their name. But why would they kill him now? Did he threaten them somehow?'

They both eyed me. 'My dear man,' said Holmes, 'must you be so obtuse?'

'But he has not heard all my evidence,' said Mrs Maxwelton.

At that moment, I felt quite warmly towards her.

'Go ahead,' I said, 'finish your story and relieve both my curiosity and my ignorance.'

'I sat in my corner,' she said, 'as the townspeople filed out, thinking hard. Soon only the justice and the constable were left, conferring quietly. I rose then, and went to the table where the striped canvas lay. In my excitement at identifying the selvedge stripes, I had quite forgotten something else.'

Holmes said, 'The stitching.'

'Correct, the stitches sewing the shroud were different this time: large, uneven, a man's work.

'The justice came up behind me. "You are done with that evidence."

'I explained, pleaded with him: "The *modus operandi* has been aped, copied. It is not the same!"

'He had found me vexing, with Atwoode the more important witness. Now he let his irritation show in full: "Do you think you can play lawyer? That is for a court to decide, man's work."

'I so forgot myself to raise my voice: "A woman or tailor sewed the first shroud. But not this one!"

'He replied: "A detail which I shall note. But now you must take your leave. You may be summonsed as a witness at the trial, but I would advise you not to expect it."'

She fell silent again. Outside it was pitch dark; we were on open sea, with only the sounds of the steamer, ceaselessly working against the waves. She turned her head to look at the stars through the porthole window, and I saw her face stricken by the memory.

'He was a worldly man, who had witnessed the Seccombes already damned in the court of public opinion. They were mushrooms, new-risen to wealth, and not Scots, like most settlers in that colony. As ex-shantykeepers, they were not respectable either.'

'Not one of us,' I said. 'The *unco guid*, as the Scots say.'

'And they hanged for it?' asked Holmes.

'I read that Mrs Seccombe died before the trial, of the phthisis behind her pallor. Seccombe alone stood in the dock, facing Atwoode and his evidence. And also that of the weeping Gretchen, babe in arms.'

She sighed. 'My one regret is that I could do nothing to help that young woman. She left the court with Atwoode as her protector and affianced husband. Seccombe left the court for prison, then after his appeal failed, the gallows.'

'Assuredly guilty,' I said.

'Of numerous murders,' Holmes added, 'but not all. Gold is a powerful motive for murder, but so is love, the romances tell us.'

I tried not to think of my inamorata of the dinner table, and her jealous cricketer.

'Was Hans's missing nugget ever found?' I enquired.

She said, 'It would have been uncovered gradually, broken into pieces.'

'So what did happen to that villain Atwoode?' I asked.

'Well done, Watson,' said Holmes.

'Some years later I read an account of accidental death, a Mr Atwoud, father of a large family. He was surely the same man, despite the spelling. By then, I was co-owner of the newspaper.'

'I did deduce something of the like,' said Holmes.

She fingered her second ring.

'My friend Jane, the editor's wife, she had cancer and worried about her girls. We all came to a mutual arrangement, between friends: that after her demise I would leave the classroom and become stepmother. I still proof-read, but also helped with the running of the paper. We co-wrote the mining news, bought shares in a quartz claim, and prospered with it. My kind Maxwelton died five years back, and now I am a newspaper proprietor, provincial but not without some importance.'

Holmes leant forward again. 'And you are acquainted with the politician whom you met on the gangplank. I saw you nod – and how he paled in response.'

'Indeed, my editorials whip him thoroughly when he proves shortsighted in the colonial parliament – opposing female suffrage! I have reminded him before of the day when he was a lowly justice, and I only a schoolmarm, a "busybody bluestocking", I heard him tell his constable.'

'You said you had sharp ears,' I said.

'As a bat's, despite my advancing years. When I sat near you on the deck this afternoon, the wind blew your words towards me. I heard your assessment of me, which was not too unflattering, and your talk of writing detective stories. Had the politician been as acute, he would have begged your autographs.'

'He did express admiration for the crime tales of your New Zealander, Fergus Hume,' I recalled.

'And hence, I proffer my own little tale, for your interest.' She yawned delicately behind a handkerchief of the finest lace. 'But gentlemen, I have diverted you enough, and the hour is late. Should you wish to make use of my story, you have my blessing.'

'And all the better if it be read by the politician, I suppose,' said Holmes.

'What, and mortify him even more?' That smile again, and then her silk skirt swished away.

We went to bed, pondering what other tales we might encounter in New Zealand. I am only sorry that she did not hear Holmes's words at the cabin door, rare praise for one of her sex: 'A truly remarkable female. What might she be, if this ladies' suffrage movement should by some wild chance succeed? A she-lawyer, a policewoman?'

'Most likely a consulting detective,' I said – and for once had the pleasure of seeing him lost for words.

CONTRIBUTORS

BILL BARNES

read all the Sherlock Holmes stories in his early teens, and enjoyed them, but they were just fodder for his voracious reading appetite inherited from his mother. The epiphany happened twenty years later when he drove past a signpost to 'Reichenbach' in Switzerland. He has been the Captain (president) of Australia's largest Sherlockian society, The Sydney Passengers, since 1996. He thinks that being a Sherlockian is one of the greatest global levellers around, an instant creator of goodwill between like-minded strangers. He edited and published *The Hounds' Collection 1996-2005* and was co-editor of *Australia and Sherlock Holmes* in 2008. He was invested into The Baker Street Irregulars in 2009 as 'The Gloria Scott'. Email: bbarnes@fastmail.fm

MARCELO BAEZ

Trained as a graphic designer, he would always have one eye on his first love, comics and illustration! Now he works as a freelance illustrator, creating work for comics, magazines, children's publications, posters, trading cards and a plethora of other print and online imagery. His list of clients includes international companies such as Marvel, Time Inc., Event Cinemas, Hardie Grant Egmont, *Popular Mechanics US*, *GQ Australia*, Microsoft, *Men's Health*, *Miami New Times*, *National Geographic*, Scholastic, *Dallas Observer*, *Time Out Singapore*, Stone Arch books, *Philadelphia* magazine and many more. Recently he has completed a set of official Marvel *Avengers* limited edition prints and he is currently working on a strange Greek myth graphic novel. Marcelo is represented in the US by Shannon Associates New York. www. marcelobaez.com and marcelo-baez.blogspot.com

LINDY CAMERON

Lindy is author of the Kit O'Malley PI trilogy *Blood Guilt, Bleeding Hearts* and *Thicker Than Water*; the archaeological mystery *Golden Relic*; the action thriller *Redback;* and the sf crime *Feedback.* She's also co-author of the True Crime collections *Killer in the Family* and *Murder in the Family*, with her sister Fin J Ross; and *Murderous Women,* with Ruth Wykes. Lindy is a National Co-Convenor of Sisters in Crime Australia, the Publisher of Clan Destine Press (www.clandestinepress.com.au), and is currently working on a series of historical novellas featuring time-travelling archaeologists, Amazons, and the great-great granddaughter of Alexander the Great and the Amazon Queen, Thalestris.

AUTHOR'S NOTE: In the story *The Wild Colonial* the newspaper article that Watson reads aloud to Holmes and Brookes – that sounds so much like a modern reaction to the internet going down and Australia losing all social media contact for a day – was published in the *Adelaide Advertiser* on Monday, 21 July 1890. It seems the more things change, the more they stay the same.

STEVE CAMERON

is a Scottish/Australian writer who currently resides in Lincoln, England. His publications include stories in *Galaxy's Edge, Dimension 6, Andromeda Spaceways* and *Australis.* Steve maintains a website at www.stevecameron. com.au

AUTHOR'S NOTE: The story, 'The Mysterious Drowning at St Kilda', is based on a series of true events, and the drowning of Mrs J. E. Roberts was widely reported as either 'The Mysterious Drowning Case at St Kilda', or 'The Melbourne Morgue Mystery'. The characters, evidence, timeline and coincidences are historically accurate, apart from a couple of minor fictional additions, such as the gardener, the assault on Watson and the hat. As a direct result of this case, the chief commissioner of police decided to purchase a camera to take a photograph of all bodies brought into the morgue. Constable Davidson, in charge of the morgue, was then instructed in the art of photography.

PHILIP CORNELL

is a lifelong Sherlock Holmes enthusiast from Sydney, Australia, where he has worked for many years as a commercial artist. A member of a number of Sherlock Holmes societies, he has appeared in Australian electronic and print news media for commentary upon Holmes several times. He is also particularly well regarded internationally not just for delightful artwork featuring Holmes and aspects of the Canon, but for the many scholarly papers he has written over the years for the premiere Australian Sherlockian journal *The Passengers' Log*. His claim to Holmesian fame is possibly capped (a deerstalker cap, we would presume!) off by the fact that a few years ago local authorities in Switzerland commissioned him to create art for a unique colour plaque depicting Holmes and Watson's arrival at the Englischer Hof Hotel as happened in the tale the world knows as 'The Final Problem', and this plaque can be seen in a public square in Meiringen as part of a series (number four, in a series of ten that are otherwise reproductions of Sidney Paget illustrations) not far from the famed Reichenbach Falls.

DOUG ELLIOTT

has been writing about the life and works of Arthur Conan Doyle for over thirty years. He is the author of *The Curious Incident of the Missing Link: Arthur Conan Doyle and Piltdown Man,* and the historical thriller *The Link*, and is co-editor of *The Annotated White Company,* forthcoming from Wessex Press, and *Australia and Sherlock Holmes.* A member of the Baker Street Irregulars (with the investiture 'Canadian Pacific Railway') and The Sydney Passengers Sherlock Holmes societies, Doug is also a founding member of the Friends of the Arthur Conan Doyle Collection of the Toronto Public Library (acdfriends.org).

JASON FRANKS

is an author and graphic novelist based in Melbourne, Australia. He is the writer of the occult rock'n'roll novel *Bloody Waters*, as well as the *Sixsmiths* graphic novels and the *Left Hand Path* comic series. His work has been shortlisted for

Aurealis and Ledger Awards. Franks' second novel, *Faerie Apocalypse*, will be published late in 2017. Find him online at www.jasonfranks.com

Raymond Gates

is an Aboriginal Australian writer currently residing in Wisconsin, USA, whose childhood crush on reading everything dark and disturbing evolved into an adult love affair with writing horror. He has published many short stories, several of which have been nominated for the Australian Shadows Awards and one, *The Little Red Man*, received an honourable mention in *The Year's Best Horror 2014*. He continues to write short fiction and is working on his first novel. Learn more at: http://www.raymondgates.com

Kerry Greenwood

Kerry is the author of 60 novels and five non-fiction books. Born in Footscray, she has worked as a folk-singer, a translator, a costume-maker, and editor. Kerry has a degree in English and Law from the University of Melbourne and was admitted to the legal profession on 1 April 1982, a day which she finds both soothing and significant.

Kerry is the beloved creator of the 20-book Phryne Fisher mystery series, the Corinna Chapman mysteries (Allen & Unwin); and the Delphic Women trilogy – *Medea*, *Cassandra* and *Electra*, *Out of the Black Land* and *Herotica* (Clan Destine Press). She holds both the Ned Kelly and Davitt Lifetime Achievement Awards for her crime fiction, and wants another lifetime.

Kerry is not married but lives with an accredited Wizard and three cats, and has no idea where she gets her ideas from.

Narrelle M Harris

is a Melbourne-based writer of crime, horror, fantasy and erotic romance. Her books include *Fly By Night* (nominated for a Ned Kelly Award), *Witch Honour* and *Witch Faith* (both shortlisted for the George Turner Prize), Melbourne vampire novels *The Opposite of Life* and *Walking Shadows* (the latter nominated for the Chronos Awards and shortlisted for the Davitt Awards for crime writing), and the short-story collection *Showtime*. Short fantasy and horror stories have also been published in Australia, the USA and the UK.

Meg Keneally

started her working life as a junior public affairs officer at the Australian consulate-general in New York, before moving to Dublin to work as a sub-editor and freelance features writer. On returning to Australia, she joined the *Daily Telegraph* as a general news reporter, covering everything from courts to crime to animal birthday parties at the zoo. She then joined Radio 2UE as a talkback radio producer. In 1997 Meg co-founded a financial-service public-relations company, which she sold after having her first child. For more than ten years, Meg has worked in corporate affairs for listed financial-services companies, and doubles as a part-time SCUBA diving instructor. She is co-author with Tom Keneally of *The Soldier's Curse* and *The Unmourned*, the first two books in the Monsarrat series. She lives in Sydney with her husband and two children.

Dr L. J. M. Owen

escapes dark and shadowy days as a public servant by exploring the comparatively lighter side of life: murder, mystery and forgotten women's history. A trained archaeologist and qualified librarian with a PhD in palaeogenetics, LJ is the author of the Dr Pimms, Intermillennial Sleuth series, a world of ancient murder, family secrets, forensic science, libraries and food. LJ launched the first novel in the series, *Olmec Obituary*, on a crowdfunding website in late 2014. It was picked up by a publisher just five days later. Described as 'the thinking person's cosy mystery', *Olmec Obituary* won a Highly Commended at the 2016 ACT Writing and Publishing Awards. Book Two in the series, *Mayan Mendacity*, hit shelves in November 2016. LJ spends as much time as possible crafting Dr Pimms' world to provide refuge for bookworms everywhere. Recipes in the series are tested under strict feline supervision. Website: www.ljmowen.com Facebook Series Page: @Dr Pimms, Intermillennial Sleuth Facebook Author Page: @DrLJMOwen Twitter: @Bleuddyn_Coll Instagram: @ljmowen

WILL SCHAEFER

was born in Perth in 1974. After finishing school he worked on farms, railways and drilling rigs before returning to Perth to study. His novel *The Wolf Letters* was published by Hybrid Publishers in 2011. Will works as an urban planner and is married with two children.

J (JOHANNES, AKA JAN) SCHERPENHUIZEN

is a writer, artist, editor and publisher. His comics, illustrations and prose pieces have appeared in Australia and the USA. Jan has collaborated with other talents but also acted as both writer and illustrator on projects ranging from picture-books series *The Wild and Crazy Dinosaurs* to the gritty horror graphic novel *The Time of the Wolves*. As an editor and manuscript appraiser he discovered Nancy Kunze, Christopher Ride, Anthony O'Neill and the late Martin Chimes, playing a significant role in their becoming professional authors. Since 2013 Jan has run small-press publisher Possible Press, which published the Aurealis Award-nominated *Bloody Waters* by Jason Franks. You can find out more about Jan's activities as agent, manuscript assessor, writing mentor and more at www.janscreactive.com and his art can be viewed at www.jscherpenhuizenillustrator.com

CHRISTOPHER SEQUEIRA

is a writer and editor who works in the mystery/crime genre and the speculative fiction realms of horror, science fiction, superheroes and fantasy, producing short stories, comic books and other entertainment formats. A Sherlock Holmes devotee, he has penned numerous Sherlockian articles, as well as pieces of Holmesian fiction, and these have seen print in Australia, the USA, the UK, Canada and Italy. Calibre Press in the USA currently publishes the graphic novel series *Sherlock Holmes: The Dark Detective* that he produces with colleagues Dave Elsey, Philip Cornell and others. Frew Publications in Australia has him currently writing both a series featuring the Victorian-era version of Lee Falk's classic, purple-suited superhero in *The Phantom by Gaslight*, as well as a contemporary take on that character. Sequeira's other upcoming works include a revival of Doctor Fu Manchu in comic books with longtime collaborator W. Chew Chan; his Canonical essay collection *Sherlock Holmes Detects: Murderers, Madmen and Monsters*; and a science-fictional anthology by diverse hands that he has edited, *Sherlock Holmes and Doctor Was Not*. He lives in Sydney with his wife and daughter.

LUCY SUSSEX

is a New Zealand-born writer living in Australia. Her award-winning work covers many genres, from true crime writing to horror. Her bibliography includes the novel *The Scarlet Rider* (1996, St Martins; reissued Ticonderoga 2015). She has published five short-story collections, and also edited anthologies, including the World Fantasy Award-shortlisted *She's Fantastical*. She has worked at Deakin, Melbourne and La Trobe Universities, while being a researcher, editor and review columnist. Her literary archaeology (unearthing forgotten writers) work includes *Women Writers and Detectives in C19th Crime Fiction: the Mothers of the Mystery Genre* (Palgrave). She has also edited pioneer crime writer Mary Fortune, and Ellen Davitt; and an anthology of Victorian travel writing, *Saltwater in the Ink* (ASP). Her study of Fergus Hume and his 1886 *The Mystery of a Hansom Cab*, the biggest-selling detective novel of the 1800s, was published by Text in 2015, and won the Victorian Community History award.

Two Author's Notes on Lucy Sussex's story:
'The Roadside Inn' is by Ellen Davitt, who wrote the first Australian murder mystery novel, Force and Fraud. *The account can be read on several levels, either straightforwardly or as the three crime buffs read it in my story. I used it as the basis for this tale.*

Women achieved suffrage in New Zealand in the 1890s, some decades before it happened in Doyle's England, and peacefully, without violence.

T. S. P. SWEENEY

is a dashingly roguish public servant by day and a roguishly dashing author by night. He can be found on Twitter @TSPSweeney, on Facebook

@TSPSweeney, or at his reasonably frequently updated blog: www.tspsweeney.com

Robert Veld

has had a strong interest in Arthur Conan Doyle's Sherlock Holmes stories as well as many of his other works for most of his life. He is the author of a number of research-based papers on various aspects of the Sherlock Holmes Canon that have been published in numerous journals and books and he is also the author of the book *The Strand Magazine & Sherlock Holmes* that was published by Gasogene Books in the USA in 2013. His other great personal interest is fishing and he has been a semiregular contributor to various of Australian fishing magazines for over 15 years. Robert lives in south-west Sydney with his wife and two young daughters.

Kaaron Warren

has lived in Melbourne, Sydney, Canberra and Fiji. She's sold more than 200 short stories, four novels (the multi-award-winning *Slights, Walking the Tree, Mistification* and her latest novel, Aurealis Award-winning *The Grief Hole*) and six short-story collections including the multi-award-winning *Through Splintered Walls*. Kaaron is an honorary life member of the Australian Horror Writers Association and the Canberra Speculative Fiction Guild. You can find her at kaaronwarren@wordpress.com and on Twitter @KaaronWarren

Acknowledgements

A WORK LIKE this is quite obviously an effort of many, but apart from the wonderful contributors within these pages there are quite a number of other people who support and encourage from behind the scenes to make a project like this become a reality.

Firstly, those whose direct efforts made this book happen need to be thanked. In this category reside my beloved brother-in-fiction and brother-in-editing on other projects, Steve Proposch, whose efforts led to the work being considered by Angela Meyer at Bonnier. I was then very much gifted to have Angela take an interest in this project; she is an absolute gem of a publisher representative, immeasurably supportive all the way, and she sourced some of the top-notch contributors for the book. The final element of the book's genesis is Brian Cook, my smart, capable and understanding agent for this and some other Australian projects: always listening, always ready to apply his considerable wisdom and experience to issues.

Philip Cornell is a contributor herein, but he must also stand in a class all his own when I turn to thank people, not a surprising thing to hear, to those who know him. Talented, calm, knowledgeable, and with a heart the size of a mountain. I have been lucky to count him as a fellow Sherlockian, thrilled to experience him as a creative collaborator, but really, above all, been most privileged to number him as a friend for many years.

Jan Scherpenhuizen is another talented collaborator who must deserve special mention beyond just being present in the page-count here; Jan and I have fought together in the freelancer trenches on many an occasion, and he was a staunch supporter of this project when I first came up with the idea. Bravo, sir!

Marcelo Baez, another trusted colleague, also deserves praise not just for illustrative acumen but also gallantly coming on board when extra hands were needed due to the dreaded curse of 'circumstances beyond one's control'.

I am blessed with a small and reliable coterie of friends from the Sherlockian scene (whether hardcore or just casual fans), from all over the world, and though they weren't all pivotal in the creation of this particular book they have been a part of the keeping alive of my love for and exploration of this sub-genre of all sub-genres of fiction (surely NOT fiction, the Holmesian says!). These people are all living examples of how this fascinating literary pastime stretches across many a divide to bring thoughtful, empathetic people together. I must name a few of them in no particular order: Les Klinger, Dave Elsey and Lou Elsey, Charles Prepolec, Baden Kirgan, Tim McEwen, Erin and Malcolm O'Neill, the late Gary Reed, Bill Barnes and Kate Dyer, Rosane McNamara, the late Frank McNamara, Jennie Leigh, Kerry Murphy and Lisa D'Ambra, the late Professor Lionel Fredman and the late Jacqui Fredman, Jeff Campbell, Jessica Quinn, Martin Powell, Kevin Greenlee, the late Howard Hopkins, Dominique Hopkins, David Lewis, and all my many friends in The Sydney Passengers.

Writers have their confidantes, their pals, their *Secret Society of People You Show Stuff To* to make sure it doesn't suck, or to just tell you not to give up. I have some amazing heroes in my team: Mark Waid, Julie Ditrich, Bryce Stevens, Chewie Chan, Paul Mason and Jason Franks.

Finally, I would never have gotten to this point in life without a loving family that supported learning, and reading, and – it has to be very firmly stressed – was fully supportive of eccentricity; for how else might a half-Indian, half-Irish-Australian boy grow up in Sydney and survive to reach his late teenage years whilst occasionally wandering around wearing a deerstalker and overcoat? That boy still has that deerstalker and now many other bits of Holmesian paraphernalia, and he still owes his family big-time: my late mother, Josephine Lydia McCarthy Sequeira (born in Dirranbandi), my late father, Jack Joseph Sequeira; my brothers Mark, Brendan, Jonathan; my sisters Ayesha, Tara, Ranee and Nalini; my late sister Kamala; my wondrous wife, Jacqui; our children, Daniel and Anita Butler, daughter Valentina Sequeira, and grandson, Hunter Butler; and many kind and loving aunts, uncles and cousins stretched across at least three continents.

Lastly, though, this book is really possible because there are millions and millions of people from every place and age since 1887 who have loved Sherlock Holmes's adventures, and who never want these to stop appearing. If you enjoy this book you stand amongst them, and I thank you.